The Sweet War Man

A Novel

by

Paul Barcelo

iUniverse, Inc.
New York   Bloomington

The Sweet War Man
A Novel

This is a work of fiction. All of the characters, names, incidents, organizations, and dialogue in this novel are either the products of the author's imagination or are used fictitiously.

iUniverse books may be ordered through booksellers or by contacting:

iUniverse
1663 Liberty Drive
Bloomington, IN 47403
www.iuniverse.com
1-800-Authors (1-800-288-4677)

Because of the dynamic nature of the Internet, any Web addresses or links contained in this book may have changed since publication and may no longer be valid. The views expressed in this work are solely those of the author and do not necessarily reflect the views of the publisher, and the publisher hereby disclaims any responsibility for them.

ISBN: 978-1-4401-1995-8 (pbk)
ISBN: 978-1-4401-1993-4 (cloth)
ISBN: 978-1-4401-1994-1 (ebk)

Library of Congress Control Number: 2009921184

Printed in the United States of America

iUniverse rev. date: 01/27/09

THE SWEET WAR-MAN IS DEAD AND ROTTEN;

SWEET CHUCKS, BEAT NOT THE BONES OF THE

BURRIED: WHEN HE BREATHED, HE WAS A MAN.

DON ADRIANO DE ARMADO,

A FANTASTICAL SPANIARD

LOVE'S LABOUR'S LOST

SHAKESPEARE

To my Four, Gregory, Catie

Bobby and Brianna

Chapter One

Waiting.

Lying fully clothed his hands behind his head, stretched full on his bed he looked at the shadowy shapes of his familiar room. Here, he had grown up. Here, he was safe, although now he felt imprisoned. It was 2:00 AM, Friday, the final one at home. The approaching weekend meant nothing to him since there was no place he wanted to go or any people to see. Again, his thoughts drifted to her.

In the rear seat of his Volkswagen Beetle where she lay, her head kept banging against the side of the car. With each thrust her head struck, sometimes twice. Alarmed that he was hurting her, he stopped. Her eyes flashed open and she growled at him to continue. Resuming, again her head was striking. He could sense her about to go off so he knew her feeling was not with her bumping head. That image was trapped in his memories. Where had they been? Was it either the small patch of dirt road in front of her tree near her parents' house, which they used so frequently, or near the school? There were many streets near Northeastern. At night they were dark, small and convenient. With caution and sometimes without, they had used many places, usually with a blanket covering them, but sometimes not. The incident of her head banging and not remembering exactly where they were haunted him. The little Volkswagen was gone. The memories continued.

It was ten days before he gave himself to the Army. Leaving Thursday morning there would be three days to drive fourteen hundred miles, Massachusetts to Georgia. Where would he be one week from today? The map said in Virginia or possibly North Carolina. Hopefully, fast asleep at this hour after driving all day. The excitement of starting the trip sent a twinge through his body.

Scotch. He could taste its tangy bluntness in his mouth. It had become his cure for insomnia and loneliness. Unfortunately, one drink would not bring him to oblivion. One would become a few. In five hours, he must be on the unyielding cement of the shipping dock. His sister Judy had helped him get the temporary job at the factory where she had worked since graduating from high school the year before. She was starting to date, seriously, their common supervisor, Al Garber. They were becoming a factory issue. Already, others who worked with him were kidding about getting extra breaks. Did it matter about the temporary job? He felt an obligation to do well in the job for his sister, despite all the enmity between them while they were growing up. What had changed that? Both were no longer students, although he knew he was to remain one in the Army for the next year. Was Judy more mature now that she worked? Or, was it because in a year he would be in Vietnam? Had that changed her? Missing a day would mean the others on the dock would have to work harder. Did that matter? When he left, no one was scheduled to replace him, so they still would have to work faster and harder.

With the urge to urinate, he got up off the bed. In the small corridor, he hesitated at his sister Judy's closed door and listened. Quiet. He had bought her a gold heart-shaped locket for her nineteenth birthday with some of the money he earned at ROTC summer Camp. He knew her windows would be shut. She slept in a sealed room. He wondered how anyone could endure that. In winter she complained of cold. In summer it was insects.

Leaving the upstairs bath, Teddy's door was open. His eight-year-old brother was nearly falling off his bed. His window, like Randolph's was open letting fresh air into the crowded room. His brother was sprawled on the small bed. Near his open mouth on the pillow was a circle of dampness from his drool. He was snoring in a delicate high-pitched tone in deep sleep. Teddy possessed the bed. His body and legs were tangled in the sheets and single blanket. He wondered if his brother could ever share a bed with a woman.

In his room, he went to the window and looked out. A slight breeze swayed the trees that were near the house, and then they quieted. In isolated places the leaves had already turned to their bright autumn colors. Parked on the street was his new Camaro, one of the few things giving him joy in the past year. He thought it strange the bank would give a new Vietnam-bound Second Lieutenant a car loan without a cosigner. The first night he brought the new car home, he was certain someone would hit it. It was parked in the same spot his battered old VW bug had resided. No one had ever hit it while parked on the street. The family's four-year-old station wagon was in the single lane of their driveway. It was his father's house. The Camaro was a suitable chariot to take him off to war.

For him, Lieutenant Randolph Thayer, it was this same first step millions of soldiers had taken. In the mid to late sixties when the war had intensified, he felt as if he was hiding in school. A lot of his contemporaries were. Then, he had met Andrea, and the war and everything else slipped from the active recesses of his mind into the totally oblivious crevasse of love. They had a year together. Physically, they were atoned, completely. It was the rest of them that did not fit. If he had not accelerated his program in college, he would be returning to finish his senior year, still waiting for his life to begin. Speeding up college to get into the Army earlier had cost him Andrea. The final link between them separated, when as a full time student, he could not take the coop job she had had her father create especially for him in his ball bearings factory. That seemed to have infuriated her further and was the final blow to their relationship.

The final parting had happened on the Fourth of July. They had spent a stubborn, seething week apart, so he went to her house for the confrontation. The traditional Tremblay patriotic party, which he had attended the year before, with kids, dogs and adults everywhere in the back yard around the pool, was in full progress. They went to that tree on their little piece of dirt road a few hundred yards from her house, away from her cousins, the vice president uncles and Frederic, her father. Under the tree, she sat and cried. She could not go through a year of agony of his being in Vietnam. She wanted them to have a future together. Flying or being an Army officer, things he wanted, she never mentioned in that final meeting. It was as if they did not exist. So, he left her under that tree, crying with big real tears rolling down her cheeks. She was a rich man's daughter, an only child. Maybe their men did things differently. For fifteen months he went into a limbo of monotonous schoolwork in order to escape the gray brick buildings of Northeastern University.

Flying. Northeastern University had only Army ROTC, so he could not think about the Air Force or Navy's jets. The Army boasted it had more aircraft than all the other services combined. His first set of active duty orders sent him to rotary wing school. Vietnam was the helicopter war. It would be his war. Weekly, they were still grinding people up.

Vehemently, she opposed him going. No compromise. He was the one who faced getting killed, not her. He had wanted her in his life. Wanted all the things men and women had and did together. Or, had it just been the flesh? Honestly, after being apart so long, he did not know. The deathly lonesomeness lead to his only solace, scotch, which erased consciousness for short periods leaving headaches but never curing them. How many anguished thoughts did he have at her unfair rejection? How many times did his stomach ache just thinking of touching her again or running his fingers through that hair.

The memory of touching lingered in his senses for months. Then, she telephoned on the Fourth of July while he was at camp. Judy had answered the phone and they had had a fine conversation lasting thirty minutes. What the hell had they talked about? Judy felt guilty. Inadvertently, she had been the one who told Andrea he was not going to work for her father but was accelerating his program at Northeastern. That would have come out, sooner or later. Judy talked to Andrea and relieved her guilt. Weeks had gone by. What was Andrea waiting for? Had she changed her mind and wanted to keep him out of her life? Why had she called? He left the window and went back to his bed. Lying flat without removing any of his clothes, he did not know when he fell back into sleep.

As he walked with the boisterous, end of the week Friday crowd, he stared at the asphalt of the parking lot. The sun absorbed the heat in the black tar and seeped up through his worn sneakers. His feet still tingled from the cement floor of the shipping dock. His co-workers, Tom and Eddy including old Herbert Trott wore expensive, comfortable work shoes. They never complained about their feet. With only three more days of work, it was too late to spend the money on expensive footgear. Each day the discomfort in his legs disappeared more quickly. He had his Army boots, worn in from two years of use, which were as soft as sneakers. There would be no more cement floors to walk on once he put them on.

"Randy, it's me." Her voice cut through his rambling thoughts. She was standing next to his new Camaro. Her long hair glistened in the hot afternoon sun. A light summer dress sculptured her frame. She stood, calmly staring at him. When he looked up hearing her voice, the sun nearly blinded him. The hair was the same. Her eyes, which had come into his dreams countless times, were the same blue. There was something different about her, but it was Andrea.

"I have my car," she said, softly. Randolph looked at the shiny Camaro as if it were a stranger's. "I know this is your new car. It should be all right here. They don't lock this lot. I know, I asked. We'll get it later." He followed her and wanted to touch her. She stared back at him. They both walked oblivious to the noisy going-home crowd. Her smile was as unsure and clumsy as their gait. "I've been waiting. I didn't want to miss you." She stopped at a new Mustang. Randolph stared dumbly at the car. "I got rid of my old one. There was too much of us in that one. My father bought me this one. Different color, that's all." Andrea went to the driver's side. "Do you want to drive or should I?"

Randolph simply nodded and opened the passenger's side. The inside of the car was hot. Andrea immediately started the motor and turned on the air conditioner. A surge of hot air hit them, but it quickly turned cool. He reached for her arm to touch her, running the pads of his fingers along her forearm. "You're thinner. You've lost some weight," he managed, finally. Her eyes closed briefly at his touch and she swallowed. He looked at her face and realized the reaction his touch had caused. He withdrew his hand. "I'm sorry," he whispered, impulsively.

"I've lost a lot of things this past year. You're thinner, too. That camp life must have agreed with you."

He laughed involuntarily. "This is my Andrea, telling me the Army did something good for me?" The laughter released something inside him and made Andrea's teeth appear in a broad smile. The tension in her face relaxed. Oblivious to the people leaving the plant he leaned toward her. She responded to the kiss. Her lips were hesitant but quickly warmed to his. Someone thumbed the car as they walked past and mumbled voices from outside ended their kiss.

"Where would you like to go?"

"I can remember when you knew the answer to that question." Randolph smiled. She inched the car forward along with the traffic leaving the plant. "You talked to my sister while I was at camp?"

"The Fourth of July made it a year. I didn't know you were in Pennsylvania."

"I can't remember what I was doing, but it was a training day. The Army didn't allow us to have it off."

"The Army made you work on a holiday?"

"Wars and training don't stop for holidays."

"My father had his party. I didn't do much that day. If I couldn't talk to you, I was glad it was someone close to you. I like Judy."

"I talked to Judy on the phone while I was still in Pennsylvania. When I didn't hear directly from you at camp, I was disappointed. Then I wondered why I was disappointed."

"Really?" Andrea turned the Mustang onto a ramp leading to Route 128, then concentrated on entering the Friday traffic. Her head bobbed back and forth several times causing her hair to flutter. He stared at it and did not look away until she turned her head briefly toward him. "I could have gone to Pennsylvania in July. I didn't think they would let me see you"

"I've been home since August first."

"That call wasn't easy for me, Randy. Know how long it took me to make it? For weeks I thought about and then decided it should be on that day. Then, you weren't home. My heart must have been beating a thousand times a second."

"You're here. Should I be grateful?"

"Would you have ever come after me?"

"Probably not."

"Is there someone else?" She looked over at him quickly and nearly changed lanes.

"No."

She turned the Mustang onto an off ramp. Within a few minutes they pulled into the parking lot of a Holiday Inn, one where they had stayed together. "I took a room here." Her face showed her sudden apprehension. "In case we want it."

"You do still live with your parents?"

"The house is my mother's now, and she's selling it. My parents separated last fall. It's part of the divorce settlement. I'm going to get an apartment." She did not turn off the engine of the car. The air conditioning was still blowing cool air at them. "Will you kiss me again, right now? I want that." They leaned toward each other over the console. Their lips melted into each other and then their tongues met. Her mouth was positive, soft and sensuous not like the first cautious kiss in the factory's parking lot.

"Goddammit, where have you been?" Randolph whispered. Her scent came back to him as it had in his memories countless times. He put his hand up to her hair, and then removed it abruptly.

"A lot of places, I guess, but never really away," she whispered softly. "I had to know that."

Randolph shifted in the bucket seat breaking their half embrace and looked out straight through the windshield. They were quiet. The only sound was from the car's air conditioner.

"I hated you, right after. It took a long time for that to go away." Her tone was abrupt, nasal and sharp. She took several deliberate slow breaths and waited. "Let's go into the lounge and get a beer or something," she said finally breaking their lengthening silence. The parking lot was hot. The lobby of the hotel was vaguely familiar to Randolph. They went into the bar, which was dark, smelled of stale cigarette smoke yet was refreshingly air-conditioned. They sat opposite each other in a large booth. Briefly, the soreness in his feet returned from standing, sitting, walking. The feeling passed quickly. Only a few people were in the bar at this early hour. A cocktail waitress appeared immediately. They ordered draft beer.

"Are you upset your parents are divorcing?"

"I blamed my mother at first. Gradually, I came to see her side of things. That took awhile especially after my father's heart attack."

"When did that happen?" His face registered genuine surprise. "Your father always seemed so much like a rock."

"Last fall before Thanksgiving. Forty years of red meat, cigarettes, and booze. Ad that to the stress of running a business. A heart attack is inevitable. Business can be as tough as being in the Army." Slowly, she lifted her glass and sipped, as she studied his face. "Now you're an Army second loo-ey. You've got what you wanted." She said earnestly.

"The training was something. I know how vulnerable the human body is."

"To something as simple as bullets? The real vulnerability is the heart. It breaks very easily. It took awhile after I talked to your sister on the Fourth, but finally I realized a lot of things. The biggest part of my anger was that I had really badgered my father to create that job. Then, you wouldn't take it. It made me feel like a big fool."

Randolph looked away from her face and down at the tabletop for a moment. He swallowed, and then looked up at her face, which had mellowed somewhat from her earlier tenseness. "I never thought of the position I put you in. You never really impressed me about being serious about your father's business."

"That's how I feel now. Maybe a year ago, I don't know." Her expression registered her confusion. "Anger mixes everything up." He looked directly at her eyes, searching. He saw pleading mixed with honesty. It was what he hoped he saw. "What I've been thinking about, even before I made that call is do we owe it to each other to find out, rather than lose it forever?" Her eyes became watery creating a camouflage for the emotion he had been following. She put her hand on his forearm, which shot numbing sensations through his body. "All I remember is us together? Does that have to be over?"

Covering her hand on his forearm he ran his finger over her skin relishing its sensuousness. Her arm was shaking. Breaking his touch, she put a dollar on the table as a tip, then slid off the bench seat and stood next to the table. She dapped at her eyes self conscientiously to stop her tearing.

"Is this what you want?"

"I don't know what I want. Right now I want you to touch me and keep touching me. I want that very much."

They left the bar and walked up a flight of stairs to her room. Her hands were trembling so much she had difficulty inserting the key. They stood a few moments after she had closed the door. Both double beds were neatly made up. Some of her clothes were visible in a closet. Embracing they pressed the length of their bodies into each other.

"Oh, I remember!" She whispered before she pushed her tongue into his ear.

They lay beside each other listening to their breathing, hearing nothing else. A long audible rumbling of Randolph's stomach brought them back to the hotel room, the bed and the twilight. Andrea turned to look at the clock on the night table next to the bed. It was after ten.

"All the restaurants will have stopped serving." She was calm and satisfied. She did not want to disturb the tranquility although her stomach felt very empty, also.

"We'll go out in the forest and stalk wild animals. We'll stew them on a slow campfire. I'll teach you some Army ways."

"Right now stew sounds very nice. It's got to be all ready, though. I don't want to wait for it to cook."

"That kills the Army method." He stroked her skin. "We'll drive around all night until we find something open. We'll barter with your plastic wampum."

"You're more confident, now." Andrea said too quickly.

"I never was unconfident." His voice was suddenly tart. "I usually didn't disagree with you. We only had big disagreements. The small things always got worked out."

Suddenly her mind like a movie film speeding up accelerated. He doesn't want to lose it either. He feels the same thing. It can't end. She rubbed his bicep and let her palm massage his skin up the rest of his arm to his shoulder. Her touch dissipated his sudden annoyance. She felt his tightness. "You're the man. The soldier. Figure out how to solve the hunger in my belly." Playfully, she smiled then sliding her hand over his chest down over his stomach, she pressed his skin. "The appetizer for whatever feast you're going to find for me." When she found his expected reaction, she climbed on top of him.

Afterwards, they rinsed quickly in the shower, each avoiding touching in order not to arouse, but obviously interested in seeing the physical changes in each other's bodies. Within a mile of the hotel with Randolph driving, they found an open fast food restaurant. Its lot was busy with groups of teenagers eating and clowning around their cars as they celebrated the end of their Friday night dates. She stayed in the car watching the antics while he went to purchase their food. He bought half a dozen cheeseburgers, two large containers of fries, and two large Cokes. She took a cheeseburger, looked at it skeptically, and then attacked it.

"Would you have rather driven around longer?"

"No, this type of hunger overrides everything." Her mouth was full and she was still chewing, quickly without formality.

"How do you like working, rather than going to school?"

"Right now, it's something to do." She wiped her mouth, and then took another large bite. "I took the coop job. My father planned it very well. I worked in every department for a couple of weeks.

After we broke up, he suggested it to keep me occupied. I needed something to keep my sanity. I actually swept floors."

"I kept expecting to see you at Northeastern. Especially when I switched to full time."

"I couldn't go back. It would have been too much. I settled in sales. Partly because I could have my own desk. Strange as that sounds, that became important. You have to have a place to go in the morning. I went to one of our industrial shows, where we introduce our new product and see what everyone else is offering. We don't put much effort into that. How do you make ball bearings interesting and desirable? Our literature for new products wasn't very appealing, so I started getting into that. Next thing I know, I'm thinking about work when I'm not at work. My uncle was kind and everything and everyone in the office helped me when I needed information or other things."

"You're the president's daughter."

"It went beyond that. They're good people. They know who I am, but wanted to help me fit in. It wouldn't have mattered what department in the company I ended up in. My uncles run all of them." She took another cheeseburger from the pile. "To think that old man made millions selling this crap to the dumb masses."

"Those dumb masses eat it right up. If he hadn't known what they wanted, exactly, he wouldn't have been successful."

"It's a good thing you didn't take my father's coop program. You would not have survived. I wanted to quit several times, but he bullied me to stay with it."

"I work on a shipping dock. At least I will until Wednesday, my last day."

"I did shipping. Harrison, my father's shipper–been with us practically since the company started–taught me a lot. There are a lot of ways an order can get screwed up right in your own factory. He knows so much. That's why my father made me work with him. He made me sweep. No way out of it, regardless of who I was."

"It'll all be yours one day."

"I can't count on that. My father will leave it to someone who can run it. It got so bad between us, once, my mother intervened. She lit into him." She took another cheeseburger, although her

11

pace of eating had slowed. "The dumb masses, huh? That's a good point." They watched the teenagers in the parking lot as some of them danced to the music on the car radios.

"Some of them may be in Vietnam in a year." Randolph said as he nibbled fries. "Maybe I'll carry some of them."

"It's definite, you're going?" Her mind shifted again rapidly.

"My orders assign me. En route, I go for two months of infantry training, then to flight school for nine months."

"That's a year you'll be in the United States?"

"Provided I don't get shot on a range in Georgia or what I'm flying can stay in the air!"

"Maybe it will be over."

"Maybe I won't mind that."

"That's a big change. I could live with that."

"I have the normal aversion to getting killed. I'd like to live to the ripe old age of twenty-five."

"Why that age?" Her face became momentarily pensive.

"That means I will have finished my tour and survived."

The War! The stupid war. If it was another girl, I could deal with that easily, Andrea thought.

They returned to the Holiday Inn. Although the bar was open and noisy, they went directly to the room and quickly got back into bed. The food made them both drowsy. They touched each other without sexual overtures, reassuring each other. Randolph yawned and stretched his feet out under the covers. He wanted a cigarette, but did not light one.

"You don't think I could have handled the coop job?"

"Business can destroy people and lives. It can be as lethal as bullets. That, I've learnt and seen. My father is a casualty. He was tough on me. I don't know if it's because I'm his only off spring and he expected more of me for that reason. He's tough on my uncles, but they've stayed with him through all the years."

"You've been in training. Mine is about to begin. Another week and you would have missed me. I leave Thursday. Why did you wait so long?"

"You'll never understand the fear I had about going to that parking lot. I wondered if you would even talk to me."

"What about now? Are you afraid?"

"I don't know"

"What are you thinking?"

"Nothing," she lied. There's a year to dissuade him. Lots of things can happen in a year. A whole year. She glanced at him quickly. I can make him change his mind. I know I can. His head had not moved and he seemed to be staring at the ceiling. "They're withdrawing troops. Is any of that going to affect you?" Her tone was subdued.

"It will take much more than a year to withdraw hundreds of thousands of troops. I will still go, like my orders state." Randolph said. "Is working better than being a student?"

"When we were in school together, I didn't need a purpose, and I certainly didn't think about it. It's all your fault. When we broke up, you made me start thinking." She poked him in the ribs, playfully, then her hand continued moving over his skin as she explored. "It's been an education to see how they make ball bearings. There're not all just little metal balls. There's a whole metal assembly that goes with them. I wasted my time going to Northeastern. I've found where I'm supposed to be."

"My contract with the Army is going to be for nearly four years. The first two of them will be the toughest. My year of training, then my tour, three hundred sixty five days." He could feel her stiffen slightly. Her hand on his body stopped, and then she withdrew it.

"What would happen if you flunked out?" She asked, finally after a lengthened silence between them.

"You mean out of flight school?"

"Yes, that?"

"I would go as a grunt, an infantryman."

"Grunt? That sounds disgusting. Are men really called that?"

"Infantry is the backbone of the Army, but I want to fly. Why did you come to that parking lot?"

"My mother actually convinced me." Andrea sighed letting her mind decelerate. Randolph felt her sink further into the bedding. She put her hand back onto him and began exploring again. "I wanted to and then I didn't. I'd think about you and get pissed. It always took time to wear that off. Then, I saw how my mother had

13

changed after she left my father. When I mentioned my feelings about you, my mother said I should find out. If I didn't, they would always nag me throughout my life. Are you angry with me?"

"When I talked to my sister at camp, it woke everything up. I had hope. I thought you might write. Never got anything at mail call. I came home after camp and waited and got more frustrated. That was exasperating. "

"You owe my mother." She giggled softly.

A year. I can do anything in a year, she thought. A whole year! It will work.

It was full light outside when Randolph gently and silently got up out of the bed. Facing away from her he pulled his pants up and belted them. He went to the balcony and pushing aside the full length drape opened the slider door. Sunlight invaded the twilight of the room. Lighting a cigarette, he took a deep drag and looked outside, his face and body profiled in the uneven light. She stared at him and her mind started to race.

My horse. What color was it? Dark, either brown or gray. The year I was thirteen, girls my age had horses. Why the hell I did I want a horse? My father tried to dissuade me. I badgered him for months and until he really thought I wanted it. He was right. I really didn't want the thing. On my fourteenth birthday, I got the horse. Maybe I rode the foolish thing twice. Finally, even before my next birthday, he sold it. I was persistent and unwavering. Made even my skeptical father believe that is what I wanted. Can I make him do what I want, not go to Vietnam? He's going to be in the Army. Could live with that for a time, if he isn't going. The clink is there in his armor. I saw it. He said it. He wouldn't be disappointed if he didn't have to go. He won't go. I can find the way with a year.

"What are you cooking over there?" He expelled a plum of smoke out the open slider, leaning his face against the door frame he looked back at the bed. "I can tell by your face when you're thinking. That, I remember."

"A horse."

"After being apart for over a year and last night, you're thinking about a horse?"

"I had a horse, once." Her tone was mellow.

"You never mentioned that before. We're learning new things about each other already." Randolph smiled broadly, and then dragged deeply on his cigarette. "I can't picture you on a horse."

"I wanted one and I got it. Then, I didn't want it. Get your buns over here." Her teeth flashed in a warm smile.

"Cigarette's almost done."

"Another bad habit you've kept. It makes your mouth taste like burnt rope."

"You been looking at other buns?" He flipped the cigarette outside then closed the glass door.

"A couple of times."

At the side of the bed he stopped, turned away from her and dropped his pants to the floor, allowing her to gaze at his buttocks for a moment. Then he slipped under the sheets next to her. "Back your ass against the wall, here I come balls and all, bye bye cherries." he sang in marching cadence.

"What's that from?"

"It's a marching song from camp. Sometimes, the cadre would make us knock it off. Don't know why, there were no women out there in the woods. They made us sing more conventional songs. Like she wore a yellow ribbon. That was from a John Wayne movie."

Andrea said nothing, but also did not look away from his face in the half light. Her look was so ponderous he was not sure if she was annoyed or happy, but he knew she was still lost in a thought.

"Shall I put my ass against the wall so you can do whatever is supposed to happen? It sounds intriguing." She giggled weakly. A warm smile spread across her face.

"It was just a marching song to help keep in step. Soldiers are soldiers regardless of what stage of training they're in." The phone rang. "Who knows we're here?" Randolph asked, startled.

"My mother." She stretched to reach the phone losing most of her covering sheet in the process, but purposely using herself to rub against his body. "I called before I went to your parking lot yesterday. She wasn't home, so I left this number." She was straddling his chest as she picked up the phone. She pushed her elbows sharply into his chest as she propped the phone against her ear. Most of the conversation seemed to be from her mother. Andrea kept saying yes, but did ask "what time." After she hung up, she slid off of him nestling by his side and pulling the sheet over herself. "She wants us to come to dinner tonight. You'll meet Scott."

"Who is Scott?"

"My mother's fiancé. We can come back here after dinner. My father bought another house. Scott lives on the South Shore. They're building down there. When my mother sells the house, that's when I'll get my apartment. Scott comes from old money. His family did not come over on the Mayflower, but it must have been the boat right after it. He's a corporate lawyer. What he actually does is handle people's money. Lots of money. He also has a lot of political connections. Much more than my father's state ones. Scott might even be under consideration for a job with the Administration."

"What Administration?"

"The Nixon one."

Randolph was silent for a full, half minute. She stared at his expressionless face.

"I came with what I was wearing and did the mission as dictated." He said absently. "I want to get my car out of that lot, anyways. We'll stop by my house and have a cup of coffee." He eyed her anticipating a protest, but she offered none.

His Friday work clothes made him feel gritty, although he had showered. At his parents' house, having Andrea with him saved a scolding. While his mother was pouring them coffee, Randolph bolted upstairs to his bedroom for clean clothes. Andrea related the major events of her family for the year she had not been to Randolph's house. There was plenty of time to bring her Mustang to the Holiday Inn lot before they started to the old Tremblay house.

"It's a lot like my Mustang," Andrea said as she settled into the bucket seat of his Camaro. "My father thinks Fords are practical and patriotic. You've seen his Continental. That's still a big Ford in his mind. Northeastern was a Ford-like college to him, also. That's why he sent me there. I've been looking at Alpha Romeos."

"What you're asking is would your father approve? You know he wouldn't, so go buy it."

"Why should I antagonize him?"

"To make him understand there is a you." He remembered the proper exit off 128 and the side roads. The Tremblay house was on a Cul-de-sac about a quarter mile from a main road with only one other neighboring house in sight. There was a small dirt path just off the pavement. Instinctively, Randolph turned onto it and stopped the car.

"There's my tree." She sighed audibly.

"We spent a lot of time here."

"We were very acrobatic in your VW." She laughed. 'I'll always remember that car."

"Maybe we could christen your new Alpha when you get it."

"Your Volkswagen had something of a back seat. The Alpha is just a two-seater. I guess you can't go back in time, can you?"

"We can do anything we want," Randolph's voice rose involuntarily. "Should we talk some more?"

"No, let's have dinner first." Her voice was emotionless.

Sylvia met them at the front door. She eyed Randolph thoroughly. Her face drifted into a natural, quiet smile. "You look healthy and well, Randy."

Outwardly, she appeared the same with slightly less makeup than he remembered. Her smile and an inner glow, which radiated from her pleasant face, were new. Without hesitation, she kissed him firmly on the cheek, something she had never done before. That startled him. She wore a thin summer dress. Her long, silky hair fell down half the length of her back, which decreased her apparent age.

"The house is as beautiful as I remember it," Randolph said.

"It's good you've come now. It's sold. In a couple of months, we will be gone."

"Who bought it?" Andrea asked.

"The couple with the three kids and the station wagon. It went back and forth yesterday. Finally, they increased their offer. The timing is right. The new house should be finished just before Thanksgiving. There will be a room for you, Andrea."

"I'm getting an apartment," she said sullenly.

"Since you're working for the company, I know living on the South Shore wouldn't be practical. Your father will be disappointed if you won't live with him."

"Then he will be disappointed."

Walking through the house, especially the living room, and seeing the large heavy table set with four places brought Randolph haunting memories. Scott Lynder was sipping from an old fashion glass, sitting in a large armchair. Rising to greet Randolph, he was bronzed from the summer sun. His full head of hair was beginning to gray along the sides. He was of medium height and dressed in expensive leisure clothing.

Andrea followed her mother into the kitchen. She departed quickly with a tall glass of beer for Randolph, and then, quickly, rejoined her mother. Sylvia watched her daughter intently while she walked quickly around the kitchen, touching counters, chairs and cooking utensils, unable to stand in one place. "You haven't been this animated in a long time." She said finally. "He looks good, maybe a little thinner than a year ago."

"I will owe you for the rest of my life, mother. Either in gratitude or damnation! You were right."

"Now you know what I've found and how much better my life is."

"He's still going. He's got training for a whole year. That's plenty of time for me to make him change his mind."

"What makes you think he will change his mind about going?"

"He told me yesterday if they didn't need him over there, he wouldn't go. It's like it was before we broke up." Andrea sighed audibly. "I don't want to lose it. He goes to Georgia in a week. Should I postpone the trip?"

"I wouldn't. I've heard about your lobbying to go to California. You will lose a lot with your father and Leland Senior if you back out."

"You got what you wanted–Scott. How do I do it?"

"Our situation developed over many, many years. We changed slowly. I earned my happiness. I'm not sorry for any hurt we did to anyone."

"I haven't got years. This stupid war just seems to go on and on. It seems like half my life, there's been Vietnam."

"I hope for Scott Junior's sake, it ends, soon."

"He's already been to Vietnam."

"He wants a second tour."

"Good God, why?"

"He's a professional, A Marine officer. All that is very upsetting to Scott."

"Give him Randy's tour. We readjusted fine last night. I'm not going to lose him, again."

"Scott and I have a lot of things we share in common. The other thing is nice. I was in a desert for years. You must learn to share other things."

"I'll never like the Army. How could anyone?"

"You'd better learn about it. Obviously, he's going to be deeply involved with it over the next few years. Your hands are shaking. Set that casserole down before you drop it. I spent a lot of time on it. I want Scott's opinion." Andrea set the casserole dish on a counter unaware she had picked it up. She stared at her mother. Her face reflected her uncertainty. "You've got time," Sylvia said in soothing tone. "Use it. Don't rush everything."

Although the room was very familiar to Randolph, everything seemed different. "Sylvia redecorated." Scott said finally, watching Randolph as he looked around. "When her husband moved out." They had both sat in huge armchairs. "Andrea is dedicated and loyal to her father." Randolph said nothing and sipped the beer. "My daughter, Allison is Andrea's age. Just graduated from Radcliff. I have two sons. My younger is preparing for the bar examination. My oldest is a Captain in the Marines. Right now, he's stationed at

Parris Island and commands a company of recruits. Sylvia told me you just received a commission in the Army."

"It's something that allowed me to get started on what I want to do."

"I've asked my son about a posting to the Pentagon in Washington. He doesn't want it. Wants to be in that miserable place."

"Training is an important part of the military. That's all I've ever had and I got another year of it ahead of me."

"I never did military service. I registered and they never called me. During the tail end of the war, I worked for the Roosevelt and Truman administrations, so I guess I was exempt. I could never understand that life, but I guess my son likes it."

"He's done his tour in Nam?"

"Little over a year after he graduated from college. 66 to 67. That was a long year for me. His company took a lot of casualties. He wants to go back for another tour." Scott looked vacantly at his whiskey glass. Dejection colored his face, but quickly he purged it. "I've met many professional military men. I've never had to deal with it this close."

"I want to fly. The Army is where I can do it."

"That explains your starting point. My unfulfilled wish is that Scott Junior would have the same feeling about the law. My father and grandfather were lawyers. My younger son wants to follow the law. The military and that kind of life are alien to me."

"Military began before they started recording history. I would like to know why."

"I've never thought about what motivated military men. Maybe if I knew the answer to your question, I could understand my son."

"Wars are major points in history. In all of man-kinds' wars, I believe some would have been soldiers, just to be soldiers."

"Are you one of those?"

"I don't know, but I want to find out if I am qualified to be in that unique fraternity."

"Most young men are trying to avoid military service anyway they can. You and my oldest son are exceptions in this strange age."

"Soldiers are soldiers and have been since the first two lined up."

"Or Marines." Scott Lynder smiled ruefully.

Sylvia appeared calling them to dinner. Scott sat at one end where Frederic used to sit. Randolph thought possibly he did not know that. Sylvia was in her usual spot nearest the kitchen. Andrea helped carry in dishes. There was baked haddock in wine sauce. There were steamed vegetables and some in casseroles, salad and bread and rolls. Andrea drank white wine with her mother. Scott accepted a glass of white wine. Randolph retained his beer glass.

During the meal Sylvia talked, something she had never done at Randolph's Tremblay dinners. She spoke of the volunteer work she did for the museums, which is how she had met Scott. Currently, there was an exhibition of Native South American art on a circuit among the museums in the eastern part of the country. Sylvia spoke knowledgeably of the artifacts and the work involved in arranging the tour. Randolph listened attentively, but was bored. Sylvia's animation and knowledge impressed him.

"Andrea knows more about ball bearings than I ever did. She got her hands dirty working in the plant. Strange, how our interests manage to surface."

"Ball bearings indirectly brought you to museums. You should love them." Andrea said, defensively.

"Your father needs to retire. He'll have another heart attack. One of his brothers can run the company."

"One of them thinks he is." Andrea said sourly. "Uncle Leslie, the finance one." She looked at Randolph.

"When are you leaving for California?" Sylvia asked.

"Tuesday." The blank expression on Randolph's face changed abruptly to surprised concern. Although clearly she saw it, Andrea ignored it. "Randy mentioned something last night that has been stirring my thoughts. Salesmanship. We were eating hamburgers that guy has sold billions of."

"An effective sales force is the leading edge of any company, "Scott said. "Sometimes it makes a difference in how quickly a company can grow."

"Growth," Andrea said solemnly. "Is good in all things." Still looking at Randolph's apprehensive expression, she smiled evenly.

They retreated to different areas to change into swimsuits. Andrea produced a few suits she had bought for him while in college. They still fit although he had to cinch the waist tighter. He changed in a bathroom while Andrea used her bedroom. They met at the pool where Andrea set up a small bar for their wine bucket and glasses. She brought beers for Randolph.

Scott's body attested to years of good diet and regular exercise. There was no fat on his small athletic frame. Sylvia wore a modest two-piece suit. Andrea wore a single-piece suit that clung to her trim body. Quickly, they got in the water, which was very warm. The pool was heated electrically. They all swam for several minutes. Sylvia pursued Scott aggressively in the water dunking, screeching and touching boldly. Randolph noticed Andrea becoming slightly annoyed with her mother's adolescent behavior. It had become cooler after the lingering summer-like day. Andrea climbed out of the pool first, and wrapped herself in a large terry cloth robe, poured herself a large glass of wine then sat on a lounge chair. Reluctantly, Randolph left the soothing warm of the water, wrapping himself in another robe against the increasing night chill and sat beside her.

They watched Scott and Sylvia cavort in the pool for another twenty minutes. They drove from the sides, chasing each other through the water as well as along the deck. They raced each other from one end of the pool to the other. They were both breathing hard when Sylvia pulled a robe over her shoulders indicating she had had enough. They said good night. Randolph formally shook Scott's hand. Andrea stood beside him as they watched her mother and Scott walk, holding hands, toward the house.

Andrea sipped her wine. She returned to the lounge chair, pulling her robe tighter since the night chill was becoming cooler. "She's planning her wedding in every detail as if she was twenty-five instead of forty-five. It's going to be sometime in November when the divorce is final. She told Scott to get a quickie divorce so he would be ready. That was part of her ultimatum. Scott's children are angry with him. Except the Marine Corps one, I don't know if the others will go to the ceremony."

"Why did your mother suddenly get up the courage to issue him an ultimatum?"

"She met Scott about fifteen years ago. He had a young family and he wasn't going to leave them. Over the years, she continued to see him. Finally, his last kid–the daughter who is my age–graduated from college. Almost to her surprise, he accepted the ultimatum and left his wife. Their breakup must have been brewing for years."

"Your mother always seemed formal. She's really different, now." He sipped his beer without interest.

"She's happy. I know now for a long time with my father she was very unhappy. Last winter, after my father moved out, we had some long talks–something we never had while I was growing up. I knew she had come from a poor family. I had never really understood her perspective. My father basically bought her affection. He was charming, sophisticated and definitely patient. Just the ingredients to win a young, naive girl."

Randolph had known nothing about Sylvia. With the exception of her behavior tonight especially at the pool with Scott, he had thought she was cold, calculating and unemotional.

"When I told her about my feelings for you," Andrea continued. "I knew it had a lot to do with Scott finally committing to her. She had not cheated my father. They lived together over twenty years and she did what was expected. She went through all the motions of wife and mother. When Scott accepted her ultimatum, she started to feel true emotion for the first time in her life. My mother made me realize I had to find out if it still existed in you."

"What's your verdict?"

"Wasn't our time together the best there ever was? Last night everything came back just like it had been. You feel it, too."

"Yes." His throat constricted slightly with his answer.

"You've changed. I can feel it in you."

"I'm apprehensive. That's all."

"Then, get out of it."

"After raising your hand, there is no way out."

"I know now what my mistakes were. You have a right to be what you want. Be a soldier. Make it the least dangerous if can be. Don't go to Vietnam!"

"That's like saying, be a cop because you've always wanted to be a cop. Put the uniform on and wear the gun and badge. But, you have to stay in the station house. Be a theoretical cop but never get to see what it's like out on the street. Suppose I wanted to make it a career like Scott's son apparently is going to?" He looked at her. Her eyes went flat and she held her wineglass awkwardly.

"Do you want to be a General or a Colonel?"

Randolph got up and walked along the cement tile beside the pool, sipping his beer. She watched him, then got up from her chair and followed him. He set his beer on the smooth cement and leaned against a fence. "This is beautiful. The pool, the house. A nice piece of property. I'd never be able to give you things like this."

"It's not mine, either. This is my parents'. We have to earn our own. I've come after you. I've changed. You've changed. You're not that gung-ho kid. Let's use this change. Let's not let it go. I don't want to spend the rest of my life agonizing over losing you, when I bent and you wouldn't."

"I have the path to follow."

"Let's work with it, together." She set her wineglass on the cement next to his beer bottle and pushed her arm around his waist. The warmth from her body pressing against him clouded his mind and then he stopped thinking.

Chapter Two

Sunday morning they ate a late breakfast in the hotel's restaurant, and then went for a swim in the pool. There was one family with three young children, who used up a lot of the huge pool. There was an obvious honeymoon couple with shiny new rings on their fingers. They ignored the family and the noisy children and were oblivious to everything except each other.

"How about transferring your commission to the Navy?" Andrea was lying on her back, stretched out on a large lounge chair. She did not see his expression.

"The Army just spent a lot of money training me."

"How many others went through your training in Pennsylvania? How many other camps pushed out hundreds of Second Lieutenants? You owe the government, not specifically the Army. Why couldn't you do it in a Navy uniform?"

"I want to fly. I'm in a program the Army has approved. It's going to be helicopters although I'd rather fly fixed wing. I might not be able to get into a Navy flight program."

"Then how about the Air Force? Don't they have what you call the fixed wing airplanes? Transfer your commission to them."

"My commission is not a subway token."

"Scott could get that done. He would know how to do it. The right people to contact."

"Why do you want me to transfer my commission, if it could be done?"

"It might keep you out of Vietnam. Most of the men in Vietnam are Army. There would be less chance of you going if you were in the Navy or the Air Force."

"I'm reporting in a week, Andrea. There isn't time to do that."

"Would you consider it?"

"Which would you pick the Navy or the Air Force? Which uniform do you like the best?" Randolph curled his lips into a ridiculous grin and glared at her.

"The Navy, I like the gold." Her face was expressionless at his levity. The sun felt good on her stomach. She watched him as he slowly lowered himself onto the lounge chair, the muscles of his arms and legs and his torso drawing her attention as he settled. It was a good point about being a cop. To make him stop wanting to wear a uniform there has to be something bigger, more exciting to him. He wants to give me things and he doesn't think he can. If he reaches for more, he can do it. I have to make him see that. Being back together is the important thing. Keep those thoughts in his mind. There has to be a way to get him off his stupid path.

Sunday night they went to a restaurant away from the hotel. They both ordered prime rib. Randolph limited himself to one scotch since he was driving his Camaro. Andrea had a gin and tonic. Back at the hotel, the combination of beef and whiskey made him pass a lot of wind, which made them both giggly. Propped up with pillows on one of the beds, they watched a color television. They were content with each other and did a lot of touching. They did not talk much. Randolph set an alarm clock, but also requested the front desk telephone a wake up message. When it came, Randolph called the plant. He was surprised to get through to Al Garber. The shift had not started.

"I won't be in today. I'm seeing an old friend who has to leave town tomorrow."

"Tom and Eddy will miss you."

"You really need a fourth person on that dock. What are you going to do after Wednesday when I leave?"

"The same thing they'll be doing today without you. Would Judy like camping? I'd really like to take her up to New Hampshire."

"Judy sleeps in a sealed room and hates bugs."

"I've mentioned it and she seems interested."

"Boss, if you wanted to go deep sea diving, she'd be interested."

Monday the pool was deserted. One white-haired, pot bellied man went for a swim in the early afternoon. They made frequent trips back to the room and ate in a restaurant away from the hotel. They spent a long, nearly sleepless night. As it was getting light outside, he pushed his arm around her shoulders and fingered her hair, which lay partially on his shoulders and chest. For a long time he knew she was awake, but still they did not speak.

"Skip going to California tomorrow."

"The reason I can't do that is I want my father to know I'm serious about the company."

"We could have two more days together. It's been a long year."

Andrea's face contorted with her thoughts. Randolph felt her discomfort, but ignored it. "If I delayed going with my uncle, my father would see it as lack of interest in the company. I can't let that happen. Not now. My uncle, who happens to be my boss, the vice president of marketing and sales, hasn't been to California in five years. There was a territorial manager for the West Coast, but the position's been vacant for the past couple of years. My father told me he wants my impression of what our customers are thinking. Except for your coop job, this is the first real business thing he's asked me to do."

"Why hasn't your uncle filled that position?"

"Most of our business out there is handled through distributors or independent reps. He told my father we have ample representation out there."

"Then why has your father asked you to G-2 the area?"

"What Army term is that?"

"Report on the area and what's going on out there. That's what an intelligence staff officer does for his commander."

"You make it sound like he wants me to spy on my uncle."

"Did he tell you not to discuss anything with your uncle?"

"He did give me a list of 'should see' customers, which I am to compare to the ones we actually visit."

"If your father adhered to the chain of command, he would only listen to what your uncle would tell him. You have a directive to go outside that normal chain and report directly what your uncle did and did not do. Wouldn't you call that a form of spying?"

"Couldn't you come to California with me and fly to Georgia Saturday? We'd have four more days together."

"I'm taking my car and clothes and stuff."

"So, you won't bend either?"

"I can't put my car in the cargo hold of a commercial airliner."

"I could pay someone to drive it to Georgia."

"That's my first new car ever. Do you think I could trust someone to drive it that distance?"

"I could have it hauled on a truck. It could be delivered to you."

"That would cost too much."

"I can afford it. There's no reason you shouldn't be able to afford it either, someday."

Randolph did not answer her. They fell into an uneasy period of silence. He continued to stroke her skin. In all their time together at Northeastern, he had never felt the presence of her family's wealth. The feeling made him uneasy. The alarm woke him while it was still dark as he dozed. Sleep had come only in jagged pieces during the long night. The wakeup call came a moment after the alarm. Having left the bathroom door open when he stepped out of the shower, impolitely, she stared at him, her eyes pensive as he dried himself. After shaving, he hurried back to the bed and sat next to her. He removed the towel and started to push his way under the bedding. "Hey, I got to get moving, too." She stopped his advance, by wrapping herself in one of the blankets. "My flight leaves at ten." She stood but did not move toward the bathroom. "I'd like to us to have the time together."

"You have commitments, too, the new Andrea." He smiled warmly at her.

"Do you have any regrets? Us being back together?"

"For months, parts of you would come to me at odd times. It was painful. These last couple of days has been a dream."

"Where ever they send you, like Georgia, I can visit you." She came to him and wrapped her arms around his head pulling him tight to her chest. She licked his ear, but then broke away from his embrace to rush to the bathroom.

In the parking lot standing next to their cars, they held each other for a long time. The roar of the morning commuter traffic came from Route 128. The sun shone in a cloudless sky, but there was a trace of coolness in the air, a warning of the coming autumn.

"I'm going to be the best damn spy there is." She looked up into his face. "I have to prove to my father I'm capable and that the company is important. That's going to be my training." They started toward their cars. "I'll call you as soon as I get to my hotel," she yelled as she was getting into her Mustang. Standing by the Camaro's door a moment watching her, he realized her face indicated her mind had shifted to details ahead of her.

At the afternoon break, Tom mischievously presented Randolph with a single cupcake with a candle in it and offered him a cigarette. It was an unspoken acknowledgement of being able to match Tom's murderous packing speed. For the weeks Randolph had worked on this shipping dock, the work never varied. Trolleys loaded with bins of subassemblies for the automotive and electronics industries appeared in a never-ending stream. Each piece had to be wrapped separately, and then boxed in larger cardboard shipping crates. For large orders, these crates were loaded onto a wooden pallet.

Suddenly, more people started to appear on the shipping dock, although the break was nearly over. Judy stood next to Al Garber. They pushed the trolleys out of the way as they crowded onto the dock. A huge cake had been set on one of the empty trolleys. In the frosting decorations was a helicopter and the words, 'Good Luck, Randy.' There was a hushed silence while the cake was cut and distributed. Randolph noticed there were many reserved expressions. Apparently there had been many similar ceremonies for young men leaving for military service.

Walking out through the parking lot of the plant now haunted for him by Andrea's return, he realized he had reached a milestone. He would never come back to this parking lot, make his way through the rows of cars to the small cement steps of the shipping dock as an employee. He was about to embark on the next course of his life, one he had sought and certainly would find more stimulating than Tom and Eddy's monotonous, but safe routines. Having Andrea again was beyond anything he had dreamed. Something made it right for both of them. Their bodies fit together so completely and naturally. Had it been that way before? Ludicrously, she had been hesitant fearing rejection from him. Of course she could not know of his months of aching. She had changed from the college student he had known. They were older, at different stages of their lives. She had no choice but to accept his being in the Army, yet still did not want him to go to Vietnam. Would she ever accept what once she hadn't? She wanted to work at it, whatever the hell that meant. He could not alter his path. Soon, he would be flying. He would begin to seek the answers to what compelled him to put on a uniform. What drove others? Her working had put rigidity in her that had not been there before. Whatever the reason, did it matter? He had her back.

On the street in front of the Thayer house next to the spot he normally took was a red Camaro, the same body style and shape as his white one. It was Faith Beckwerth's. She worked for a law firm, did a lot of overtime, was well paid and so had a new car. It was not unusual to see her in the Thayer household. She often played Monopoly with Teddy, when she wasn't visiting his sister. She had been a fixture since the sixth grade. Going in the back door, Judy still wearing her work smock was busily cutting up lettuce which was to go into the huge seldom used vase-like dish which was stored in his mother's hutch. His mother still wore her powder specked, bakery uniform. She was busily cutting up potatoes, which had been boiled for potato salad.

"Bring this apron out to Faith. She's still in her work clothes. She'll get them all greasy. She's doing the grill." His mother indicated an apron draped over one of the worn kitchen chairs.

Picking up the apron he went out and around the house to the back yard. Faith wore a dark blue dress, the hem conservatively dropped below her knees. Her back was to him as he came around the corner of the house. She was attempting to light the coals using lighter fluid and dropping paper matches. When a small blue flame started she sprayed more fluid in an attempt to enlarge the burning area on the coals. He came up beside her. Her dress had an open neck displaying a hint of her collarbone. A pearl necklace and earrings with the dress made her appear older than her nineteen years. Her brown hair, which touched her shoulders, longer now than he remembered it, was still work-ready combed. When she had just turned sixteen on a couch in her parents' basement cellar playroom within sight of all her father's Japanese and Marine Corps souvenirs hanging on the walls, she had allowed him to pull her panties completely off. For the next several weeks, as he commuted to classes at Northeastern whenever he saw her, he stared only at her belly, which remained, comfortably and reassuringly flat.

"My mother wants you to put this on to protect your clothes."

She took the apron after shifting the lighter fluid can in her hands. "I brought shorts. I'm going to go change after I get this started."

"I can finish it for you."

"Gee, I wish you would finish it." She grinned revealing her brace-straight bright teeth. Randolph took the lighter fluid can.

"You've got it going. We won't need this anymore."

"I wish we did. Oh, the fire. Yes, that's going." The smile never left her mischievous face. Randolph blushed.

"How is Arthur?" Her brother Arthur, a Marine Corps lance corporal had had his leg blown off by a land mine in Vietnam.

"I went to see him Monday. It's been three months since he got here from Japan. He's still resisting the therapy."

"Still won't use the artificial leg."

"He's had it for weeks. He has no excuse not to try it. He fights the shrink, and they're talking about discharging him. One nice

31

thing about the Marine Corps, when they're done using you, they throw you away." Her bright smile had faded from her face.

"What else can they do for him? That's why there's the Veterans Administration. They'll send him to one of their hospitals."

"I've heard they're hell holes. I don't want that for my brother. They wanted to give him a medal."

"What medal?"

"The bronze star. They wanted to have a ceremony to present it to him. My father was all excited. Arthur said he wouldn't accept it. Says it's an insult and a mockery to other Marines. I don't know what we're going to do with him. He's getting more unpredictable each time we see him. Never know what he's going to do or say." Her eyes watered and she turned her head away from him. "My father wants to bring him home. My mother says no way because of the younger kids." Faith had two younger sisters and one brother. One sister was Teddy's age. The other, Sarah, was sixteen and gorgeous. The baby brother had just started kindergarten. She took a deep breath and sighed, then looked back at him. Her face again noticeably brightened. "Will you get home for Thanksgiving or Christmas?"

"I don't know. I have to show up this Sunday. Then I start finding things out."

"Put more coals on, so they'll be burned when we're ready for the hamburgers. I'm going in to change out of my work uniform." Looking at Randolph she smiled fully but turned quickly away from him and started for the house. As she came into the kitchen, Mrs. Thayer stopped mixing the potato salad.

"Are you all right?" She asked Faith.

"Got some smoke from the charcoal." Quickly, she picked up a small cloth bag that had her change of clothes and darted up the stars to Judy's room. Mrs. Thayer looked at her daughter. Judy merely shrugged then continued with her food preparation.

Upstairs in Judy's closed room she stepped out of the sleek, expensive work dress. Tears rolled down over both cheeks. Quickly, she stepped into the shorts, and then added a sleeveless blouse. Judy's window overlooked the back yard. From it she could see

Randolph, sipping a beer and still tending the coal fire on the grill.

She was gone. Out of his life. I could sense his eagerness to get started with the Army. He was beginning to notice me, again. Idly, she looked around Judy's crowded room at the wiggly cot in the corner. It was her cot, really. No one else ever slept on it. How many times had she endured that falling-apart, squeaky, uncomfortable cot just to be near him sleeping feet away down the small hall? Why couldn't she ever decrease the distance between them? So many times he was leaning toward me with a comment, a look, and some laughter and sharing something only we knew together.

Stop kidding yourself. Was anything ever really there over the past year and a half? All that hoping and wanting. Wise up. If there ever was a chance, it's gone now because she is back. Her crying had stopped and she made a conscious effort to insure there was no residue left on her face. She studied her image in Judy's mirror. It would be so easy to just kiss him off. Now it's really hopeless. If I give up, there will be no more me. Can't let that happen. A smile slowly kept across her face as she looked at herself in Judy's mirror. I have no choice, the words formed slowly in her mind. I'm not going to give up.

"You have a telephone call," Judy stood at the corner of the house. After putting more coals on the grill, the fire was beginning to whiten some of the coals. Randolph walked quickly into the house.

"These calls are going to cost that poor girl a fortune." His mother paused in her cooking preparations as he passed through the kitchen. "You were on for twenty minutes last night."

"These are business calls, Ma. She doesn't have to pay for them. Her company does." In the living room, where his father was dozing in his reclining chair in front of the black and white television set, was the single Thayer phone on an end table next to his mother's couch.

"My uncle says my father has a lot of state political contacts." Her voice sounded inquisitive. "He could get you a position in the National Guard. You transfer your Army commission to a National Guard one."

"You gave up on Navy gold?" He laughed.

"I didn't." She matched his laugh. "You might even be able to continue flying, depending on where they can get you in."

"That's a part time job. What do I do with the rest of my time?"

"Your coop job could probably still be arranged." Andrea giggled.

"I'm not doing anything if I can't fly."

"My uncle thinks it would be a pretty sure thing. The wheels would have to be started. Can I ask my father when I get back home?"

"You should be able to ask your father anything." Randolph looked at his father, who was definitely sleeping in his recliner. His mouth was open and he was snoring lightly. "I'll let you know when, if I want to pursue that."

"My mother wants to know where you're going to be on November eighth. Now that the house is sold, they set the date for the wedding."

"I'll be at Fort Benning, Georgia."

"I'll have to check the map to find out what city that place is near. I'm sure the Army will give you weekends off."

"We didn't have weekends off when I was in Pennsylvania."

Faith walked slowly down the stairs, pausing on the last step until Randolph's eyes met hers. She did not return his smile. She had long shapely legs and had added a bandana to her hair, tying it into a ponytail. Her change of clothes took her away from her profession in an office and put her back into their neighborhood on a late summer day. When Randolph turned slightly away from her, she continued on toward the kitchen.

"Let me know if you can come to the wedding. Something very interesting happened today." Her tone changed becoming almost conspiratorial. "A call from one of our customers got directed to my room by mistake. They asked why we had cancelled our visit.

I said I thought it was still on for Thursday afternoon. My uncle cancelled it. This was one of the "should see" customers. What should I do, Randy?"

"You're out there for a reconnaissance. Didn't you learn anything at your company's coop job? Like, how to avoid walking into an ambush? Stuff like that is useful. "

"This is serious, Randy."

"Tell your uncle you're not feeling good and you want a nap. Tell him anything, but get in a cab and go to that customer on Thursday afternoon. Something is being hidden. That's what your father wants to know."

"What should I bring?"

"What do you usually bring on these visits?"

"Literature on the latest product stuff."

"Bring that and see if that's been seen recently. If they haven't seen any of it, whoever's supposed to do that hasn't been doing their job. That would mean you uncle hasn't been doing his part because it must be his job to see they get that kind of information. I'm promoting you to Second Lieutenant in the spy corps. Remember, they only shoot spies in the movies."

"What if my uncle finds out?" She did not laugh.

"He will eventually. Let's hope you're back in Massachusetts and you've been able to report to your father. Otherwise, I'm sure he will want to line you up against the nearest wall."

"I can't do that to my uncle. He's been so good to me."

"You are the one who wants to make your father think you are serious about working for the company. He gave you the spy mission. That costs us two days together. Remember, he is the commander."

"Maybe that's why sales out here aren't what my father wants."

"Don't lose sight of the objective. Scott told you growth can happen through increased sales. Your father knows the same stuff as Scott. Spy on."

She was silent a moment. "You have a feeling for what's going on out here. I wish you were here with me."

"I'm with you in spirit. I'm about to put the uniform on. We know that's going to change things. Only geographically. I will help you all I can." After he hung up, he went back into the kitchen. His mother was molding hamburgers with her hands. Judy was finishing the tossed salad.

"Judy, your father bought a case of beer for the men. Better get some ice and put it in the cooler."

"I'll do that Mrs. T," Faith said. She would not look at Randolph. She hefted the case of beer and took it out the back door. Judy watched her departure, and then looked at her brother's bright face.

"Who else is coming to this thing? You have enough hamburgers for a platoon."

"Betsy is bringing her boyfriend." Judy said. "Her school in New Hampshire just started. She wanted to see you off. Connie said she might bring someone. Probably that Tina. She's just coming from Boston."

"Is there someone from Northeastern?" His mother asked. "If you hadn't disappeared this past weekend that was one of the things I wanted to ask you."

"The only other person I want here is in San Francisco."

"The other most important guest just arrived." Judy announced. Al Garber was standing in front of the screen door. Quickly, Judy opened the door, and kissed him lightly on the cheek. He was in his mid-twenties, of medium height and muscularly slender. He had short hair and wore a blue business shirt with a solid color tie. There was a plastic pencil carrier in his breast pocket, which was filled with pencils and pens. "I keep wanting to do that at work." She giggled. "Can you get a warning for kissing the supervisor?"

"Hi, ex-boss. Faith is putting the beer on ice," Randolph leered. "Want a warm one?"

"Sure," Al Garber said. "Is there anything I can do?"

"Are you a grill man?" Mrs. Thayer smiled at him.

"Don't take that away from Faith." Judy said tartly. "She always does a good job, Ma. Let her do it."

"Are you implying I can't cook?" Al smiled.

"Yes, I've seen what you bring for lunch."

Randolph led Al Garber out through the back door he had just come in. In the backyard he poked at the coals in the grill. Faith had set up a cooler and was putting the beer in it. She handed beers to Al and Randolph. Al led him further into the yard away from Faith.

"I want to take Judy to the White Mountains. We could hike a mountain and sleep in tents. Here's the problem. How can I get Judy away overnight?"

"Ask her?" Randolph sipped his warm beer.

"We're going to do the Blue Hills this weekend for practice. We can do that in a couple of hours. That's just a day trip. We'll be back in the evening just like going to the movies."

"My sister Judy said she'd climb a mountain?"

"I took her Monday to buy hiking boots."

"Fifty bucks." Judy walked quickly toward them. "He bought me the top of the line, the best."

"He also wants to go to the White Mountains and have you sleep in a tent." Randolph said quickly. "It's the Ma problem, though."

"I'll tell her I'm sleeping over at Faith's."

"I don't want to lie to your mother." Al said solemnly.

"Faith's from the neighborhood," Randolph said. "Too easy to find out you weren't there."

"Betsy's going to school in New Hampshire. I'll say I'm going up to visit her and spend the night in her dorm. Betsy will do it. I want to go, Al."

"The last thing I want to do is get in trouble with your mother." Al looked suddenly depressed. "I don't want to ruin that relationship before it's really started."

"I want to go hiking in the White Mountains with you. And sleep in a tent. We could set it up here in the backyard and practice." Judy giggled.

"There's bugs out in the woods." Randolph taunted.

"Al will protect me."

"You'll end up carrying her."

"That's fine with me." Al smiled at Judy.

"She even sleeps with her windows closed."

"You can zip the tent up, right?"

"After hiking all day, it won't make any difference. The clean, cold air will wipe you out. I know another couple who hike and camp. If they'll come with us, then I could say men in one tent, women in the other. Would your mother go for that?"

"My mother would pick that one apart in a minute." Randolph said.

"It doesn't matter," Judy said evenly. "I am going with you whether it's with another couple or not."

While the coals were burning down, they arranged beach chairs near the table with the salad and condiments. Al and Randolph drank their beer. Faith and Judy drank soda. Mrs. Thayer remained in the house. They saw Betsy's convertible with its roof down stop on the street. She was in the passenger seat. A young man was driving. Betsy Croteau leaped out of the car and ran toward Faith and Judy. They hugged each other as if it had been a lot longer than three weeks she had been away at school. She introduced her boyfriend, Andrew Tanlewood. Judy introduced Al Garber to them.

Betsy's blonde hair was nearly white. Her skin was bronzed from spending the summer on the Cape. Andrew had the same deep tan and his darker blonde hair had bleached also. Both were wearing designer summer clothing. Betsy wore long pants with low heels and a sleeveless jersey. Andrew wore slacks with a matching jersey. Neither looked like college students, but rather like young professionals. Andrew still showed a lack of expression as he accepted a beer from Randolph. His bored look came either from the long ride south from New Hampshire or his tolerating Betsy's desire to visit. Betsy requested a Coke. They sat next to each other in beach chairs.

"Andrew's finished taking a summer course," Betsy said. "Then we went straight into fall classes. He hasn't had a break."

"Randy did a summer course, too." Judy snickered. "What did you take?"

"Latin. I needed a refresher."

"I played in the woods. How's the draft treating you?"

"I have my student 2S. I'm safe as long as I keep that."

"Al's a veteran." Judy told Betsy. "He did the Air Force for four years. He was in Thailand. He didn't have to go to Vietnam. He says Thailand is a beautiful country." Judy beamed. Betsy eyed Al Garber thoroughly obviously tallying his presence to Judy's gossip.

"I'd like to go back some day when the War is over." Al announced through Betsy's leering scrutiny.

"Now, he's doing school at night. His classes just started, too."

"Is Connie coming?" Betsy asked. "That should be interesting with Randy." She smiled at Randolph.

"I told her no anti-war crap." Judy said.

"Knowing Connie, she will ignore you." Faith stood up. "The coals are ready. Who wants cheeseburgers? Hotdogs, what?" Faith went to the grill with determination on her face. Betsy and Judy disappeared into the house.

"Judy didn't tell me you were Air Force." Randolph said to Al.

"I made it to illustrious pay grade of E-4. I was in communications. I got to see Texas, California then Thailand. Thailand was the best. Even a lowly enlisted could live like a king. They could make some wonderful resorts over there. Maybe they will when the war is over."

"They launch B-52s out of there to hit the Ho Chi Ming Trail."

"Most of those came from Guam. I did see some B-52s."

"Could you have gone on any of those missions?"

"No!" Al laughed. "Those crews are all highly trained. Even though they were six miles up, they got shot at."

"Lot of people don't know that."

"I was very content to stay on the ground. They were professionals. I admired the crews. I was a tourist. I just passed through the Air Force."

"Summer Latin guy, you want another beer?" Randolph got up out of his chair to go to the cooler. "Al?" Al nodded.

"I'm fine," Andrew shook his beer can to emphasize. "Who did you pledge?"

"Just the flag."

"What houses, I mean." Andrew persisted, annoyance registered plainly on his face, as Randolph sat again.

"The house of green."

"Who was that?"

"The biggest fraternity in the world, the Army."

Andrew was sullen, his expression registering displeasure of Randolph's patronization. "What sports did you play?"

"I tried skiing in the Army."

"Army has a ski team?"

"It was a Rotsee weekend. A tactical problem. We hardly got to use the skis. We lugged them halfway up a mountain in New Hampshire. No one could ski with them. Even experienced skiers said they stunk. Then we ran down the mountain carrying the skis."

"Sounds exhilarating. I'll have to cut back my senior year. I need the time for courses. I'll miss them. Sports are a great mental diversion."

"What did you play?"

"Tennis, golf, crew."

"Good thing for a prospective doctor."

"Yeah, or I might be wearing one of those green suits very soon."

"Especially if you can't get into medical school."

"It's only a matter of time. I will." Smugness returned to his facial expression.

"They draft doctors, after they've been trained."

"There's got to be a way around it. I'll be damned if I'm going to spend all that time in school and then get drafted. With a residency to do, no one is going to draft me."

Connie Anacio's gait was recognizable as she strode around the house coming into the backyard. She was two inches over five feet. Her shoulder length dark hair was shiny and robust, but she had tied it behind her head and it stuck out like a horse's tail. She wore no perceptible makeup. Her steps were small but determined. They had parked a ten-year old, rusting Ford in the driveway behind the Thayers' old station wagon. With her was Tina Michaud. Although the summer was nearly over neither Connie nor Tina Michaud had any signs of sun. Tina was a full head taller than Connie and wore an exorbitant amount of makeup. She looked like her face had been painted with several layers. Dark eye makeup encircled her eyes. Connie was studying on a full academic scholarship at Boston University. As part of his sister's circle of close friends, Randolph knew her as very articulate and brainy. With them was a young man their age with long hair tied into a neat ponytail hanging to his belt. His skin looked bronzed from the summer sun. Connie introduced the pony-tailed man as Kevin Bolkanwicz, but addressed him as Skip.

There was no hugging, as there had been when Betsy arrived. There was an unbelievable coolness with Judy and Faith. They knew of Tina, but nothing of the young man. Faith asked them what they wanted to eat. Hamburgers and hot dogs were still cooking on the grill. The three took paper plates from the table with the salad.

"How is school?" Judy asked, affably.

"It's still there," Connie said tartly. "We're preparing for a colossal march in D.C. in November."

"Hey," Judy said coldly, staring at Connie. "Cut out the anti-war stuff. Maybe it's an important part of your life, but not this afternoon. This is Randy's party. You're here because we all grew up together. That's what I want him to leave here with."

"The biggest thing of our lives–and poor Randy is about to be sucked into it. That's your attitude. Let's be quiet and applaud him as he goes off to face the worse thing our country has ever been apart of. That's why we have to march."

"It's not just students involved," Skip interjected evenly but firmly in an attempt to break up the confrontation between Judy and Connie. He had started to eat his salad. He set it down on the condiments' table. "This movement has involved everyone from business presidents to janitors. Even soldiers although out of uniform. Everyone is marching with us." Skip looked hopeful as he scrutinized the cold stares. He was not intimidated and seemed accustomed to hostility. Undaunted he continued, "Slowly, a huge diverse group–the real feelings of the majority of the people-are beginning to speak as one. End this war."

"People's lives are at risk." Connie lectured, her voice rising, looking from face to unfriendly face. "They are dying every day. Soldiers, civilians. We have to do whatever we can to put a stop to it. Our support is growing, daily. It's amazing how you can feel it–that people know what we are doing is right. They want to end the war."

"I have an announcement to make." Randolph stepping forward held up his can of beer waving it to gain attention and silence. Everyone looked at him their expressions becoming momentarily bland. No one moved after Randolph's sudden surge. "I've been waiting for the right time to tell everyone. I love you all greatly–because of those sleep over parties Judy had–that forced me to sleep on our lumpy couch. Just so my mother would keep me from getting a glance of some colorful panties, which I knew you girls all wore." Turning to Al Garber, he saluted by raising his beer can to him. "Now you're the only one, Al, who's going to get to see those panties." He swept the air using his beer can as emphasis. "So, it's fitting for me to tell you all. Tomorrow, I'm not heading for Georgia and the Army. I'm going to sneak into Canada, renounce my American citizenship, throw away my commission, and save my ass from getting shot at." No one said a word, nor moved for several very quiet seconds. Randolph looked from face to face, elongating the silence. Judy and Faith's faces looked like they had been slapped. "And, if I do all that, I can't march in any demonstrations. Sorry, can't be in two places at the same time."

Betsy's face was the first to loose the solemn gaze as her lips curled into a wiry smile. "How did you find out what color panties we wore? You were always the most solemn guy. Who would have thought?" She started giggling softy. Her smile spread to Judy and Faith. Her boy friend Andrew looked at her, but his face remained neutral and emotionless.

"Faith," Connie turned to her. She had ignored the colored panties comment. "With what happened to Arthur, you should want to see this war end. That shouldn't happen to any other boys."

"My brother is a Marine. His price was steep, but he's a man. We're proud."

"Leave it to those Commie bastards." Randolph said in his newly acquired ironic tone. "They can't win on the battlefield, so they're trying to win here. Problem is some of those Commie bastards are right here."

"All right, Randy!" Judy exploded turning all her attention to her brother. "We don't need it from you, too. Enough of the anti-war and war crap. Let's get some music out here." Judy started toward the house, but quickly stopped when no one offered to follow her.

Skip had evaluated his audience. His face melted into sobriety. His eyes hardened. He backed away, leaving his half eaten salad on the table and walked toward the side of the house, then around it. Connie and Tina did not follow Skip. Connie's facial expression returned to intransigence and anger. Tina munched her salad glancing from face to face, but remaining expressionless. She seemed to enjoy the food and quickly shoveled it into her mouth. Faith did not follow Judy but inched protectively closer to Randolph.

Without a word but after a quick surveillance of everyone, unexpectedly Randolph followed Skip with a determined gait. The long-haired young man leaned against the old Ford, lighting a cigarette. There was a pensive and hesitant expression on his face when Randolph suddenly appeared.

"You came here to recruit us?"

"I came because Connie asked me. She's very dedicated as you can see. We get support. It comes from all kinds of people. Some from where you'd never expect. I have an open opinion of everyone—at first."

"You were hoping?"

"We don't have to hope. More and more are coming over to our point of view about the war. It's inevitable, we will end it."

"Even girls like Tina." Randolph also lit a cigarette. "Where did Connie find her?"

"She's a special person. May not look like it, but she has opinions, too."

"Makes it easier to knock of f a piece of ass, now and then."

"If that's what you want, she might be gullible and impressionable. I have more important things to think about and do."

"Connie's intelligent but also very impressionable. She more your type?"

"My girlfriend's name is Susan. I live with her. She had other commitments, or she would have come with us."

"Good, old, painted Tina. Under all that make up she wears, she's sort of what you need for the 'chicks up front' mentality."

"There is a tactical scenario. You're a military man. I shouldn't have to explain that to you."

"Would you fight for this country?"

"I believe I am in a battle. We're trying to save lives."

"Not for an Asian who wants a democratic form of government?"

"As an intelligent person, you can't believe those corrupt governments our government props up, are democratic? Let the Asians decide for themselves what type of government they want to live with. I hate seeing this country torn apart by a war created by politicians for their own, unclear ideals."

"Aren't there bigger issued involved?"

"What's a bigger issue than an unnecessary war?"

"Better red than dead?"

"Propaganda! Clichés! Words make us do a lot of things." Skip dragged deeply on his cigarette and looked away from Randolph.

"What about traitors? Americans are dying because of what you're doing. Doesn't that bother you?"

"I was in D.C. two years ago during the riots. I saw the troops on the steps of the Capital. It looked like a banana republic with the troops taking to the streets to keep the government in power. That was more frightening."

Randolph was quiet a moment and dragged deeply on his cigarette. "Why do men put on uniforms? Why do they become soldiers?"

"Governments will punish them, if they refuse."

"Oh, there are laws to make you serve. That happens in any country. That's practical. There are men who put on a uniform merely to be soldiers."

"Mankind is a beast. Without laws, there would be anarchy. Mankind also uses laws to corrupt–to make what he calls legalized barbarity–War. Men who put those uniforms on willingly are real beasts. Didn't we learn all that from World War II? With all those uniforms and the raising of the arm in the heil. It's the ultimate insult to mankind. They banned together to stop anarchy, but permit it on a gargantuan scale. That is legalized anarchy."

"Still, there are men who will go. They would go under any conditions." Again Randolph paused, paying attention to his cigarette.

"I know what is wrong and evil." Skip said smugly. "Are you an intellectual soldier? That's a rarity. Also a big contradiction."

"Too bad your recruitment was a failure today. You need better training. The Army is very thorough when they train us."

"We learn to adapt to accomplish goals." Skip said defensively.

"You'll be using the same recruitment techniques ten years from now to sell marshmallows. You'll probably be good at it."

"You should know what war is going to be like. You don't seem to be a fool."

"No one knows what war is like until they've been there. Not even the most dedicated and pure soldiers."

"I pity you." Skip eyed him sharply.

"Don't. In your Army, you don't get combat pay. We do. It's actual money. You can buy beer with it." With a final harsh glare at the pony-tail hair man, Randolph turned and went back around the house.

Andrea sat cross-legged on the spacious bed in her hotel room in Los Angeles. The day had been spent in airports departing from San Francisco and dragging luggage as she and her uncle continued their sales and marketing trip. She had changed into two-piece, comfortable pajamas, which she preferred. Her legs began to tingle thinking about Randolph. She wished he was there to rub his legs against hers and create the warmth that always escalated between them. Possibly they needed a break after the intense sexual activity in the short time they were together, although she felt no abnormal discomfort. Eying the big bed brought a smile to her lips. We would have made good use of it, she thought.

Four days ago they had last touched. It seemed longer. She had flown across the country to two major Californian cities, visited a dozen customers and had kept a hand written journal in keeping with Randolph's instructions of what she thought her father wanted to know about this trip. Her uncle was concentrating on certain older customers and their needs. Many were traditional, manufacturing plants producing capital machinery for heavy industry. These were Tremblay Bearings staples, their oldest customers historically going back to the company's founding. That seemed normal, yet something was missing along with his refusal to visit particular customers. His claim was time constraints. Their itinerary was vigorous and some customers had used more time than they allocated. That reason seemed plausible to Andrea as to why they had skipped some customers. She had sales figures which indicated some of her father's must visits were minor and easily handled by distributors or reps. It was a question for which she wanted to elicit Randolph's thoughts.

Staring at the phone and at the clock on the end table next to the bed, it was nearly the agreed time for him to call. For two days he had been driving alone but had called her each night. He should be in Georgia and close to Fort Benning.

It was hard to believe their reunion had been so easy. He was right about the time from that Fourth of July call through the rest of the summer being lost. Why had she been so hesitant? Anger had caused so many negative images. He had left her at her tree in such a vulnerable position with her heart open and pleading. Without commenting or even saying good-bye, coldly he had left. That had hurt so, it turned to antagonism which solidified and further alienated her.

The Army was about to possess him. We've been that way before, butted heads and lost time together. I will not let that happen again, she told herself sternly. To seduce him away from the Army she wanted to know more of how Tremblay Bearings operated. This trip had shown her how the practical side of sales operated. It was people, meeting them, getting involved with them and their need for Tremblay product. She had learned a lot from her uncle on this trip. He had been doing this all his adult life, but still it had all been revealing to watch it transpire.

Randolph's suggestions concerning this trip had been beneficial. He seemed to grasp her father's reasons. How could she seduce his interest to Tremblay Bearings? That had to be the way to divert him, even while the Army had him. She felt so much depended upon her ability. There was no one else to change things. When the phone rang, her heart quickened. After he had given her his telephone number, she quickly dialed him back.

"I know how much time you'll get off on the weekends." She teased. "You'll have duty Saturday. Maybe half a day, but Sundays you'll have off. We'll have plenty of time to be together."

"Who told you that?"

"They want Scott in the Nixon Administration. So, they've assigned a mentor to make Scott's life as pleasant as possible. Someone who works either for the Nixon Administration or the Republican Party called me in San Francisco the day we got there. After introducing himself and convincing me he wasn't a deranged nut, he informed me that they know about us and that you are just entering active duty. If I wanted any Army information he would provide it. So, I tested him. I asked what course you were taking at Fort Benning. He didn't know, but called me back within a couple of hours and told me it was IOBC. That stands for Infantry Officer Basic Course. Aren't you impressed, I've learned an Army acronym."

"Why would they do that for Scott?"

"He has international and legal banking connections, everywhere. It's a very prestigious position. He'd even get a title. They want his pre-eminence and influence in certain areas of the world. They're willing to do whatever it takes to make him change his mind. That's why I got a call."

Randolph was silent for a moment. "Anything else happen your last day in San Francisco?"

"That company we discussed on my father's list, I called. As you predicted they had no appointment with my uncle and didn't know he was in the bay area. In fact, they haven't heard much from Tremblay Bearings in the past couple of years. No problem reordering their usual traditional bearings, but they know nothing of recent products."

"That was the definite third company in the San Francisco area that's been neglected."

"My uncle considers them an OK account."

"In your uncle's terms that must mean a self administered account. Is there the potential for growth? There's no one to find that out. Maybe you need a salesman just to cover California."

"This week in LA is going to be a waste of time. I know it already."

"How many companies in the LA area are on your father's list?"

"Five."

"How many has your uncle scheduled to visit?"

"Two. They're the largest, though. That's just what we did in San Francisco. Just the important ones. Why would my father want to know about small accounts? All the sales figures indicate what they do. He knows what they are."

"The reason has to be hidden in those numbers. Did you look at history or just current sales? Even the guys I worked with on the dock over the summer knew the history of who was getting what and how much. That was useful information even to us dock jockeys. Advance info told us when we'd be hit with a lot of stuff to package."

"We have the last two years figures with us. They must have been bigger customers at one time. Obviously, that's why he wanted me to visit them. You've given me the reason and why."

"Right up an Army officer's lists of must accomplish, sell ball bearings."

"Remember every time you get on a train, most likely you are riding a Tremblay Bearing."

"Problem is I can't remember the last time I was on a train. Cars and trucks do everything today. Get your ball bearings into them."

"When we get through this week, I'm going to tell my uncle I've decided to fly to Georgia to see you. You're going to be my camouflage. How's that for Army talk." She giggled. "What I'm going to do is stay here and visit those other companies. I may even go back to San Francisco and hit those other places we missed. I'm going to find out the reason for the neglect and give that to my father."

"That's the way to be a spy. Do you want to be the salesman out there?"

"No! I like the way you do it on the phone. You ask all the right questions. You're the one giving the orders. I want to be that person. Maybe with your help, I can do it. My uncle is a good man. My father has always respected him. He gave me Barbie Dolls when I was growing up. He's a real part of Tremblay Bearings."

"Why hasn't he been doing his job?"

"There has to be a good reason why no one has been doing anything out here. I need to find that out, too. Maybe with this additional time, I can."

"Will that delay your first visit down here?"

"When I've finished out here, I've got to go home to report to my father."

When she hung up the phone, she laid her head on the comfortable pillow. Closing her eyes she could feel him as if he was lying beside her. It set her skin to tingling. His interest is in the company. He is such a natural. The key will be to keep that interest alive, regardless of what the Army is making him do. My responsibility is to get more involved. This trip has made me see that. She started to drift into sleep weighed by the fatigue of the strenuous traveling day. Smugly, she felt confident she could pull him onto her path. The way was through and with the company.

Chapter Three

The gates of Fort Benning were manned by impeccably uniformed MPs. They admitted him once he produced a copy of his orders. The streets were named after renowned military leaders or places with battle significance to the Army. The jump towers for airborne training were the most prominent structures. Temporary signs for Infantry Officer Basic Course students directed him to the building, which housed the student brigade's orderly room. There was no feeling of beginnings. Sparse Sunday activities greeted him. There were no companies of soldiers marching. Few people were visible on the Post. Infrequently, World War II temporary buildings caught his eye. Most of the architecture of the Post was modern.

The student brigade was quartered in a large suite of offices in a multi-storied red brick building. There was a counter which several enlisted clerks manned, very efficiently. They collected copies of his orders, issued and made him sign for a numbered room key, handed him directions to the BOQ, which was within walking distance and directives on where students were permitted to park. Hours of operation for an Open Mess dinning facility completed the clerk's logistical briefing. His time was free until a mandatory formation at 1900 hours in a building, which was also within sight of the orderly room. Had the enlisted clerks been wearing ties and coats instead of khakis, it would have seemed he was registering at a Holiday Inn as he had the night before.

Olsen Hall was the bachelor officer's quarters for student officers. It had been a troop barracks several decades before. It was a three-story structure with broad cement balconies on each floor. The horseshoe shaped buildings interior parade ground had been paved for a parking lot. As he carried his duffel bag filled with uniforms and a suitcase with civilian clothes he noticed the parking lot was filled with sports cars like his Camaro. He counted a dozen Corvettes, all current models as well as Firebirds and Mustangs, and a few foreign two-seaters.

He passed several other student officers moving in and was panting slightly when he set his bags down on the third floor to open the door to his room. The open bays on each floor had been enclosed and divided into two-occupant rooms. There was an individual sleeping area separated by a common bathroom. The room looked bleak. Its walls were painted pastel colors and were bare. On the back of the door was a plastic enclosed note informing the occupant that no cooking or heating apparatus was authorized for use in these quarters. Penalties were not mentioned but hinted at being severe. There was a bed, a bureau, a desk and a chair for the desk. There was no radio, but he could hear the sound of one somewhere close. His roommate greeted him from the open door of their common bathroom.

"Heard the door open. Name's Jerry Thompson from Marion, Ohio. ROTC from Ohio State University." He extended his hand to Randolph. "I've got a cooler with some soda. Want one?" Thompson's half of the room was identical to his side with the same furniture. He turned the volume of the radio down. "Better than a tent." He handed Randolph a Coke then sat on the bed. The layout of the room reminded Randolph of a college dormitory. Thompson apparently had not been there very long. He was still unpacking. He extended a round tin filled with cookies. "Chocolate chip, my favorite. Can't go off to war without your cookies. My girl made them. Went to Indiantown Gap in '68. These nine weeks shouldn't be bad. I mean, we're officers now. What can they do to us? Send us to Vietnam." He laughed.

"You sign up for Airborne or Ranger training?"

"I'm strictly a two-year straight leg infantry. The sooner I get out of the Army, the better my girl and I will like it. All the RAs go to Ranger School. I don't think they have a choice. Why anyone would want to go out to those swamps, I'll never understand. All that for a little tab to wear on your shoulder."

"The RAs get everything. I wanted active duty right out of camp. They got it like they get everything."

"You graduated this year?"

"And commissioned at IGMR."

"I was going to request a delay, but I figured might as well get it over with."

"What's your girl think of the Army?"

"She kind of looked at the Army like I did. Get it over with. Got a ring before I left. We're officially engaged, now."

"Your fiancée isn't opposed to The War?"

"We both support the government. I'll do my part. Figured when I got down here, maybe orders or things could change. They are withdrawing troops. After these two months of school, we'll probably get three or four months of troop duty. Then you have thirty days of leave before you go over. Twelve months over there. That's your two years. They got it all figured out."

"I'm here en-route to flight school. Rotary wing."

"You're either very brave or crazy, Thayer. Brave to go to flight school. Crazy to go beyond the mandatory two years. I'm in shock seeing all this Army stuff again."

"I forgot to bring an alarm clock."

"The main PX is closed, but there is a small one that might still be open. Bring a copy of your orders and you can buy something. I've had enough unpacking for now." Thompson drove a Mustang, the same model and type as Andrea. As he got into the car, a sense of familiarity gripped him. "It's not really a practical car. There's very little room in it. When I go overseas, I'll give it to my fiancée. When I get back, I want a truck."

At the small PX there were some men and a few women in various uniforms from TWs to fatigues. Although it was Sunday, obviously some had been on duty. This mini PX featured quick items, like cigarettes, but it also had some small appliances and radios. Thompson looked around the small store, and then joined Randolph who was examining radios, which had alarms in them.

Two Second Lieutenants in very starched fatigues were in the next aisle.

"Wish someone had given me a commission."

"Some people get everything given to them."

Their voices rose. Both were glaring at Randolph and Thompson.

"Wouldn't last a week as a candidate."

"ROTC garbage. Proves anyone can get a commission."

Randolph did not feel intimidated, only rather embarrassed. He picked up one of the radio-alarm clocks and started for the cashier. As they walked out into the parking lot, they were silent until they got into the Mustang. The two OCS graduates did not follow them.

"Probably newly commissioned," Thompson said as he started the car. "What assholes. Did they expect us to pick a fight with them in the PX? I guess if you spend six months having drill sergeants scream into your face, you'd resent us when we show up with our gold bars."

"Where were they on the night it rained and I was in a foxhole with six inches of water?"

"You have to understand the Army's mentality. They need officers. So, the standards get lowered. If you can pass a test and have the endurance, you can get a gold bar. They must be crackers from someplace out of the hills."

"Fortunately, they'll only Second Lieutenants."

"There's a shit-load of Captains with the same backgrounds running around. You get the railroad tracks in twenty-four months. You'll make it being in flight school. I won't. I'm going to get promoted back to civilian. Unfortunately, we're probably both going to bump into a lot of those Captains and wish we hadn't. For me, this is going to be a long two years."

Thompson's voice rose as he sang off-key while shaving. The count-down had been going on for the past couple of days. It was Saturday. He was planning to pick up his fiancée at the airport. She was due to land at one in the afternoon.

"You'd think we could be in a classroom in dry fatigues on Saturday, the half day before a holiday weekend." Columbus Day was Sunday. The rest of the country celebrated it on Friday. Training was not interrupted. Friday, the half day Saturday and Monday were normal training days. They would have the usual Saturday night and Sunday, free. The training schedule indicated drawing weapons and proceeding via bus to a field site for river crossing.

"We have to get back here, turn in the friggin weapons, get changed and before twelve-thirty. I need at least half an hour to get to the airport."

"The training schedule says its commanders' time from thirteen hundred to fifteen hundred." Randolph said.

"Well this time, Goddammit, it's my time! I don't want any of those crackers bothering my girl. She's flaky enough about this trip. Hasn't flown that much and she was concerned about the changeover in Atlanta."

"Mine will rent a car when she gets to Columbus. She's used to traveling. We'll be at the Holiday Inn tonight. You staying there?"

"I checked their prices. That's an awful lot of money for one night. If you go out of Columbus a few miles, it gets much cheaper. Last weekend I did some checking."

"I don't pay for it, she does."

"As well as the ticket down here?"

"She's probably made this a business trip. That's how the rich keep getting richer and we're in the Army and keep getting poorer. Her father owns a company."

"Money too, that's even better." He laughed. "I'm just a poor boy from Ohio who would like to suck the public payroll as an educator of our public, collective children."

"She hates the Army."

"We have something in common. I'll have to meet this woman."

The training routine had become a mixture of some classroom lectures and hands-on demonstration. For subjects requiring all students, they used a huge amphitheater auditorium where they had received their first orientation briefing on the Sunday evening of their arrival. Building number four was known as Bedroom Four. The seats in the auditorium were very comfortable. Field training demonstrations and exercises were well organized. Training was Fort Benning's main military occupation. The instructors were dedicated, serious career professionals. All field-training sites were permanent and used year round. Instruction was by the standard Army formula. There was a briefing covering the subject, followed by a demonstration, and then performance with hands-on participation. The majority of instructors and student cadre, as professionals, were recent Vietnam veterans. Many had been through numerous and various counter offenses including the Tet Offensive. They spoke in respectful terms about the NVA. Most said nothing positive when they spoke about the South Vietnamese. This was Randolph's first introduction to what the Army termed its 'Allies'. There were many of them on the post taking various Infantry instruction. They wore khakis similar to American uniforms. Occasionally, there were strange uniforms of officers from other friendly countries. The Infantry Center hosted international training.

For the first time Randolph trained using the standard issue infantry rife, the M-16. It was incredibly accurate and lightweight. Firing it for the first time, he hit targets at 300 yards. Its rate of fire was so great accuracy did not seem to be stressed although he qualified as a sharpshooter, the middle firing rating. Not all the ranges had fixed positions to kneel or lay while firing. Some were designed for jungle and close proximity contact such as the jungles of Vietnam. Walking in lanes, camouflaged, silhouette targets popped up for them to shoot. There were about two hundred students in the class. The majority were ROTC graduates starting their two-year active duty commitments. There were several with direct commissions. The basic officer course was designed to teach company grade tactics. Leadership was not stressed since these students having obtained their commissions were deemed to have already acquired it. Gradually, Randolph learned there were four other student officers, graduates of the ROTC flight program at their colleges who were on orders for the Rotary Wing course after Infantry Officer Basic. One afternoon, they filed into Bedroom Four for an extended lecture on additional tactical and firepower support available to the normal infantry platoon. He sat next to another Second Lieutenant whom he had seen in class but never been introduced to.

"Name's Randy Thayer. I'm from Massachusetts." Randolph sunk into the comfortable seat. The Second Lieutenant did not answer him. Randolph thought he might not have heard him, so he introduced himself again.

"This is the call down the world lecture." The lieutenant said, ignoring Randolph's self-introduction. "When you're out in the boonies, if your radio is working, this is everything that's available to you. Artillery to the Air Force fast movers."

"Have you heard this before?"

"This will be my fourth time. I was with the previous increment. And the one before that. I got recycled."

"You injured or something?"

"Last spring when I got here, a few weeks into classes I got acute appendicitis. Spent a week in the hospital and then they didn't want me to go out in the field. Missed most of the course, so they recycled me. Second time around, my father died. I got emergency leave. I got it extended because of the situation at home. They recycled me again. Started figuring out the time. I was getting pretty much through my first year. Third recycle, I asked for more leave due to my family situation and I got jaundice to put me in the hospital for three weeks. They didn't catch on until the course was nearly over. The dumb bastards. They called me into the old man's office and read Article 31 to me. You know what that is?"

"Nothing to fool around with. Legal stuff."

"They said they'd recycle me to this increment. If I didn't make it, they'd court martial me for malingering. Know what malingering is? Old term associated with the Army a hundred years ago. You don't hear that term much these days. Our modern term is Gold Bricking. I'm sure you heard of that. I've used up nearly seven months in Officer Basic. Do the math. Almost don't have time for a complete Vietnam tour. If I used up more than eleven months of the two year Rotsee commitment, they might not send me over. They caught on, though. The bastards!"

Randolph was shocked by the open admission and thought at first the lieutenant was joking. He avoided any further contact with him, fearing any association might be harmful. Thompson was skeptical also when Randolph told him the story, but confirmed its truth.

The student company commander had been a Sergeant First Class, and had received a direct commission to Captain. He was Special Forces qualified, wore his green beret and had done two tours in Vietnam. He wore a Silver Star, the CIB, jump wings and three rows of other medals and ribbons. His chest was also covered with Vietnamese jump wings and some other Vietnamese decorations. He was lean and reserved. Next in line as the student XO was an aviator First Lieutenant, who had taken a direct commission from CW2. Another aviator, who had only been able to get a commission to Second Lieutenant, was Randolph's student platoon leader. Although they were students, the student cadre commanded as in all Army units through rank and seniority.

"You're either a very good Non Commissioned Officer, which is what he should have stayed," Thompson commented dryly when they discussed their student commander. "Or, you've been trained for leadership. He'll never know what lieutenants should be or how they should think."

"He's seen it, though." Randolph said.

"As an NCO. He skipped being a lieutenant, like us. It's just another example of what the Army has to do when they get desperate. They need officers, so they take them wherever they can. They also need qualified NCOs. Who replaced him? One of the crackers who put shoes on for the first time when he went into the Army. Look at OCS. Those guys are going to be more concerned about their troops polishing their boots rather than if they're keeping their ammo clean or changing their socks regularly. Don't be surprised if there is a pile of wet fatigues on this bathroom floor. I got to get to the airport on time. I don't want her wandering around with all these red-necks down here."

They went to the Open Mess for breakfast. The formation was at 07:00 after which they formed a line to the arms room, which was in the basement of the building. Olive drab painted buses were lined up to ferry them to the field site. Once there, they had a lecture about the tactics involved in crossing waterways from squad level up through company. The class was uninspiring but presented with the usual professionalism. The two hundred students listened respectfully with very subdued enthusiasm. Most were anticipating the evening and Sunday, their second full day off since the course had started. Eventually, they got to the climax of the training, wading through a foot-deep stream. Since it was mild and sunny, the wet pants and boots were minor nuisances. Erik Blaisedale from Arizona, also on orders to flight school en route to Vietnam, sat with Randolph on the bus back to the parking lot.

Getting off the bus there were two hundred Second Lieutenants with soggy boots and pants, holding M-16 rifles. There was some minor confusion about a formation, which was quickly cancelled and a lot of milling around while individual decisions of what to do next were made. A line to the arms room formed quickly and soon snaked out of the building. Several students carrying their rifles walked to the BOQ to change out of the wet fatigues. The arms room line did not seem to be moving. Randolph saw the Green Beret student company commander, who had not drawn a rifle for the exercise, or waded through the stream since his fatigues were still starched. His student platoon leader, the Second Lieutenant aviator, was nowhere in sight. He saw Thompson briefly then lost him in the milling crowd of Second Lieutenants.

Randolph went to Olsen Hall carrying his rifle. It was quarter past eleven. In his room, he leaned the M-16 against the wall. Somehow, Thompson had been there and left, since as he had predicted there was a pile of wet fatigues on the bathroom floor in front of the shower. The puddle was still forming on the floor next to the heap of wet uniforms. Randolph changed into dry fatigue pants and put on his second pair of boots. He wiped the wet ones down and left them in the bathroom. Squeezing out his fatigue pants, he slung them over the shower stall. He took Thompson's wet pants, squeezed the excess water out in the sink and threw them next to his on the shower stall door. Andrea was due sometime in the afternoon. She had not been more specific. His thoughts raced at the prospect of seeing her again.

Stepping out of his room, he closed his door, hearing it lock, and went out on to the balcony. The line for the arms room was still outside the building. Many of his fellow student officers also realized the line was stalled and were heading for the open mess, which was also in sight of the orderly room.

Blaisedale in dry fatigues met him on the balcony.

"I was second in line at the arms room door. The armorer is making everyone clean them. That's why the line isn't moving."

"You got yours turned in?"

"Yes, but they were turning guys back to the cleaning tables. There isn't enough room down there. They'll be in that line forever. I'm going to get something to eat. You want to go?"

"I'm hungry." Randolph said. "The arms room is open until four, like last week?"

"I don't know. Probably. Let's go to the Club. They have a brunch there on Saturdays."

"It's got to be quick. I have to get in that line."

"That line is not moving. That armorer is an asshole."

Randolph drove his Camaro to the club, a half-mile from the red brick student brigade headquarters. There were plenty of empty tables. They were seated quickly.

"There's no quarters at Wolters. Everyone lives in trailers." Blaisedale said. "They charge quite a bit because they know what we're making. They usually have two separate bedrooms." He was not married. "We'd save a lot if we roomed together." The waitress came. They ordered sandwiches and beers. The beers went down quickly. They were on a second round when the sandwiches arrived. Randolph heard the loudspeaker page for Lieutenant Thayer. His first thought was that something must be wrong at home. Panic shot through him. Quickly he hurried to the club's foyer to answer the telephone.

"Where is your rifle, lieutenant?" It was his platoon leader, the aviator Second Lieutenant. He sounded flustered and disgusted.

"I'll turn it in right after lunch after I clean it."

"Yours is the only one that has not been turned in."

Randolph looked at his watch. It was twelve thirty.

"That whole line is gone?"

"Get over here now and turn it in," he snarled.

He put a five-dollar bill on his plate next to his half-eaten sandwich and told Blaisedale about the call. After retrieving the M-16 from his room, the arms room NCO was standing at his cage door. His platoon leader and the Special Forces student company commander Captain were also waiting there. Both had long, stern expressions. There was no one else around. The few cleaning tables were empty, although there was cleaning debris scattered on and under the flimsy tables.

"I can clean it." Randolph offered.

"I'll take care of it, Lieutenant." The armorer said dryly.

"I assumed you'd be open all afternoon. Like last weekend."

"I'm sure the sergeant is as pleased as the rest of us. We were released at 12:00." His platoon leader said sarcastically. "Not very impressive planning, Lieutenant."

The student company commander said nothing but looked at him with clear disapproval then walked away.

He was angry. The previous weekend, it had been three o'clock before weapons had been turned in and they were released. He went back to his BOQ room and changed into civilian clothes. He pulled out the training schedule. Clearly, it read 13:00 to 15:00 as commander's time. The turning-in of the weapons must have speeded up considerably after they were released. Cleaning must have either been ignored or suspended. They had not fired the weapons so extensive cleaning did not seem required, as it had been the previous Saturday when they had range fired.

Waiting in his room he found himself staring at the two sets of wet fatigue pants slung over the shower stall. His concern was had he ruined his career, which had hardly started. The room, his dark thoughts and the musty wet smell of the fatigue pants were too confining. He went outside and walked around the parking lot several times. It was emptying quickly as the student-officers departed. The orderly room was busy as many signed out for the evening indicating they were not going to be in their assigned quarters. Andrea ignoring his concern had said she would meet him on the Post. He had no idea how she would find him.

When she arrived, it was with a sudden squeal of tires. She drove not the usual sleek Mustang but a Ford Maverick, a boxy two-door sedan. Randolph climbed into the passenger seat.

"No Mustangs. What a clunker." She slide across the bench seat and wrapped her arms around his neck. The kiss was wet and sensual. "We were late getting into Atlanta. What is wrong?" She pushed her head back in order to look at his whole face. "You look like you're the one who almost missed the connector flight."

"I left my rifle in my room while I was eating lunch. I though we had until four o'clock to turn them in. That's what we had last Saturday. They released us at noon."

"For Christ's sake, did they think you were trying to sell it to a Mafia guy?" She giggled. He was still solemn, his face a mask of dejection. "You've been in the Army two weeks."

"You don't understand," he said irritated. "I wasn't thinking. That's unacceptable for an officer. My roommate also has his girl coming down here from Ohio this weekend. That's all he's been talking about all week."

"Did he turn his rifle in or bring it to the airport?"

The sour expression he gave her killed any remaining levity. "I could be in serious trouble. My roommate must have been first in line. He was out of here like a bolt of lighting. If he had been here, I'm sure he would have turned mine in for me. Once we got released, the armorer stopped giving everyone a hard time. I wasn't there and I should have been. I was at the Club."

"I can call my contact about this. Let's go get a drink. You need one."

"The only place around here that serves alcohol is the Club. The very place that put me into trouble."

"They need lieutenants." Andrea tried to distract his dejected mood. "They aren't going to fire you. I won't let that happen." She turned the car around and following his directions drove the short distance to the Officer's Club.

"Your influence won't help me down here." Randolph sat hunched in the passenger's seat; his head was bent forward half on his chest.

"You'd be surprised what influence does." She spotted an empty parking space in front of the club and quickly pulled the car into it.

"Do you see the sign?" Randolph's head jolted up and he pointed at the sign prominently displayed at the curb, reserving the space for the post commanding general.

"How the hell are they going to know this isn't his car?" Andrea smiled, trying to draw him from his gloominess. People entering and leaving the Club and walking through the parking lot were staring at them.

"You have no sticker. This is a military post. Not the civilian world." Randolph's voice rose. "I don't need any more trouble today. Move the fucking car!"

Her playful smile abruptly disappeared, again. "Look what the Army is doing to you? I'm so glad you're in it." Andrea backed out and found another parking space in the main lot. When she turned off the ignition, they both sat still for an extended moment.

"I'm sorry. This is my problem, not yours. You've come a long way to be with me—and I'm being an idiot."

"I understand your concern. We can face this.'

"A drink would be pretty good right now."

There was activity in the club. The bar was only half occupied. Easily, they found an empty table.

"Do you want a beer?" They sat with the corner of the table between them.

"A gin and tonic. Make it Tangueray, if that's not too exotic for this place."

Slightly annoyed, he ordered a scotch and water and her gin. After the waitress departed, he stared at Andrea's legs. "That is a short skirt."

"In California, it got me in to see who I wanted, usually very quickly." Again her face became a warm smile in another attempt to change his bleak mood.

"Is that how you conduct business?"

"In business, you use what works. I'm learning that."

"So, the trip was successful?"

"My father was very pleased with the information I brought him. We had lunch yesterday and he wants me to continue spying. Well, not spying but getting information he wants." Their drinks arrived. They each finished half of them quickly. So much for his interest in Tremblay Bearings, Andrea thought. His sour expression was starting to dissipate. "Scott's mentor has been telling me there are a lot of different career paths to take in the Army."

"This is the Infantry School," Randolph said in a low tone. "I need combat, if I'm going to stay in the Army."

"Eisenhower commanded nothing until he wrote the plan for the invasion of Europe. Then they gave him the job." He looked sharply at her face, which had a smug expression. Her eyes were exploratory. In all their time together at Northeastern, academics were purely a secondary interest. He was very impressed and felt his gloominess lifting.

"He wasn't a Second Lieutenant at that time. He had a star. The way I'm going I'll never make First Lieutenant."

"I'm sure it already is forgotten. In twenty-three months, you'll be a Captain." She said earnestly. "With that rank, there's a lot of things open to you." They ordered more drinks. The first for both of them had gone down quickly. The sun was shining through the glass wall that looked out onto a huge lawn.

Their telephoning had lapsed to every other day, partially due to her strenuous schedule. He knew she had been discovered her second clandestine day in Los Angeles. A customer had called the company. She had unearthed more potential neglected sales, not for the traditional bearings Tremblay Bearings produced, but for a new and cheaper bearing made of low-cost alloy materials. It was sweeping the bearings industry and opening up new markets the company had never served. These inexpensive bearings could be used in a multitude of commercial products. Potentially, this was a whole new horizon that could open for Tremblay Bearings. They needed special capital equipment, which Tremblay Bearings did not possess. The main reason her uncle had limited their visits was to avoid talk of these new products. Most customers they had seen used the traditional products, which Tremblay Bearings could still support.

"Yesterday, my father brought me out to lunch." This was news Randolph had not heard and apparently unexpected. "It was interesting." Her face became pensive. "Order us some more drinks. They're good after a zillion miles in an airplane." Without hesitation he ordered them another round. "Again, my father thanked me. It proves the potential is there. He didn't have any confirmation except media literature until I gave him my numbers. My uncles oppose it. While he was recovering from the heart attack he read up on these new developments and metals going into these new types of bearings. The information I gave him–that some of our customers are looking for this new type of bearing–confirms what he suspected. There's a big potential market out there. He wants Tremblay Bearing to get into it. My uncles' resistance is based on staying in the old, sure markets. My father wants to jump into the new metal alloys and increase sales, dramatically. Some are saying bearings with these new materials aren't as good as ones with traditional materials. They won't last in the market. Even if it's only temporary, a couple of years, maybe ten. Then he told me what he wants to do with the company. He wants the sales to double before he retires."

"What's the sales, now?"

"We're at about ten million. Sales have to increase especially in those areas we've been dropping off in."

"Those short skirts will help." Randolph's expression was still sour.

"Walking around naked wouldn't help. We need the new equipment."

"Can't you rent it or lease it?"

"This equipment is not like you get at the local rotor rooter store. Use it, then bring it back. If we could do that, it would be easy. This is capital equipment, big bucks. You have to buy it. That means capital investment. He wants me to go to the mid west where our business is also falling off and see if I can get the same interest in the new alloy, cheap bearings. He also wants me to call on some companies we've never done business with to gauge their interest."

"The spy in the short skirt."

"My father has arranged for me to be investigating a trade show in Minneapolis as cover for my trip, although I don't think its much of a secret any more. Let's get another round. Unbelievable how good these taste? I also need to go home to get fitted for my dress for my mother's wedding. We better make the most of me being here. It might be awhile before I can come down again."

"Do you want to eat here or go someplace else?"

"Another place, this is too Army." Andrea's expression was still light and she smiled. "Hey, do you want to stay in VIP quarters? We're entitled to stay in Distinguished Visitors Quarters, the Guest House or something called that. It was arranged for me. I have a reservation. It's probably just around the corner out there someplace. We could go there and I could take a little nappie. Goddamned long flight to get here." Andrea yawned. The waitress brought them another round of drinks. "They said protocol office of something. I didn't confirm it. They were arranging the whole thing. I was saving that as a surprise for you."

Randolph paid the tab and they went outside into the warm air. Leaving the air conditioning struck them both. It was muggy. Their cheeks were flush. Randolph stumbled on the flat surface of the parking lot while they were walking toward the car. It caused Andrea to laugh. He looked at her with a sour expression. "Give me your keys."

"If you hit anything," she said. "They will take your driving privileges away. I'm going home, Monday." She smiled, touching his outstretched hand. "I drive. We'll be careful."

They got into the car. When she started the motor she moved the shifting lever and stepped on the gas. The car went up over a curb in front of them. The engine raced knocked out of gear. Andrea turned off the key to silence it. "I thought that was reverse." Randolph's face reddened from embarrassment and the alcohol he had consumed. He put his hands on the dashboard to steady himself. She started the motor again, pushed the shifting lever through its entire range of gear positions, and then settled it on what she thought was reverse. Turning in the seat, she laid her arm along the bench seat and looked out the rear window. Stepping on the gas, the car lurched forward, the rear wheels going up over the curb and the car going forward over grass. Quickly she stepped on the brake. The entire car was now up on the grass, the paving behind them. "Where the hell is reverse in this thing?" Again, she giggled. "Nothing like my floor shift. They put it in a different place."

"Great, you can't find reverse. Take it slow, let's get off the grass."

In neutral she pumped the accelerator causing the engine to race. This time she found reverse and started back toward the pavement, but too rapidly going over the cement curb. She hit the pavement hard, causing a loud metallic crunching. Stepping on the brake quickly, the car stopped before hitting one of a row of parked vehicles. They both saw the flashing lights on the Military Police sedan as it pulled into the Club's parking lot and headed straight for them. After the MP car stopped, the driver got out and went to Andrea's side. He was a SP4 and wore a black and white armband and a belt with the usual police equipment. Randolph quickly got out of the car.

"May I see your ID card, sir?" The young Military Policeman eyed him thoroughly.

Randolph dug his wallet out of his rear pocket. Andrea was still sitting behind the wheel.

"I put the car in the wrong gear, officer. It's a rental. Not like mine at home."

The young MP stepped back and thoroughly surveyed the car. "You may have done some damage underneath." Andrea had turned off the engine. The SP4's partner got out of the passenger side of the sedan. He was a Private First Class. He stared at them, saying nothing. The SP4 asked, "Are you all right, Mam?"

"I am in the pink, officer."

"Would you please step out of the car, Mam?" The SP4 handed Randolph back his ID card after having written on a note pad.

"I don't want to get out of the car. I am comfortable in here. Listen soldier, get on your little radio and tell your boss that you are talking to Andrea Tremblay, that's T-R-E-M-B-L-A-Y, who has a VIP reservation at your Guest House, Distinguished Person place. The White House arranged it."

The SP4 was startled temporarily, and then seemed to accept her explanation as if he had heard it all before. He wrote more on his pad. The PFC, who could plainly hear them, reached into the sedan for the microphone to his radio. Randolph saw him repeating Andrea's name.

"What is your rank, soldier?" She was annoyed clearly by his lack of indicated respect of her disclosure.

"I am a Specialist Fourth Class, Mam."

"Well, Mr. Specialist Fourth Class, I am a first class." Inadvertently, she giggled.

"I understand that, Mam. You are a first class."

"No, I mean a VIP first class. You are confusing me, Mr. Fourth Class. Don't do that."

"Oh Jesus, Andrea!" Randolph muttered. His heart was fluttering. The alcohol euphoria was completely gone.

"Neither one of us will drive. We'll call a cab." Andrea smiled, ridiculously, at the military policeman.

"Please get out of the car. You are on a federal reservation subject to its regulations."

"No, I'm not. I'm sitting in a car and my feet are off the ground. I'm not on federal property." Glaring stares were coming from people in the Club as well as those walking through the parking lot.

The car remained in a driving aisle, clearly in a blocking position. The MP Lights remained flashing. Andrea leaned her chin on her left hand with her elbow resting on the sill of the driver's window.

"Mr. Specialist? What comes after Fourth Class? Third Class? Second Class? Fifth Class?"

"Sergeant, if I'm lucky."

"Sometimes luck has nothing to do with it."

"Andrea, for Christ's sake!" Randolph said. He had come around the car and was standing next to the MP.

"Your car may be damaged." The SP4 said.

"Perfectly good rental. It got me from your quaint little airport down here in this wonderful southern country. You like Georgia, Mr. Specialist?"

"I'm from California."

"This is getting us nowhere. Call the rental agency or a tow truck." Andrea was suddenly flustered. "Get on your little radio and call the Protocol Office and ask them why you're delaying one of their guests? See what they say."

Two more sedans appeared in the distance. Neither their lights nor sirens were on. They quickly pulled into the Club's parking lot. An MP Captain got out of the passenger's side of one of the vehicles.

"Here comes the Calvary." Andrea called loudly. Randolph thought of saluting the Captain but decided against it since he was not in uniform. The Captain surveyed Randolph from head to foot. The PFC who had radioed still held the microphone. There were now six MPs standing next to the sedans in addition to the Captain. Silently, he looked over the car as the SP4 had done.

"What have we got here, Specialist?" Only the lights of the first vehicle were still flashing. "Kill the lights." He growled at the PFC.

"Suspected operation under the influence, sir."

Andrea stuck her tongue out at the Captain. He did not smile. "Who are you?" He asked Randolph.

"That is Lieutenant Thayer," the SP4 said.

"She had a long flight from New York. Fatigue got to her, sir."

"You've been in the Club at the bar. How long you been in there, lieutenant?"

"You don't have to answer that, Randy." Andrea had taken her head off of her hand, and glared at the MP Captain. "That's a lawyer question."

"We both had a few drinks, sir. I'm sorry about all this."

"No, you're not. You don't have to be sorry. We didn't do anything except drive on their grass, a little. If there's any damages, we'll pay for it."

The Captain smiled, but then the smile disappeared. "From your accent, Mam, you're from Boston?"

"I don't live in the city, but close enough. You are one smart cookie, Captain." Andrea smiled warmly. "How do you like it out here in the boonies?" She laid her head against the window frame of the car door. There was a playful twinkle in her eyes.

"This is a fine place, Mam." The Captain smiled back at her.

"Sir," the PFC called. "They're calling for you." The MP Captain walked toward the first MP sedan. Randolph watched his face as he took the microphone from the PFC.

"Why won't you get out of the car?" He whispered to her.

"I have to go to the bathroom. I should have gone before we came out."

"I'm dead! They'll be putting me on the plane back to Logan with you if I'm lucky and the stockade down here is full."

"So far you have done nothing wrong. I drove over the curb. You have been an innocent passenger. Besides, I won't let them do anything to you. We have Scott and his buddy. They'll save us. You watch how I'm going to handle this." They looked at the Captain as he quickly finished his radio conversation and came back to the rental car. On his TWs he had silver jump wings, but wore no other decorations.

"Would you like us to take you to your quarters, Miss Tremblay?"

"How about calling us a cab," Andrea opened the door and climbed out. Yawning sleepily, she looked at the car. "I should have got a Mustang. That's what I drive. This one is confusing. Pisser of a place to put reverse."

"Can I see your license?" The Captain asked, politely.

"No, you may not." Andrea smiled. "You know who I am. Don't press it. You can call us a cab."

"We will escort you to your quarters."

"I don't want to go to my quarters. Call the cab and we'll be on our way. I will tell the cabbie where I want to go. Do you want to be the one who interrupted my travel plans? Call the cab, Captain."

The Captain signaled to one of MPs who picked up the radio microphone.

"I would like to get my suitcase out of the trunk."

"Of course, Miss Tremblay."

"I'll get it, sir." Randolph's throat was dry. After getting the keys from Andrea, his hands shook as he opened the trunk.

"Would you like us to move the car to your quarters?" The Captain asked.

"No, we'll leave it here. We'll pick it up tomorrow."

"We can't leave it blocking the aisle, Miss Tremblay. It has to be moved."

"You are right about that, Captain. That's one for you."

"I'll move it." Randolph said quickly. He had set her suitcase down and started for the driver's side of the car.

"No, you will not!" Andrea hissed and pulled his arm as he was about to open the driver's door. "Get away from the goddamned car! One of these fine officers will move it for us. Right, Captain?"

"Yes, Miss Tremblay." He again signaled to one of the enlisted MPs, who got in the rental. It coughed once, but then started. The soldier drove the few feet into a space. Getting out, he handed the keys to the Captain, who put them in Andrea's outstretched palm.

"Where the hell is the taxi?"

"It's on its way," the Captain said softly. The cab arrived. Clumsily, they got in. Randolph bumped his head on the doorframe. The driver took the suitcase. As the taxi drove them off post, the three MP cars followed it to a gate, and then stopped. They were deposited at the entrance to the Holiday Inn. Andrea had money in her hand to pay the driver before Randolph could think of it. The cabbie handed him the suitcase, then quickly got back in the cab. Randolph was still very tense.

"That's how influence works." She laughed, uneasily, seeing the anguish on his face. Andrea registered for them. Dumbly, feeling the effects of the scotch he stood watching her sign the register then followed her carrying the suitcase. "I registered us as Mr. and Mrs.," she giggled as soon as he had closed the door. The drapes over the sliding glass doors opened onto a small balcony. They were shut, although the room was still bright. She slide her arms around his neck and pushed him onto one of the beds, then began licking his ear. "They can't touch you," she said huskily and looked into his eyes. "They won't. I won't let that happen. I will keep you safe."

The rumbling of deep-throated snoring woke her. Randolph was lying on his back. Each breath brought a vibrating rattle. She pushed at his body, until he reluctantly rolled on his side, facing away from her. The snoring noise stopped and she listened as his breathing settled into a normal rhythm. She was wide awake.

Even with the amount of alcohol they had consumed, they achieved an impassioned coupling. She remembered his sudden release drenching her inside. It was a feeling she lived to anticipate, which sent shivers through out her body. This one was more intense, it had seemed. She decided it was the two and a half week separation with the tension over their escape from the Army's arm of law. At home, even if they had been arrested, she was sure her father's connections would nullify it. With the impending relationship of her step father-to-be, Scott, she felt they were safe. She had handled the situation, although possibly without tact. Had she gone too far with the MPs? Why had they acted so meekly? Military police must be like any other policemen. It was the White House connection. What, sane career orientated soldier would dare butt his head on that linkage? For anyone else, they might have sent a Sergeant. We got a Captain and he was informed. Scott has got to take that job. She would join her mother in urging him.

She glanced at Randolph's back. He was still and she felt his steady breathing. Suddenly, she felt possessive. She had let him slip away before through her own intolerance and ignorance. That would not happen again. I can take on the Army and tonight was the first step, I won. That Captain knew he had to act passively. I need to make the Army treat Randy that way.

On the phone for the past two weeks he was so light and airy. Starting the Army made him slightly anxious. That was to be expected. He used to get that way before finals. As if a college exam really made any difference to what you had to confront in the real world. All that talk and help he had given her about the sales and spying trips had faded by two weeks in the Army. During their whole abbreviated evening together, he had made no mention of what she was doing or of Tremblay Bearings.

Slowly, she got out of the bed. Her head banged, the uncomfortable aftermath of excessive alcohol. Aspirin, she thought and went to her pocketbook. Next to her traveling bottle of aspirin were her birth control pills. She was not sure if she had taken them the day before with all the packing and rushing around to make plane connections. She checked the slot for yesterday's pill and sure enough it was there and she had forgotten it. Taking them with the aspirin bottle, she went into the bathroom.

Looking at herself in the mirror she noticed her face was puffy and slightly tinted pink. She began combing her hair with her hand, putting it in the proper places and then going on to touch her skin mentally noting which cosmetics to apply to achieve the desired tones. Randy had never seemed to care what type of makeup she wore. Once or twice he had complained about the taste of lipstick, so she had used very little or none to please him. Getting ready for business meetings required beauty preparation. Appearance had to fit the setting and the impression to achieve. It often meant different application, depending on the age and gender of who she was going to meet. Cosmetics had never been a big part of her life. Now they were part of her daily preparations.

Frederic was pleased with the information from California about the potential markets for the new alloy bearings. It was her first positive achievement for him. Everything else she had done for the company really had no meaning and little purpose. Randy was right. They had found a place for her on the payroll. This mission, as Randy termed it, was different. How was that important? What did success and pleasing her father mean? It had to be something she could use to get Randy away from the Army. If he is undedicated then he will not want to go to Vietnam.

At Northeastern we were never unfaithful to each other. I didn't give him the chance to go elsewhere, she smiled. When we broke up, did he? He must have been too busy at Northeastern, finishing two years in one. I could have had the opportunity. None were interesting. There must be something to get his attention away from Vietnam. It's got to be Tremblay Bearings. That's the only thing that is bigger and more important. My uncles will oppose the new alloy bearings. It will be me and Frederic. The horse thing is way in the past. In the mid west I will find the same sort of information. He will not be disappointed. If he wants these new alloy bearings, I will find the potential new markets. Randy was right about the salesman for California. That person will work for me. Expanding my authority beyond being on the payroll is the first step. That will get Randy's attention.

Viewing herself in the mirror, she ignored the puffiness caused by sleep, alcohol and fornication. Her lips parted into a slight smile backed with confidence. She shut off the lights in the bathroom, gently opened the door and trotted back to the bed.

Chapter Four

Riding in the olive drab buses to the Monday morning training site, Randolph sat with the other bleary eyed, frequently yawing Second Lieutenants. Thinking about their final kiss in the half-light of the Holiday Inn room, her mouth after their intense night was still soft and sensuous. With daybreak lightening the shadowy room, he had crawled out of bed to shower, shave, and dress in his fatigues. Wide awake, lying still under the bed clothing, her eyes followed all his movements as he dressed. Since she had a morning flight, they said their farewells in the hotel room. They had retrieved the Maverick from the Officers Club lot Sunday without incident. It was difficult for him to believe only a mere three weeks had passed since she had come back into his life. He felt a strange awe toward her now, in how she had handled herself in the parking lot of the Club. At first he attributed it to her being slightly drunk. Silently, as he thought about the incident during Sunday, he realized she had demonstrated a profound sense of un-drunken cognizance during the whole episode. She had counseled him on speaking with the MP Captain and prohibited him from touching the steering wheel of the Maverick, which could have landed him immediately under arrest. Her possessiveness once they reached the safety of the hotel room was slightly intimidating, yet also made him feel intensely loyal to her. Their bond had to be strengthening. With her physical appetite as intense as he remembered, this was a different Andrea than the college student.

Stumbling off the bus with the other sleepy lieutenants he climbed onto the open seating for the first narrative class of the week. Slumping on the back-less bleachers, he hooked his foot under the bench in front of him as he had learned to do in order not to accidentally fall off if he dozed. A tugging at his shoulder at first felt as if the student next to him was about to ask him something. It was the Green Beret student company commander. His face was expressionless, it's normal appearance. He indicated Randolph should follow him out of the bleachers. The unit's company commander, another Captain, wearing TWs and looking very out of place at a field site, was waiting for them. He was very agitated. The aviator First Lieutenant, the student XO, was also present, standing unobtrusively observing the Captains.

"Leaving your assigned weapon in your quarters, unsecured, is a serious offense, Lieutenant." He turned and started toward his civilian car, a Camaro. The Green Beret Captain gestured for Randolph to follow him. The two Captains took the accessible front bucket seats leaving him to squeeze into the small rear seat. He had to turn sideways since there was no room for his feet. "One of my biggest problems in the field was unsecured weapons. I couldn't stress security enough. The last thing I needed was my men getting shot with their own weapons by NVA infiltrators." The company commander's tone became more menacing as he related more detail. The Green Beret Captain said nothing as they rode over the dirt roads past other training sites. Randolph wondered where they were going. His heart seemed to be beating faster and blood pounded near his temples. Deep within him, he knew they would not let it pass. That was not the Army's way. He had left his rifle in a secured, locked room. The only thing he had done was made the wrong judgment about waiting in an endless line, when he thought there would be ample time to return, clean the weapon, and turn it in before the anticipated 16:00 hours turn-in time. Randolph was frightened but strangely not intimidated.

The Green Beret Captain with his silence seemed to be endorsing the philosophy the company commander espoused.

Although both were Captains, the cadre company commander was a veteran of commanding troops in CONUS and Vietnam. The Green Beret, although a Vietnam veteran, was new to his rank. Since the Green Beret Captain had been present when he turned in his rifle, he hoped for some supportive comment indicating it was a mere unfortunate mistake. He, Lieutenant Thayer, was one of his troops. Didn't a commander stick up for his men? His silence weighed heavily. Maybe Thompson was right, Randolph thought. Possibly he had returned to NCO status where he politely and respectfully endured the ranting of a military superior. Once an NCO, you were always an NCO. They arrived at the multi-storied red brick building, which housed all the units' offices. The Captain parked in the spot reserved for him as the unit commander. He was silent; his monologue about security had worn itself out. The three emerged from the small car. Again Randolph had to struggle awkwardly to get out from the back seat. One leg had gone to sleep and he staggered several steps making him feel more clumsy until the blood flow returned to normal. Meekly, he followed the Captains as they started for the battalion's orderly room.

There was another student, a Second Lieutenant also dressed in fatigues. They stared at each other in silent anxiety. Unplanned visits to the battalion commander's office on a Monday morning, when classes were scheduled, was not career enhancing, Randolph though. A SP4 clerk, seeing them arrive, announced them over an intercom. Randolph sat on a straight-backed chair after the Captains had seated themselves on the single couch. The unit commander in his TWs no longer looked displaced.

The SP4 received a command over the intercom to have the other Second Lieutenant report. With resolve, the student opened the battalion commander's door and entered, closing it firmly behind him. For the next twenty minutes, the two Captains and Randolph sat quietly exchanging hostile glances. The clerk ignored them while he worked at a typewriter. The unit commander became silently agitated with the wait and kept fidgeting, and checking his watch, although there was a huge round wall clock in clear view. When the Second Lieutenant emerged from the battalion commander's office, his face was a lot brighter. The unit commander Captain jumped to his feet and they had a whispering conference. Randolph heard him instruct the student to wait in the company's orderly room for him, so he could drive him out to the class's field location.

The clerk told the two Captains to report to the battalion commander. They entered in the same manner as the student Second Lieutenant. Their conference lasted about five minutes. When they came out, the Green Beret's face was its usual expressionless blank. The other Captain was plainly more agitated, than when he had been waiting. He glared angrily at Randolph, but left quickly.

"Lieutenant Thayer, report to the battalion commander," the SP4 clerk said, unemotionally. Randolph went in, closing the door behind him as seemed to be the custom. His palms were sweating. The room was well lit. The walls were covered with black and white photographs, some of which had autographs written across them. There was a large U.S. flag and the battalion's standard behind the battalion commander's desk. Randolph walked to the front of the desk and stood at attention. He saluted and stated he was reporting, as ordered. Lieutenant Colonel Somabee without looking at Randolph, started to read Article 31 of the Uniform Code of Military Justice, which stated he had legal rights to remain silent, and request legal representation during the interview. Randolph swallowed several times as his throat dried. A dozen disconnected thoughts shot through his mind. Most prominent was Andrea's admonition that he had been in the Army only two weeks. What could they do to him, he wondered? Anything, he answered his own thought.

"Do you want a lawyer present, Lieutenant?"

"Do you think I need one, sir?"

"I asked if you want a lawyer," the Colonel asked tautly. "It's your right under the Code."

"No sir." He felt as if a weight had suddenly been lifted from his back. His legs twitched, but held him standing.

The battalion commander had a leanness of the life of imposed physical regiment. There was a hint of jowls at his cheeks, which made his face square. The southern sun had also tanned him to a healthy hue attesting to his frequent outdoor activities. The rest of his nondescript face was that of a bureaucrat. Near his writing hand was a yellow legal-sized pad of lined paper. He studied Randolph silently without moving any part of his body. Randolph sweated under his fatigue jacket and felt the moisture on his flanks.

"Stand at least, Lieutenant." Randolph moved his left foot six inches and meshed his palms behind his back. He tilted his head down slightly, and his eyes met the Colonel's.

"It isn't often a name appears twice on my Monday morning list. You have won that distinction, Lieutenant." Randolph said nothing. His mind was still gauging liabilities, now that he had given up legal representation. Requesting a lawyer would delay a resolution and prolong everything. "Leaving a weapon unsecured is a serious breach of security."

Randolph's thoughts stopped racing. Imprints began to click, defensively. "I'm here to develop my leadership skills."

"Leaving a weapon unsecured is a clear indication of failure to develop those skills, Lieutenant."

"Leadership means following directives and tactics when there are clear directives."

Colonel Somabee's thin eyebrows rose as he studied Randolph's face. "Explain that."

"In ROTC at college we always cleaned a weapon when it was taken out into the field, before it was turned in."

"After range firing, yes." The Colonel wrote some quick notes on his legal pad. "You're not in college now, Lieutenant."

"My weapon was secured in a locked room. I knew exactly where it was. No one indicated when we had to turn them in. My roommate had to go to the airport to pick up his fiancée. Otherwise, I'm sure he would have turned it in for me."

"Nothing was said at the formation?"

"There wasn't much of a formation. We barely got into position when they dismissed it."

"What was said about cleaning weapons?"

"Nothing. That's why I assumed I had until 1600 to clean and turn it in, as we had done at the previous Saturday's training. The line formed right away, and a lot of guys went to change their wet fatigues. They brought their rifles to the BOQ. I did too."

"Your two hundred class mates managed to turn theirs in. Were you at the club getting drunk?"

"I ordered a beer with a sandwich. I didn't get to eat the sandwich. Sir, I picked infantry because it is the Army. Everyone else works for us, so we can do our job. They exist for us, so we can meet the enemy and crush him. When I'm told properly what to do, I'll do it. And, I'll lead my men the same way. When they know what I've told them to do, they'll do it. I wouldn't expect them to conduct an operation without a proper briefing." His legs were trembling and he could not stop them and was afraid it would show. His hands were all sweat and sticky. A hardened resolve settled over him. If they were going to persecute him, he was not going to be passive. The Colonel was writing again on his legal pad.

"The second entry I have here is you were involved in a motor vehicle incident at the Officers' Club. You were intoxicated at this incident?"

"My girl and I had a few drinks in the Club, sir."

"You and alcohol don't seem to mix, Lieutenant. The woman you were with is Miss Andrea Tremblay?"

"Yes sir!"

"There was damage to the vehicle?"

"We ran over a curb. If there was damage, it was very minor. We drove it away the next day."

"Where the MPs improper in any aspect?"

"I'd say they did their job correctly."

The Colonel's hand exploded with movement as he scribbled more notes.

"Why was Miss Tremblay upset?"

"The Captain was very polite and even offered to drive us to the Guest House. She was embarrassed. She had to go to the bathroom."

"The MPs wouldn't let her go?" The thin eyebrows squinted again.

"She didn't tell them, only me."

"Are you aware Miss Tremblay's reservation for quarters was arranged by someone from the White House? The Commanding

79

General is concerned why she did not stay in those quarters. Do you know why?"

"She decided to stay with me. I would have felt uncomfortable in those quarters."

"Why is that, Lieutenant?"

"I'm a student here. I have quarters. She came to see and stay with me. We found another place to stay."

"That's the only reason?"

"Yes sir."

"Did the MPs act improperly in any way?"

"They didn't, sir. They were professional in all aspects."

"It was Miss Andrea Tremblay you were with?"

"It was Andrea, sir."

The Colonel wrote more notes, slowly with some deliberation. His eye brows moved at the same pace as his pen.

"I have decided not to impose Article 15 non judicial punishment for careless and negligent security of your issued weapon, an M-16 rifle. A letter of reprimand will be placed in your 201 file for the remainder of your training on this post. I don't want to see you before me again. Do you understand, Lieutenant?"

"Yes sir."

"That's all." Randolph came to the position of attention and saluted.

"What are those shits trying to do to you?" Was Andrea's harsh comment when he told her about the summons of the battalion commander. It was very late Monday evening, the day Andrea had traveled. When they were finally released from training at 17:00, he had skipped evening chow and gone to the informal lounge in the basement of the officer's club. For two hours he drank draft beer and played a pinball machine, letting his mind blissfully go into an unthinking stupor. Finally a couple of tippling Captains indicated they wanted a turn at the game. Surrendering the machine not because of their rank but more due to their over bearing manner, he left the club and went to the phone booths outside Olsen Hall.

The night air was cool. Still wearing his fatigues he shivered slightly.

"The Colonel read Article 31 to me. He could have given me an Article 15."

"What are Articles?" Her tone was still tart, but inquisitive.

"It's legal stuff, the Uniform Code of Military Justice. I could have had a lawyer, but I said no. I turned it around on them. I said no information was given out or orders to turn in the weapons. Then he brought up what happened at the Club."

"I was at the wheel of the car."

"I was there. I was responsible for what happened. You were my guest. That's the way they look at it-and that's right. They were concerned about your influence. They're bureaucrats. The last thing they want is trouble from above. Way above!"

"That Captain knew." Her voice resounded with vindication.

"Don't you think anyone who refused to show a driver's license probably would have been cuffed and arrested?"

"Will that be the end of it?"

"The Colonel told me not to show up in his office again. You have arrived safely?"

"Through one time zone, four airports without losing my luggage. That's an accomplishment. It's chilly up here after Georgia."

"Hard to believe we actually kissed very early this morning, before my career went in the toilet."

"If you are really worried, I'll call Scott, right now."

"You do anything, and you'll stir up the bureaucrats. Nothing else can happen, unless I'm stupid enough to pee on my own boots." She was absolutely quiet for an extended moment to the point of hearing her rhythmic breathing. "It's over. Leave it that way." He said with resolve.

"I've got an interesting company lined up for tomorrow. They make conveyer belts for farm machinery. They're expanding in their overseas markets. Anything that cuts costs will interest them. This is the market for the new alloy bearings my father is looking for."

"Are you going to wear that skirt you wore in the club?" The hairs on the back of his neck suddenly went taut.

"I buy my skirts off the rack. That's current fashion. Next year it could be skirts that cover your ankles. I need to know if this company will use the new alloy bearings. If a short skirt can get me that information, that's what I'll wear. I've learned you do what you have to for business."

"That skirt got the attention of everyone in the club."

"There were other women with short skirts."

"Tell your uncle to wear the short skirts. That will get their attention."

"Sales is such a huge subject." She ignored his comment. "How do you know where to direct your attention? What's important? What isn't? What gets their interest? What do you concentrate on? I'm learning that's what made my father capable of creating his company. He made the market by creating a better product. Scott said growth is the key. Before growth, you've got to have increased sales. We need new and bigger markets for that. My father has seen that with the new alloy, cheap bearings."

"You're beginning to sound like a broken record about those new alloy bearings."

"You're the one who set me on this path."

"A month ago I didn't know you were on any path."

"It's for both of us. My mother's wedding is coming up and I've got to do some apartment hunting. My mother will be out of our house in three weeks. I've got furniture and stuff to either get moved to my new apartment or put in storage. I can't go back to Georgia after this trip. I still have to investigate the trade show being held here. That's still my official reason for coming to Minneapolis."

When Andrea hung up the phone, she noticed how cool her room was. Hugging herself, she set the thermostat warmer and put on a bathrobe. Flannel pajamas will be fine for these solitary trips. Still, no suggestions about Tremblay Bearings or to help me out. Other than the length of my stupid skirt. His mind is sinking into this soldier crap. What the hell are Articles and this Code stuff? Doesn't sound healthy. She scratched a note to herself in her calendar notebook for the mentor.

When Randolph hung up the phone and stepped out of the booth, the cool night air struck him. In all the books and movies the new officer always did something wrong that made him seem stupid. How the hell had it happened to him? He had been careful as a cadet. Was it being around Andrea? Had he been anxious about her arrival like Thompson was about his girl? He hadn't thought so? His loins felt battered after the intense sexual activity. Was that the only feeling a soldier felt after a short overnight pass? He did feel something more for Andrea, didn't he? How long would be have to wait before she returned? Was that more important? As he walked up the three flights of cement stairs, his thoughts bounced off the thought of merely missing her or just the sex. He had just laid on his bed, still fully dressed when Thompson appeared in his opening of their common bathroom.

"What happened to you this morning?"

Randolph looked at Thompson's curious expression. His face reminded him of a little old lady interested in gossip. "I was the last one to turn my rifle in, Saturday. They didn't like that."

"I ran to the head of the line because I knew I had to get out of there. I had to argue with that E-6 armorer. No one was taking my spot in that line."

"Did you see guys taking their rifles up here to these BOQ rooms?"

"A few. They were probably going up to change before turning them in."

"This room can be locked and is secure."

"Sure. Why did they give you a hard time about that?"

"I was at the Club with Blaisedale. I was only gone a half hour. I left the M-16 here."

"You went to the Club? Thayer, that was dumb."

"The Saturday before, we had to clean the Goddamn rifles. It was after four before we got released."

"We range fired. They had to be cleaned." Thompson was quiet a moment.

"Why was that armorer giving everyone such a hard time?" Randolph asked.

"He is a cracker. The Green Beret got the deal to get us released as soon as weapons were counted. When that word came down, that armorer just started reading off weapon serial numbers. There was no more hassling about dirt. What did they do to you?"

"I got chewed out. Strongly implied I should not get into any other trouble while here."

"Don't feel bad. I heard some other poor bastard got drunk at the Club with his girlfriend and smashed into an MP sedan. Slatton wasn't in class either this morning. I'll bet it was him."

The next day, an arms room SOP appeared on the unit's bulletin board and outside the arms room. It was mentioned at the first formation, and each student was given a mimeographed copy. The unit commander, the nervous Captain was at the morning, noon, and final evening release formations, lurking in the background, although he never interfered with the Green Beret Captain's functions as the student commander. Randolph knew he was the cause of the special attention for weapons handling. He wondered why a rather formal and standard procedure had been allowed to be overlooked. It was the student company commander, the Green Beret's fault. While he should have been supervising the formation, and the uniform dispensing of instructions, he had gone off to get them permission to get released early. Thompson was right. He had done things like an NCO rather than an officer. That explained why he had not been chewed out by the Captain when he stood by the armorer's gage as he turned in his rifle.

After evening chow he lay on his bed scanning training manuals, which had been amply supplied to every new Second Lieutenant. Nothing looked very new. In some manner, Randolph had seen most of the material before. It was two days since Andrea's departure and an agreed telephone night. Glancing at his watch, the time was dragging. Nothing unusual had happened to him. He was beginning to feel normal, again. Thompson appeared in the bathroom doorway. He had not heard him come into his half of the room. He looked up at him, but did not say anything. He was getting used to Thompson materializing suddenly and silently.

"Heard a good one today. It fits with the mentality here. This two-year Rotsee guy went on active duty. He requests to have his commission transferred to the Air Force. Of course, the Army laughs at him. He starts a Congressional. There's a whole department in the Pentagon that handles congressional inquiries. They have lots of top brass, colonels, and stuff from all the services. Congressionals get top priority. Commanders have to answer them within twenty-four hours or something. No one can sit on them. Anyway, this guy does his OBC and then starts his troop duty. He gets the Air Force interested, and they say they will do it. In the meantime, the paperwork is going back and forth and time is passing. They don't send him to Vietnam pending his transfer to the Air Force. He eats up most of his first year and well into his second of active duty. He has to resign his Army commission to accept a commission in the Air Force. So, with all the delays by the time the paperwork is ready for him to sign, he says no, I've changed my mind. I want to keep my Army commission. There isn't enough time for a tour in "Nam." Thompson laughed.

"You'd like to beat the system? Get sent home."

"I'll do my part. If my orders direct me to another place, that won't bother me either."

"Old men don't fight the wars. Haven't you heard the protesters use that?"

"Yeah, I heard that. You're the crazy one. A well thrown rock could probably bring one of those helicopters down."

"Why did you become an officer?" Randolph persisted.

"I didn't want some red neck cracker telling me what to do."

"They'll still be there, only wearing railroad tracks. You told me that."

"There was that fifty bucks a month in Advanced Rotsee. I had to plan on every nickel I could earn. There was a chance to get paid to go to class, rather than paying."

"That's a hell of a commitment to make for fifty bucks a month. This is infantry, not transportation or adjutant general. Why did you pick this branch?"

Thompson was silent and looked around the room with a vacant stare. "Maybe you'll laugh at this." He blurted, suddenly.

"The Commies are trying to take over the world. They got Russia and China. That's most of the world right now. What's next? They're trying to get it a little piece at a time. We have to stop them. Vietnam seems like the place to do it. We have to say no more. It stops here. Our way of life will end, if we don't. I don't want some atheistic Commie bastards raising my kids."

"Why not war simply because it's war? For the true soldiers."

"Maybe you're a soldier, Thayer. I'm a civilian wearing a uniform for two years. We have to be soldiers to fight the Commies in a place like Vietnam. You're the one who says a lot of them wearing uniforms are only bureaucrats."

"Beating the Commies is your only reason to wear a uniform?"

"Our fathers beat the Nazis and the Banzai Japs. Our grandfathers beat the Germans before they became Nazis. Our generation has got the Commies. There is no such thing as a true soldier. After we beat the Commies, there may be a period of Eisenhower peace. Then, there will be some other group that wants to conquer the world, and push their thoughts and ideology on the rest of us against our will and desires. They'll have to be stopped. There is a perpetual soldier. For me it's two years. For others down through the ages, it was for the duration or an enlistment, whatever the period of time. When that term is over, you take off the uniform and become a civilian. You've taken your chances. Now its time for the next guy to take his chances. There is no true soldier. There are perpetual ones that rise up to meet the occasion, and then they disappear."

"They'll always be there, though."

"Until the time comes to melt down the swords and make them into plow shares. In between, Armies become slack, corrupt, and bureaucratic. They're unprepared for the next war. Look at history, it will tell you that. We've never been ready for the next conflict. The Army always has to catch up and relearn."

Randolph searched for his cigarette pack, found it and lit one. Thompson's face, again, had a vacant look and he stared blankly at the wall. "We're getting it from everyone since her trip down here."

"Getting what?" Randolph was puzzled.

"A lot of flak."

"You're engaged. Good thing you didn't try living with her while you were in college. Christ Thompson, this is the era of free love."

"Not in our families. They wouldn't have allowed us. My parents have been everything for me. They sacrificed to help me. My future in-laws are the same way. My girl couldn't turn her back on her family. I wouldn't expect it. If I do buy the farm over there, we would have missed everything."

"That's the way it's been through all of time. Haven't you read books? Seen movies?"

"She's the reason I'll get through." Thompson ignored Randolph's comment. "I won't take unnecessary chances. I'm applying for leave during Thanksgiving. We're going to get married. I don't care what it takes. We're going to do it. Then, the families will settle down."

Randolph laid the field manuals on his desk and swung his feet over the side of the bed. He still wore his fatigues. "Call time." He announced.

"She pays for the calls?" Thompson came out of his sudden trance and looked at Randolph. "You got it made." He retreated through the common bathroom to his part of the room.

Randolph picked up his field jacket and cap. Outside it was dark and cool. The glow of cigarette butts indicated occupied booths. There were plenty of vacancies.

"The next time some one reads you Article 31, you demand a lawyer?" Andrea's tone was scolding. Stars filled the clear, fall sky. "If you need a lawyer, I will get you one. A civilian one who knows what the hell he's doing. You have rights. You should know and exercise them."

"The mentor guy again, huh? If you had hired me a lawyer, there would have been some sort of hearing, which would have tied me up here for God knows how long. Maybe enough time to get me bounced out of flight school even before I start. It got resolved, it's over. You stick to new alloy bearings and trade shows."

"If you get in that situation, you call me, and I'll get the help, We don't need you thrown in jail to ad to your Army time."

"It was a paper spanking. They still need bodies in Nam. And there's enough guys trying to get out of going even though they're wearing gold bars." He told her the story Thompson had told him about the Second Lieutenant who tried to transfer to the Air Force.

"I gave you a chance to transfer your commission to the National Guard."

"People in the National Guard go into it to escape going to Vietnam. There is some National Guard there, but most are individual volunteers. This war is being fought by draftees and two-year men like Thompson, my roommate here. He says he's one of the perpetual soldiers. They wear uniforms, do their thing while it's their turn, then take off the uniforms. It becomes someone else's turn. According to him, there are no true soldiers."

"He's right, listen to him. You're a perpetual. Only you've got more than two years to do."

"You think so?"

She was silent a moment, and he could feel her anger.

"There's two main ways Tremblay Bearings can raise money for new equipment for the new alloy bearings that are what everyone is talking about especially up here in Minneapolis." Her tone indicated her anger had dissipated. "The Company is private. If he goes public, we sell stock and can raise money easily. You lose some control making your company public. The government has the right to look over your shoulder. Or, he can get some loans using his assets as collateral. Some of it would be my inheritance. If could affect me. Would you mind that?"

"Would that mean according to some ancient custom, you come to me naked in your shift when you're broke, so I wouldn't have to assume your debts?"

Again, she was silent and he could feel her resentment at his humor attempt. Their non conversation silence dragged nearly into a full minute. "I'm convinced we need the new equipment." Her tone was strained and back to her objective. "I've been to five companies in the last two days, and all of them are considering new products that could use the new alloy bearings within the next two to five years. My father's hunch is right. If the company is going to go to twenty million, we have to have these new products."

Briefly, he thought of more sarcasm, but resisted it. "What do your uncles think?"

"They're conservative. They don't trust the new products, and if we go public, they're afraid their share of the company loses value."

"If you get the new equipment, sell the new stuff and start reaching your father's goal, everything has to have more value, doesn't it? That means more sales, increased quantities, more money coming in. Bigger volume means their shares have to be worth more. How would they lose?"

"Profits have to go to shareholders. They have a point about reduced value. If the new alloy bearings were to flop, we'd be out a lot of money spent on capital equipment that won't produce. They are conservative. My father is the only one willing to take the chance."

"Your father sent you there to find there is a market. You've done that. Obviously, Uncle Leland isn't telling him that. Rich people stay rich by using other people's money to make more money. Haven't you ever heard that?"

"We should go public, then?"

"Either way. That new market is the future, as you keep reminding me."

When she hung up the phone, Andrea stared out the window of her hotel room, watching some trees sway slightly in a gathering breeze. She felt serene and satisfied. At last he had given her some solid advice about Tremblay Bearings, although he really didn't understand the complexity of her uncles. She would handle that. It felt so good to have him back with her thoughts on her side. He's right. My father will use other peoples' money. This is the first time since his two weeks in the Army that he has had any opinions to share. She lay on the huge bed and stared up at the ceiling. If only he was a two-year man. Causing a hearing might have been the way to disrupt his path. No flight school. The Army would not mean anything to him. There was a chance, but it's blown. He saw it, too.

Still it was an opportunity. If there was one, there will be another. The next one I've got see ahead of him.

One sunny, humid afternoon, they were attending a series of classroom lectures on artillery support available to an infantry platoon. The buildings were old, and next to shady trees. There was an undergrowth of vines and bushes, which made a good nesting area for beehives. There were several in the immediate area. During the mandatory ten minute break for each hour, the students rushed outside to light cigarettes. The sweet-smelling heavy autumn air had stirred the final serge of activities from the bees and hornets. A bee settled on the collar of one student and dropped down his back. Frantically, he pulled at his fatigue shirt attempting to extricate the angry insect. It stung him several times before he managed to expel it from his clothing. The student readjusted his uniform and returned to the classroom. Within ten minutes of the stinging, his eyes, nose, and ears began to ooze liquids. His skin turned pallid, and he started to go into shock. An ambulance was called, and he was carried out of the classroom on a stretcher.

"Imagine, going through four years of Rotsee and a couple of physicals before commissioning, and they didn't discover he was allergic to bees." Thompson was standing in their common bathroom.

"Hard to believe you can get through your life without a bee sting." Randolph lay on his bed, smoking a cigarette.

"They said if he hadn't gotten to the hospital as fast as he did, he could have died. Imagine, going into the Army and getting killed by a bee. At least that's one thing we're going to have in Nam. Good medical support. There are Field and Evac Hospitals all over the place. That guy has a ticket out of the Army. Not only is he getting out of going, he'll get a medical discharge. If he does it right, he could get disability, which will mean money every month for the rest of his life. The lucky bastard. He'd probably stuff that bee and hang him over his fireplace if he could."

Randolph set the telephone contact for every other night. Habitually without realizing it, Andrea retold the same information about her sales probing activities. Only the companies' names were different. Randolph began to yearn for something out of the ordinary, although after two long days he was enthralled simply listening to her voice. Conversation was mostly by Andrea. One night after one of those lengthy phone booth calls, he called home using a pile of silver coins. Dutifully upon arrival at Fort Benning he had sent home his mailing address. His mother and Judy had written short notes to him. He had not answered either. A telephone call was more expensive but easier.

"Ma had to go to Teddy's school tonight for a teacher conference." It surprised him having Judy answer the phone. His mother was always home. "Betsy stopped by last weekend. Andrew's mentioned a ring."

"Is someone else mentioning rings?"

"Not that I know of." She giggled. "Do you know someone who is?"

"Not from down here."

"Faith's here, she wants to say hello."

"What are those Southern Belles like?" Faith's voice was light, fluffy, and caused an overwhelming serge of homesickness. He could picture exactly where she would be standing as she held the Thayer phone.

"They'll all sitting on their porches with their mint juleps. We pass them while on the buses heading for training sites." He laughed, releasing something inside that made him comfortable, a different type of relief that he did not feel when talking to Andrea. "All I see all day long is other Second Lieutenants in fatigue uniforms trying to act like Second Lieutenants."

"Isn't it more advanced training than Rotsee camp?" As usual Faith was interested in what he was doing, and asked a question that meant something.

"They made us do more in Rotsee camp. We had to practice leadership. Here, we're just students. They seem to be just demonstrating everything. They want us to absorb. How is your brother doing?"

"Arthur is being nasty to everyone who comes to see him, resisting all help from whoever tries to give it, and being his usual, stupid, selfish, self. What do you do for excitement down there?"

"Try to stay in one piece. Stay alert. Stay alive! That's the motto. I'm getting very good on a pin ball machine in the club. Or, the thing just likes my money. What do you think about Betsy?"

"All Andrew wants is to insure he'll become a doctor. He wants Dr. Croteau to get him into medical school. Betsy is his ticket. He's very obvious. Judy doesn't believe that, though. All she can think of is true love, since that's what she has. What about Thanksgiving? Will you be home for that?"

"I have the day off, but that's all. Time's almost up and I'm out of coins."

"You be sure to duck if those pin balls get loose. Loose balls could be dangerous." She started laughing so hard at her wisecrack Randolph could not help joining her. The operator broke in asking for more money. He ended the call. As he replaced the receiver, he stopped laughing. The sound her voice remained in his thoughts as he trudged up the cement stairs to his room.

"Oh, it was so good to hear his voice. Sounds like he's enjoying what he's doing. And, I like what he's doing with all his free time."

"The Army is what he wanted to do," Judy said laconically.

"It's the flying he really wants. Have you ever heard his flying stories about Norwood airport when he was first learning?"

"You're my best friend. I love you dearly. I probably will all my life. Andrea is back in his life. You know that."

"They broke up. That could happen again. If she really cared about him, she'd be with him now in the time he has before he goes to Vietnam."

"How do you know she isn't there with him?"

"I called Tremblay Bearings a few days ago to find out where she was. I told their receptionists I was an old school friend and wanted to get in touch with her. She gave me a telephone number in Minnesota, and said she was on a sales trip until the weekend."

"You did that?"

"She's a fool. If it was me, I'd be with him, even if I had to live in my car."

"You need to go out on some dates. If you put on an 'I'm available sign,' I bet you'd get dates. Your law firm is huge."

"Half the proposals would be from married guys."

"You know how to find out paper-wise if they're married."

"Why bother?"

"You've got to."

"Hearing his voice means I'm going to have a hard time getting to sleep tonight."

Chapter Five

Thompson's leave for Thanksgiving was granted by the battalion commander after a face-to-face interview. The story he told Randolph was that his finance had agreed to marry him in secret during the leave. This plunged him into the myriad numbers of forms and prerequisites the Army required for the proposed transaction. To Randolph each night with wild hand gestures, Thompson would explain the latest administrative snag either with the Army or at his finance's end. Complicating the situation, his girl still lived with her parents. Their telephone conversations required colorful and elaborate encrypting descriptions, which often, frankly, confused Thompson as well as Randolph who was hearing them second hand. A wedding could not be planned like a raid or a clandestine operation, which were the alternating methods Thompson seemed to be employing. Randolph was sure both families had deciphered the elaborate plans and would be ready to ambush him.

The previous night during their usual telephone conversation, Andrea had given him the flight number and arrival time. They coincided roughly to Thompson's planned departure. Randolph offered him a ride to save the nominal cost of garaging his car at the airport during his Thanksgiving leave. Upon his return a bus would be available for Fort Benning. After watching Thompson depart, there was an hour to wait for Andrea's arrival. He bought a paperback and settled in a chair. His interest soon drifted from the book to the substantial holiday crowd, most of it obvious military. People greeted each other renewing reunions in varying degrees from nonchalance to direct, unrestrained passion.

Holding the paperback, trying to read, his peripheral vision absorbed the holiday reunions going on around him. Did Thompson's plight and his with Andrea have any similarities? How did he manage intimacies when she still lived with her parents? Thompson complained of the cost of a motel room. As far back as college, although they often used a car, Andrea usually paid for a room with her unlimited plastic. She didn't care what her parents' thought or what his parents thought. He knew his mother strongly disapproved. Her eyes betrayed her. He had decided he could live with her cutting glances. He had no moral restrains, as apparently Thompson did. Once he was with Andrea, the sheer physical drive took over in both of them. Knowing where he was headed and the type of profession he had chosen, made no difference. That made him very different from Thompson who threw political influence into why he wore a uniform. To settle the question of sleeping together legally and cementing feuding families seemed to be Thompson's reason to get married. That would solve Thompson's moral dilemma. His girl was a student. Would she leave school to come and live with him while he finished his troop duty? Or, finish school wearing a ring? Getting married was Thompson's only objective. There was no after-planning.

Did he have to consider that with Andrea? What was a marriage proposal worth? Would it entice her to come to Georgia and spend the time together until going to flight school? That was six weeks. What would they have him doing since the schooling was finished? He would have lots of free time. What would she demand of him? Preventing him going to Vietnam was what she wanted. He had no control of where he was going, so possibly it would be worth it to ask her. It might gain him his objective, which was to have more time with her.

Since the Columbus Day visit, she had found an apartment and furnished it. The distance from Tremblay Bearings and where her father lived, was the major element of her selection. She had been in her mother's Saturday afternoon wedding. Then had got on a plane and flown back to Minneapolis for the final day of the Industrial Show. That had been the original objective of her clandestine sales exploratory trip, which no one in the company believed any longer. Tremblay Bearings, which had previously nearly ignored this trade show, was rewarded with some increased business. Andrea was lauded for her efforts. The reward for her industrial show success was to be given complete control of the major trade show Tremblay Bearings attended in New Jersey scheduled for the second weekend of January, a week after Randolph was scheduled to start flight school. She had already been directed to attend two pre-show conferences, one of which was on a weekend. Randolph knew of her hectic program since she reported it during their now daily telephone conversations. He could hardly fault her failure in mounting a second visit. With the Thanksgiving Holiday approaching and her mother still on her month long honeymoon in Europe, she had informed her father that she would be spending the holiday time in Georgia. He, like his roommate Thompson, had started ticking off the days until their rendezvous.

When she appeared coming through a crowd, his attention was drawn to her long, shapely legs. Her face exploded into a smile when she first saw him, and her gait increased to shorten the distance between them. She wore a maroon business suit with a mid thigh skirt. Their first touching denuded his thoughts. They kissed, open-mouthed standing among a crowd, which due to frequent passionate greetings ignored theirs. Randolph now felt be was part of what he had watched with interest, earlier. The touch of her lips awakened every sensual junction. So entranced, he left the newly purchased paperback on the seat next to where he had sat. Later when he realized it, he could not remember the title. They walked toward the baggage area.

"Stop staring at my legs. You're making me self conscious."

"Neither have the lengths of your skirts."

"I keep telling you that's current fashion. Wearing something non fashion gets unwanted attention. I don't want that."

"I've always liked your legs. I dream about them."

"Your dreams have been answered. They are here with the rest of me." With continued minor annoyance, her face indicated her awareness of his open attention. Suddenly she stopped them by putting her hand on his arm. "A lot of my time I'm pushing off unwanted advances."

"Who makes advances at you?"

"Men in airports. Men at business meetings. Most of the time I know it's not genuine. I just ignore it."

"Live with me, Andrea. We could find a place off post. We'd have more than a month before flight school starts."

"That doesn't make sense. Do you know what it takes to set up an apartment? What would we live in—a motel? I see enough of them, now." Forcefully taking his arm she pulled him to get started for the baggage area. "I'm not interested in anyone but you. There is no one for you to be jealous of."

"I want us to be together, and this is time I'll be relatively free."

"There are meetings in December for the Jersey trade show, and I've got to be in Massachusetts at the plant some of the time. I don't want them to forget me. I wouldn't have much of that month here."

Randolph fell silent as they retrieved her suitcase. He was dejected by her clear refusal. He tried to think of her part of the rejection. There were business meetings for her to attend. Did she have to be in Massachusetts, though? They must know what she was doing, and it was only a month. His silence continued until they arrived at his car.

"I wish you could have been at the wedding." Andrea said when she had finally settled into the bucket seat of the Camaro. "Everyone asked about you. Scott's son wore his Marine Corps dress white uniform. Pretty snappy. Does the Army have dress uniforms? Have you got one?"

"It looks like a Civil War uniform. Same colors too."

"Scott even had a sword." Andrea giggled. "It kept getting caught in things. Have you got a sword?"

"Army Second Lieutenants no longer have use for them."

"Scott's getting more pressure from the Administration. He took my mother on a month-long honeymoon just to get away from it. My mother told me while they were in France, a special courier found them to deliver an invitation to a diplomatic party."

"Did they go?"

"Scott though it would be an interesting way to pass an evening. My mother was knocked over by it. There was a prime minister as well as some royalty there. She wants him to take the job in Washington. I do too. It would be good for both of them. Give them a chance to start their marriage in new surroundings."

"Don't they have the new house they just built on the South Shore?"

"That would remain their legal address. They'd get some fancy apartment in D.C."

"Expensive way to live."

"Scott is money. The only problem money presents to him is how to manage it properly. He's delaying an answer to keep his son from a second Vietnam tour. At the wedding Scott Jr. told me when he gets to Vietnam he wants to command a company in the field, and then get transferred to a battalion or regiment staff as a something. Then, he can get promoted to major before he leaves Vietnam. It's all a career path for him."

"Could Scott actually stop those orders sending his son to Vietnam?"

"The mentor said if Scott took the job with the Administration and asked for that, it could happen. That could cause a lot of bad blood between father and son. What I think Scott is hoping will happen, is that someone will know what he wants and orders for Scott Jr. never get issued. Then he could honestly say he had nothing to do with it. So far, Scott Jr. is still commanding recruits on Parris Island. Maybe they are giving Scott what he wants."

"Does the Captain expect the orders?"

"At the wedding he told me he expected to escape from Parris Island within thirty to sixty days. As of last night, he still doesn't have orders."

At the Holiday Inn while Randolph carried her baggage, Andrea quickly produced her credit card, and paid for the room she had reserved four weeks previously. Randolph felt awkward while they stood in front of the check-in desk. The feeling passed quickly. As soon as he had closed the door to their room, he dropped her suitcases and wrapped his arms around her. He remembered feeling the coolness of the sheets, when they pulled back the bedspread. Their bodies wedged into each other fitting perfectly. Afterwards, for a long time gently caressing with soothing touches they held each other. Each rediscovered the other's body after the six-week absence. Long into the night, they were both wakeful.

They ate their Thanksgiving meal at the hotel's restaurant. They had drinks in the bar before going into the dining area. It featured a turkey entrée. They had prime rib. For their meal they ordered a bottle of wine. Since the Officer Basic Course had reached its ninth and final week, the Friday after Thanksgiving was declared a non duty day. Saturday morning, they had a rehearsal for the graduation ceremony, which was scheduled for early in the next week. There were many young women, some with young children roaming through the Holiday Inn.

"Scott gave me the name of a guy really qualified to be our California salesman."

"Aren't they still in Europe?"

"They are. There are telephone cables under the Atlantic ocean."

"Expensive call."

"An important one. That's why he made it. I'm going to contact the guy, and see if he is interested." Andrea had selected a red wine. Randolph was half way through the bottle when their entrées arrived. It was Saturday night, their final evening together.

"I thought you were the trade show guru?"

"Trade shows are something that's been neglected at Tremblay Bearings for so long, that doing anything was an improvement. It's how you view trade shows. Some think they're a waste of time. We brought in sixty K in sales for that Minneapolis thing I did. The detractors said we would have got that business eventually.

Most of it was repeat stuff. I made it happen because I was there. That's active sales. When we introduce the new alloy bearings, we are going to have to be there to get first sales. That will mean real growth." Andrea still nursed her first glass of the wine. Randolph's face had flushed to a warm glow from the alcohol he had consumed. "There's a lot of potential in California. The industrial base out there hasn't been tapped by Tremblay Bearings either old or the new products. With someone devoted entirely to California, that could really boost sales. That is going to happen."

"Who is going to do the trade shows?"

"I'm not sure who my uncle will give them to. I've got some cousins on the payroll who could be stimulated to do something useful. I've shown them that they are important. At the Christmas party, which is one of my father's favorite functions, he hands out bonuses—envelopes full of cash no one has to pay taxes on—and announces promotions for the coming year. That's a party you better plan on going to, if you're home at Christmas. There should be a special announcement concerning me. I've been told the Army allows a lot of leave during Christmas time, especially for someone like you, going from one assignment to another. With travel time you could probably take two weeks. Plenty of time before your reporting date in Texas on the fourth." Randolph sipped his wine making a small ceremony as he balanced the glass between two fingers and gently set it down on the table. Andrea stared at him, impatient with his non response. "My father still hasn't decided how to raise the money for the new equipment. The only thing is that he has decided to enter the new alloy markets."

Randolph knew this and said nothing.

"A week ago he told me there are some other options to raise the money. He's still sensitive to his brothers concerns. There's been a lot of tension over this. I even heard there could be a challenge to my father's control to stop a public stock offering. It's his company. He controls most of the stock. My mother would support him just to spite my uncles. Of course, I'd vote my shares for him."

"You have stock?"

"I'm coming into part of my inheritance. What would you think of me sitting on the Board?"

"Watch out for splinters with those short skirts." He poured more wine. She glared at his wine glass. "I wonder if Thompson managed to tie the clandestine knot." Randolph had told Andrea his roommate's plight. "And if they got to consummate, legally. Wonder if that takes the fun out of it? Suppose he'll bring her here to Benning? I could lose my roomy."

"They'll continue doing what they're doing with their lives. She's a student. He's in the Army. The Army squashes a lot of plans."

"Sort of like us."

"Not quite like us. He still has a better situation, only two years, and then he's free. What do you think about me on the Board?"

"What are you bucking for?"

"Our future."

"Here's to our immediate future tonight, since I may not be seeing you again until I get to Texas." He pushed the wine glass away.

"Leave at Christmas time would mean you could see my new apartment."

"And utilize it to its full potential?"

She smiled just before she filled her mouth with pink prime rib, noting with satisfaction he had pushed his wine glass away. Randolph's face went blank as he thought about the marriage proposal. It had to be worth more than a month together. Since she was not going to stay with him in Georgia, it would have gained him nothing. She saw the sudden change in his mood. Looking at her eyes, they bore into him.

"What do you want to be in your father's company?" He avoided her harsh staring.

"For now, I want to control all domestic sales. That's eighty percent of our business."

"That's a big bite."

"Nothing is assured in business. Maybe I'll get half of it from the Mississippi to the Coast. Even after the decision has been made, you have to look over your shoulder, constantly watching for an ambush. How's that for an Army term?" She smiled sarcastically. "If he makes the announcement about buying the new capital equipment in December at the Christmas party, it could make my

New Jersey trade show really active. People will want to know when it will be available. That will mean definite schedules. That's easier to deal with. In Minneapolis, I got a lot of questions about the new products, and I had to play dumb. I need something to knock the wind out of Leland Jr. He's bucking for something. I'm not sure exactly what. He's got his sights on climbing higher in operations. He's been eyeing senior materials positions. The current director of materials might be thinking of retiring soon. He's been with the company over twenty years."

"You're not too young to control most of sales?"

"I'm the president's daughter," she smiled with a sneer. "I'm going to use every advantage I have to get what I want for us." Her intense gaze cut through him. It felt like being hit by something. "Do you plan to work on that shipping dock again when the time comes, and you're allowed to grow your hair longer?"

"I do need a haircut. Thanks for reminding me."

Her expression shifted to a phony pout. "You have less than four years to go. You've been here two months. Time is passing. Think future!"

"I've done pretty good in the last four weeks. I haven't had to see any Colonels."

"Apply for leave at Christmas. I want you there at the company party." She picked up her wine glass.

"Yes mam." In defiance, he took another sip of wine.

After a gratifying session in their Holiday Inn bed, helped by Randolph's inhibiting his intake of alcohol, it was Andrea who rolled onto her side and fell into a deep slumber. He was wide awake. It was good that the infantry training was coming to an end. He felt confident. The Army knew how to train. He could lead a platoon, if required. For the first time the girl lying next to him seemed strange. Physically, she was the same; a lean body proportioned exquisitely, especially the legs. They were the standards by which to judge all females. She was more confident. She ordered not asked him to apply for Christmas leave. Her pursuit of business interests was becoming all consuming. It overshadowed chances to be together. A few things like her mother's wedding and getting an apartment were realistic demands on her time. Of the six week separation, she could have used two, possibly three to accomplish those tasks. The other eighty percent of her life was Tremblay Bearings. It had crept into her thoughts, speech, and mannerisms, and was slowly pushing him away from access to her. Why wouldn't she give it up or at least put it on hold until he went to Vietnam? He knew she wouldn't. Stubbornness was a major cause of their breakup. She expended her efforts for them, she kept expounding. How could he make her change direction and share his time at flight school, one of the momentous experiences of his life? Had she stayed a student after their breakup instead of dropping out, giving up or postponing school would have been easy. His future was now. For the first time, he felt some resentment for her wealthy background. There would never have been these problems if she came from a blue collar neighborhood. Was a marriage proposal the only weapon left to him?

Sunday, Randolph drove her to the airport in the early afternoon. She was stoically mellow. Sensing her uneasiness, was it her refusal to live with him? In her practical terms, it made no sense to come to Georgia. Texas was a different matter, and he had still to mention it. They checked her one piece of luggage then stood in the busy, holiday-crowded terminal. She wrapped her arms around his neck, and they kissed passionately, oblivious to the crowd. Each felt the impending separation, knowing it was to be another long period.

When her plane lifted off, he felt suddenly intimidated. He couldn't understand it. He had never felt that way when with her. Was Tremblay Bearings his real enemy? She seemed to be pushing him toward choices, when he felt he had no choices. The Army had him for the next several years. It, not Andrea, determined his future.

At the seven o'clock formation, their last Monday of the course, there was an unpretentious animation among the Second Lieutenants. Anticipation for the end of the course was contagious. The majority was about to embark upon their first real Army unit assignments. Infantry branch offered to a few of the student officers some additional schooling. About a dozen were staying at Benning for the short three-week parachute course. For a select few, there was jungle survival school in Panama. Two Regular Army in the class had been designated for Ranger training. Those facing the greatest amount of schooling away from the guardianship of infantry branch were the five graduates of the ROTC flight program. The student executive officer First Lieutenant aviator, who usually handled announcements, began calling off names, Blaisedale, Cooper, Dean, Jardin and Thayer. The five named were being sent to the post hospital for Class II flight physicals the following day, Tuesday the last day before graduation. All were due flight physicals before arriving at Fort Wolters. In its mysterious ways, the Army shadowed them.

"At Christmas, we're getting married." Thompson said as he began packing that evening. He had been assigned to a training brigade stationed at Fort Benning. They had to vacate Olsen Hall within three days of graduation. It belonged to the next officer basic class. Randolph stood in their common bathroom, watching him. During his Thanksgiving leave Thompson had not been married, although he had done everything necessary including getting the license, finding a Justice of the Peace, and selecting a hotel for their one-day honeymoon tryst. Both sets of parents were against the ceremony at Thanksgiving. His fiancée also wanted something approaching a normal wedding where she would get to wear the traditional white dress. Christmas was the next compromise. This time both sets of parents were working toward it. "She has a semester break. Hopefully, I can get leave at Christmas. Talked to my new CO. He said he could probably spare me, seeing how I'm getting married."

The next morning Erik Blaisedale rode to the hospital in Randolph's Camaro. They wore fatigues; their duty uniform and each carried a manila folder with the flight medical forms. He was not sure how much Blaisedale knew about the rifle incident. Would be judged harshly as Thompson had done? During their frequent encounters after that fateful early October weekend, it had never been mentioned. Blaisedale did not express any curiosity about the reason for leaving the Club so abruptly that day, when they were having lunch, other than Randolph's explanation of turning in his rifle. He was from Arizona. That was all Randolph had learned about him in the nine weeks of OBC.

"Did you get your single engine land rating from the flight program?" Randolph asked as he drove toward the hospital.

"Had to buy twenty hours, but I got it. Needed it. I'm going to be a state trooper when I get out of the Army. The flying ones make more money. I'll be getting flight pay long after you've stopped collecting yours."

"I might stay in."

"Good luck to you. As a trooper, they can only send me from one end of the state to the other. That's all the moving around I want to do after the Army. Are we rooming together at Fort Wolters? The trailers are rented all furnished. All you need is your clothing and personal gear."

"How did you learn all that?"

"Stopped by there on my way here. Asked questions. Drove around. Got some telephone numbers. With non-availability of quarters, which we'll get, rooming with someone means about breaking even on rent. I know you're single. Cooper and Dean are bringing their wives and kids to Texas."

"What about Jardin?"

"I couldn't take those aviator glasses he must wear twenty hours a day. California sunshine boy. You strike me more as a conservative type, although you're from the East where all those faggots march in the anti-war demonstrations." Randolph grunted but said nothing. "I'm going to be a public servant, and I don't want nothing to screw that up. Take it easy, Thayer. If you ain't got a sense of humor, this will never work. They want a month's security deposit. Are you in?" Suddenly, Randolph knew Andrea would not come to Texas to live with him. When she visited, they would use the local Holiday Inn. He nodded. "I'll need some money once I make some calls. I'll let you know how much."

The five arrived before seven as they had been directed, although all the hospital personnel were at their morning formation. Other uniformed soldiers had gathered in the waiting area. Some were waiting for sick call to begin. Outside on a grassy area, they watched the hospital personnel in formation.

"Only the medical corps would allow all those motley collection of uniforms in one formation," Blaisedale said as they watched through the huge windows.

"They all have different duties and responsibilities. Each is in their duty uniform."

"It still looks sloppy. Un-military."

Cooper moved closer to them as they stood by the large windows. He was from Pennsylvania and had an infant daughter. His wife had accompanied him to Benning. They lived off post. Dean was also married with two small children. His wife had remained in Idaho since he could not afford to bring them with him. They were going to join him when they went to Texas. Seldom did he speak about his family. Jardin was also single, although the rumor was he had been through a divorce. His aviator sunglasses were put on the moment a formation broke up. He drove a new Corvette.

"You people on your way to Fort Wolters?" A Second Lieutenant dressed in TWs came toward them. He was lean with that OCS, recent graduate appearance. The five ROTC flight candidates stared at him with guarded vigilance waiting for the usual challenge. He also wore jump wings and a single ribbon, the National Service Defense Ribbon worn by everyone on active duty over ninety days. Soon, they would be entitled to wear it. "Name's Todd Richner from Richmond, Virginia." He took a step toward them as if to shake hands. No one offered. No OCS graduate ever offered any sociability in conversation or mannerisms. Randolph and his four classmates were stunned. "Rotsee flight program graduates?" Again, no one answered. "You guys are lucky being on orders for flight school. Before I went to OCS, I probably could have got Warrant Officer Candidate School. Almost wish I had done that. At least I would have been flying during all the bullshit."

"Bullshit ain't allowed in ROTC, although many exalted members have a habit of stepping in it. Name's Erik Blaisedale. We're all from the just graduating OBC." Blaisedale extended his hand to the Virginian.

"I've been out of OCS for three months, now." With southern courtesy, Richner shook each of the others startled hands. "There's a slowdown. Things have started to tighten up. If I had known about that ROTC flight program, I would have done that in college. I'm still holding out for fixed wing. Allocations from infantry are getting tougher to get. I might have to take rotary wing."

"How do you get fixed wing?" Dean asked.

"It helps if you're Nixon's illegitimate son." Cooper said. The others laughed further melting the still simmering tension. Todd Richner smiled broadly.

"Do OCS guys get sick?" Dean asked. "I thought you guys ate snakes and stuff like that out in the woods."

"You're confusing OCS guys with Rangers. Snakes slither away from them 'cause they knew they'll get eaten." Cooper said.

"I'm only here for a flight physical," Richner laughed softly realizing he had broken some of the inherent resistance.

"You're the first OCS guy I ever talked to. I really wondered if some of them could talk." Dean said.

"I spent six unforgettable months because I didn't have your foresight. Didn't think I needed it. There are all types in that program. Some good and some odd ones. I'll always remember them. You're going to be aviators. You're in the pipeline for that. I have to ask for it. You have to be in the right place at the right time. Branch controls where you go. I was working on my multi-engine instrument when my draft notice arrived. I've got about six hundred hours. About a hundred and fifty of that is multi engine."

"What kind of ratings do you have?" Randolph asked.

"Commercial, but for cargo only."

"Thayer, you got a license?" Dean said. "They have an aero club here. We could have rented a plane."

"I'm signed off over there. I'd rent a plane if you guys want to go." Todd said quickly.

"Is it possible to swap your slot? Rotary for fixed wing?" Dean asked.

"If you could get the allocation, you could get your orders changed. You are an allocation right now. Armor has some unused fixed-wing allocations. I'm hoping to get one of them. There are still infantry allocations for rotary wing, although there're drying up fast. I've been sitting on the fence long enough. I have to do something, soon. First thing is get the physical out of the way. If the Army is going to keep all the helicopters, what they need to do is activate the old Army Air Corps."

"They have. Only Warrant Officers are in it." Cooper said. The others laughed easing more of the latent hostility.

"With all your time," Randolph said to Todd Richner. "I should think the Army would want to put you in fixed wing?"

"I've been trying since I graduated from OCS. They keep sending me little barbs about keeping up with branch, and becoming a pilot is not the way to do it. I want to fly. Fight school is getting tougher. They're pink slipping more people out."

"What is a pink slip?" Cooper asked. Todd Richner had gained all their attention.

"Unsatisfactory flight or a violation of safety rules. Get three, and you're out. A couple of years ago, in 66 and 67, once you got to flight school, you stayed until you got your wings. They needed the bodies. They kept recycling you. They even lowered the eyesight requirements for a short time. If they gave you a few more hours, maybe you'd get over whatever the problem was. All that is gone now, from everything I hear."

"Infantry considers you a second class citizen as an aviator?" Randolph asked.

"If you're going to wear crossed rifles for a career, stay here and wear them. They want you to be a platoon leader, then a company exec, then a company commander and then on a staff at battalion or brigade. That's the career path course. Aviation is a side trip that keeps you away from that important stuff. After your short tour as an aviator, you'll come back as a Captain who hasn't done what they expected you to have done. You're an odd ball as far as infantry branch is concerned. You'll have to catch up. You probably never will. They will tell you, if you want to fly become a Warrant Officer."

"How do you know so much about the flight program?" Jardin asked suspiciously.

"My brother went through the WOC program in '67. Did his tour in 68-69. Now, he's an instructor pilot at Rucker. Warrant Officers fly each assignment. As an infantry officer after your Vietnam tour, you'll have to fight to land a flying slot. Wolters is the primary rotary wing school. You do what they call Primary One and Two. Each is fifty hours. You have to pass a check ride with each one. Then you go to Rucker to finish with instrument and contact."

"What's contact?" Cooper asked.

"Transition into UH-1s."

"We don't start out in Hueys?" Jardin seemed surprised.

"Trainers," Todd Richner said. "It's TH55 or OH-23s. Piston driven, not turbines. For the Army that's a lot cheaper. You have to get two hundred hours of dual and solo flight time to become a rated military pilot. Things are slowing up over there with the pullouts. They won't need as many pilots in a year or so. Flight school is getting tougher. They'll cut the numbers down through forced attrition and by higher qualifications and standards. That's not just the infantry way, that's the Army way."

A Colonel from the Infantry Center came to the auditorium of Bedroom Four and presented completion certificates. IOBC was over. Like un-penned birds, the students began to scatter immediately after the ceremony going to their first duty assignments. Cooper and Dean requested leave immediately and departed for their home states to spend an extended Christmas with their families. The next Christmas they would most likely be in Vietnam. Jardin and Blaisedale remained with Randolph as unassigned personnel who still belonged to the student brigade. Forced out of Olsen Hall, they were sent to a transient BOQ, a converted World War II barracks. Rooms for bachelor officers were the same size as at Olsen Hall, but had beat up furniture and lumpy mattresses. In disgust, Jardin quickly asked for leave, got it and soon departed for his home state of California. Blaisedale, like Randolph, was concerned with using up too much leave and remained. Each morning, they reported to the company orderly room, where Randolph went through elaborate concealment maneuvers to avoid the nervous company commander. He spent a lot of time in the latrine. Usually, by eleven they were released and told to report again the next morning. Randolph drew duty officer for a complete weekend, which caused him to sleep on a couch in front of the bench where he had signed in. Nothing happened, and only one telephone call came in which he recorded in a log.

His only distraction other than the pinball machine in the basement lounge of the Officer Club was the daily collect call to Andrea. She was in New Jersey several times during the beginning weeks of December making arrangements for the vital January trade show. Each night she reiterated details of ornery carpenters and contractors, leisurely scheduling, and often non-showing electricians. There were battles with trade show officials over the best geographic location. From originally being assigned a wall deep in the exhibit hall, she had inched toward a prime spot in front of one of the large entrances. It had been a tough turf battle, which she won while also enhancing her determination and persistence. The tradeshow officials all knew Andrea Tremblay, the tigress in the short skirts. After the trade show in Minneapolis, she was convinced that a new, portable showcase was essential. Finally during a confrontation with her father, who approved the appropriation of twenty thousand dollars for the new case, her uncle-boss was compelled to take the budget hit. Again, Andrea prevailed. The elaborate display case was to make its first appearance at the New Jersey show. Its manufacture and promised delivery to the hall caused some additional trips from Massachusetts to New Jersey and added more rounds of verbiage with the tradeshow officials over her primary piece of real estate. It made Andrea's life full.

In contrast to Andrea's frenzied activity and the end of daily orchestrated training, Randolph found his existence boring and hollow. Blaisedale was affected similarly. Randolph applied for leave to begin one week before Christmas Day. Blaisedale actually left the day before him. Coupled with his travel time from Georgia to Texas, he would have over two weeks before he reported to Fort

Wolters. Andrea, due to the mentor's information, was right. Packed days in advance, armed with directions to Andrea's apartment, he drove by the statue of the Infantry Leader, Iron Mike as he was leaving Fort Benning. He stopped his Camaro and got out to look at the statue. The young officer had his arm raised as he looked back over his shoulder, while shouting the slogan of the Infantry, "Follow Me." It haunted Randolph. The statue was appropriate and captured the spirit of the American Infantry. For several minutes he absorbed every detail. The artist had caught the essence of the young officer's determination. Missing were doubts and although there was anxiety on the bronze face, there was no uncertainty. The path was clear.

When he crossed the Massachusetts border two days later, he had a day's growth of beard, griminess from a missing morning shower, and an arousal that erased sleepiness. At five in the morning, he woke her from a sound sleep. She met him at her apartment door where he dropped his duffle bag by her feet. She was wearing flannel pajamas.

"You said you'd get here Sunday," she protested meekly, through a sleepy smile. Her mouth tasted dryly of sleep.

"Where did you get this thing?" He was helping her take off the top of the pajamas. He tossed them aside onto the floor as she was leading him to her bedroom.

"They're warm, especially when you sleep alone so much."

He thought of commenting, thoughts about Texas that had traveled with him for two days, but decided against it. "It's freezing here. What a big difference from Georgia. Is this a bed or a football field?"

"I got a king size. There's plenty of room in this bedroom."

"I can feel where you were laying. It's still warm. Is there a flap in the back of that thing for quick potty forays?" He tossed the garment over the side of the bed.

"You're fresh, but you don't smell that way." She pushed her tongue deeply into his mouth. "I'll take you anyway you are." She said in a husky voice. When their breathing returned to normal, the sense of finally being together again revived in both of them. The pale winter air became dawn outside the shuttered windows.

"When you come into me, I can't explain what it does to me." She said breathlessly, breaking a long silence between them. "I don't know what would happen to me, if I could never have that again." When he did not answer, she turned her head to look into his face. Her long hair slid over his chest.

"I kept my accelerator floored for fourteen hundred miles. We can't have any more of these long separations. You've had a hell of a lot of things to do this past month while all I've had is thinking about how I screwed up."

"That's all in back of you. Leave it there!" Her low and seductive voice had disappeared completely. "You made some minor judgment errors while you were in training. I've made a heap of mistakes dealing with those tradeshow jackasses. I try not to make the same mistakes twice. Sometimes I do. Regardless, you pick up and keep going."

"I've learned that OCS hates ROTC. That airborne thinks it's better than straight leg infantry. Lording it over everyone are Rangers. Then there's two year guys like Thompson my roommate who have to fit in some place. That's what I learned about Infantry."

"Forget all that crap!" Her eyes lit up with sudden ferocity. "Forget about the Goddamned Army for these two weeks. You're mine and I want you without Army." There was a moment of stilted silent tension, and then she forced her facial expression to relax and her lips turned into a conciliatory smile. "The party is coming up Wednesday Christmas Eve. My announcement is coming. I'm expecting Western Territory Sales Manager."

"What happened to getting all of domestic sales?"

"If I can turn things around in California, increasing sales, that will be the proof I'm capable. Eventually, I will get all of domestic sales. If I get increased sales even my uncles would have to admit to my success. After the announcement, the Mississippi to the West Coast is going to be mine. I've got to get that sales candidate Scott gave me. Jonathon Dawes sounds really qualified. Finally got through to him today. I think I made him interested. I couldn't talk money with him because I don't have the title yet. Told him I would call him the day after Christmas. Scott said expect him to be expensive but worth it. I'm going to get him regardless of what he asks for."

"Who's going to do the trade show stuff? One of your cousins? You're the one getting all the praise for the shows. Did you ask your uncle or father directly about the western sales job?"

"No. Everyone else in the company knows what I want. They would have to be deaf and dumb not to know."

"Your uncle, who has done a shitty job on trade shows, finally gets someone who can handle them well, and he's going to allow that person to leave? You better talk directly to your father."

"I'll get it. I always get what I want." She yawned sleepily and climbed on top of him letting her hair tease and caress his face. "You do need a bath. After this, I'll get in the shower with you. Enough business."

After showering they got back into the huge bed. Finally, Andrea lying on her side slipped into sleep. Her breathing became regular and measured. Sitting behind the wheel of the Camaro for two days made him want to stand and walk. Careful not to disturb her, he climbed out of the bed, and then slipped on his pants and shirt. Barefoot, he set out to explore the apartment. She had hung prints in heavy expensive frames in the bedroom. The prints were black sketches by Picasso which broke up the white monotony of the walls. He recognized none of her bedroom furniture. All of it was new, still without much dust. In her closet he saw her clothing. Obvious business attire was at one end of the large closet, the other end held her leisure clothing. All had dry cleaning tags still attached. Looking closer the tags were different and from a variety of states. He wondered if she sent her underwear out for cleaning.

The apartment had two bedrooms opening onto a huge open area, which served as living room and kitchen. All the walls were white. In the large common room, there were more framed prints, more Picassos and some other masters he could not recognize in tones of light browns. These complimented the leather sofa and two easy chairs. A large wooden console contained a color television and stereo system. In the kitchen end was a new table and chairs. There was ample counter space including a dishwasher. It all looked like a magazine advertisement. Nothing was out of place, and there was no clutter from living there. Opening the door to the second smaller bedroom, he found an office. There was no bed. A huge desk, full sized couch, an arm chair, and a large coffee table filled the small room. Papers and ball bearing reference materials were neatly arranged on the desk. The only thing out of place was a take-out paper container of Chinese food. It was half filled with dried out fried rice. Back in the kitchen, he found coffee but little else. Her refrigerator was nearly empty. He started a pot of coffee.

To have more time together, like the wonderful stuff upon his arrival was his objective. How could he get that? Putting it into military thinking, there was a clear and precise objective. What would it take to get her to live with him in Texas? With the mission defined, good staff planning would devise a usable plan. What did he have in his favor, and what was there to oppose it? The coffee slowly started to perk. He stared at the pot, blankly. There was not much in his favor. Andrea believing what she was doing in Tremblay Bearings was for their future, was a heavily defended emplacement. There didn't seem to be any flanks to probe. A frontal assault would be risky and improbable. She had refused to live with him in Georgia for a month. That made sense. The New Jersey trade show had caused additional trips. Then there was the actual tradeshow the first week in January. If she drove with him to Texas, she would shortly be on a plane back east. The only heavy artillery he had was the marriage proposal. Fort Benning had not been the right place. What other place could he use? This new apartment was so new, she had not spent much time in it with the hectic business travel. Would its newness make it neutral to her? Did that give him an advantage, a breach in the embankment? Was the timing advantageous? No, she was about to get a big promotion at the company. Would his proposal only equal it? Marriage had to mean more than a promotion at work, especially his proposal. It should overwhelm every other thing in her life. In the least, would it be enough to get her to move to Texas? His marriage proposal could not be a dud, an unexploded round. A dud would remain there until an ordnance team came to remove it. It would be there, but you could get around it, harmlessly. Tactically, Andrea could easily out maneuver that kind of dud. There seemed to be no positive aspects he could count on. She might neutralize them all.

Without real positives, he still had to consider the negatives. Todd Richner had told them flight school was going to be tougher. Possibly, if he told her, having her in Texas with him would help him. It might sway her. If she was with him, and it became difficult, it might be like having a counterattack at his most vulnerable point. There would be numerous attacks. She would harp on the difficulties and take advantage of them to suit her objectives, which were, after all, to separate him from the Army. Her being there would make it easier to shoot at him. Flight school might be in jeopardy.

"I smelled the coffee." She had put a bathrobe on and was still yawning slightly, but went directly to him for a kiss. Her mouth tasted of toothpaste.

"I don't recognize anything of yours from you old house."

"My bedroom stuff went to that room my mother saved for me in her new house. I bought from stores that would deliver, set up and take away the packing materials. I haven't had that much time here." She set the table with coffee cups, milk and sugar. "I didn't get the chance to go to the supermarket, so I don't have anything else. There's a donut shop about a mile away."

"Maybe later." He sat in front of his coffee cup.

"Scott's looked at Tremblay Bearings. He thinks if it's handled right in the next ten to fifteen years, it could easily double or triple in size. With the proper financing at the appropriate times, he thinks it's very possible. Leland Jr. has the same ideas. Unlike all my uncles, he's dying to go public. He's already chomping at the bit to leave the assistant production manager's job. Purchasing director seems to be out, but he'll get something. We'll know at the Christmas party."

"I got you something." Pushing his chair back, he got up quickly and went to his duffel bag, which lay where he had dropped it in front of the apartment door. He set the small package on the table next to her coffee cup. "You don't have a tree to put it under."

"Next year I'll do Christmas decorations. No time this year." She eyed the small wrapped box hungrily. With no taxes and very competitive prices, the PX had been an easy place to shop. With all his free time he had completed all his shopping before leaving Fort Benning. Andrea's eyes widened as she picked up the small jewelry box. Her hand started to shake. "Can we open them now?"

"You're supposed wait until Christmas. Won't your mother have a tree?"

"She has a fake tree." Ignoring him, quickly she tore at the wrapping and opened the small box. Her deflated expression was allowed to last for only a fraction of a second. Quickly her face returned to exhilaration. Her eyes gleamed again. They were diamond-studded earnings. "They're beautiful, Randy." She looked into his face, and projected her sincerity. "I have a lot of things they'll go very well with." She wiped a tear from her eye. She stood rather stiffly and went into the bedroom. Coming back, she carried a small wrapped present. "I thought quite a long time what to get you. It's something you can wear, too."

Her gift was also in a small jewelry box. Quickly he opened it. There were a set of regulation-size dog tags, not of the usual aluminum, but gold plated with his name, religion and serial number. On the back of the tags was her name. Under that was a heart and below the heart she had inscribed 'Follow Me.' Holding the tags in his hand and reading them made his throat dry.

"That is the Infantry motto." Her face remained inquisitive as he studied the gold dog tags.

"I am Infantry. When they turned in the swords and started using firearms, that was a change. They were still Infantry. The real Army is the Infantry. Everything else helps them. They are the last to stand on the real estate. There have been soldiers through the ages from the first recorded history. Where did they come from? What made them soldier? It isn't just rules and laws, or loyalty to one man or a tribal group. Something made them. I want to know why."

"Armies are mans' stupidity." Her tone was suddenly bitter. She hesitated seemingly regretting what she had just said. "Didn't we agree to forget the Army for these two weeks?"

"Come and live with me in Texas." He blurted quickly.

Andrea had to set her coffee cup down. "What the hell would I do in Texas?"

"Sell ball bearings. You've got an office set up in this apartment. You could do the same thing in a trailer in Texas. Make it headquarters for the western sales territory."

"In a trailer? I wouldn't live in a drafty trailer. I just set this place up."

"Rent it as is. It's all furnished. Make it a short lease. You'll be back in nine months when I get my wings."

"I spent time selecting this furniture and everything. It means something. I don't want strangers here. I'll be on the road a lot when I get my new title and I will visit you in Texas."

"You want your job?"

"If my father sees I can handle responsibility, and even manage some growth, I may, I mean we may one day have the opportunity to run the company. It isn't going to come to me because I have the name and am the only off-spring. The Tremblays—my father and his brothers-are the company. They are not going to give it to someone who isn't ambitious and smart enough to run it."

They did not go out for dinner, but had pizza delivered. Most of the afternoon was spent in the bedroom. During the night he woke and could not get back to sleep. He knew she was sleeping since he listened to her steady breathing for a long time. Occasionally he heard autos pass on the road in front of the building.

He would never be able to make her understand his feelings about Infantry. She disliked everything about the Army but had bought him special dog tags. How could he make her understand he had to remain a part of it? The crossed rifles were part of him, yet he would not be an infantryman. He had the knowledge and the ability. Something was missing, deep inside him. Possibly it was heart. That is what made a good Infantryman, a good foot soldier. His heart was in another area, in the spinning rotors that had made a different Army that needed a different soldier. Pilots who sat in armor plated seats facing their enemy as they drove their machines toward the firing. He wanted her to come to Texas for selfish reasons. Perhaps it was better that she not come. She was too involved with her father's business. Hopefully, she would honor her pledge to visit him. Was that the best solution? He should keep his final cartridge–the marriage proposal–until he really needed to use it, and there would be some chance of success. His thoughts trailed off but sleep would not come. He was awake for a long time.

Chapter Six

They lay close together in the huge bed. The apartment was snuggly warm. Outside was a pale, chilly December day. It was mid morning.

"I usually get the Sunday paper. It's my motivation to get up and get moving. Now that you're here, I can send you out for it." She pinched his thigh, playfully. "I can stay warm and comfy."

"What's in the papers except gloomy news?"

"Information about the world we have to live in, so you know how to plan to exist in it." Randolph stared at the new white paint of the ceiling and lay perfectly still. "You're the lucky one. You've got nothing to do for two weeks." She added in a conciliatory tone.

"I told them it would take me three days to drive home. They'll be expecting me this afternoon. My mother probably will hold the pot roast until I get there."

"You have one commitment." Sarcasm dripped from her tone.

He did not answer her immediately but thought of her expression when she opened the jewelry box the night before. Maybe she was hinting for a ring, and maybe that could be another round he could have to fire. This marriage proposal thing had multi layers, all of which he had to be prepared to use. "Yes, I do. They're my family, and they matter." Again, he began to think about the improbable possibility of her coming to Texas.

"You have another commitment on Wednesday. Your schedule is starting to fill up. Plan to come to work with me in the morning. Some guys are half plastered by eleven. The caterers will be there by ten and serving by ten thirty. Everyone is out of there by two."

"All I've got is one suit my mother bought me my second year at Northeastern. Last time I had it on, it was tight and uncomfortable."

She slid her hand over his belly, exploring, also seeking to arouse. She pinched some fat. "You're right, I've seen that suit. I don't want you to wear it. Weren't there any social functions you needed a suit for in Georgia?"

"No," he said bluntly. "I've started to pay off some of my college loans. I haven't allotted any money for clothes."

"Plenty for pinball machines and beer." Again she picked at the fat on his stomach.

He pushed her hand away. "I had to have something to do at Benning. I didn't have much company."

"I'll take you shopping tomorrow after work. That will be some more early Christmas presents from me. I want you to feel comfortable."

"No gold bars on the collar?"

"You're a civilian for these two weeks!" Her annoyance rose so abruptly it startled him. He felt her entire body tense. "We agreed, no Army." Then he felt her start to relax slowly, expelling it lying perfectly still.

At one in the afternoon they had finished reading the Sunday paper, which Randolph had not seen in almost three months. The familiarity of the paper brought pleasant nostalgia as he read about places around Boston. Al Garber's Firebird and Faith's cherry red Camaro were parked on the street where he normally put his car. Walking toward the house over the worn frozen path, everything seemed the same. Opening the door, the smell of his mother's cooking struck him first. It was pot roast. His mother was standing before the stove, stirring something. Her blank expression slowly changed into a warm smile. Her gaze settled on Andrea.

"How good to see you once again," Maggie Thayer smiled graciously at Andrea. "Merry Christmas." She laid down her cooking utensil and came toward them. She surveyed her son from head to toe. He knew he was being silently reprimanded for not coming directly home.

"You look healthy and well," his mother said, and then took Andrea's hand in hers and kissed her cheek. "It's very good to have you back in this house." Randolph knew in that moment his mother had accepted Andrea back into his life. Judy, Faith, Teddy, and Al Garber crowded into the kitchen having come from the living room where they had been watching television. Judy hugged him, briefly and kissed his cheek. Faith's sunny face quickly changed to stiffness as she stared at Andrea. The harsh glare was returned. Abruptly, Faith forced a smile. When it was her turn, she hugged Randolph wantonly, placing her lips then pressing them against his cheek. Randolph felt the warmth from her breath, which startled him, unexpectedly. Formally and hastily, Judy introduced Faith to Andrea. The dour looks returned in both women. Al Garber shook his hand. "Your mother insists I come for Sunday dinner. I like real food."

"Everything he eats comes from tin cans." Judy said. If she noticed any hostility between Andrea and Faith she ignored it. She retreated to Al's side.

"Let's hope the supermarket's roast isn't tough this week." Maggie Thayer said. Randolph had taken off his jacket and helped Andrea remove her coat. She wore a sweater and a modest, but colorful seasonal skirt that hide her knees.

"Do you remember me?" Andrea said to Teddy, who was staring at her.

"Yes," Teddy said cautiously, "Randy's girlfriend." His gaze remained fixed on her.

Randolph hugged his brother, awkwardly while holding his jacket and Andrea's coat. "You got bigger. You been eating all the potatoes?"

"Teddy, get your father." Everyone moved on Maggie Thayer's command. The dinner all prepared and ready had been waiting, pending his arrival. Judy and Faith took dishes and pans from the stove and counter to the table. Al Garber got out of their paths, retreating to his chair. Teddy rushed out of the kitchen.

"What's up with Teddy?" Randolph said to his mother. "He seems a little sour."

"His bike's in the cellar again. For three months, this time."

"It's going to be snowing soon. He wouldn't be able to use it." Randolph smiled.

"I know that." His mother matched his smile. "March is soon enough. He almost got hit, again. Still doesn't look." Randolph followed his brother's path to hang their coats in the hall closet. Surprisingly, Andrea remained with him.

"Who is that girl?" Andrea whispered.

"Faith and my sister have known each other since first grade. This is like her second home."

"She kissed you."

"She's like another sister."

"She didn't kiss you like a sister."

He smiled cruelly at her anguish. "She's an extra my family is lucky to have. Does all kinds of things for my mother."

They met Frank Thayer on their way back to the kitchen. Obviously, he had been dozing in his chair. Some of his hair was matted to the side of his head. His appearance had not changed. He acknowledged his son's arrival, noticed Andrea and grumbled an audible, pleasant greeting to her, as he self consciously patted his mused hair. He took his place at the head of the table. Maggie Thayer asked everyone to hold hands for the brief meal prayer, a ceremony used only on special Sundays when either an event or holiday was given special observance. Frank Thayer offered the prayer in his usual, plain tones. His father added the news of Randolph's safe return after his long journey from Georgia. Faith crossed herself before beginning her meal. Surprisingly, Randolph found he was hungry. They had finished the leftover pizza from Saturday night. His stomach was empty. The meal centered on the pot roast beef and boiled vegetables and potatoes. There was one casserole of green beans with slices of nuts mixed in a creamy sauce. Randolph knew it to be one of his mother's stables. He noticed Andrea seemed to dig into her food with familiarity as well as real hunger.

He remembered the Tremblay dinners he had at first endured, then rather enjoyed when Andrea's parents were still married. The beef, usually prime rib, always perfectly cooked, was her father's specialty. Ceremoniously, he enjoyed carving the meat, which many times was tender enough to cut with a butter knife. His mother's pot roast was faintly salty and disintegrated when touched. He wondered if Andrea made any comparisons. Watching her eat, he didn't believe so.

When the meal was finished, his father stood and padded back to the living room. Al sipped coffee. Judy and Faith began clearing the table. Andrea started to rise from her seat next to Randolph to offer cleaning help, but Maggie Thayer signaled her to remain.

"Please come to see my brother, Arthur." Faith had interrupted her clearing and cleaning to stand on the opposite side of the table from Randolph. She still held a dishtowel. Her face displayed her anguish. "Judy and Al said they are coming. My parents are. I want as many of the people he knows, that I can get. He needs help. All the therapy is not working. He's getting worse. Something needs to jar him back into wanting to recover and resume his life. He only lost a leg. There's still a lot more he can do in life."

With his peripheral vision, he saw Andrea's sudden tenseness. "We can't go tomorrow. We're shopping." Andrea said in a low tone.

"When?" Randolph ignored Andrea's warning.

"Day after tomorrow," Faith eyed Andrea directly. "Tuesday, after work at six. The hospital people will let us in to see him, anytime. It's got that bad! He's been reading this book, Waiting for Godot? Some people at work said it's a strange book. Do you know what it's about?"

"Existentialism," Randolph said. He felt Andrea's continued hostile gaze but did not look at her.

"He's got enough problems. He doesn't need that too." Faith laughed nervously and squeezed the dishtowel making her knuckles turn white. "What is it?"

"An obscure literary philosophy."

"Philosophy he can take. That doesn't hurt you. You're in the Army and everything; I thought that might help seeing someone else in the military who he knows. You're not a Marine. Maybe that won't matter."

"I'm not a veteran. I haven't seen what he's seen."

"Any spark that gets him started. He acts so unnatural."

"Of course, we'll come." Randolph reassured her.

"Yes, you come too!" Again Faith shifted her attention directly at Andrea. "Anyone who can offer help, I want to come." Some of the agitation had left Faith's face replaced with a hardened resolve. Judy had finished the clean up and washing dishes and quietly sat next to Al Garber. Her attention was on Faith. The gentle wrapping at the kitchen door went unnoticed at first. It was Betsy Croteau. Maggie Thayer, who had been listening intently to Faith's plea, was closest to the door and opened it for her. Betsy walked quickly into the center of the kitchen. Her pale skin abruptly turned pink from the sudden house warmth and her long winter coat, which she made no attempt to take off. Her face slowly changed into a broad, but stiff smile. She brought her hand up to display her huge, gaudy engagement ring. Both Judy and Faith rushed to her side for a closer view of the ring.

"I wasn't supposed to get it until Christmas," Betsy said. Her voice was strangely distorted. The stone was over a karat. Another half karat in chips made up its ornate setting. "That's when our engagement becomes official. See, the dates engraved on the inside." She pulled the ring off her finger and showed Judy and Faith. Their eyes were still wide as they examined the delicate craftsmanship of the ring. When she put the ring back on her finger, again she held her hand at arm's length.

"Are you sure?" Judy asked, staring at her bleak face.

Betsy said nothing, and then looked around the kitchen as if seeing everyone for the first time. Her lips quivered, then shook, and tears rolled down her cheeks. Faith and Judy hugged her at the same instant and possibly kept her from falling. The three stood together as Betsy's sudden outburst overtook her. Her shoulders began to heave as sobs contorted her whole body. Judy and Faith guided her out of the kitchen. They heard their footsteps going upstairs.

There was stunned silence in their wake. Maggie Thayer's face was blank and she remained standing. Al Garber's face was pensive. Idly, he dipped his spoon in his coffee. Andrea moved in her seat, creating the only noise.

"Judy's been telling me about Betsy," Al Garber said morosely. "I could go home and study. We were only going to a movie. All the Christmas shopping is done."

"Thank goodness, you manage the important things, Al! Christmas shopping? Studying?" Maggie Thayer laughed at his sober expression. "That poor girl is about to fall apart. Betsy needs them. I'll go up and see what's what. I wouldn't count on seeing Judy much more tonight." They heard her footsteps on the stairs.

Al's face remained pensive. His spoon slipped out of his cup, spilling coffee on the table. Awkwardly, he grabbed a paper napkin. "I hope Judy doesn't react the same way." Al said when he had finished mopping up the spill. "Did you see her face when she was looking at that ring?"

"The guy wants to be a doctor," Randolph said. "That collegiate sun-god thinks that's the way he can dodge the draft. That ring is an investment for his future."

"I'd have to sell my car or get a loan for a ring that size." Al's face remained gloomy

"Judy's too practical. If it came with a big bill, she wouldn't want it."

"The sentiment is more important than the size," Andrea said. "It's what it means that really counts." Randolph looked at her, but said nothing.

"I haven't talked about an engagement. Everything she does or says seems favorable. She wants me to finish school, first. That's going to take years. I don't want to wait that long. I want a life with her now."

"That's what we all want. Sometimes there are obstacles in the way you can't ignore," Andrea said.

"When Judy knows what she wants, I've never known her to hesitate going after it." Randolph said.

"I can't remember one real disagreement. We sort of think along the same lines. That's been one of my biggest adjustments.

I've done whatever I wanted so long, it's hard to have to consider another person."

"It's easier when you both think alike," Andrea said. "Your foundations become solid. Some couples have multiple foundations. They have problems." Quickly, she threw a glare at Randolph. "That makes it difficult, but nothing that can't be overcome."

"She certainly saw that in Betsy. That question she asked was all it took. Judy knew. Her perception blows my mind."

"Did you get her a ring?"

"It's my main present to her for this Christmas. My parents are retired and living in Florida. I can't get the time off from work or school to go down there—so they're coming up here to meet her. She doesn't know about that yet."

Monday morning he felt Andrea climb out of bed. Lazily, half awake he listened to her preparations for work. Her shower was mechanically short. Toweling her wet skin was another function she skimped on to save time. He caught glimpses of her towel wrapped body, followed by flashes of skin as she changed into a fluffy bathrobe. Her hair was encased in another towel as she padded toward the kitchen for a cup of coffee, which had been started by an electronic timer set the night before. Returning, as she sipped her coffee, she dried her hair using a blower and two mirrors allowing herself a view of all angles of her head. As she worked, he realized she was allowing the dampness of her skin to dry in the towel bathrobe, saving her toweling time. Her morning ritual had evolved to maximum efficiency. She applied makeup while still naked under the robe and only when her face and hair were complete did she dress. Again there were views of her lean, unclothed body as she removed the robe to put on her underwear. After watching all her preparations, he had an erection so strong it reminded him of when he woke alone thinking about her when they had been apart for weeks.

Finally, she sat on the side of the bed next to him letting her loose hair tickle his face, neck and shoulders. She kissed him wetting his tongue with hers, and then sliding her lips over the edge of his cheek until she reached his ear lob, which she playfully chewed before thrusting her tongue into his ear. Her lipstick and perfume flooded his senses. When he attempted to wrap his arm around her legs, firmly she broke his grasp, standing up and backing away from the bed. At the bedroom door she paused, looking back at him. "I should be back by three, so we can go shopping. I'd come back and kiss you, but I really have things to get done. Be ready to shop." Then, she disappeared into the living room. The apartment door closed and he listened for the sound of her Mustang's engine. The heat clicking on grounded out any possibility of hearing her departure from the parking lot. He lay comfortably in the bed for a long time while his arousal slowly eased and disappeared. When thinking finally kicked in, he knew where he had to go. Things needed to be sorted out. Without reluctance he left the comfortable bed. Outside, the cold air made him feel he was New England home.

At the lake in the parking lot of the recreational area trees stood naked without their leafy cover. There was ice on the lake, which was too thin to walk on. Huge floats used in the summertime lay beached and abandoned on the sandy shore. Easily he found the well-trod path he had often used. Passing the sleeping, bare trees there were occasional evergreens giving the appearance of a wooded area and some sanctity and solitude. The path lead to a huge rock at the water's edge. Although on town property, it was his rock. Here he had contemplated many momentous events that had shaped his life. There were many thoughts about his opposite sex, and the campaigns he had waged in pursuit of them. The first time he had encountered flesh making him a man had been Faith. That inevitable rendezvous had caused many apprehensive hours, innumerable cigarettes, mosquito bites and cramps from remaining in one position too long. Strangely, he remembered committing himself to the possibility of a child. That one time with Faith, unplanned and unforeseen, might have altered his future. That was the reason it had caused so much fear and unease. There had been several campaigns after Faith, and before Andrea. One became a sexual conquest. Faith was the only girl he had thought about the possibility of creating a child. She had been the first, and they were so young, although not really so young. A rationalization he was sure, since his other conquest was planned, calculated and aggressively sought for the known physical pleasure it brought. Otherwise, he had been a normal, sexually aggressive adolescent and then young man. Possibly the real soldier did not consider children since his child was his military organization. All creative energies were devoted to it. Did that rule out the possibility of any family for the true soldier?

Why had these thoughts about children never surfaced with Andrea? They made love for the physical and mental pleasure it gave both of them. Not to make babies. While at Northeastern, there had been the mysteries of learning about each other. That seemed to be a relatively short period, and then their relationship turned physical. Their logical energies converged on how and when they could be together. There had been cars. His old VW bug, as small as it was, often had frost on the inside of the windows. Occasionally they would get a motel room, if she had an overnight excuse. Now, although she rambled about their life together, there was never any mention of children. Should he ask her about that? Somehow he felt he shouldn't since it might taint their sexual relationship, which he wanted to maintain. Babies and thought of them could wait. After their breakup, he had dissected every moment he could remember them sharing. Returning to that possibility was bleak. He wanted to enjoy her as much and often as he could. There was nothing else. Was that the feeling and thoughts of the true soldier?

How many decisions had he made on this rock? One had brought him to Northeastern and not to another college, which ultimately had brought him to Andrea. In many thoughts and deep contemplations, there was his strange fascination with soldiering. What had brought him to the Army? Was it the physically demanding requirements? For all of his life he had been a sedate student, sitting in a classroom absorbing thoughts. He disliked sports and didn't play them in high school. The Army made him do things with his body, which often put painful stress on his non athletic limbs. That was acceptable and expected as part of soldiering. His father had never been in the military. His maternal grandfather was an organizational National Guardsman who became a reluctant WWII veteran. Perhaps it skipped a generation. There had to be more of a reason.

It was buried in the deep recesses of the brain of a man, but not in all men. In some there was no hint of it, like Betsy's doctor-bound boyfriend. Some even wore uniforms. That is the truth he sought. Infantry was the Army. He had sorted it out in his head, and this sacred place finalized it. He wore their insignia and would support them, but would never be one of them. That was one thing Fort Benning had given him. Possibly it was the only thing. He was to be a different kind of a soldier. To him, Lieutenant Randolph Thayer, that was acceptable. He would fly a machine while some real Infantryman shot at him. What made soldiers, soldiers? He was a student and destined to be a student for another nine months. He would have to wait to see the real Army. It would be in Vietnam when he was trained and ready. There was still a long path to follow.

He stared at the gray frozen water and shivered in his thin field jacket. Andrea would never understand what he felt about soldiering and the answers he sought. She did not want to understand. That life was alien to her. She deplored it. That was the basis of their breakup. Nothing was new about that. How could he reconcile himself to what she felt? Could he coexist with that dislike and hate for something he believed he loved? There must be coexistence or they would fail again. Why had be made so many stupid mistakes at Benning? Strangely, Andrea seemed to be indirectly involved, and possibly that was an omen of their relationship. Either he was thinking about her, or she was there. Was it her fault? He must take responsibility. Like any male when the blood thickened with lust, thinking decreased. Bodily functions and desires were the drivers not rational thought. Yet, that was why he was there on this cold rock with winter tearing at his thin clothing. He did not want to give up the opportunity of her body once again. Selfishly, the sexual demand that was their relationship surfaced. What was he willing to sacrifice to maintain it? At this period in his life, his sacred rock gave him no answers. Woman made you do stupid and dumb things to achieve that sexual objective. What a brilliant thought.

Had he come out on a wintry, chilly day to discover men did stupid things when under the influence of lust?

Was Andrea only the satisfaction of lust in his life? He did not want to think so. There had to be more. To have more, they must be together to see if they really liked being together, doing all the things a man and woman did when together. Living together in Texas was not gone. He needed her there to discover what their true relationship really contained.

The wind stirred, cutting through his lean Army covering as it blew across the gray frozen water. He had had enough of deep thinking, and he was getting numbing cold. Back in his car, the eight cylinders quickly invigorated his heater, and pleasantly warmed the inside, thawing him out. Some things about the Army felt settled. Others issues remained clouded.

Mr. Beckwerth still had the lean frame of a Marine. With each of twenty-five passing years he had added a pound which had blended well. His hair had grayed at the temples, which polished his middle age. The walls of the den in the Beckwerth cellar, where Randolph had deflowered Faith, were filled with souvenirs of his combat in the South Pacific. Most of the artifacts be had picked up personally from dead enemy. They included Japanese uniform insignia, a personal flag and other small pieces of equipment he had been able to stuff into a duffle bag. There were also a few officially sanctioned war souvenir bolt action rifles which had been the equipment of the Japanese forces. Over the years a few items had been purchased. They were careful purchases of specific insignia or equipment that had been used on the battlefields where Mr. Beckwerth had fought. Every piece had a specific history. Randolph had spent a great deal of time in the Beckwerth house as he grew, and he knew Mr. Beckwerth's narratives of each piece. All the souvenirs were lovingly cared for with a reverence reserved for sacred objects.

The inspiration and experience of being a combat knowledgeable Marine had governed Mr. Beckwerth's life. Seeking solace with the millions in similar circumstances, he found it in the innumerable veterans clubs that sprang up following World War II. There was alcohol and stories, which changed perceptively with each telling through the years. His first born, a son, Arthur, named for him was raised in the towering shadow of his beliefs in freedom and the Marine Corps. His second child was Faith. She drew heavily from his features. Two more daughters followed, Sarah and Meredith, years apart, who drew their appearances from the long, slim lines of their mother. A final son, Matthew came fifteen years after the first, attesting to the erratic romantic path of the former Marine.

Mr. Beckwerth mourned the tragic wounding of his older son. The cost of a leg, the young man had paid, was a grave price. He had seen it before in some of his comrades who had been as grievously wounded. Some had survived and recommenced their lives accepting their expenditure for liberty paid their country. A few had not survived Mr. Beckwerth acknowledged. He did not think they were bad Marines. They had done their combat. They lacked something. It made them imperfect in the world that glorified perfection. Mr. Beckwerth knew imperfection existed, but he would not accept the fact it had struck his oldest son.

Andrea was mellow and had been since getting out of work and arriving at the apartment. Quickly, she had changed from her work clothes into slacks and a sweater. Her mood was a great contrast from the previous evening, which they spent among the desperate last minute shoppers in a crowded mall. It had been a creative and enjoyable task for Andrea to purchase Randolph's Christmas party attire.

"I'm hungry and pissed!" Andrea said finally breaking a moody silence as he parked on the street in front of his parents' house. Al's Firebird was also parked there. "I'm doing this as a favor to you."

"Hunger I can understand. We'll go out and eat after. The visit shouldn't take that much time. Why are you pissed?"

"I found out what Leland Jr. is getting. Senior Metals Buyer. That's number three in the materials group. I couldn't get a hint at what I'm getting. No body would tell me anything."

In the Thayer kitchen Al Garber was the only one seated at the huge table. He was drinking coffee while Judy and Maggie

Thayer washed dishes from the supper meal. Within minutes of them sitting, coffee cups, milk, sugar, and a small frosted cake appeared. Randolph sipped the coffee. Andrea took a piece of cake and gobbled it down quickly. The Beckwerths arrived twenty minutes later. Faith was the first to enter. Her sister Sarah was a sophomore in high school. Tall from her mother, she was the same height as her sister, Faith. Her face was drawn attesting to the long, dragged out period of supporting her older brother. Within the strain reflected in her eyes there was a visible determination. Both the older Beckwerth girls had it. When Sarah first saw Randolph she came toward him hugged him tightly and pecked his cheek lightly, then politely stepped away from him. The two younger Beckwerth children, Meredith and Matthew were to be left with Maggie Thayer. They darted past the adults to find Teddy. They were thoroughly at home in the Thayer house.

As they were getting their coats from the closet near the living room, Andrea hissed at him, "I suppose that's another sister, too. That was a pretty tight hug."

"Surprisingly, you can see the faint family resemblance that they are sisters, but they do look so different."

"Have you got sisters all over the place?"

"Only in the Beckwerth family." Randolph smiled at her annoyance

The hospital at Chelsea Naval Base was on a hillside overlooking the Mystic River. The Marine guards at the gate knew Mr. Beckwerth and chatted with him. Randolph with Andrea in his Camaro and Al with Judy in his Firebird waited behind their station wagon. Only when another car came up behind them, did Mr. Beckwerth enter the base. Several of the Marines stationed at the base knew Arthur. A few without prompting had visited him. Hurrying into the old granite walled hospital to get out of the cold; Mr. Beckwerth had no great urgency to get to his son's room. Most of the Navy doctors, nurses, and corpsmen knew the Beckwerths. Their bending of visitations rules was only one of the many things they did attempting to start Arthur back on the road to recovery. Mr. Beckwerth loitered visiting briefly with several patients, cheerfully reliving the camaraderie of his Marine Corps past. His wife, Sarah, and Faith were adjusted to the routine. They passed greetings to many of the patients. Al Garber and Judy endured the delay as if it were part of the visitation ceremony. Randolph watched Andrea's face as it passed from impatience to annoyance. Sights of the wounded and sick, young military men filled her with an irritable gloominess, which stayed on her face. After the lengthy detours they arrived at Arthur's room. Mr. Beckwerth paused outside his son's room. He wiped the weary severity from his face and smiled bravely for everyone, then proceeded into the room.

Sitting on his bed in hospital uniform, Arthur was reading and seemed annoyed with the intrusion. He glared at his parents. "I am free," he said finally and then looked out the window. The bright expression on Mr. Beckwerth's face fell, but only momentarily. His smile returned, and he went to the side of his son's bed.

"They told me you did well at therapy this week." Mr. Beckwerth said.

"They can't make me wear that thing," Arthur said stubbornly. He would not look at his father.

"You've got to put it on to get used to it. What is this you're reading, 'Waiting for Gau-dot.' What's it about?"

"I have no one to be responsible to. I can do as I please."

"Once you get out of this hospital, of course you can. You've got to work at that therapy, and then you will be out of here." Mr. Beckwerth persisted.

Arthur remained sullen. He ignored his mother and sisters, and shot suspicious glances at Randolph, Andrea, Judy, and Al Garber. He knew Al Garber. His gaze briefly settled on Andrea. It looked for an instant as if he was about to ask who she was, then his attention wandered. Andrea's irritability intensified as she stood in the small, crowded room with the visitors. When he tried to take her hand, she swatted his away. Sitting rigidly on his bed, occasionally turning his head to scan those in the small room, finally Arthur looked out the window away from his visitors.

"What kind of Marine are you?" Finally, Mr. Beckwerth became flustered.

"Not a whole one. Therefore, they have no rights over me. You must have a complete body. Don't you know that? It's in the regs. Since I am not complete, I am not a Marine. I am me. I have the right to do as I please."

133

"What are you talking about, Arthur?" His father snapped at him.

"I choose. That is my right. No one has the right, not to let me do as I prefer."

Mr. Beckwerth left the room. There was twitching in his face, and all could see plainly the tears in his eyes. Arthur turned to his mother.

"Why did you bring me into this world?" His voice cut through the heavy silence that had descended after Mr. Beckwerth's departure.

"You are our gift from God, our first born." She started to cry. "We love you, Arthur." She followed her husband, audibly sobbing.

"Arthur, you have to stop this!" Faith said angrily. "We want to help you."

"Give me back my leg."

"You have to be reasonable. This thing has happened. You have to live with it."

"I am free. You are not."

Faith left the room. Her face was dark and hard. She did not cry. Arthur glared at his sister Sarah, whose eyes were twitching as tears formed in them. Stubbornly, she would not move.

"The war is wrong, Arthur. You are right!" Sarah said. Her eyes overflowed with tears, and they rolled over her cheeks. Her lip quivered as she tried to hold her ground. Arthur's harsh glare bore into her. Suddenly, she ran from the room. Judy's eyes started to tear. Al Garber pulled her following Sarah.

Arthur's hostile gaze settled on Randolph. "What do you want, Lieutenant?" He was surprised to be addressed so clearly and factually. Moving closer to the bed, he stared at Arthur's eyes. There was no anger in them. Something seemed to be missing.

"You're an asshole."

"I know what I am." Arthur said without any anger. He smiled oddly. "They didn't get my asshole, just my leg. You're going to find out, Lieutenant, I did."

"Did they take your mind, Arthur?"

"I wish they had. Then it would be easier."

"Get it back. Be the Marine your father is so proud of."

"I want to rest. Run from it. You don't want any part of it. It never sits on you right. "

"Your only weapon is your mind. Don't point it at yourself."

Slowly, Arthur turned his head away from Randolph. "You will find out, lieutenant," he said blankly.

Suddenly, he realized Andrea was no longer standing behind him. In a sudden panic, he rushed out of the room. Only Faith was waiting in the hallway. Her eyes were dry, but her face was dark with gloom. "Where is Andrea?" Randolph demanded.

"She said she'd meet you at the car. Each time it gets worse. He won't help himself. Do you really care, or are you just more concerned about her?"

"You and Arthur I've known all my life." Randolph looked at her hard glare. "We all are one."

Suddenly, the hardness left her face. Tears welled in her eyes and over flowed to her cheeks as her sister Sarah had done. She looked so vulnerable Randolph instinctively wrapped his arms around her shoulders. Faith melted into his embrace.

"I heard you. You got the closest, Randy. I thought for a moment he might bite. He didn't though."

"He needs good doctors. They know all this stuff. We tried. I'm sorry."

She did not move from his embrace, but nestled closer to him. "He's Catholic. He won't do anything to himself." Her tone was defiant.

Randolph did not answer her, but continued to comfort her.

"I can feel him sinking," she whispered. "It's such a helpless feeling."

"You see it. I don't think your parents do. Get him the help. From professionals. Don't wait. Do it." Randolph's tone was low matching hers. She moved her head to look up into his eyes. Pain was etched into her face. For a reason that wracked his thoughts for weeks, suddenly he lowered his head meeting her lips. Her mouth opened, and he tasted the sweetness within her mouth. He held the kiss for a long time. Her taste traveled throughout his senses. As quickly as he had started, he broke both the kiss and the embrace pushing her away from him. Blankly, they stared at each other. The pain was gone from Faith's face replaced with a serene look. Without another word, Randolph started down the corridor leaving her.

Andrea got out of bed at six thirty. After her showering and hair preparation ritual, she dressed in a sleek but conservative blue dress, which showed only half her kneecaps. Meticulously, she prepped herself to include Randolph's earrings. Allowing him to sleep until half past seven, she laid out his new Monday-night acquired clothes on her side of the huge bed. Watching her, comfortably stretched out under the covers, she searched for and removed tags from the shirt, tie, and leisure suit, which had come off the rack. Fortunately, it had not required tailoring.

"Isn't there a tag on the bottom of the new shoes? They are going to hurt like hell after two hours." Andrea actually picked up and turned over the shoe before she realized his sarcasm. She threw the shoe at him, purposely trying to miss him. It hit the pillow he was laying on. "Why so early? I've met your uncles before. They know who I am."

"There's a lot of people, who work at Tremblay Bearings, who know about you. They want to meet you."

"Andrea's show and tell."

"You got it. Now, get moving, Mr. Thayer."

The Tremblay Bearings plant moved from Everett, where it had been founded and outgrown its crowded birthplace, to a Route 128 North Shore town in the early 1950s. When Route 128 was widened from a two-lane road into a divided, multi lane highway, it prompted many similar businesses to move from the inner cities to the suburbs. The sprawling, roomy plant was now crowded from the natural growth the company had undergone in the last two decades. Andrea told him the plant would have to expand physically to accommodate the new alloy capital equipment.

They arrived at eight thirty. The majority of the employees were dressed for a holiday. With some obvious pride and certainly with a lot of knowledge, Andrea conducted a personalized tour of the entire plant. He saw the production facilities, the raw materials storage areas, the inspection and finishing departments with their specialized tools, the finished product storerooms, and the executive and business sections. At the shipping and receiving dock, Randolph met the grizzled foreman, Harrison, who had compelled Andrea to sweep floors. Already, he smelled faintly of whiskey. Frederic had been by and presented him with his Christmas bonus envelope.

There were a lot of devouring stares for Randolph. His cheeks became partially numb from the constant smiling and sheer number of people he was introduced to. His feet started to ache in the stiff, new shoes. At eleven, they arrived in the company's spacious cafeteria where the caterers were dispensing the Christmas feast. Randolph was glad to sit in one of the metal chairs.

"That's where he makes all his pronouncements?" Randolph pointed to one end of the room where a single podium had been placed.

"If he makes the announcement of the expansion of the plant, that's the signal we are going into the new markets. That will be heard in New Jersey."

"Will he announce the company is going public?"

"No, that's a board of directors' type of announcement." Andrea seemed suddenly annoyed by Randolph's naiveté. "Certain things need confidentiality because of a lot of unpredictable factors. You've got to know and understand business," she lectured quietly.

"There is an SOP for that sort of thing?"

"Business is not the military. Scott has told me about the timing of the announcement to go public and sell stock. That timing can affect the price of the stock. Incidentally, I won't do any more visits to that Arthur kid."

"He's a wounded Marine, not a kid. I know it affected you. Why didn't we talk about it last night?"

"When my father had his heart attack, most of the patients were older. You expect to see that in a hospital. Most of those we saw were young men, maimed by war. I don't need reminders what the cost of war is."

"Military people fall off of ladders and have car accidents, too. Some of them were there for those things. I'm not an Arthur. You met Mr. Beckwerth. He saw combat in the South Pacific. Arthur is obviously a lot different than his father. If Mr. Beckwerth had lost a leg–as long as it was with the Marines–it only would have made him walk a little slower than he does now."

"Didn't we say no Army?" Andrea's tone turned icily contemptuous.

"We're not talking about the Army. Arthur is a Marine."

"It's all the same. I don't want anything else to do with him."

Frederic spotted them from across the huge cafeteria. Briskly, he strode toward them. There was a party smile on his face. In the lapel of his suit coat he wore a sprig of mistletoe. He pumped Randolph's hand. Frederic was a little thinner than Randolph remembered him. He thrust an envelope into his daughter's hand. "I'm looking forward more than ever to my Christmas address."

"I'm expecting a lot." Andrea answered her father, bluntly.

"You will have plenty to do. You won't be bored."

Frederic hurried away to avoid further conversation. He had mastered the art of short, non-entangling dialogue. More were gravitating to the cafeteria. The food was flowing smoothly as were occasional paper bags of liquor. Waiting lines had formed. Andrea still held the envelope her father had given her. The flap had come open. Randolph could see that the top bill was a hundred. Andrea had left her pocketbook at her desk.

"Here," she handed him the envelope. "Put this in your inside pocket." Randolph took the envelope.

"Don't you want to know how much it is?"

"It's only money."

As noon approached, the cafeteria had filled. Conversation died when Frederic stood behind the podium. His brothers, the vice presidents, stood silently behind him. The message was cheery indicating they had a good, profitable year. Nothing was said about the well known and unaccountable individual envelopes. The list of receivers was highly select. Everyone else would expect a separate bonus check through payroll with taxes deducted. He expressed the wish that the coming year would bring good health to everyone. Then he announced promotions, which came with comical suggestions of how the gaining department would cope. His remarks prompted canned, polite laughter. He named an obvious long term employee to become assistant production foreman. There was more than the expected response from the audience, which caused Frederic to pause and smile broadly. This position was Leland Junior's old job. Leland Junior's promotion was next. He would assume his new duties as senior metals buyer. Then he stopped his speech and looked with anticipated expectation at his employees. This created some forced tension, which Frederic knew how to play.

"Finally, it is my great personal pleasure to announce a promotion for my daughter. You all know she's been with us for some time and been away from her desk a lot over the past few months. She's been churning up new interest for Tremblay Bearings by running one of our most successful trade shows, ever. With deep personal pride, I'm proud to announce that Andrea assumes the title of Director of Industrial Relations. She will be responsible for running and directing all of our industrial shows and upgrading company literature. Please give her a well earned round of applause."

Andrea had to smile, as she stood to accept the acclamation. Randolph had never seen her face so twisted with anguish mixed with forced levity. Her shock and anger momentarily had to be suppressed. After the polite applause ended, Frederic announced it was time to eat, and then left the podium. Nothing had been said about the impending expansion for the new alloy product lines. Randolph noticed Andrea was mumbling inaudibly through her artificial smile. Her head turned to glare directly at her father. "Nothing about the new alloy products." She hissed at Randolph. Before he could comment, she left his side. Going directly to her father, she propelled him into a small, unoccupied office. Loudly, the door closed behind them. Meekly, Randolph followed her taking a position almost as a guard near the closed door. Randolph and others near him could hear raised voices. There was no discerning who was yelling at whom. The different pitches in tone indicated both were presenting a boisterous argument. After a few minutes of relative silence from the sealed office, Andrea emerged first, her face clouded and scowling. Frederic's face as he stepped through the threshold changed from grave to his office-party flamboyant smile. Ten minutes after the closed-door meeting, his Camaro sped them to her apartment.

Other than snarling commands to prompt them to leave the Christmas party, Andrea had said nothing during the short drive to the apartment. Her face was still a dark scowl. In the bedroom, she marched in small tight circles as she shed the Christmas outfit and jewelry. Her gait became more confused as she stumbled, while trying to remove pieces of her clothing.

"You never told either one of them directly." Finally, Randolph found the opportunity to break into her intemperate mood. He caught her when she fell as she was struggling with the blue party dress. As he pulled her toward the huge bed she was finally free of the dress, which she threw across the bedroom. It hit the wall and sunk to the floor in a disheveled heap.

"No one wants to do the stinking trade shows. Oh, Andrea will do them. She does such a great job with them. My father and goddamned uncle were hoping I'd accept it. And, keep quiet. Well, I wasn't quiet!"

"Colonel, they underestimated you." Randolph smiled at her anger. "What about the candidate out in California? Are you going to lose him?"

"My father gave me the OK to hire him. He'll work for me. I have to do the New Jersey show, and then I can have Western Sales Manager. It's mine, and I'm going to have all the authority I want out west. He'll make the announcement after the trade show."

"You did get what you wanted?"

"I told you, I always do."

Her anger began to dissipate. She started untying his tie, which accelerated into a lascivious de-clothing spectacle. Sufficiently naked she initiated a savage and very colorful, wanton physical session, matching her inflamed mood. It was not yet two in the afternoon. She was somewhat calmer an hour later when a call came from Frederic who was at his brother Leland's house. He wanted to know if she would come to a Christmas Eve dinner. In a calm and overly polite tone, she refused the invitation indicating she had a commitment with Randolph.

"Shouldn't we have gone? My mother would understand. That is your father." Randolph commented when she had hung up the phone.

"The last thing I want today is to be around those two. I'm going to be overloaded, and they know it. They'll just gloat at me hoping I'll fail. Well, I won't fail. I didn't lose anything. I'm still the Director of Industrial Shows and Company Literature. I have to handle that too."

"Call your stepfather and get a name for trade shows. If the California sales guy can work for you, why can't a trade show person be sales, too? Aren't all the trade shows in the United States? That's not much of an interloping area. It will also be a first step to all domestic sales, some day."

Andrea stared at him, her eyes crafty and alert like a cat of prey. "For a non business sophisticate, you do come up with some meaty ideas." She pushed her arms around his shoulders and hugged him tightly.

"See, lieutenants are useful."

"No Army, remember." She hissed.

At four, they got out of bed to shower and dress. Maggie Thayer had prepared a ham for their Christmas Eve meal. Al Garber was there when they arrived. The meal was quiet and orchestrated by the informal pace of the Thayer household. Andrea seemed to slip into a more tranquil mood either from their extended physical workouts during the afternoon or Randolph's stimulating advice. Clearly, he observed it had hatched thoughts which brewed in her mind. With silent amusement she watched Teddy's growing excitement over the prospect of presents to open in the morning. It was the first time he had seen her pay any extended attention to a child. Al Garber was somewhat fidgety, unusual for him. After the meal Andrea insisted on helping clear the table and clean up, although she produced many awkward motions among Judy and his mother's industrious activity. When the kitchen had been sufficiently cleaned, they went to the living room where a well known singer-entertainer had a special Christmas Eve color spectacular, which they were forced to view on the black and white console set. As they watched the clouded shades of black Randolph felt Andrea truly relax in both mind and body for the first time that day. Finally, all the tension of excitement and confrontation had seeped from her body. She seemed to be at rest.

Al Garber waited until the program had finished before he asked Judy to go out into the kitchen with him. She had been sitting curled on the floor beside him with her head on his legs. With a startled expression, she got up and followed him looking with a curious expression at his smiling face. Maggie Thayer nearly came out of her couch seat as she strained to hear any conversation. The television's commercials drowned out any sounds from the kitchen. A moment later, Judy walked back into the living room. Her arm was extended in front of her just as Betsy had done as she looked at the ring on her finger. Al Garber materialized behind her, his face cut with a broad smile. Judy went directly to her mother. They embraced. Joyous tears began to form in Judy's eyes.

"You knew." Judy managed to say.

"Al's a good man. You are going to be a lucky woman." It was the first time Randolph had heard his mother elevate his sister to an equal status. Andrea also received an embrace, then Randolph. Frank Thayer got out of his easy chair and shook Al Garber's hand. They went into the kitchen for coffee and dessert. When Randolph excused himself to go up to his room for a pack of cigarettes, he was surprised to find Judy in the narrow hallway in front of his bedroom door.

"I've never felt this way about anyone. What will happen in a few years if he hates me? I couldn't live." Her lips quivered as she probed her brother's face.

"Why would he hate you? The only thing he wasn't sure of was should he give you that ring or buy a bigger one like Betsy's."

"He can't afford it. He's paying for school. I want him to finish."

"He will. He'll listen to you."

Apprehension spread across her face. "I see it with the women I work with. They all said, oh, the men make all these promises, and you'll see what happens to them. All the promises their men made, they broke. That's why they end up working in a place like that factory."

"You have a bright future together. He's done his military. He has a good job. He's a supervisor. People look up to and respect him."

"He needs to get his degree. What if I'm the reason that gets screwed up? That's what is making me scared. I love this ring-his ring-and I wouldn't want a bigger one. We'll get married. We'll have kids. The degree will get pushed aside. Then, he'll have to stay in that factory. Eventually, he'll blame me. He'll be right. It would be my fault."

"If you didn't take his ring, you will still work in that factory. So won't he. You'll have to look at each other every day and wonder what happened. Al comes from our same kind of people. You get by. You do the best you can. You try to enjoy it as you go along. That's what life is for us. This is Judy's time. You enjoy it, every minute of it."

"I know Betsy isn't sure."

"If she's smart enough to know that, then she's wrong. You're lucky you're not faced with her situation."

They went downstairs together. Their mother was waiting at the bottom of the stairs. Her face was pale. His father was not laying in his recliner. Randolph saw him in the bathroom standing before the wash basin, washing his face.

"Faith called. Arthur killed himself. We have to go to the Beckwerth's. Faith asked for you, Randy, specifically. You have to go to her. Judy, you stay with Teddy."

"Ma, I need to be there, too." Judy protested and then started to cry.

"Mrs. Thayer," Andrea had come out of the kitchen. "I'll stay with Teddy, if you'll allow me." Plainly, she had heard Maggie Thayer's command to her son. His mother put her arm around Andrea's shoulder, hugged her lightly and whispered a thank you, then went to get her coat. Judy bolted toward the closet for her coat. Andrea's stark gaze remained fixed on Randolph. He had not moved from his spot at the bottom of the stairwell. "I can't do a wake and a funeral for that boy." Andrea turned away from him and went into the living room. Standing in the middle of the darkened room, shadows from the glow of the television danced throughout room. The sound from the set had been turned off. The news was on. The shades of gray showed an urban area in Vietnam and the aftermath of the war's violence. It was so common it did not capture Randolph's attention. "I can understand that girl wanting your sister since they are so close. Why did she want you?" Her voice was still very low.

"We've all been close. I don't know why she asked for me."

Her eyes remained dry and clear. "Don't stay all night. I want to go home." She walked slowly to the couch and sat, folding her hands in her lap. Suspicion showed clearly in her face. Plainly, she had very little feeling for Corporal Arthur Beckwerth, Jr. whom she had met only once.

Faith had hugged Randolph when he went through the formal receiving line in front of Arthur's closed, flag-draped casket. Only three years out of high school, Arthur had been a star athlete. Many of his friends and former teammates, including a few who had gone on to college, were home for the Christmas holidays. A few in the military had managed leave. Everyone from the neighborhood came to the small funeral home. The director had to hire a policeman to manage the traffic. The mourners spilled into the unused sections of the funeral parlor. Since the majority of the mourners were young people, who had not seen each other for months and in some cases years, it soon became a social event. The chatter in the unused sections of the funeral home rose.

Randolph was standing alone. Judy was showing off her new ring and Al Garber to several friends. His parents had stayed briefly, signed the register, then left. Faith waited until there was an appropriate slowdown in the receiving line, and then went directly to him. This time she hugged him more directly, harder, and intimately. Randolph finally had to break her embrace.

"You have been so much for my family. I will always be thankful to you." Faith stayed physically close to him. Her sweet perfume filled his nostrils. "Andrea couldn't come?"

"She's afraid I'll be the next one in the box." Randolph said bluntly. "She said she couldn't handle it."

"Did you see Connie?"

"I missed her."

"I knew she would come. Her anti war-crap is just school thinking. She's really one of us. Her parents gave her an ultimatum. Stop the anti war activities and concentrate on school, or they'll cut off her financial help. I'll bet that turns her around."

"Connie's been academically smart but stupid in a lot of other things." Randolph said tartly.

"Judy's ring is beautiful. Al picked out a pretty stone."

"It's only about a third the size of Betsy's."

"Betsy's may have a lot of sparkle. Realistically, it could end up back with a jeweler."

"Judy had some doubts."

"Never! Those two were meant for each other."

"She's afraid if he doesn't finish school, he'll be stuck in a miserable job all his life."

"Even if he finishes school, he'll still be stuck with a miserable job all his life. Nothing new in that."

"I could end up in one of those factories."

"You've got a good chance at beating that."

"I could stay with my green suit. Maybe the only difference is the factories look different."

"That's a special life that takes a lot of dedication. It won't work for everyone. You must be excited about flight school."

"It's been a long time since I've been at the controls of an aircraft. Yes, I am getting excited." He realized she had dug into his hidden thoughts.

Faith looked around absently at the crowds of people. Although subdued, the atmosphere was definitely of a party. "I can't cry anymore. My father called the hospital to find out about getting

Arthur's dress uniform to the funeral director. I never heard my mother scream like that. She absolutely refused to let him be buried in anything from the Marine Corps. I never saw my father so shocked. My mother was adamant. My father said a Marine should rest in the uniform he had worn proudly. My mother just screamed at him, that her baby was not going to lie throughout eternity in a uniform that had killed and cheated him of his life. My father went absolutely pale. They got his last high school suit. That's what he's wearing. I still can't believe he did this. Especially at Christmas. What could torment him that much to make him do this?" Faith's composure started to shatter, but she resisted it. Her face remained somber.

"He wanted to be at peace. He knew he had made a mistake by being careless and triggering that mine. Careless soldiers or Marines can't make mistakes and survive. His body had survived, but not his spirit. That's what he was trying to tell me. He was a real and true warrior. He couldn't live with himself for that reason. He's as good a Marine as your father."

She stared at him for a moment. "That Gaudot book. I started to read it, and it didn't make any sense."

"Arthur found the philosophy that allowed him to do what he wanted. Take his own life against all the principles he had been raised with including the Marine Corps."

"God won't forgive him for that."

"Suppose he'd died when he stepped on that mine in Vietnam. You would not hesitate in believing God would welcome him immediately. His body didn't die, but his spirit and will did. So finally, months after stepping on the mind, his body found his spirit and joined again. Why should God deny accepting him for finally coming to where he felt he should be?" Faith was silent. She stared into Randolph's eyes.

"Maybe you're right," she said finally, ignoring the steady low chatter around them. "My father took down all the Marine Corp things and the war souvenirs on the walls in the playroom, and put them in the attic. Those things are sacred to him. He was my brother." Faith's lips quivered. This time the hard façade of her face dissolved. She could not stop the tears. "I loved him."

"He's with those, he should be with." Impulsively, Randolph put his arms around her shoulders to comfort her. She pressed into him, and he felt her whole upper body shake. Not all of it was grief. "That's good for me to hear," she whispered. "That's two good things I've heard."

"Two?"

"You don't know how much sleep I've lost thinking about that kiss, and what it did to me."

"I'm sorry. I shouldn't have."

"Don't you ever be sorry. It's my life."

"It can't be."

"If Arthur could do such a stupid thing with his life, why can't I? That will always have some meaning to me."

Finally, their embrace ended, dissolving slowly so that neither could tell who broke it. They stood facing each other a long time, neither speaking.

Monday was the funeral. Several burly cousins and some uncles, many who had been in the military, were Arthur's pallbearers. There were a few in military uniforms from those at home on leave. Several of the gate guards at the Naval Base came in their dress uniforms. They were the only Marines visible. Randolph wore his uniform and was the only officer present. An honor guard from Mr. Beckwerth's veterans club fired the volley for Lance Corporal Arthur Beckwerth, Jr. In the bitter December cold, the graveside ceremony was mercifully short. The next day, Randolph started for Texas.

Chapter Seven

"So, you wannabe a helicopter pilot, lootenant?"

Wearing a standard issue two-piece Nomex flight suit, Randolph was strapped into the middle seat of the three-place, rotary wing aircraft. The Army named it after a bird. To those who flew it, it was always referred by its numeral identification an OH-23. Randolph straddled the console while the instructor, with his dual set of controls huddled in the left seat. The cyclic was the stick held by the right hand, controlling the direction of the main rotors. The left hand held the collective, an up and down lever controlling the pitch of the main blades. A manual throttle at the end of the collective could add or subtract motor rpm. Both feet rested on pedals that controlled the pitch of the rail rotor, which allowed stability, direction and power. Everything about flight controls had been covered in the first two weeks of ground school, which were non fly weeks. This was the third week of primary one. They had to solo within fifteen hours of dual instruction. His class had drawn these piston-engine aircraft. Others, most of the Warrant Officer Candidates and Vietnamese Air Force classes flew the Hughes TH-55, a two-place trainer, smaller and with more of a whine to it's three main blades.

It was Randolph's second dual lesson. At the Main Heliport, starting, taxing, take off procedures, and navigating to the stage field where most of the instruction was to be given was crammed into the first orientation flight. It had been a busy flight with him making approaches and takeoffs from the six-lane practice field. For separation and safety, half the lanes used left-hand traffic, the other used right-hand. It was exciting, challenging, and took the combined concentration of both student and instructor to stay away from other aircraft.

"You're drifting. You're drifting right. Correct it, stupid! You wanna be in the other lane? Correct it now, loo-tenant."

To Randolph's unmitigated annoyance, most of his instructor's corrective commands were loud, coarse and derogatory of his abilities to handle the aircraft. The instructor had demonstrated the first simulated engine failure and power recovery from autorotation. This maneuver allowed the helicopter to maintain flight characteristics and reach the ground safely, if the engine suddenly quit, either through the myriad number of possible mechanical problems or a bullet. Ordering Randolph to keep his hands on the controls to follow the maneuver, the sudden loss of power startled him. The aircraft nosed down and seemed to pummel straight toward the ground. As they were falling, they turned 180 degrees into the wind. As this was happening, the instructor calmly read off which instruments to monitor. Randolph's eyes were wide staring at the ground coming rapidly at them. He saw nothing else.

"That weren't bad, loo-tenant. Some nearly crap their drawers the first time. Y'all sitting in something mushy that gonna stink up this cockpit?" The little man chortled, a half laugh and half sneer, which Randolph was quickly growing to despise. "I'll be on the controls next time. I don't want any rotor over-speeds. Understand loo-tanant?"

It was the last time the instructor announced the maneuver. Thereafter, Randolph's reactions to simulated engine failure were part of his grade slip. The OH-23 with all the moving pieces of machinery was a new and strange experience to Randolph. It was very different than his experience in the civilian fixed wing. Flying in a helicopter was fluid. Above and behind them were the mechanisms, the engine, and transmission along with the couplings and gears, which, together, satisfied the mysteries of flight. Sitting in a plastic bubble beneath it, they sat with a clear view of the ground. Gone was the fixed wing stability of sitting on a solid wing and flying in an aircraft. Even in level flight, the helicopter vibrated as it moved through the air.

This second flight he had ridden to the stage field in the bus while one of his stick buddies got the orientation ride. Carefully, after he completed the start up procedure, the instructor had let him make a few takeoffs and landing, growling at him for any slight drifting after his turns over one of the stage field's six lanes. On the third circuit of the field, while down wind, he had rolled down the throttle. Randolph felt the instructor's firm hands overriding his unsure reactions to complete the recovery back to powered flight. There were more, instant and nagging corrections, some Randolph was beginning to sense rather than understand. Quickly, he found himself looking outside the aircraft not in awe but to gauge the rate of descent and his movements on the vibrating controls to control the aircraft's flight. Again, he was told he had no coordination between his hands and feet.

"You got to use that gray matter between your ears, loo-tenant. Get your head outside this cockpit, or else you going to be using your feet, only."

The criticism seemed almost an after thought, as if it was part of the instruction. There did not seem to be anything personal to it. On the ground the instructor spoke in normal tones, and as if Randolph was another person. The instructor hovered the aircraft at three feet. At the takeoff pad, he turned the controls over to Randolph, and began a continuous low mumble of corrections and criticisms as he started to pull power for the takeoff. The scream echoed in the cockpit outside the headset as he grabbed the controls before the aircraft had gone five feet forward.

"You want to get us killed?" He screeched as he hovered rearward back to the pad. "You ever do that again, and it's an automatic pink slip."

Randolph had forgotten the pre-take off clearing and safety checks. It was a Cardinal Sin against the God of Safety. It had caused many expulsions. Using heated air just as an automotive heater does, the instructor kept the inside of the bubble comfortably warm in the cool Texas air. Randolph started to sweat. He could feel his flanks as moisture trickled down his sides. When he tried ignoring the loud criticism, there was a comment.

"You listening to me, loo-tenant? Your headset turned on?"

"Yes sir," he answered, automatically.

"I don't think you can hear me, because you're not doing what I'm telling you to. Get that helmet checked, loo-tenant."

After the next landing, the instructor had taken the controls again without explanation and hovered the aircraft to a portion of unused taxiway. There he had given the controls back, and told Randolph to keep the aircraft at a three foot hover over one spot. Fifteen minutes later, with sweat slowly dripping from his scalp under the plastic helmet almost into his eyes and down his sides and back under the Nomex flight suit, he was still holding the controls maintaining the three-foot hover. His left hand was cramping from squeezing the collective with the throttle, and his right was numb from holding the cyclic.

"Lay your right arm on your thigh. That way your hand won't go to sleep." His instructor had the ability to invade his thoughts.

Randolph gingerly allowed his right forearm to come in contact with his thigh. He could feel the continuous vibrations through the cyclic. His right hand felt immediate relief, and there was no hindrance to his control movement. He had little trouble stopping any drift to either side or forward. It was rearward motion that he was fighting. The aircraft had clearly drifted back a foot, which Randolph had not recovered. The instructor had to have noted the rearward motion.

"Relax on the controls. Don't squeeze them. Think movement rather than try to do it."

Going through Randolph's mind over his concentration on maintaining the hover, was the grade he was to receive. He did not want to believe he could be flunking after the second session.

"Why should he be yelling at you? He's supposed to be teaching you how to fly." Andrea seemed genuinely puzzled. It was Wednesday night, the day of his second flight. She was at her apartment. Their telephone conversations had become erratic during Randolph's two weeks of ground school. Andrea had commuted to New Jersey several times at the end of December and into the first week of January. The new showcase arrived only hours before the four day show began. Andrea's days sometimes stretched into twenty hours. Her reward, as she had squeezed it out of her father, was being named Western Sales Director. There was very little fanfare about the announcement. Her authority as a supervisor was established.

Blaisedale had purchased a long cord for their communal telephone. Randolph had pulled it into his room and closed his door. "My instructor is a civilian and works for the company the Army hired. They tell you, and you listen. You don't converse, other than to say, 'yes!' I'm not the only one getting screamed at. We've got two full Colonels in our class. At first we thought they were VIP visitors or part of the school. They're students. They ride the buses with us to the stage field, and they come to formations in the morning. They don't stand in the formations, but they come."

"Do they yell at the Colonels?"

"Probably not. They're still smiling after flight periods. There's a couple in each class. They wear colored hats like us." Each class wore a bright colored baseball cap.

"What color is yours?"

"Yellow! Some guys think they're gold. They'll yellow. You can't get any more yellow than our caps. We finally got a chance to ask our Colonels why they were being sent through flight school. One of them said, when you give it too much left pedal, you might over-torque the rotor system."

"What did he mean by that?"

"The Army is going to keep helicopters. There are very few senior officers with practical flight experience. They're going to be needed to develop tactics and strategic planning at higher levels. Some of these guys will wear stars. Our two seem like normal types, though."

"I got tickets on a Friday afternoon flight. Jonathon wanted to meet this weekend. I called him today and reset the meeting for

Monday. There's a lot of things he wants to do. He's full of good ideas. Wants to get started."

"On the weekend?"

"He's used to working six days a week. The whole week, if necessary. How do you think he got to be a top notch salesman? He's not cheap, either. He negotiated a hell of favorable contract with Tremblay Bearings. I thought my uncle was going to have apoplexy. My father was impressed and gave him all he asked for. I told him our first meeting had to fit my schedule. How's that sound for someone who is a new boss? I've got a Sunday afternoon flight Dallas to San Francisco."

"What time Sunday? That's my only full day off. Why couldn't you have made it for Monday morning?"

"It takes some time to fly from one major city to another, then get into a hotel room, and unpack, and get ready for the next day. You don't just hop off the plane and go right into meetings." Last week Andrea had finished the post New Jersey trade show briefing to her uncles and Frederic, and then had Jonathon Dawes fly to Boston for his formal hiring and orientation meetings. They had dragged into the weekend, which was to have been her first visit to Texas. Sunday, Andrea showed her new salesman some of the highlights of Boston. "We'll have Friday and Saturday night together. We've got reps and distributors bent out of shape because they're learning I hired Jonathon. Most of them know him. They know he's going to cut into their business. They tell me my uncle has got several scalding calls already complaining about him."

"I can't pick you up Friday afternoon."

"I'll rent a car. What town is Fort Wolters near?"

"Mineral Wells."

"Sounds delightful. I'll find it. One other thing, Mr. Thayer. I got approval to hire someone to do trade shows. This will be my second employee. My uncle didn't object at all. The only hitch is the salary has to be in a certain range. I've already been talking to Scott about scouting out a good candidate for us."

"Good, I'll see you in two days, then?"

"Do they have a Holiday Inn?"

"It's actually in the flight pattern at the Main Heliport."

"I'm not going to get out of bed while I'm there. You can bring me my meals."

"You expect to get rest in our bed?" He chuckled.

"You can find out what it's like to make love to Sleeping Beauty."

When she hung up the phone, she remained sitting on her couch. The apartment was quiet. He had been the only one, other than her mother, who had spent some time here with her. She wanted him back in it, not in some motel room. He had made it more than an apartment. He should understand all the sacrifice, so that one day they would have a comfortable life. Why would the Army allow screaming while he's trying to learn something as complicated as flying. That was the stupid Army. If he can't make it, he might lose interest in the Army. I may have to do nothing. Her head ached. Standing, a slight wave of nausea swept through her. She had to put her hand on the couch to steady herself. The feeling did not pass quickly. She shrugged if off. All the preparations and the trade show were behind her. Jonathon was on board. She had her title, the actual authority to go with it, although her uncle, the VP of marketing and sales remained her nominal boss. He would not oppose her plans for California since her father backed her. Randolph had been right about slowly gaining more ground now that she was authorized to hire a trade show coordinator. He does possess the right instincts. Only he needs to apply them to something that will mean something, not the Army. My father has the right instincts about the new products that will break Tremblay Bearings up and out of its confining industrial base. His brothers, my uncles still don't see it. At the trade show, one of the main new topics was new alloy, inexpensive bearings, which Tremblay Bearings still could not provide. She had learned that some of their competitors would be able to produce them, soon. The company had remained quiet on these new products. The stock offering was also becoming only a whispered banter.

Going into her bedroom, she looked at the huge bed and remembered when Randolph was there with her. The bed did not seem so big, then. She smiled with the thought, and then her head started pounding again. She had wanted to start her packing this evening rather than leaving it all for tomorrow night. There was aspirin in her bathroom. After taking two tablets she laid on her bed. Although she felt warm, she pulled her comforter over herself.

"Did you hear about the Jesus Nut?" Tim Covington asked. He was one of Randolph's two stick buddies, assigned the same instructor. It was Thursday of the first flight week. Students and instructors were going through the introduction phase of working together. They were waiting in the briefing classroom at the Main Heliport.

"It's that big retaining nut on the top of the mast," Randolph said. While they were waiting in silence his thoughts had drifted to the chance of seeing Andrea within twenty-four hours. Covington's comment jolted him back to the briefing table. "It kind of looks like it holds everything together. They call it the Jesus Nut because if you lose that, that's all that stands between you and Jesus."

"He's a real confederate. That war's been over for a hundred years. They lost. Why can't they forget it?" Mike Riard said. Both Randolph's stick buddies were Field Artillery Second Lieutenants fresh from the schools at Fort Sill, Oklahoma. To escape his draft board, which was pressuring him, Mike Riard had enlisted to insure a slot in OCS, and then had managed to get one of the dwindling Artillery Branch rotary wing flight allocations. Tim Covington was from Indiana, an ROTC flight program graduate who had finished his officer basic course at about the same time Riard had been commissioned. Like Randolph, he was in the pipeline and had not been offered a choice between rotary and fixed wing schools. If there was any hatred between Field Artillery OCS and ROTC graduates, it was not apparent in Randolph's stick buddies. They kidded him mildly about being Infantry. "Other guys say their instructors scream, too. They all must." Riard added.

"It's to prepare us for 'Nam," Covington said. "They want to see how much pressure they can put us under."

"I could do without the screaming when I'm trying to concentrate." Randolph said. "The guy's an asshole for no reason."

"He doesn't need a reason. He's there, has been there, and done it all, and you ain't!" Riard said sounding like a genuine OCS graduate. "He does a good preflight, and is real good explaining things. When I started off with him here at the Main Heliport, he's in no hurry and checks everything. It's in the air he makes you feel like an idiot."

"He doesn't trust their maintenance. Said be your own maintenance officer. Your own standards will always be higher than theirs," Covington said. "You see that TH-55 they left on the ramp? The one with the skids curled up to the doors. That happened yesterday. It was a solo student. The write-up was 'a suspected hard landing.' I heard he broke his back."

"Maybe he was drifting off his lane," Riard snickered, which caused them all to laugh, harder than they should have.

"Or something broke. Maybe something structural." Covington added in a melancholy tone. They stopped chuckling. "I heard he was going about sixty knots when he hit the ground. Fixed wing is a lot easier and safer. Not that much can go wrong. How often does a wing fall off an airplane?"

"Once would be enough to ruin the flight." Randolph said. "And, maybe get a safety violation." They laughed again, uneasily. "As my Benning roommate would have said, that is his ticket out of the Army."

"Use that gray matter between your ears, lootenant." Riard imitated the instructor's southern drawl. "What the hell are they doing in there? Did he go off to take a shit? Suppose he shits the same way we do in the North?" He looked at the closed door to the instructors' room.

"They kept the Marines together," Covington said. "They didn't split them up with us."

There were eight Marine Corps Second Lieutenants fresh out of their basic six-month course at Quantico. They spoke of earning Naval gold wings rather than the silver ones the Army would award. There was also a group of foreign officer students from Armies and police forces friendly to the United States. Another separate class consisted only of Vietnamese. Since anything that flew in Vietnam belonged to their Air Force, these students had American Air Force officers rather than Army officers as advisors.

Their student company leader was a senior Captain with six years of service and one tour of Vietnam as a signal officer. Although there were two full Colonels in their class, the formations and other administrative details were left to the senior Captain. There were several other Captains and a few First Lieutenants caught in the twelve-month window before they would become Captains. The majority of students in the Officer Rotary Wing class were Second Lieutenants, like Randolph, with minimal service experience. All had attended basic branch schools or were recent OCS graduates.

As silence descended over their table while they waited, again Randolph began to think of seeing Andrea. His loins shivered with a pleasant tingling sensation. When their instructor approached their table, conscientiously they stood, as if he were an officer senior to them.

"He chops the throttle."

"What does that mean?" Andrea's voice reflected unusual fatigue.

"He rolls it down. Did it second time around at the stage field today. I've started squeezing the throttle so when he goes to roll it down, I can feel it. It gives me a few seconds head start on the maneuver. Collective down, right pedal, get the turn into the wind. Keep the nose down. We go into autorotation."

"What is autorotation?"

"If your engine quits, the transmission disengages allowing the blades to free turn. The turning blades act like an airplane wing. That keeps you from becoming a rock in the sky. Then, you look for a place to put it down."

"What happens if the blades stop turning?"

"You meet Jesus."

"I can't get everything in this damn suitcase. I need more luggage. Haven't had a chance to get to a store." He heard her sudden struggle with the phone receiver as she cursed from nearly dropping it. Then, she sat and lay back on her bed. "I need things for California. I don't know how long I'll be there. Leland Junior has been appointed New Construction Coordinator. He's going to oversee the details of the building expansion. My father's is adding almost a third to our current square footage. He still hasn't made the announcement about going public and selling stock."

"Is that a promotion?"

"That snake! No. It's just more visibility."

"Your plate is full enough." Randolph was thinking about promised trips to Texas.

"My mother says there are going to be a bunch of social activities, cocktail parties, and such in D.C. on the weekend of February fourteenth. These are high level must attend affairs. If Scott doesn't go, it would be like saying he's not interested in the Nixon job. His two younger children said they are going. Scott Jr. will probably get a pass from the Marine Corps. It's all VIP stuff. The Marine Corps encourages things like this."

"I have a Saturday morning ground class."

"You wouldn't even be missing any flying, then. This is Washington where the power is. If you tell them that, no one is going to deny you a weekend pass."

"I'd miss a Monday. I don't know if I can do that. Things are tight down here."

"Look into it. I still have all my packing to do. I didn't do anything last night."

After they ended the call, Randolph held the twenty foot cord and started swinging it like a jump rope. The other end of the makeshift jump rope was jammed under his bedroom door. When she gets here the first time, he would force the issue about her living with him. Blaisedale would get his half of the rent. He would slow down paying off his college loans. She could find an apartment in Mineral Wells. Should he expend all his ammunition to insure success? The last round before the position became untenable would be the marriage proposal. That would be the end of his arsenal. He was tired of telephone conversation.

After replacing the receiver on her bedside phone, she remained laying on her back, which felt unusually comfortable. A long night's sleep had not made the symptoms dissipate. If anything they were getting worse. After eating a sandwich at lunch she had to dart into the bathroom, where she lost it. She had no appetite when she arrived at the apartment and was afraid to put anything else in her stomach. If I tell the mentor, maybe he would make the Army give him a pass. No, he is there only to give advice. He has no real power. As she started to sit up, nausea overwhelmed her, and she laid down again. Her head had started to pound furiously. More aspirin, she thought and get more sleep. I can beat this. Put off packing again. What I need is a maid. The thought made her giggle, which caused her head to move and pound again. Too many things to do before the airport, tomorrow. When the throbbing in her head seemed temporarily to subside, she rolled off the bed and went into her bathroom for the aspirin. Standing to gulp some water with the pills, her legs felt rubbery and weak. There will be everything to do tomorrow. Holding onto walls and furniture, she made her way back to her bed. It is more than a cold. Shit of a time to get it. There is so much to do in California. Sleep came rapidly.

By Friday of the first flying week definite flight procedures and instructor idiosyncrasies had formed. The first student who went with the instructor from the Main Heliport went through the intensive preflight. After cranking, there were the normal delays involved in getting permission to taxi, taxing out to the colored takeoff pad, and flying to the stage field. Randolph and his stick buddies realized the instructor was allocating those first flights evenly. Those originating and terminating from the stage field allowed more time to improve rudimentary flying technique.

When Randolph's flight was to or from the Main Heliport, he began to anticipate the expected simulated engine failure, which students called splitting the needles. The rotor and engine RPM needles were in the same instrument face, and while in normal flight were synchronized. During autorotation, rolling off the throttle caused the engine needle to drop rapidly splitting away from the rotor RPM needle. Dipping the nose caused the blades to speed up which made the rotor needle rise, hopefully to stay in the green arc. When rolling on the throttle for a power recovery the engine needle rejoined the rotor. When the instructor began checking for clearance from other aircraft, it was Randolph's clue to squeeze the throttle tighter. Each time he managed to turn the aircraft properly into the wind, keeping the rotor speed in the green and on the power recovery, rolling on the throttle to bring the rotor and engine needles back together. The throttle seemed to turn only a half inch through the maneuver. Randolph began to feel the effect of the collective, and how it influenced the rotor speed. To avoid a rotor over-speed-which could cause immediate damage to the aircraft-pulling up on the collective or raising the nose slightly slowed the rotors down. Suspected rotor over-speeds like any other malfunction had to be written up in the logbook on post flight. Additional inspections would be made before the next flight. He noticed with satisfaction there was less instructor overriding on his control movements. His debriefings were shorter than Covington's or Riard's. Friday, at the stage field, he was telling the instructor when he began an approach if he was over or under arching, then made corrections.

After the final formation, he raced to the trailer to await Andrea's telephone call. After changing out of his Nomex and wolfing down a plate of macaroni, patiently he watched the color television with the silent Blaisedale. By nine, he was concerned from the lack of a phone message wondering if something had happened to her flight, or that she unfortunately missed it. Knowing she would not be at her apartment, he tried her mother's phone. An answering service received his call. The woman was polite asking if it was an emergency. Stunned into silence, Randolph said it was not. The Lynders were unavailable that evening. Saturday after the morning ground school class, again he raced back to his trailer. Neither Sylvia nor Scott was home, the kind female voice of the answering service reported. In desperation he called Andrea's apartment letting the phone ring until an operator broke in to announce the obvious, which was no one was answering that line. He started another non-talkative, television-viewing session listening to Blaisedale as he munched potato chips. He could not concentrate on any of the programs and found himself gazing at the colors on the screen. When the phone ran, Randolph pounced on it.

"Randy," Sylvia's tone was not the ebullient one of a newly married woman, but of a concerned parent. "I got your phone message. Sorry I could not get back sooner. I'm with Andrea at her apartment. She stayed overnight in the hospital. We didn't get released until late this afternoon. She insisted I put this call through. I'm with her in the bedroom. When I give her the phone, I'm going to the kitchen for some coffee. Please don't make it a long conversation. She needs to rest."

"Is she all right?" Panic raced through his thoughts.

"At the plant yesterday she fainted. She was badly dehydrated. She had to have fluids intravenously. Her temperature was nearly 103. The doctors think it's an extremely bad case of the flu. She needs bed rest. If it had been up to me, I'd have made her stay in the hospital another day. She wants the phone. Remember, no long conversations."

"I'm sorry, Randy." The weakness in the tone of her voice was apparent. She sounded defeated, something he had never experienced with her.

"You had a suspected hard landing." He tried to be cheerful, hiding his disappointment.

"My mother is exaggerating. I didn't need to be taken to the hospital. I have a bad case of the flu. They got scared and rushed me there. It was over my objections, which I don't think they heard." She laughed strangely, and he could feel her frailty.

"Still, you fainted?"

"Just a little." She giggled. "It's like the old saying—you either are or you're not. Isn't that virginity or something?"

"What the hell are they giving you?"

"Yellow pills. They're as big as cough drops. Hard to swallow."

"You take them and get better."

"Maybe next weekend. In a few days, I'll know better."

"What's next weekend?"

"Me going to Texas. I want to see cowboys, and cows, and stuff like you've said you see from the helicopters."

"I've only seen cows from the air, Andrea."

"Good, I'll see them too."

Sylvia took the phone from Andrea. "She did all that trade show in New Jersey by herself without any help from anyone at the company. I know what it's like to put on exhibitions for the museum. I've only been involved with a small part of it. Andrea did that whole show with all the monstrous problems. Her father and especially her uncle should know better than to let her drive herself so hard. They are blind at times. She's insisting on going to California early in the week, then going to see you next weekend. That's too much for her, Randy. You must convince her to rest."

"I'll do my best," Randolph managed to say. She had never been sick since they had met, always the healthy and indestructible Andrea. Could a flu bug take that much out of her? Sylvia was right. She needed at least a week to rest. That put the next weekend into jeopardy. She could skip going to the west coast until after her visit here in Texas. He did not want her to leave after she arrived. That was to be his big surprise to her. Its impact, he realized, was not going to be strong.

Late in the week over her mother's strenuous objections, Andrea flew to San Francisco. She landed to turbulence caused by Jonathon's energetic activities. In the Bay Area, he disenfranchised the main distributor by visiting nearly a dozen companies they represented, asserting his contract rights, and offering better prices, which had not been reviewed in several years. He had even managed a trip to the Seattle area where he reestablished tarnished links with a few old Tremblay customers. His efforts in the few short weeks of employment had resulted in over fifty thousand of undisputable new business. Frederic sent him a congratulatory personal message.

By Friday of the second week of flying, two yellow hat students soloed. One was a transportation First Lieutenant who had a commercial fixed wing rating and over seven hundred hours. The other was a Second Lieutenant of Armor who was a natural. Flying was second nature to him. The controls were an extension of his hands. Other students recognized his flying ability when watching from the stage field. Hovering, approaches, and landings were done with double proficiency. Randolph realized he was not one of these types of pilots. He was mechanical, manipulating the controls stiffly, but still efficiently. All the students had acquired two digit flight time by the end of the week. Fifteen, the maximum number of dual hours allowed to solo, hovered on the horizon for all of them. That accumulated flight time would be reached by most of the students early in the next week.

The sick-bed promise of coming to Texas for the weekend evaporated during their nightly telephone conversations. Randolph hoped it would be renewed for the following one. His Saturday night was spent watching the colored television with the uncommunicative Blaisedale. When she arrived in California Randolph could not help being drawn in by her boisterous enthusiasm. His concern had been about her health. She seemed to have recovered quickly from her flu symptoms and was resuming her strenuous pursuits. Listening to her narration of Jonathon's sales' feats was captivating. Their conversations often became planning and operational conferences. As the newest member of Tremblay Bearings management, she had been thrust into the realm of problem resolution, which Jonathon passed on to her, especially when it interfered with his sales itinerary. Some problems were simple requests for technical information, which she could easily obtain from the plant in Massachusetts. Others were managerial, which she discussed with Randolph. Some of their evening phone conversations neared two hours. Beckoning her was the larger California jewel Los Angeles which accounted for the bulk of Tremblay Bearings West Coast business. Jonathon was eager to begin his assault, especially to test the potential market for the new alloy bearings, which Frederic encouraged by hiring several new engineers with specific knowledge of the new materials.

The stock offering to raise funds for the new capital equipment was set for early in March. In the small community of industrial bearings manufacturers, the publication of the news was like the first shot of a revolution. The quality conscious, austere Tremblay Bearings was plunging into the open market of cheap bearings designed to reach commercial markets. Ground breaking for the expansion of the plant was ambitiously scheduled for the end of that month. Scott informed Andrea that none of the usual, legal steps toward making Tremblay Bearings a public company had been started. He indicated, since Frederic had made selling stock known, possibly he was going to Europe. It would be a step to keep the company private avoiding many regulatory rules of the federal government. Although known in Europe as a quality high-priced manufacturer of mostly railroad bearings, Tremblay Bearings had never established a good foothold in that continent. Scott was skeptical about meeting Frederic's goals in raising money. He attributed it to some unknown source which forecasted success with the proposed offering. Frederic made no announcement although expanding the plant was moving from planning to actual contracting with construction companies.

With her daily telephone contact they seldom talked about his flying. The impact on the ball bearings industry of Tremblay Bearings announcement and Jonathon's bold west coast sales assaults filled their conversation. Randolph's optimism of being with her during the approaching weekend mellowed.

Monday, the opportunity to solo didn't happen for Randolph. A dozen of his classmates including Riard soloed. Riard was ecstatic. Temporarily, his pressure was relieved. Tuesday Randolph rode the bus out to the stage field while Covington got the first flight from the Main Heliport. Watching from the stage field his aircraft hovered to a taxiway, and the instructor got out. Covington soloed. His permanent gloomy mood temporarily evaporated when he came into the stage field hut.

Randolph had the second flight period. He concentrated. Calmness overcame him. His starting procedure was flawless. Picking up the aircraft to a hover, he executed all the clearing safety procedures, and made several approaches and takeoffs, some his best. His angle of descent was like walking effortlessly down a staircase as the instruction manual dictated.

"Hover over to that apron." The instructor said after his fourth approach. "It's going to act differently without the extra weight. Once around and then come back here to get me."

Adrenaline shot thought him when he realized he was going to be allowed to solo. Although he felt the hair prickly on his head, he maintained his calmness. The instructor climbed out, being careful to buckle his empty seatbelt. Without the extra weight, his sense and touch on the controls quickly readjusted. Again carefully he hovered to a lane, went through the clearing procedures, well aware that the eagle eye of his instructor was watching each move, then pulled pitch, thought the cyclic forward, and added some left pedal. He was kept busy feeling the vibrations and keeping visual contact outside the cockpit. His turns in the pattern while climbing out and leveling off felt the same. When he turned onto a lane for final approach, he had to lower the nose of the aircraft slightly to initiate the maneuver. He had the immediate sensation he might fall right through the bubble and out of the aircraft. The feeling passed quickly as he realized his approach speed was too fast, and he was going to overshoot the spot on the runway he had picked to touch down. He thought there was no way for the instructor to know about which spot he had picked. That was the first thing his instructor mentioned after he had hovered over to pick him up.

"Everyone does that," the little man said in his southern drawl. "It's the difference in the weight without another body in there."

The solo wings were oversized and colored gray, black and white. When earned, they were sewn onto the front of the colored caps. Each new starting class was easy to identify because of the absence of these wings and the clean hats. Harry Cooper offered his wife's services to sew the solo wings onto his yellow baseball cap. They lived in a trailer also. Their trailer was sparsely furnished like the one he was sharing with Blaisedale. Cooper had rented a u-haul. They were acquiring so many possessions, he said he might have to rent a truck and tow his car to Alabama. Their daughter was round-faced, smiling and plump as Cooper said from, a steady diet of breast milk.

"We take turns." Cooper said making his wife blush. "Amanda does the first approach. I get whatever is left after her go-arounds.

We have to be concerned with simulated titty failure. Gretchen needs time to do a power recovery fill-up."

It took Gretchen longer to set up her portable sewing machine than it did to sew on the wings. Cooper had soloed Monday and his wings were already in place on his yellow cap.

"It's been five weeks, Andrea."

"I've lost time. I have to make it up." If there was any residue of her flu it was not in her voice. She sounded like the old Andrea.

"That was good for last weekend. Two weeks ago you got sick. It's early in this week. Do whatever you need to do and be on a flight Friday night. Start Los Angeles, Monday."

"There's one rep my father has been doing business with for over twenty years. He insisted I meet with him. We're having dinner together Saturday night. Jonathon is coming with me."

"Jonathon?"

"He calls me Andrea. He knows I'm his boss. This rep has had three wives and wears a toupee. Tells me he'll be ruined financially if he loses Tremblay Bearing business. Says his kids are in college and his X-wives want back alimony."

"How much business does he generate?"

"Last year did somewhere between two hundred thousand and a quarter million. He's a major player. That's why my father insists. Jonathon thinks we can easily double that in the coming year. Sales have stayed stagnant with this guy. If he won't get off his ass, especially when we get the new alloy stuff on line, Jonathan will make it happen."

"That's what Jonathon thinks?"

"He's been selling industrial products for twelve years. There are trends in the manufacturing cycle. That's essential for new sales. The new alloy bearings open up the potential for enormous growth. Jonathon is thirty-five years old and has two daughters, eight and eleven. They play soccer. I'm going to a game Thursday afternoon."

"I soloed today."

The entire contingent from Fort Benning, Blaisedale, Cooper, Frank Dean who had brought his wife and two small children, and Jerry Jardin, still sporting his aviator glasses rather than the Army issue ones, had soloed. The two full Colonels to no one's surprise earned their solo wings. As the week progressed, there were only a few yellow hats without solo wings. By Friday, they were no longer riding the bus to the stage field. Their names were not recorded during the brief, morning formations. Among them was one of Marines and a Minnesota National Guard Second Lieutenant who had been waiting two years for a slot in an ORWAC class. He shook hands and said good-bye to everyone in the class on Thursday when it became apparent his instructor was not going to allow him to solo. Unlike the other non soloist he was going home to resume his civilian life. His main concern was that he would probably lose his slot in the aviation unit in the National Guard.

"I understand the pressure on you. I know pressure, too. Have you looked into getting a pass for the following weekend, the fourteenth?"

"I can't."

"Did the Army tell you that?"

"Why can't you meet with that rep from LA during the week?" He ignored her direct question. "Why does it have to be on a weekend?"

"I'm in a rigid environment too. It seems I solo into something new almost every day. My father ordered it. You're told to do something, you do it. Haven't I heard you say that before? It fits into Jonathon's schedule, too."

"So you don't miss the soccer games."

"Since he came to work for us, he's dedicated himself and missed a lot of time with his family."

"His kids will be playing soccer next year. Isn't our time as important?"

"There's still D.C. and the weekend of the fourteenth. My mother wants Scott to take the Administration job. I've got to be there for her. Work on the pass."

After they ended their call, he wondered if everything she was doing took precedence over them being together. Her getting promoted and taking on more responsibility was too powerful for her to resist. She loved what she was doing as much as he loved what he was doing. He wondered if she felt as terrified as he did at times. Even if he used the marriage proposal, the strongest shot, would she accept it? His apprehension had not changed since Fort Benning.

On Friday, Riard took an aircraft solo back to the Main heliport from the stage field. The instructor rode the bus. "Suddenly, there's aircraft everywhere. You have to get into the daisy chain. It's hard missing it, but you suddenly seem very close to a lot of other aircraft." Riard was still pumped with adrenaline when the bus picked him up at the Main Heliport for the short ride to the company area. The bus went silent as everyone listened to his commentary. It stopped at the Holiday Inn near the front gate. They went directly into the motel's yard where the swimming pool was not covered, although it was winter. It was the end of the flying week. Since it was a dry county, someone had brought a case of beer, some of which went into the pool. All including the Colonels were thrown in, a tradition for all the new solo pilots.

During the Saturday morning class, Cooper invited Randolph for dinner at his trailer that night. Without Andrea and without her visiting the next weekend, his only other prospect seemed watching Blaisedale's TV, so he accepted. He brought a bottle of white wine, which Harry Cooper gracefully accepted, placed on the small kitchen's counter, and promptly forgot as he handed Randolph a beer. Another yellow hat classmate, Sam Napin had been invited. Also an ROTC flight program graduate, Napin was a Medical Service Second Lieutenant who had come directly to flight school after finishing OBC at Fort Sam Houston, the Army's medical training center. Lois Napin had shoulder length blond hair and was in the sixth month of her first pregnancy. She was anxious to hold the Cooper's baby, Amanda. They were from Delaware.

Harry Cooper and Sam talked sports, barely mentioning flying, which briefly left Randolph out of their conversation. Gretchen refused a beer saying it affected Amanda. Lois Napin being six months pregnant decided to abstain, until she spotted Randolph's white wine. She asked for a glass. They had to squeeze in around the small kitchenette table the trailer provided. Randolph ate a plate full of vegetables, food his system sorely lacked. By nine o'clock, Lois was yawning profusely, so the Napins said good night. Gretchen went into their bedroom to nurse Amanda. Randolph refused another beer since his stomach was so full and also said good night. The night with young married couples was fulfilling for the vegetables, which the next day shot through his system. Andrea would have been bored silly. It was an interesting evening although not very entertaining for him, and one he decided he did not want to repeat. Randolph wondered why these two men, with the responsibilities they had with their spouses and children and near children, wanted to go to Vietnam, when there were so many obvious ways to avoid it. Cooper, he knew, wanted to fly. Napin had not revealed it during that social evening.

Neither was close to any definition Randolph had of the true soldier. They didn't fit into Thompson's definition of the motivated volunteer. As usual none mentioned politics or the world situation. They were young married men wearing uniforms and learning how to fly. They knew where it would lead them, and that didn't seem to bother them.

Frank Dean sat next to him on the bus going out to the stage field. Neither had drawn a first flight from the Main Heliport.

"How do your kids like Texas?" Randolph asked. Dean was quiet and reserved.

"Give them their toys, and a back yard anywhere, and they're happy. They won't remember any of this." As usual, Dean seemed annoyed to be asked a personal question. His face was pensive for a moment. "The four-year-old asked where the mountains went." Randolph remembered he was from Idaho. "Cooper's going to get grounded."

There had been a near miss incident the day before at the Main Heliport involving Harry Cooper. All departing traffic had been stopped for five minutes. Those who still had not taken off before the incident brought the story to the stage field. At their final formation, the cadre company commander, a Captain whom they seldom saw, had lectured them on safety while informing them about the incident.

"He'll get an FEB." Dean added.

"Army lingo for what?" Randolph asked.

"Flight Evaluation Board." Dean seemed annoyed further with Randolph's lack of Army knowledge. "Rated pilots not commanders judge whether he's fit to fly. At least, he's got a chance of a fair hearing. Cooper told me the instructor is trying to cover his ass."

"What can they do to him?"

"Throw him out of the program. A Flight Evaluation Board can do anything it wants to."

Randolph went directly to the Coopers' trailer after formation. Cooper was wearing civilian clothes watching TV. Gretchen was cooking their supper.

"We just took off from the pad. It was south take-off. We were doing the red poles from pad number one for west traffic departure. I was still pulling power. My instructor was going through the clearing procedure for climbing out. He pointed to the right and-you know how they do it in a singsong tone-and asked, you clear right, then above and-then I interrupted him. What about this guy underneath us, I said? His blades were about to come up through our skids. My instructor grabbed the controls, pulled an arm full of pitch and turned to the left to get out of the way. Then, the tower told everyone on take off to hold where they were and shut down the field. I should have initiated the climb to get out of the other guy's way."

"The instructor was in charge of the aircraft." Randolph emphasized. "That was his job."

"You think so? He asked me several times during the interviews why I hadn't started an avoidance procedure. I had the controls, until he jumped on them."

"How many hours have you got? How many does he have? You were listening to him giving the clearing instructions."

Cooper pondered that. "You're right, I was. Maybe I wouldn't have turned far enough. It was a solo student. We chased after him and followed him into a strange stage field. That was enough for my instructor for the day. We never flew back from that stage field. We took a bus. They came out there to interview us. That took hours."

"How do you feel?"

"I didn't need to change my pants afterwards," he laughed. "My instructor might have. Like they say, it was over in a few seconds. You think about it a lot afterwards, and each second seemed like an hour. I'll never fly with that asshole again!" Cooper said with sudden vehemence. "I'll be leaving the yellow hats," he added morosely.

"They'll resolve this and you'll be back."

"I'm grounded until this is over. I'll miss over a week and be way behind on time and stuff. What the student did was, after we took off, he took the pad and did the clearing turns, but I guess I was climbing more vertical. He claimed he didn't see us. It's hard to see directly up through the rotor system, and you can't see anything in back of you. We were blocked from his view. Basically he didn't give us enough time to clear. We were hardly over the first outbound pole."

"What are they going to do to him?"

"He was crap. It was his third pink slip. He's gone."

With the trauma of solo behind, earnest progress began on acquiring the level of proficiency required to meet the next gating event, the Primary I check ride at the fifty-hour level. Each week they had to acquire ten to twelve hours of flight time, either dual or solo. Ground Saturday classes would continue until the end of Primary I. To obtain maximum use of classrooms, personnel, and aircraft flight scheduling alternated each week, mornings or afternoons.

Although there were rows and rows of helicopters at the Main Heliport, as well as two other large heliports, Dempsey and Downing with similar large numbers, aircraft availability was a factor. Classes started every two weeks as a smaller class minus the failures departed for Fort Rucker, Alabama for the second half of rotary wing training. For each morning or afternoon flight schedule, each assigned aircraft could be used for two flight periods, each not exceeding an hour and a half flight time. During these intensive weeks, each stick got at least two aircraft. Sometimes one period was available on a third aircraft. Although some sticks were down to two students, the majority still had three. Some days, depending on aircraft availability a student might fly two periods, a combination of dual or solo. The instructors had to assess the progress of their students and keep everyone at the same level of flight time.

As he entered the trailer, Blaisedale surprised him by indicating he had received a letter. Although they went to the same place each morning, they drove their own cars. Blaisedale got regular mail from his parents and other family members. He seldom used the phone. Randolph concluded it was because his calls would be long distance. Letters were cheaper. That situation worked fine for Randolph with his long evening conversations with Andrea, all collect calls. Although he had received a few letters from his mother and one from Judy, this letter with an obvious feminine script perked Blaisedale's interest. Randolph picked the letter up off the kitchen table and went into his bedroom, closing the door behind him as he did when on the phone to Andrea. He chuckled at Blaisedale's cut-short curiosity.

The letter was from Faith. As soon as he picked it up, he had recognized her handwriting.

Dear Randy,

I got your address from your mother. I told her I wanted to send you a card thanking you for the help you gave me during Arthur's funeral. If there's no card in this letter, I forgot to enclose it. I really did buy one. (There was no card.) If I had asked Judy for your address, she would not have given it to me. I do have your phone number, but I thought a letter might allow me to express myself better.

It's hard to believe it's been seven weeks since Arthur's passing. My mother is not coping very well. I've had to step in and help with Mathew and Meredith doing things a mother should do. Meredith understands what happened but still cries a lot. I try to explain it, and comfort her as much as I can. Mathew doesn't say anything, but you can see it in his face. Sometimes I'd like to make him talk to me so he can get it out. There weren't much of Arthur's things to put away. When he went into the Marine Corps, Mathew kind of took over all his space in their room. Most of his things went into the attic. They're still there.

I'm a little concerned about my father. I know I told you he took all of his war souvenirs out of the playroom. Now he is talking to Vietnam veterans who denounce the war. Sarah has become more openly anti-war with my mother kind of in the doldrums. The only good thing is that Sarah has gotten closer to our father in all this. Of all the members of my family, those two seemed to be the furthest apart in thought and action. Arthur gave them something in what he did.

I've come to the point where I have accepted he is gone. All the energy used in trying to help him left a void. That took awhile to get over. I hope you are right, and that he really is with God. It goes against everything I've learned from the Church. I've thought about that a lot, and I've come to the conclusion you are right despite the Church.

I haven't been able to spend that much time with your brother, Teddy because of everything happening in my family. He's been swiping his bike from your cellar. Him and some neighborhood kids like to ride their bikes down the sled hills instead of using sleds. There is little snow on the ground. It's been a mild winter so far. He sneaks the bike back into the cellar thinking your mother doesn't know what's going on. Nothing gets by your mother. I mean nothing! She is some smart woman.

Judy and Al haven't set any real wedding date. A year from this summer seems to have surfaced. I think it's your mother's idea. She wants them to have a long engagement, so that Judy is very sure and doesn't make a mistake, like Betsy will do if she marries Andrew. I think that's influencing your mother a lot. Poor Al, he's panting like a dog who smells a bitch in heat. He certainly doesn't want to wait more than a year. Those two were meant for each other. You can tell about certain couples. Sometimes they are not right together, like Betsy and Andrew.

When I told Judy if she got married a year from this summer, you would probably not be there, she got a little upset. When she marries, she definitely wants you there. I remember you told me flight school is about nine months, so by the calendar, that means sometime in September you should get your wings. Then you'll have leave before they send you to Vietnam. I told Judy that in the Catholic Church you have to reserve time for a wedding six months in advance. I don't know how you do it in the Protestant church, but that got Judy all excited. There are a lot of things to do before a wedding, like hiring a hall for the reception. Those get booked up real quickly. Maybe I set her to thinking.

Now that you are flying again, which I know you must really be enjoying, you must be acquiring a lot of new stories. How I wish I could hear them. I really loved all those you told about learning how to fly at Norwood. Helicopters are certainly different than airplanes. It was so good when you were commuting to Northeastern, and I got to see you once in awhile. You will never know how much that meant to me. I know you are pursuing what you really want to do. I am happy for you. Save me some choice tidbits for when you come home on leave. I will always want to hear them.

The neighborhood is about the same since you left at Christmas. Connie is still going to Boston University. She must have stopped her anti-war activities to keep her parents' financial support. If she hadn't, I think I would have heard about it by now. I've visited Arthur's grave twice. They got him into the ground when it was half frozen. It still looks kind of chopped up. In the spring it will thaw and then some grass will grow, and it will look natural. Then life will go on.

Remember me, I am always,
Faith

"Can you get a weekend pass?"

"We're flying our asses off, Andrea. Some days it's two periods. That's three hours in the air."

"I did." She ignored his comment. "This is something that could be considered beneficial to the Army. The Marine Corps is highly encouraging Scott Junior to go. He has his pass already. Seventy-two hours. Your name has been mentioned. They know you're an Army Lieutenant."

"They're just cocktail parties not official functions."

"This is where influence and power can be exchanged. Scott still hasn't committed yet. My mother told me he's purposely holding them off. Scott Junior still doesn't have his second tour orders. Scott is still hoping they will stop them. If you can leave Dallas Saturday morning, you'll be back Monday night."

"They're bouncing guys out of this program for the first time. They haven't done that the last couple of years. Missing a day could be crucial."

"What if you were sick for a day?"

"You don't get sick during this training."

"The influence you'd get from D.C. would mean no one would mess with you. We already proved that at Benning."

"One of the guys who went through Benning with me had a near mid air. It wasn't his fault, but he could still get thrown out of the program. If I'm absent from flying, I could fall behind. I'm not going to allow that."

"You don't want to be with me?" Her tone was icy.

"You have freedom of movement. Last weekend you just had to be in Los Angeles. After three bottles of wine and some prime rib, you finally discovered the guy wasn't really going to be suffering all that much from Tremblay Bearings loss of business. You were only one of his many accounts."

"My father wanted me to meet with him. He found customers for us in lean years. Twenty year associations have to mean something."

"Twenty years ago, he was probably like Jonathon and wanted the business. That's why he hustled for Tremblay Bearings. You could have ordered Jonathon to meet with him. He's the one who is taking over this guy's accounts. You are his boss, aren't you? Ever heard of delegating to your staff. That's what a commander does. It's been seven weeks!"

"We could have a weekend together, one that really counts. I want Scott to take this job as much as my mother does."

"Why?"

"Connections and political influence."

"Every four years it changes and a new set of assholes get in."

"The sub levels remain. That's where the power is. I want to cultivate and maintain that."

"For what?"

"Business reasons," she said tartly. "Why are you so dense, at times? Can't you understand what I'm trying to do?" She was silent for a long time. Her breathing into the receiver told him their connection was still good. "All right," Andrea said softly. "I will come the following weekend."

When he hung up the phone he felt satisfied. The victory seemed cynical. Why did she find excuses not to come? When they were together, they couldn't keep their hands off each other. Didn't she miss that, too? He reevaluated his proposals. He did not want to miss on a single shot. Possibly they had to be layered. He would lead her up a set of steps to force a capitulation. Should he get her a ring? He had looked at them in the PX. If he did, it had to be at the top of the steps. It had to be so powerful and overwhelming she would submit to his wishes. Then, he realized, she had become the fireball Western Sales Director, and she might submit to nothing. The thought depressed him.

Faced with the prospect of listening to Blaisedale munch potato chips Saturday night, he accepted an invitation from Riard and Covington to go to Fort Worth to investigate the local bars. There were glimpses of long hair, shapely legs, and gyrating bodies. Although the scenery was a welcome relief, his heart was not with it. While Andrea rubbed elbows with the powers of Washington, his major bitter thought was that they had lost another opportunity, another potential weekend to her misguided business appetite. The missed weekends were piling up.

Sunday night the phone ringing surprised him. It was his sister, Judy.

"When do you graduate?"

"If I'm still in the program with my class, the first week in September."

"That means you'll be home the second and third Saturdays in September."

"It's possible. In the Army, you don't plan that far ahead because things can change quickly. What's going to happen on those Saturdays?"

"I'm getting married, and I want you there."

"Who else knows about this?"

"No one because I just made up my mind, now. If Ma doesn't like it, tough. She can miss the wedding."

"Faith told you about the timing before I go to Vietnam."

"Have you been calling her?"

"No."

"Writing?"

"No."

"You have Andrea. Leave her alone so she can get on with her life."

"I haven't seen Andrea since Christmas. Does that tell you how much she's in my life?"

There was a dead silence from Judy. Finally Randolph prompted her to see if she was still on the line.

"I'm not going to tell her anything about this call. Don't you either. You hurt her, and I will never forgive you. This is long distance, and I have to pay for the call. We have to hang up." Judy hung up the phone before he could answer her.

At the beginning of the following week the nightly phone conversation of the cocktail parties remained the exhilarating topic for Andrea. There were three distinct parties, which the mentor, who didn't rank sufficiently to attend, had arranged for them. An under secretary accompanied them to the three parties, two held in elegant, private palatial residences, the last in a large downtown hotel. Their focus was on the international banking which was the interest they had in Scott. Scott knew many of the attendees from his own professional associations. Andrea reported a lot of their conversations centered on the mundane about offspring and their activities. Sylvia, the new and very attractive wife, was also a major topic. Andrea heard the names of prominent foreign bankers and financial wizards from the Orient from which they gauged Scott's reactions. Scott's tidbits of personal details of many of those individuals seemed to wet their appetites even further. There were several high ranking appointees who would be Scott contemporaries. They had been unofficially urged to attend, specifically to meet and hopefully influence Scott on the seriousness of his direct participation. At one of the gatherings, the Secretary, himself, appeared briefly, staying only a half hour. His arrival was highly orchestrated since he was lead directly to Scott. Each member of Scott's family was introduced to him. Andrea told Randolph in detail the Secretary's mannerisms as well as the clothing he wore that evening.

The extended weekend had also exposed to Andrea to conditions in Scott's family. Both his younger children, Sandra and Samuel opposed the war, and did not want their father to work for the Nixon Administration, even in an area not involved with The War. Scott Junior was becoming disgruntled over his lack of expected orders for Vietnam. He still had no inkling or did Scott, that possibly Scott's vacillating was holding up the orders. Scott Junior still believed it was the Marine Corps bureaucracy. Through most of their telephone conversations Randolph listened, patiently believing they would be together at the end of the week. He still was not sure of how to mount his assault and what proposals to utilize.

His brief telephone conversation with his sister about Faith lingered in the back of his thoughts whenever there was down time from flying. He did not want to hurt Faith. Selfishly, he liked the idea that she was there.

It was not unusual Andrea did not call on Thursday night. His evening had been spent waiting for the phone to ring watching the color television with Blaisedale. Their conversations were a daily experience, but often her schedule precluded their nightly contact, which would be explained in minute detail the next evening. Sylvia and Scott remained in D.C. Andrea was still trying to influence her stepfather to take the Administration job. He did not think it made much sense for her to fly back to Massachusetts that late in the week only to be on another plane to Texas by Friday. As he dressed in his Nomex, the sun rising outside the small trailer's windows seemed clearer and fresher. They would actually be together that evening, probably at the local Holiday Inn which was in the Main Heliport's traffic pattern.

Many times, he had departed the Main Heliport with the instructor. He had studied the traffic schematic intensely. The take-off and landing pads were colored the same as the poles, which guided departing or entering traffic. All entering traffic went to an area marker labeled East or West at different altitudes, then to an outer marker where the colored poles began, and then to an approach marker. Take-offs were handled the same way with specific turns required upon reaching the outer marker. Brightly colored poles were the most efficient way to handle the hundreds of aircraft using the field.

With growing anticipation Randolph waited for his first solo flight into the Main Heliport. In their stick, Riard had been the first to get that flight. Early in the week, when they had been assigned two aircraft, he and Riard had solo flights from the Main Heliport. The outbound flight had been stimulating, as several hundred trainer helicopters departed in the short frame of time. Randolph still plotted short flights to the stage field with written compass heading on his kneeboard, although after the flight he could not remember ever looking at his kneeboard. Following the horde, and straining to keep separation from other aircraft, took all his attention outside the aircraft. By the time he had climbed to en-route altitude, he could see the stage field and had to start his descent. As the week progressed, their stick drew from the plentiful supply of aircraft allotted for this period of their training. On this Friday morning, he was not surprised when the instructor told him they would fly dual to the stage field, and he would solo the second period back the Main Heliport.

Walking casually by the rows of aircraft beside his instructor they passed a new class. There were Captains, First Lieutenants and many Second Lieutenants. Their colored hats were clean and new, and there wore no solo wings. The students all looked very attentive as their instructors gave detailed preflight lectures. Finding their aircraft, he started the preflight by opening the logbook and checking the maintenance entries. Patiently, the instructor waited for him to finish reviewing the logbook before he reviewed it. A week before the aircraft had been red-Xed, which meant its status was un-flyable. The rotors had been replaced. His attention heightened when he climbed up to inspect them. His instructor climbed up with him, pointing out the painted hash marks on the newly installed blades. Slippage marks on these paint smears could mean a loosening of the rotor mountings. Their preflight lasted forty-five leisurely minutes. Every instructor seemed to have one area of the aircraft they were particularly sensitive about. Students exchanged their own information, while they waited between flights, or rode the buses which enhanced their own safety awareness.

He started the aircraft, going through each step of the start up procedure as he did when solo, ignoring the instructor's presence. His wry comments had shrunk considerably since their first screaming sessions together. RPM 3200. Let it settle. Magnetos, switch each side off. Check the tip path plane. Randolph's eyes automatically shifted to outside as he rocked the cyclic slightly and watched the blades dip. Roll off the throttle to split the needles. To Randolph the engine always sounded like it was passing wind when he did this. Idle at 1650 to 1700. The controls were loose and free, unlike the Piper Cherokee. In the fixed-wing, the pilot could take his hands off the controls for a moment, long enough to light a cigarette or sip a cup of coffee. In these training helicopters the controls had to be manned continually. When solo if there was a need to scratch, and it was in a difficult place to reach, it itched. The pale Texas sun had warmed the bubble to a comfortable temperature, yet he had begun to sweat. As he picked up off the pad to a hover, he felt rough air, more than he anticipated. It startled both of them and, although not graceful, Randolph kept complete control of the aircraft. Carefully, he pedal turned remaining over the center of the parking space. Another OH-23 was hovering on the lane he would have to turn onto. Randolph had caught his rotor wash. It was another instructor and dual student. The instructor motioned for him to go in front of them. There were several aircraft in front of him when he reached one of the take off pads. He set the aircraft down on the tarmac while he waited. When one aircraft departed, he picked it up and moved forward, then set it down again.

Traffic jam. Just like Boston, he thought. Each aircraft went through the safety turns and then the pre take-off list. His checklist card had been bought in the PX. All students bought them. The official take off procedure was in a thick book in his flight bag. There was no place to put it on the small console. To turn the pages, the student would have had to take his hands partially off the controls. That was a definite no go. The instructors hinted the card was more efficient. The PX had an un-ending supply. The card easily jammed into a slot next to the radio on the small console.

Each pilot pulled pitch and guided the cyclic slightly forward to gain some take-off momentum to get into translational lift when hovering ended and true forward flight began. He sensed the impatience of those waiting in line to move onto the take-off pad. It was clearer how Cooper's near mid air had happened. Calmly, he waited reviewing the turns, course and altitude he needed to fly to reach the stage field. He had another plastic coated card clipped to his kneeboard with the Main Heliport's traffic pattern.

When it was his turn for take off, he remained at a hover over the pad until the aircraft that preceded him had climbed out passing two colored poles. After safety clearing turns, he pulled up on the collective hearing the change in the sound of the rotors as they cut into the air. Glancing briefly at the few mechanical instruments on the panel, his attention shifted fully to outside the cockpit with an eye on the aircraft that had taken off before him. Again as the nose dipped slightly, a rush of adrenaline shot through his body. With the added weight of the instructor, the sensation of falling over the console and out through the bubble did not occur. He finished his climb out, concentrating on the turn at the outer marker and maintaining the course climbing to the pre-assigned altitude. His instructor had no comments about his departure procedure. At his cruising altitude within a few minutes, they could see the stage field, and Randolph began mentally calculating the turns necessary to enter the traffic pattern. In the stage field pattern, he had an hour of flight time to practice take-off and landings. His instructor seemed to wait for an opportunity to snarl at some minor infraction.

After the dual flight while his aircraft was being refueled, he watched other aircraft making approaches and landings. Tediousness from the weeks of work at this stage field was becoming apparent in many of the student pilots. There was more joking and laughter in the non-flying time on the bus rides or while waiting for fuel or a stick buddy to finish his flight to free up the aircraft. After getting his aircraft for the second period, he spent the first hour in the pattern doing more take-offs and landings. With only his weight the aircraft responded quickly to his control touches. Occasionally, he would dump the nose on an approach, and then slow the aircraft when it had started to gain downward momentum. On other approaches, he slowed his descent more than required to stretch the landing time as much as possible.

As with his other solo flights, he had written departure headings and altitudes to the Main Heliport on his kneeboard. The flying time from the stage field again was minimal. Still, he had calculated the time on his hand held flight computer. When he finally departed from the stage field pattern, a new sense of exhilaration surged through him. Getting closer to being with Andrea was part of the elation. That very night he would actually touch her flesh. Unlike her visits to Benning, she had given him no flight times of her departure from D.C. Their last, long conversation two days before had still centered on the cocktail parties, and Scott's reluctance to give in to Sylvia and accept the position.

Straining to see the Main Heliport, within the few allotted minutes of straight and level flight, he could see it plainly in the hazy distance. There were aircraft in his sector and some very close to him also going in the same direction. Quite suddenly, there were dozens of aircraft heading for the traffic entry outer markers. Plainly, he could see daisy chains, little strings of aircraft forming informal lines, heading toward him and the traffic entry. He began to gauge his spacing. Suddenly, he was very busy sorting out aircraft that seemed to materialize from nowhere. Panic shot through him. He did not want to cut anyone off, so he slowed his airspeed, but other aircraft cut in front of him. The outer marker panel was coming up fast. Seeing a spot, he manhandled the controls to insure taking it, finally ignoring all other aircraft around him. As he passed over the panel, heading for the inner marker the daisy chain of aircraft had compacted as they entered the downwind portion of the landing pattern. There were dozens of aircraft ahead of him. He sighted the Holiday Inn, which was a reference point in turning crosswind. Andrea could be there waiting for him which caused another shot of adrenaline to course through his body. Straining, he tried to pick out the familiar dark green, emblem sign he knew was in front of the motel. Suddenly, he realized he had drifted left out of the line of aircraft flying the downwind pattern.

There was a solid line of aircraft to his right. He could not see behind, so he was afraid to turn right fearing getting too close to another aircraft. He estimated where he would have to return to the daisy chain, spotting a slight opening interval between two aircraft. He pushed the hose over slightly increasing his air speed to insure he could slide into it. When he completed his turn, he was back in the line of traffic. Briefly, he wondered how badly he had cut someone off, but realized he had no other choice to get back into the line. Going down over the colored poles, he terminated on the landing pad and quickly hovered off finding an empty parking spot. Being in the wrong place had sent chills up his back and caused his hands to sweat in his gloves. As he finished the shutdown checklist, his heart returned to its normal pace. Walking around doing his post flight calmed him further. By the time he reached the classroom, he felt normal.

The summons came from his instructor, and he was ushered into the sanctity of their private meeting room. There, his instructor solemnly handed him the notice of a safety violation, a pink slip. An instructor from another flight had seen him inside the assigned ground track on the downwind leg and recorded his tail numbers.

On the short bus ride though the post to the company area, it registered slowly. Everything seemed to have slowed. Details of winter leafless trees created stark images in his mind. At the last formation, his name was called to report to the orderly room. His classmates eyed him sympathetically. He was not the first one to get a pink slip. Since the student detachment Captain as usual had held the formation, Randolph assumed the cadre company commander had summoned him.

A Lieutenant Colonel has had a go at me, Randolph thought as he headed slowly toward the orderly room. His helmet bag flopped casually against his thigh. Being chewed out by a Captain did not seem as ponderous. It was not a summons from the unit commander. In the orderly room a SP4 clerk handed him a slip of paper, which had a scribbled, unofficial note. His fiancée, Andrea Tremblay had cancelled her flight to Texas due to an invitation for a private tour of the White House.

"Is that the actual White House, she's going to?" The clerk's eyes expressed his curiosity.

"No," Randolph said sourly. "Her grandmother's house is painted white. Naturally, they call it the White House. The old lady-or some lady-must be sick!"

Chapter Eight

"You coming with us?" It was Riard. His invitation to go bar hopping in Fort Worth had been extended during the morning ground class when he learned Andrea had cancelled her trip. "Did you ask Blaisedale?" With Randolph's inclusion into the group, Riard's excitement about the abundance of women and potential prospects from the previous weekend's foray had been a major conversational topic all week. Mineral Wells was in a dry county. There were no rows of bars and strip joints outside the Fort Wolters gates, as there were with many other Army posts. Riard was seeking to enlarge the number of potential drivers, who had to be sober enough to drive on the return trip.

"Hell yes, I'll go. I like the way these Texas women talk on the television. The only problem is they're not talking to me." There were clubs on the post catering to each military group, enlisted, NCO and officers. In the first weeks of the course, his stick buddies Riard and Covington had found and explored the on-post possibilities. With a few others, a group that constantly changed, they had started the Saturday night trek to Fort Worth. Without enthusiasm Randolph climbed into the cramped back seat of Riard's Mustang. There was a repeat of loud music, dance floors and various colored lighting schemes, which he had seen the previous weekend. The locals ranged from blue collar to young professionals. If there were college students among them, they blended. The women favored long hair and mini skirts. After weeks of Andrea's enforced deprivation, the chance again to see thighs, legs and long hair created welcome images in Randolph's dormant memory.

They spent no more than half an hour in each place gauging the prospects. They met other groups from Fort Wolters which stayed in informal formations. When ready, like a flock of birds, they departed seeking better possibilities at the next watering hole. In each new place there was more elbowing at the bar to order drinks, while a quick reconnaissance of new faces and possible targets was hastily tabulated. There was much gesturing and talk among the student military aviators. Success was varied. Mostly, they observed from distances and verbalized about the splendor of the females. The bolder among them plunged onto the dance floor and were rewarded, usually very briefly, with wild gyrations and contortions. Intermingling however was brief. Generally the women tended to return to their own groups. Short haired young military officers stood out like rotating beacons.

After the fourth or fifth club Randolph was mildly inebriated. Riard was relatively sober since he was driving his car. Covington was flagrantly drunk, but could still stand on his own. Blaisedale looked sober, although he finished every drink in each bar. He spoke infrequently, but his eagle, future law-enforcement eyes dug out every potential target. A minor amount of dancing seemed to be their only success. He remembered waking when they stopped at his trailer, and he and Blaisedale climbed out of the Mustang.

Sunday morning the phone woke him. Blaisedale did not even stir. Randolph's head pounded as he got out of bed.

"I tried calling you last night." Andrea said.

"Had a mission."

"What do you mean, a mission?" he felt the sarcasm in her voice.

"To find loud music, strobe lights, and activity to break up the terror and loneliness of flight school."

Andrea was silent.

"I learned last night there are people with long hair and short skirts. I remember one particular girl who used to look like that. I hear she sells ball bearings."

"Did you dance?"

"Yes," he lied. "It was all fast music. No rubbing bodies together. I used to remember what that was like, but that's just a memory, too. How was the White House?"

"Impressive!" She exhaled audibly. "This was a last ditch attempt to influence Scott. Scott Jr. got his orders. He'll be in Vietnam by April. That shook up Scott. I don't think he's going to take the position. If Scott refuses the job, it could screw up the surprise I was working on for you, getting you into the diplomatic corps."

"I'm struggling to become an Army aviator. What makes you think I want to struggle to get into another Army program?"

"There are military attaches in every country. All you need to be is a Captain. You'll be that in eighteen months. Without Scott in the Administration, that's going to be difficult to arrange. You could continue to fly. That would be looked upon as an asset in being a military attaché. We could pick out almost any country in the world. I want a European country, because in about two years I want to start expanding sales in Europe. By then the new alloy bearings should have taken hold in this country. It will be time for Europe."

Randolph was silent. His head still hurt.

"I had to support Scott and go on that tour. It was The White House. How many people get the private tour?"

"Maybe as many as tour Mineral Wells. They also have a Holiday Inn, which I haven't seen the inside of."

"There is another important reason I couldn't get down there this weekend. A candidate Scott recommended lives in Pennsylvania. I called her, and she drove down Saturday for an interview. Sam is a hell of a person."

"Sam is a she?"

"Samantha Brown is my new trade show coordinator. I'm at her apartment in Pennsylvania. She's a single mother. I drove up from D. C. last night after the tour and spent the night. We stayed up half the night talking. She's got wonderful ideas that will really help put some 'umph' into our shows. We're going to meet her ten year old son today. He's in a private school here."

Again Randolph refused to answer and remained quiet. He could feel the blood pumping in his head from last night's alcohol.

"You don't turn down the White House. There was just the three of us, my mother, Scott and me. Scott's younger children should have been there to go on the tour for their father. They are so against the war, they refused. Scott's really bummed out about Scott Jr's orders."

Anger and resentment bubbled inside him. He said nothing.

"I'll be there next weekend. I had to do this. The White House!"

"And business as usual. Good night!" He hung up the phone cutting off any response.

"He's pissed at me." Andrea still held the phone as Samantha Brown rejoined her in the modest living room. Samantha's ex-husband was an active duty Army sergeant currently serving somewhere in Southeast Asia.

"It was the White House tour, not you." Andrea said in a mellow tone. "I was supposed to be in Texas with him this weekend."

"Soldiers are always pissed at something," Sam said cautiously. She felt a little light-headed from being up most of the night engaged in stimulating discussion with her new boss. Already, she had decided to move to Massachusetts, and was wondering how she could move her son from the private school he attended. The money was to be better than she had earned before. This new job presented many interesting opportunities. This young woman, her boss, seemed concerned and pleasant.

"I need to be in Texas next weekend."

"Then go." Sam said in a mellow tone.

Monday, Randolph rode the bus out to the stage field. He had passed the forty-five hour mark and had only one flight period scheduled. Covington was solo from the Main Heliport with their stick's second aircraft. Riard was dual with the instructor from the Main Heliport. Randolph was to have their aircraft, and Riard was to take over Covington's for his second flight period. There was a subdued feeling of anticipation among all the students. The expectant look was in all faces and eyes. This was check ride week, another opportunity for each student to demonstrate his prowess or face expulsion. There were no check pilots at the stage field. Anxiety replaced by forestalled relief made the day a normal training period.

The next day the first indication the check ride evaluators had arrived at the stage field was the unusual number of civilian autos parked near the hut. Most were CW2s with Vietnam tours, hundreds of hours of flight time, and exposure to the Army's methods of instruction that specialized in how to evaluate students. Flight Eval Instructor pilots were a social class onto themselves and had no other function than giving check rides to students and other military rated and instructor pilots. The civilian instructors were safe from them having only to deal with their employer and the Federal Aviation Administration, which issued their licenses and ratings.

The IPs stayed together in one part of the hut, smoking and talking. Their leader had a star over his wings indicating his rating as a Senior Aviator, a rarity especially for a Captain. He introduced himself to the student flight leader. With proper military protocol the Colonels were introduced separately. With the exception of their school badges and Army wings, the evaluators could have been another class of students. They were the same age. Their faces, however, separated them. They had lines of expression and experience missing from the faces of the students.

A few selected students along with the Colonels got the first rides. The Transportation First Lieutenant with the hours of civilian flight time and the natural Second Lieutenant of Armor were among these. No one from Randolph's stick was in that group. There were more solo and dual flights, while the check rides were in progress. High on time, Randolph drew a second period dual, which meant he would practice landings and takeoffs at the stage field before bringing the aircraft back to the Main Heliport. Outside in the cool February sunshine Randolph preceded his instructor to preflight. As he stood near the aircraft while the refueling was finishing, one of the Colonels joined him. With formality Randolph saluted, since they were outside. Nonchalantly, the Colonel returned his salute. Affably, he started talking about the next phase of training, Primary II, and how much more interesting it was going to be. They were to do more practical navigation to out-lying areas, and land in natural settings, among trees, hills, other special terrain features and cows. The last subject made the Colonel chuckle. Randolph listened to the breezy chatter, commented on a few things with correct military etiquette but was still stunned with the pre check-flight fright. The Colonel did not seem tense or even worried about his impending check ride. His casual attitude indicated the flight was to be like any other. His check pilot was to be the evaluator detachment commander, the Captain with the Senior Aviator wings.

The era of instructor yelling in the cockpit seemed to be in the past. Randolph knew as did the other students, the civilian instructors could not afford having too many of their students flunk. The FAA would easily yank a rating which was the basis for their employment. In particular, his instructor scrutinized Randolph's execution of the simulated engine failure. Twice, he instituted the maneuver at the stage field, and once on the short flight to the Main Heliport. Everyone given a check ride on first day passed. Morale and hope for the balance of the students was raised to an optimistic level.

That night Andrea called from her apartment. "Scott has turned down the job."

"That means your potential influence has failed the power recovery."

"My mother is really bummed out. She really wanted to move to D.C. and get into that social scene. Scott's taking her to the Caribbean for a week to cheer her up. The diplomatic thing is going to be difficult. Scott still has contacts, but he bashed our best chances. The mentor said he would try to stay in touch."

"He just auto rotated out of your sight." Surprisingly, Randolph felt some degree of relief with this news.

"If Scott had taken the job it would only be for a few years. Nixon will never win reelection in seventy-two. Scott told the Secretary, he would offer his advice on specific areas concerning China and its banking industry. They won't trust him if he's not part of the Administration. They were stupid enough not to realize the one thing he really wanted was keeping Scott Jr. out of Vietnam. Now, it becomes very difficult for us. All the vibes were there to line up a very good Army job for you."

"I have an Army job. You'll be happy to know my three years could be starting this week."

"What's that mean?"

"This is check ride week. I flunk, I wear the crossed rifles. I could be in Nam in a couple of months instead of eight."

"Why is taking a check ride difficult? They're only measuring what you know. That's what Sam says."

"If you had been here in Texas just once in the past two months, you wouldn't be asking that stupid question."

She did not answer and fell silent for a moment. He had decided to give up asking when she would come to Texas, wondering when she would offer.

"Leland Jr. has got contractors lined up already. He's the new golden boy of Tremblay Bearings. Since my father announced the expansion of the plant, they say he's been working twelve hour days. The new machinery for the alloy stuff is going to be put on order the third week in March. That's two weeks after the stock offering. Even Scott thinks that's pushing it. The money could come from Europe. I've been told that's how to avoid Federal intrusion into your business. Tremblay Bearings is known in Europe. There's going to be a strong market for the new alloy bearings. My father is being mysterious about wherever it is. Sam's here with me now. We ditched my rental and I drove up with her. My couch in my office is a fold-out bed. It didn't make sense for her to stay in a hotel. Sam thinks Scott might change his mind after a week in the Caribbean with my mother. She can be persuasive when she has something in mind, and she definitely wants to go to D.C."

"You think Scott will mellow over the Captain's orders?"

"Sam thinks that also. He was determined to go, and nothing his father could do really would have prevented it."

"You two seem to find a lot to talk about."

"We're finding we have a lot in common. We both have strong feelings about the Army. She's on her way to Atlanta. We have a show coming up in a few months, and she wants to do some scouting. Sunday, when I leave you, I'm going to California. Jonathon says he's getting hit with a lot of interference. There's still a lot to do out there."

Long after he had hung up from her call, he was staring at the phone. He had apprehension, not from the possibility of seeing Andrea in a few days, but of what he had finally voiced to someone about the upcoming check ride. She still did not know or really care about what he was going through. There had to be someone. Faith. Although there was an over powering sensation that surged through his body as he thought about her, something held him back. She was the right one to call to be his sounding board for his unsure thoughts. She would understand. What prevented him? He had not answered her long letter that must have taken her some time to compose. That was rude. He was not sure he would have answered it, since his sister did not want to encourage her.

He returned the receiver of the phone and did nothing.

When Andrea hung up the phone, she remained seated on the couch. Her face was pensive. Samantha opened the door of the office bedroom where she had retreated during the call to Randolph. She studied Andrea's foreboding expression.

"Let's open that bottle of white wine I saw in the kitchen." Quietly, she disappeared, returning with two filled glasses. Andrea accepted hers, but did not sip nor even look around. She held the glass over her lap. Silently, Sam studied her pensive face further awaiting a suitable opening but her face remained stony.

"Before my ex made sergeant, and right after my son was born we needed money, so I started having Tupperware parties." Impatiently, Samantha had waited as long as her impulsiveness allowed. "You never asked me about my early background during my interview, but that's where I learned sales. Some months I did better than my husband's Army pay. Then, I started selling cosmetics. It was a natural for southern women. I learned to give them what they craved."

"Scott's resume gave me every company you ever worked for," Andrea said coldly. She started to come out of her reflecting stupor. "Plus contacts to call. I did." She forced a smile and faced her. The impenetrable mask dissolved from her face. She sipped her wine for the first time. "I called the three industrial ones. One even wanted to know if you would consider coming back to work for them. You wouldn't have got my job if all you ever sold was home products."

Samantha sipped her wine. She was beginning to see the different facets of Andrea's personality and was still confident of having made the right move.

"I like you, Sam." Andrea had seen the reflective expression. "You are what Tremblay Bearings needs for trade shows. What really impressed me at our first meeting was your ability to cut through all the crap and get to the point. When you meet Jonathon, you'll see he's like that, too."

Sam's expression relaxed slightly. Drawing on Andrea's compliment, she used the salesman tenacity to push into uncharted territory. Samantha was a risk taker. "What did he say that's got you upset?"

"It's his mood because of the damn flying. I need to make him more concerned with Tremblay Bearings. The Army will never do him any good."

"If he becomes a professional, like your stepfather's son or my ex., you will never get him away from it. It does something to their brains. They're what the insiders call lifers. Do you want him out of that uniform?"

"I don't want him to go to Vietnam."

"With a future with Tremblay Bearings, you can offer him a lot more."

"If he was as perceptive as you, I wouldn't be having this problem."

"He's a man. You can wave good things in front of their noses, and they'll refuse to see them."

"If he flunks his checkride this week, that might be good. He's Infantry and knows what that means. He doesn't want to go as a grunt. That might make him change his mind about Vietnam."

Samantha paused a moment as she studied Andrea's reflective gaze. To gain time, she sipped her wine. She was very aware of plunging into a hole filled with double-edged daggers. "The true lifers are all grunts." She said cautiously.

"He wanted to be a soldier. There's been problems which I helped him out of with Scott's influence. "Now it's this checkride thing. What makes them persist with something that continues to make their lives stressful?"

Samantha sensed another opening and without caution decided to take it. "My ex before he made sergeant was a good husband. Then we had my son. I had to be wife and mother. As he got more stripes he was less interested in wife and forgot about being a father. Pretty soon there wasn't enough room in our bed for wife and mother duties. The Army pushed everything out of our bed, so I made it official with a divorce. Mix with a soldier, and you have that possibility. The best thing you've got going is your stepfather–if he would take the job with the Nixon Administration."

"My mother certainly wants it."

"That was very obvious when I met her over the weekend. Scott seems to be doing everything within his power to satisfy her. I wouldn't be surprised if he reverses his decision."

"It didn't keep Scott Jr. from going back to Vietnam. Scott wouldn't have approached any one directly. They must have known how he felt."

"They are starting to bring troops home. On my ex's first tour in '63, things weren't as bad. I survived that year. When he went back in '66, there was a lot of combat. I got put through it again, only it was a lot worse. I was still living on an Army post and was with a lot of women who lost their men. It was always ugly. Then he went back again in '68. Basically he hasn't been back since."

"His main interest is flying. I've tried to maneuver jobs in the Army that would allow him to continue that. Without Scott in the Administration, it's going to be useless."

"I wouldn't give up on your mother's ambitions."

"I'm just as concerned he ignores the fact Leland Jr. might be eclipsing me."

"You are doing the right things for the company. Leland is just an errand boy, getting things delivered for you. Your father is the company. Everyone does what he dictates. What you're doing has foresight." Samantha sipped her wine. She felt confident she was trotting on the right path.

Wednesday morning when they met their instructor at the Main Heliport, Randolph was informed his ride would be that day. His stick buddies had not been scheduled. Covington, who was lowest on time, drew the ride out to the stage field with the instructor, and then had a solo period. Randolph and Riard rode the bus. Riard was solo the second flying period. When their instructor arrived from the stage field flight line, Randolph was ushered into the presence of one of the check pilots, a CW2. He was about Randolph's age, slightly shorter. On his Nomex uniform, he wore a First Aviation Brigade patch on his right shoulder and a school patch on the left. Formally, he shook Randolph's hand. They went to a table and sat opposite each other.

Looking at Randolph's face impassively, he covered all the safety procedures he expected to be used, passing of controls with both visual and audio confirmation and detailed all the maneuvers to be judged during the ride including the simulated engine failure. The IP used checklist notes from the evaluation form, leaving nothing to memory. That part of the briefing in his monotone voice sounded almost like a recording.

"You will recover the aircraft to powered flight upon my command. The flight will not exceed one period. I will debrief you after the ride at this table. Do you have any questions?"

Randolph did not have any questions.

"You can begin your pre flight as soon as the aircraft is refueled." The CW2 Eval instructor slide the logbook across the table to Randolph. "The pre flight will not be evaluated."

The air outside the stage field hut was as cool as usual but surprisingly did not sting Randolph's face. He conducted his usual thorough pre-flight slowing his pace and looking at everything completely. When the evaluator walked out of the stage field hut, again his face was expressionless. He carried a helmet without a bag and his kneeboard. Ignoring Randolph's pre-flight, he conducted his own, without using the regulation logbook or even a PX card. His examination of the aircraft lasted only a few minutes. It included all the vital areas and was done with a veteran's confidence. As they strapped in, Randolph noticed his name and rank written on the evaluation form on the kneeboard. He felt calm. When he had finished buckling his shoulder harness, he sat still.

"Start her up." The IP finally said. Randolph had decided to do nothing unless directed. The IP began writing notes on the evaluation form, although all they had done was strap in. Suddenly Randolph realized this pilot could be the only other person he would fly with. This man held that power over his future. A sudden chill shot up and down his spine. Then, his mind dived into the startup checklist. When the rotors and engine were running smoothly, and after reciting the pre-takeoff procedure and safety checks, he lifted to a hover, and was relieved the aircraft reacted the same. At least he's not a lard ass, Randolph thought and smiled. The evaluator did not notice. He continued to speak in monotones and made no attempt at any other conversation. Any communication was to clear the aircraft and issue commands for each maneuver.

On the stage field they did normal, steep, and max performance takeoffs. His turns and climbs in the pattern were smooth and coordinated. His handling of the controls was positive. The aircraft went where he directed it, and he kept his mind and attention ahead of his flight path. On each down wind leg of the pattern, his left fist on the throttle squeezed slightly in anticipation of the tug that would announce the simulated engine failure. In three circuits of the field, it did not come. Dutifully, Randolph recited the pre-landing checks and announced which lane he was going to for each approach.

Calmly, the evaluator wrote on the form on his kneeboard during each maneuver. He even wrote while on some of the downwind sections of the pattern, which gave Randolph an added indication he was not going to split the needles for the simulated engine failure. Then, quite suddenly after he had instructed a normal take-off, he took the controls, and they left the pattern. Glancing down at the radio control head Randolph noticed all his receiver switches were off. He had not heard the radio conversation for the departure from the stage field. He could hear the Eval pilot's faint conversation above the noise in the cockpit as he continued to talk to the tower. A short distance from the stage field, he was directed to take the controls back. They went through a series of climbs, turns, straight and level flight, and then Randolph was directed to turn over the controls again and look at the floor of the cockpit as the Eval pilot set up the unusual attitude maneuver. Randolph could feel exactly how he set up the maneuver, getting out of trim using the tail rotor petals and pushing the cyclic in the opposite direction. Randolph's recovery was quick, positive and smooth. His receiver switches were turned back on and the evaluator directed him to reenter traffic. Seeing where he was, he planned his reentry, then called the tower for permission.

As they entered the pattern, the evaluator ordered him to make a normal approach and then a take-off. As he turned onto the down wind leg, Randolph was again slightly squeezing the throttle. The evaluator pilot did not have his pen out to write on his kneeboard. The yank on the throttle over rode Randolph's slight squeezing pressure. Suddenly it was very quiet. It startled him. When his instructor rolled down the throttle, there was always some engine noise. His response was automatic after nearly six weeks. He began the turn, added right pedal. The nose had dropped so quickly and uncharacteristically he had to give it a little aft cyclic. His turns were rough. He manhandled the controls using pedal and cyclic to complete the turn. The aircraft felt completely different without the usual couple of hundred RPM his instructor had always left. The one hundred eighty degree turn, which should have been smooth and coordinated, resembled a horseshoe. The power recovery was also different. Being accustomed to the throttle in a certain power setting, it required only a certain distance to move it back to get the required engine and rotor needles comfortably back together. This time they fell short of the required operating RPM. Randolph realized it just as the check pilot rolled on more throttle. As the needles started through the red arch on the instrument, he was beginning to pull up on the collective when the evaluator overrode him there also keeping rotor RPM in the green operating arch. The only consolation Randolph felt in the ragged maneuver was they were at the same recovery altitude as normal, but further outside the traffic pattern than usual. Forcefully, Randolph completed the power recovery overriding the check pilot's guiding hands.

"Power recovery. Execute a go-around."

Randolph said nothing, but swallowed hard. Although he had started the power recovery, it was the normal command at this part of the maneuver. He began pulling power, slowly and smoothly and beginning a climb. With power from the engine back to its usual setting, the aircraft responded to his control movements, normally, gaining altitude smoothly. They reentered the traffic pattern and landed. The evaluator's last command was to hover to a parking spot. After they had shut down the aircraft, the CW2 quickly got out and told him to meet him in field house after completing the post flight.

Randolph climbed out of the aircraft at the same time as the Eval pilot. He walked slowly toward the building, carrying his helmet and kneeboard in one hand, wiping his hair and forehead with the other. Momentarily, there was hollowness in Randolph's chest. He started the post-flight perfunctorily, but then decided not to finish it. The check pilot as the pilot-in-charge had to sign off the post flight in the logbook. Students only signed them on solo flights. In the stage field hut, the students who were not flying studied Randolph's face, which was still expressionless. Another student at a table at the other end of the building was being debriefed on his flight.

Sitting opposite the CW2 Eval pilot, his head was inclined forward and Randolph could still see some sweat on his forehead. Quickly, he looked up and began the debriefing in the same sing-song audio tape monologue voice, starting with his start-up and safety procedures. He told Randolph he had observed him taking-off the rotor tie down and rotating the blades 90 degrees from the tail. That comment struck Randolph as comical. How else could you start up the aircraft, and it was in the pre-take off checklist, which he used, line-by-line. Randolph did not smile. All his maneuvers were satisfactory. Some received praise. He started to relax. The check pilot's voice became a soothing hum, which lulled him.

"But," his tone struck him like a punch. "I can't pass you. Your turn on the simulated engine failure was very uneven. I had to almost completely override you on the controls during the power recovery."

"That was the first time I've had the throttle rolled completely off." Randolph was suddenly exasperated.

"It was a simulated engine failure. You don't have any power when that happens."

"The aircraft reacted differently. That's why I had to add collective for the recovery. I felt you there too, but I added it!"

"I'm sorry. I still can't pass you on that maneuver. Everything else was satisfactory."

Randolph's face fell. Everyone in the stage field hut knew it immediately.

The CW2 stood up, pushing his chair back slightly, which screeched hollowly against the floor, and joined some of the other flight evaluation pilots who had gathered at one corner of the room. There was a lot of low mumbling. Stunned, Randolph still sat where he had received the briefing. The student flight leader, their senior Captain, approached his table.

Randolph looked up at his face. "He chopped the throttle entirely. That was the first time I've had that happen. It wasn't taught to me that way."

The Captain looked sympathetic, but said nothing.

"Do I get a make-up ride? I got the fucking thing around on the turn! It was sloppy, but I did it! Even he said I did it." Randolph looked over at the evaluation pilots. Some of them returned his look, stonily.

"I'll find out for you." The class leader said softly. "Take it easy, Lieutenant."

It was a long ride from the stage field back to the Main Heliport, then to the company area. During the last formation, Randolph was numb in body and mind. He fell in, came to attention, but heard very little. On his way home, he stopped at the class six store and bought a fifth of scotch.

Blaisedale's hand was poised to take another potato chip from the translucent, plastic bag when Randolph opened the door to the trailer. Sounds of the television separated their stare. Blaisedale's check ride had been taken after his. He had passed. Randolph walked to the sink, setting the bottle of scotch on the counter. Deliberately, he took it out of the paper bag, and then twisted the cork top off. The aroma of the whiskey assailed the scent glands in his nose, making him squint. Opening the cabinet, he took a glass and placed it on the counter next to the bottle.

"You may get another ride," Blaisedale said in a soothing tone. "Better stay sober, at least until Friday night."

Randolph stood looking out the small window above the kitchen sink peering into the dwindling light. The dimness mirrored his feelings. Without a word to his roommate, he went out the door, shutting it firmly behind him. Behind the trailer was an open field, which he had never explored. With the lengthening days of the coming spring, there was still twilight. Pulling his flight jacket tighter over his Nomex uniform he walked through the field. His boots crinkled the dead tall grass. At the other end of the field was a dirt road, which stretched through the flat landscape. There was nothing to see in the approaching darkness except the open Texas fields with occasional houses or farm buildings in the distance.

Even if it was snowing in Massachusetts, he would have gone to the rock by the lake. Nothing in his life like this had ever shaken him, as it had, and as he felt now. The Colonels passed. Those Flight Eval wonders would not have the balls to flunk a full Colonel. How would they explain that? Not very good career enhancement. That Captain with the star over his wings knew the right moves. A nothing Second Lieutenant was just that, a big nothing. They could flunk. They could be part of the failure statistics without detrimental side effects. When the Army says reduce the numbers, it is done. With half the rides given, only he, the lowly Lieutenant Thayer had flunked.

It was still early evening when he found his way back to the trailer. Leaving a light in the kitchen Blaisedale had shut off the color television and retired. The walking had tired but not fatigued him. He was still very much awake. Without taking off anything, he laid on his bed. His flight jacket warmed him comfortably, so he did not take if off. He looked at his boots covered with some dried Texas dirt. *The only thing I'll be using out of this place.* They were shined but would never have passed an ROTC inspection. Mud. He would get to fight the war with muddy boots. He would see plants, insects, mildew, reptiles, and other strange animals, up close. Barely, he would know what was going on except for the several feet in front of him. Lieutenant of grunts. He had the job, now. Rolled the throttle completely off. Never heard the engine that quiet. Was there any hesitation in the maneuver? Maybe the lack of engine noise sound had made him hesitate. He fought the aircraft, making it turn into the wind. The needles wouldn't joint as they usually did, since there was lower RPM. He should have cranked on that throttle a little more. Maybe that would have meant the difference.

How would Andrea react? When he had learned to fly while at Northeastern, they already had parted. Flying had been the main reason he was able to get over her loss. It transplanted the emotion he had felt for her and for the breakup. It had filled him when he had been absolutely empty. All the exhilaration flight had given him never touched her. Would she try to use his dismay to sway him into some non combat job? Should he allow that? If he couldn't go as a charioteer, then would it matter if he missed it? Should he let her have her way? Then, there would be no him. One slippage would become another until there was no longer anything left of him.

Looking up at the ceiling of his trailer bedroom, it did not say anything to him. Feeling warm in the flight jacket, he got up to take it off and noticed Faith's letter on top of his bureau. Really, he was not suppose to answer it. It had been a good letter. Laying back on his bed, he reread it. Judy would be upset if he answered the letter or telephoned. She had been pissed at him many times in their lives. She would get over it. Now, he had a flying story. It was the last one. Retrieving their phone with its long cord, he settled on his bed. For a long time he just looked at the phone. He knew the

Beckwerth number. Through all their growing up, it had remained the same. He dialed. Sarah answered commenting to him that it was ten o'clock before getting Faith to the phone.

"Hi." Randolph said and waited for her response.

"What's wrong?" Her tone was clear, crisp, and concerned.

"I have a flying story for you. You said in your letter I should save them for you. I'm through. It's over. I busted a check ride."

"Tell me what happened."

For the next better part of an hour, he told her the details of the ride as she often interrupted him to ask short, quick questions to clarify his narrative.

"Doesn't it have to be reviewed?"

"It's a go or no go. I was a no go."

"You need to go higher up in your chain of command."

"The student flight leader said he would find out about another ride. No one has had a second ride."

"Then a decision hasn't been made. There's still hope. I believe it. You must too."

"I'm going to be a grunt."

"You're going to be a helicopter pilot. We need someone with knowledge of how the Army bureaucracy works. You told me, they teach you pilots no matter how bad it looks, you don't give up. Even when disaster is coming up fast. Give up and you have no chance."

"Did I tell you that?"

"Yes! You know it is true. Pilots don't give up."

"Right to the end?"

"You're not there, yet. The way you explained it, you weren't tested as you were taught. That has to be grounds for an appeal. I hear that all the time at my office. Lawyers grab onto anything they think they can use."

"No such thing in the Army."

"It's past midnight. I have to go to work tomorrow. You call me as soon as you know. Promise me that. I won't sleep much the next couple of days if you don't."

"I promise, Faith."

After he had hung up, the trailer fell into its deathly middle of the night silence. His thoughts drifted to how the aircraft would react and his movements on the controls. Of course the aircraft would act differently. More pedal. Get the nose down. More turn to the power recovery. Perhaps a little sooner. Goose that throttle. Risk an over speed. No one was going to accuse him of not reacting, if they gave him another chance.

After the morning first formation, the class leader told him his status had not changed. He had failed to pass the check ride. However, the cadre flight commander was going to Flight Evaluation that morning. Randolph's explanation of having the throttle rolled completely off by the instructor pilot differed from the method of instruction presented by the civilian contact instructors. It offered only a slight glimpse of hope, the class leaders said. No re-take had been scheduled for that day. Still, as an unclear part of the class, he rode the bus from the Main Heliport. Riard was to have his ride and flew with the instructor to the stage field, where they terminated the flight and turned the aircraft over to the evaluation pilot. At the stage field, their instructor ignored him. Their stick drew only a single aircraft. Covington had it solo, the second period. Riard passed his ride. Covington still had his, which meant he would go on Friday, the last day of Primary One. During the long afternoon, more briefings and debriefings at the tables meant more students had taken the check rides. Two others failed, creating awkward company for Randolph. The Eval pilot, who had given him his ride, was not at the stage field with the others from his detachment. It was an extremely long day for Randolph. He avoided everyone as much as possible and smoked a full package of cigarettes. The sight and sounds of the helicopters in their numbers coming into the Main Heliport sent a longing that lingered in every part of his body. After evening formation, he hurried to the orderly room. The commander was not there. There was no new information about him.

At his trailer Blaisedale arrived after him with a fast food hamburger. The aroma of the meat and fries made Randolph's stomach rumble. As usual, Blaisedale turned on his color television. Randolph made a peanut butter and jelly sandwich to alleviate his grumbling stomach. When the phone rang, Randolph briefly wanted to avoid it thinking it must be Andrea since they had not talked since before the check ride. When Randolph remained seated ignoring the ringing, Blaisedale looked at him sharply a sour expression on his face. He never got calls. Reluctantly Randolph got out of the easy chair to pick up the phone. It was Grandmother Willis.

"Faith told me you have some questions about Army bureaucracy. Having lived by it for over thirty years I do have some experience with it."

Randolph stumbled into his bedroom pulling the long cord behind him. As usual his grandmother was positive and concise. "Who else has Faith been talking to?"

"Wait, I'll ask her." After a moment of silence she came back on the line. "No one, just me."

"What do you think a Roman Legionnaire felt like when he flunked the chariot course and knew he was going to be returned to the sword-carriers?"

"Your grandfather loved the Artillery. In the few assignments away from it, he always strove to get back to it. Have they notified you, officially?"

"They said I failed my check ride."

"You are still with your class?"

"They called my name at formation, and I went out to the stage field on the bus."

"Some higher up is making the decision. That takes a little time. Army decisions always take a lot of time. Was there a technical question raised?"

"One of the maneuvers, the engine failure, wasn't the way I was taught."

"Faith explained that. That goes in your favor, too, if they're fair. There's no guarantee about fairness."

"If they won't let me do another ride tomorrow, I'm gone. They're reducing numbers. That's Army policy now."

"Your grandfather was very familiar with that type of reduction. It hit him several times for things he really wanted. You have to be resilient, Randy. Throughout your grandfather's National Guard time, we often sat and talked when things didn't go as he wanted. My interest helped him. It brought closure to decisions, which were way out of both of our hands. Faith is solid, Randy."

"Grandma, she isn't my girlfriend."

"That girl thinks an awful lot about you. You'll never find a more steadfast one than her."

"I know about Faith."

"Tell her yourself." There was a pause as the phone changed hands.

"You're still in the running. Your grandmother is right."

"Grandmothers are always right. Thanks, it has cheered me up, a little."

"You have to hang in there."

Strangely, Andrea did not call. Blaisedale had not left any notes about messages from the previous night when he had explored the dirt road and dead grass fields. At nine o'clock more in resolution than desire, he called her apartment. An answering service like the one that serviced the Lynders took his call. Very recently she must have added this service since it had not been there earlier in the week before his check ride. It gave him a reprieve. He could avoid telling her for anther night what would obviously make her happy. She must still be in Massachusetts, although he was not positive. He decided not to leave his name or telephone number. Let her wonder which call she had missed.

Friday unraveled the same as Thursday. His instructor again ignored him. On the bus to the Main Heliport, he listened to the conversations of his classmates. They were making plans for the upcoming weekend, or talking about flying. Again, as a non-person everyone ignored his presence. Covington had his ride. After it, his check pilot spent a long time with him at his debriefing. For a time, it looked as if he might flunk, making it four from their dwindling class. Finally, he got up from the table with an odd half smile on his face.

At the final formation the class leader Captain, since it was Friday, reminded everyone to sign out if they were going to Dallas, since it was beyond the fifty-mile radius. All bachelor officers, Army and Marine Corps, had been invited to attend an ROTC Ball at a local university. Dress could be informal, a business or leisure suit. Tickets had been put in the mail boxes of those eligible. There were some catcalls from the married officers, who supposedly felt left out.

"Flight detachment commander will address the formation. Class, attention." The student flight leader Captain saluted the cadre Captain, who came to the front of the formation.

"Stand at ease." He looked at the formation a moment in silence. "Training is my mission. Standards should be uniform, and we do all in our power to keep them that way. However, we have no authority over the civilian contract instructors. We do, however, closely monitor their methods of training, which have to be in accordance with the Federal Aviation Administration. Regrettably, there are gaps, which we are made aware of from time to time. That happened this past week. Lieutenant Thayer, the decision on your check ride has been reevaluated. Your check ride was a go."

The formation exploded with howling, stomping, and cheering, lead by the two full Colonels, who seemed to have been waiting. Everyone shook his hand and congratulated him. Numbness overtook him, and his smile soon hurt the muscles of his face. The cadre Captain shook his hand and said something, which he completely missed he was in such a daze. The formation broke up, and the students drifted off to their cars.

It was the class leader who brought him the details. "The flight commander really chewed on them. It was the contractor's company regulation; the throttle could only be rolled down so many RPM. Your evaluator didn't know that. The other IPs did."

"I'll bet the asshole knows it now." Randolph commented. The class leader agreed.

At the trailer, he pulled the cork stopper out of the bottle of scotch. They ordered delivery pizza. As it was being delivered, Riard and Covington drove up. Each had brought a six-pack of beer.

"You had a long debriefing." Randolph said to Covington, whose face was drawn. He smiled weakly and gulped his can of beer. "Since I had nothing else to do, I know everything that happened in that stage field hut today. Only two guys failed. One of them was one of the Marines."

"It was almost three." Covington said. Carefully he set down his beer and looked at everyone. "The evaluator didn't like some of my approaches. I thought they were pretty good."

"The engine failure is the important thing." Randolph said.

"He was careful to keep the minimum RPM. What happened to you, Randy probably worked to my advantage. He over-road me a little, but said it was a sufficient execution."

The whiskey warmed him. Setting his glass on the counter Randolph excused himself and dragged the long corded phone into his bedroom. Momentarily, he was reluctant to make the call but thought he owed it to her. Faith picked up the phone.

"They reversed the decision. I didn't even have to take another check ride. They told me two hours ago. Primary-Two starts Monday. Thank you for believing in me."

"Oh Randy, that's wonderful news. I couldn't sleep and I called in sick for work." Her voice was gritty. "I'm so proud of you. I'm so ashamed of my father and Sarah. They actually marched in an anti war demonstration. I'm embarrassed. My father has changed so much since Arthur's death. For him after all these years, and all the sacrifice, the war is completely wrong. How can he change what he believed all his life? Have you been getting any mail? Are you homesick? I could write to you, if you want me to."

"This isn't World War II. We are not saving the world. We have prosperity, plenty of gas, and telephones. You can call me any time you want."

"Connie's friend Tina Michaud is pregnant. She either doesn't know or can't say who the father is. She's going home to New Jersey to have the kid. Says she's going to keep it. Maybe that made Connie straighten out and stop all that anti war crap."

"You really sound tired. Go to bed."

"Oh, I've got more news. Big news! Judy asked me to be her Maid of Honor."

"Do you qualify to be that?" He laughed.

She giggled and sounded like the teenager he remembered. "It's a wedding term. If I'm disqualified, you're the one who did it. When do you go to Alabama?"

"End of April."

"Texas to Alabama, that's a long drive." Randolph did not answer immediately. He could hear her breathing into the receiver.

"My stick buddies are here. They're helping me celebrate."

"She's a fool."

"You helped me through this thing. Now go get some sleep."

When he hung up, he stared at the wall, seeing nothing for at least a full minute, but still hearing the craggy tones of her voice. Images rushed through his mind of their growing up together, as children then as adolescents and then of that one time in her cellar playroom.

Where the hell are you, Andrea? He called her apartment. The answering service told him she was unavailable. His annoyance was tinted with a slight concern. Listening to the sounds from the common room of his stick buddies and roommate, he wanted to share his triumph. When the voice prompted him again for a telephone number, he hung up.

"At least this gets me out of the trailer." Harry Cooper smiled, ruefully. Standing outside the classroom next to Randolph, who was smoking a cigarette, they were on a ten minute break of the last Saturday ground school class. Although not flying, Harry still wore a yellow hat. "They haven't had me on any type of duty. Every time Amanda's down for a nap, we jump in the sack. I might have started another kid. Just what a grunt needs. It's set for Monday, two weeks exactly from the day."

Randolph felt a mutual bond to Cooper. They had both received persecution, unwarranted but unavoidable. He felt a deep sense of relaxation with his check ride behind him, something he knew Cooper still could not feel.

"I got a flight surgeon's recommendation. Basically he asked me if I wanted to continue flying." Cooper smiled wryly. The look on his face indicated he missed being in the cockpit.

"Instructors think they can read your mind." Randolph stated.

"If my last one could read mine, he'd get out of town." Cooper laughed sarcastically. "We've having two couples over tonight. You know the Napins. You're welcome if you want a home cooked meal."

"I'll pass but I'll be thinking of your vegetables." Their class leader, the Signal Corps Captain gestured for everyone to return to the classroom. After the class, when they had been released, Randolph stopped at the main PX for cigarettes. He began browsing the jewelry counter looking at engagement rings. He had looked before settling on the largest one in the display case. Still, it would pale in comparison to the one Betsy wore.

"Thayer, you look like a lost, tired hound dog." Todd Richner in civilian clothes smiled broadly. They shook hands. "Those solo wings look good." He indicated the wings on Randolph's yellow cap. "I gave up on the fixed wing slot. Rotary wing ones are getting tougher to get. I decided it was time to un-ass Fort Benning. Infantry was starting to hint strongly that I should start working as an infantryman. What are you flying?" His voice had that homey southern polite twang.

"Twenty-threes. Harry Cooper was one of the guys with me when we met waiting to take the physicals at Benning. He's sweating out an FEB, a near mid air. His instructor is trying to cover his own ass." Randolph told him the facts of the take-off and about the solo student. "What do you know about FEBs?"

"My brother said he's sat on one once. The Army never says, politely, we no longer require your services. They say, you can't do your job and fire you. If this had happened two years ago, he probably wouldn't even have been recycled. An FEB would have been a next day formality. It's not healthy taking two weeks. Things have certainly changed since my brother's time."

"Has he got a chance? The other aircraft almost hit them."

"I would suppose it depends on the pilots involved. Are they lifers? You know, guys that want to stay in. Was the IP civilian or military? Makes a difference what the feeling is about the civilians. If the lifers know they need to cut they'll cut. Sometimes they do it because they think they're following unwritten orders. Fairness has nothing to do with that."

At the trailer, Blaisedale was in civilian clothes, eating potato chips, and drinking soda, watching his colored television. He belched and laughed. This was the usual, Saturday afternoon ritual Randolph had watched for the past six weeks. After changing out of his Nomex, he sat but could not get interested in the program Blaisedale was watching. He eyed the phone. It was strange for this much time to pass without conversation with Andrea. Their last contact had been before his check ride on Wednesday. When the phone rang suddenly, he answered it quickly. It was Riard. His invitation to go bar hopping in Fort Worth was open ended. Randolph agreed to be the driver on this trip. Riard and Covington squeezed into his Camaro's rear seat. Blaisedale because of his size had the front passenger side.

The tension of nearly being expelled from the program created restlessness in him. Sitting in the trailer alone waiting for a phone call that might not come would relieve no stress. If he could not touch feminine skin, noise, conversation and viewing would expend a long dull Saturday night. As they neared Fort Worth, Riard and Covington's open jubilance became infectious. Even the usually staid Blaisedale joined their exuberance.

Their method of operation remained the same. They stayed in each bar while all prospects were thoroughly analyzed, then moved on. Randolph bought ginger ale in every other bar. At first, he merely observed, letting the visual and audio stimulus engulf his senses. In one dimly lit place, a girl with hair cascading halfway down her back, wearing a mini skirt and a blouse that displayed her dark under garments, approached him to dance. Without hesitation he followed her onto the dance floor and gyrated wildly following her movements. She remained with him for a second, slower dance. Wrapping his arms around her, he smelled her perfume and then her hair. This sent pleasurable but taunting sensations through his body. It was a clear signal to pursue, which he ignored and which earned him open sneering from Riard and Covington. Even Blaisedale gave him questionable looks. Riard remained the most vigorous pursuing any possible and some highly improbable targets. Covington got mildly drunk, which slowed his pace but made him more audacious. Blaisedale seemed to disappear in each place until it was time to leave. In one, almost as soon as they walked in, he sighted a lone woman sitting at the bar. She looked slightly older than many of the other women, perhaps in her late twenties. She was dressed more conservatively. Her skirt was longer. A blouse had long sleeves that covered her arms. Blaisedale remained beside her, until Riard signaled it was time to leave. He whispered to Randolph to check this place before they left, and if he was not there, he would get a bus back to Mineral Wells. That was the last they saw of him that night.

The sight of bare thighs and gyrating bodies, and the touch from the one woman he had danced with then abandoned, awakened a competitive and dark urge. Being relatively sober and to amuse himself, Randolph began to view their evening in tactical, military terms. What was their objective? Intimate sexual activity? Of course, that was not his objective. He had a woman, who happened to be in other parts of the country, continually. He had a phone link which suddenly and unexpectedly had temporarily broken. He had memories, which were receding into the nether areas of his brain. His triumph over the check ride created in him a wanton desire to share and celebrate the victory. Where was Andrea? The scent of perfume of that strange girl and the silkiness of her long hair taunted him.

Successful hunters stalked alone. These unsuccessful student aviators had one car with three or possibly a fourth temporarily AWOL passenger stuffed into it. Acquiring another body would cause more logistical concerns. All the senses were needed for the hunt. He was the only one with senses intact or at least minimal to pilot an automobile. Covington could barely walk. Riard was boisterous and nearly giggling from his alcohol consumption. He fell asleep in the passenger's seat on the way back to Mineral Wells.

Covington stretched out in the cramped rear seats and was soon snoring. Mission accomplishment meant going someplace after the bars. Militarily, they were not exploiting their government financed education. Their planning was inept and inadequate. The Army should be ashamed of these Second Lieutenants who didn't know how to plan and execute a simple pick-up-a-girl mission. Possibly Blaisedale was the only successful officer in their midst. And, he wasn't around to report on anything. Randolph was squinting at the solid white lines on the Interstate when they reached Mineral Wells.

The majority of the women in these bars remained clannish. They came to be with people they choose, not obvious Army Second Lieutenants from remote corners of the country. The overview of this tactical scenario gave his restless energy something to plot. There was the texture of that girl's hair and her slim, curvy, and firm body. Clearly, she would make a good objective for potential intimate activity. He wondered what her voice sounded like. Barely had they spoken during their brief encounter. A good military scenario could apply to closing with and capturing the attentions and anything else obtainable during the pursuit of females. It was all amusing and academic to him since he was not participating in his fellow students' hunt. The evening passed.

Chapter Nine

Mid morning Sunday Randolph was summoned by a telephone call to the bus station at Mineral Wells to retrieve the sleepy-eyed, but uncommunicative Blaisedale, who upon arrival at the trailer immediately went into his room closing his door firmly. The squeaking of the springs indicted he had settled in his bed. Briefly, he wondered what sort of adventure his reticent roommate had encountered. Then, quiet except for occasional gusts of wind that struck and caressed the metal skin of the trailer, enveloped him.

Randolph made instant coffee, and then sat next to the telephone and stared at its' shinny black plastic. The slight pressure he had applied to the mysterious, long haired girl's back floated into his memory, as they had danced slowly to the second song the band had played. His stare shifted to his hand, open palmed. He picked up the phone. A voice identifying herself as the answering service was interrupted by another female tone. "I've got it." The second woman said, and the first voice left the connection.

"Where is Andrea?" His concern quickly swelled into apprehension.

"You're Randy? We've been trying to reach you. Your orderly room didn't contact you?"

"We were dismissed Saturday morning from a class site. No one went back to the company area."

"They should have telephoned you. My message was pretty explicit. Sounds like the Army to screw things up."

"Who are you?"

"Samantha Brown."

"You're the one Andrea just hired?"

"She is in great need of help. If you had heard the desperation in her voice, I couldn't ignore her. I drove home to Pennsylvania Friday morning. When she called me, I got back in my car and drove back up here. You can't be here, being in the Army."

"Where is Andrea?"

"She's sleeping."

"Could you wake her up? I haven't talked to her since early in the week!"

"She hasn't slept in forty-eight hours. Her father had a heart attack Friday, and she's been at the hospital since then. I checked on her ten minutes ago. She's out cold. I'm not waking her up."

"Frederic?"

"A major one. Was this a second attack?"

"He had one over a year ago."

"At the hospital no one would come out and say that directly, but I assumed from listening to everyone that was the case. They wanted to move him to Mass General. It got quite confusing. The vice-presidents—I mean Andrea's uncles-thought he should be moved. Since her mother divorced him, his closest relative is Andrea, his daughter. Her mother was there, and that made it even more complicated. Andrea could become her father's guardian. The local doctors sort of fought for their own respectability and didn't want him moved. She was upset she couldn't contact you. Where the hell have you been?"

"If Andrea was directly related, the Red Cross would have called, and then they would have tracked me down."

"I'm very familiar with how the system works. Typical Army bureaucrats. A man had a heart attack, and you needed to be informed. They didn't do it on a technicality."

"For two months, I've been trying to get her to come to Texas. She's had some legitimate reasons not to come. Some haven't been, especially recently."

"She actually asked me if you could get emergency leave."

"If you know the system, you know the answer to that."

"We both have the same objective. That is to help her get through this terrible time. The impression I got from waiting around that hospital, is that her uncles are suddenly more concerned with running the company than their brother's health. She has to deal with that, too. There's a lot going on with the impending expansion."

"There's a stock offering coming to finance the new equipment. Her uncles oppose it."

"I knew about the expansion, but nothing about a stock offering. Something beyond normal operations is why the vice presidents were so vocal at the hospital. Not a good time for her father to be out of the picture. As soon as she wakes, she'll call you. If you saw her, you wouldn't want to wake her. Please don't insist."

After hanging up from Sam, he listened to the silence. Occasional bursts of wind rocking the trailer were the only reminder things existed outside. His coffee untouched had turned stone cold. Frederic had always been a rock throughout the time he had known him. At the Christmas party, there was no hint of his heart attack. With a second one, Andrea would get pulled into everything. Would he ever see her again?

He turned on the colored television, but found he was watching the colors only without any regard for the program. Was Faith's hint about the long drive from Texas to Alabama genuine? How would she handle it? Get away from Massachusetts and home to come to Texas. She is a legal secretary in a big firm. A business trip could be her cover. Their lawyers must travel some of the time. She would be going with one of them to a big conference, where they would need a secretary. Would she generate that big of a lie to be with him? She wanted to be with him. Was he imagining the hint?

What would happen to Faith if she did break with her upbringing and morality? There would be a cost for her. If she could know what Connie Anacio was doing in the anti war movement through neighborhood gossip, wouldn't she be risking herself and reputation? Gossip in their neighborhood was like blood in the veins. They would find out. The Thayers and Beckwerths were lifelong friends due to their children's' associations with each other. How severe a strain would this be on that relationship? Could it even survive?

How would his mother view a Faith visit? She knows about his cohabitation with Andrea, but she was not of the neighborhood or of their blue collar values. She was a rich girl from an alien world. The case of Faith was very different. Like Faith said, his mother would know everything. He could stand his mother's reaction to it, but not the price Faith would eventually pay. A cost that would continue for many years. He would not put Faith through that.

Very late that evening Andrea called. She sounded exhausted and emotionally drained; a way he had never heard her before which also affected him. Their only topic was Frederic. She planned to return to the hospital that night to continue the vigil. This was the first time he had heard her voice since taking his check ride. Nothing of the turmoil he had gone through was in their brief conversation. Afterwards he realized there had been two days before Frederic's attack she had neglected calling him. He felt it had worked to his advantage not having to tell her about the initial check ride failure. Yet he also wondered what had filled her so much she had neglected him during those two long days in his life.

Monday morning the first day of Primary II, there was a realignment of sticks. With more military instructors available, most sticks consisted of two students. Covington was moved. Riard and Randolph remained together. With an agile pace, CW2 Shanke walked from the sanctity of the instructors' room to their table in a classroom of the Main Heliport. On his right shoulder was a First Aviation Brigade patch. He shook hands and introduced himself, then sat and began explaining, very plainly, the purpose of Primary II instruction. They would concentrate on navigation, pilot technique for tactical take-off and landings in open terrain areas, aerial recovery from stimulated engine failures, and for the first time touch down autorotations, the realistic termination of an actual engine failure. Although he retained the military formality, his manner was easy and pleasant. While they were being briefed, Randolph noticed Riard eyed him cautiously. Randolph drew the first ride. Riard got the first long bus ride out to the new stage field.

"There are three colors of tires," Shanke said. They had flown from the Main Heliport to an area, which Shanke seemed very comfortable. Randolph noted passing his Primary I stage field and feeling relieved he was not heading there to do any more tedious take-off and landings over the six asphalt, short runways. "White, you can go into any time solo. Yellow, you can go into once you've been in there with an IP. Red, you are not authorized to go into solo. I'll take you into one to show you how tight they are. The trees keep growing, so the open area doesn't stay the same. If you violate any of that, it's safety violation."

Randolph had the controls and had flown from the Main Heliport. He knew Shanke was scrutinizing his actions and techniques, which had started with pre-flight. His opening tenseness when he started-up the aircraft quickly left. He expected criticism. It did not come.

"All right, I'll take the controls," Shanke had not stressed the passing of the controls. Randolph glanced at Shanke's hands and feet to insure he was on the controls before relinquishing them. If he noticed Randolph's caution, he did not mention it. "You watch. That's why I'll do the flying for this first one. There's a white tire area over here," he indicated to their right. "Are we clear right?"

Randolph turned in his seat and looked to the right of the aircraft, where Shanke's view was obstructed since he was in the left seat. Randolph cleared them for the right turn.

"There's the tire." They flew over a small hilltop that had medium-sized trees around its sides. The top of the hill had an oval-shaped clearing with an automobile tire painted white clearly in view in the center. "The stage field is easy once you get into the pattern. You don't really have to think about setting up an approach. You line up on the lanes. Out here, you've got to make imaginary lanes when you're setting up your approach. Look for the signs that will give wind direction. Smoke-that's the easiest-or flags, and sometimes you can tell from the leaves on the trees. Once you've determined wind direction, then you set up an approach. Enter on the downwind just like at the stage field, and judge the barriers you've got to clear, and how steep the approach you'll make. You want to plan your touch down for the upper third of the landing area."

They touched down in some dried foot-long grass. Beneath it, new growth had started. Shanke picked up to a hover and slowly taxied to the center of the clearing. "Now, you're planning your take-off. You want to check the barriers you have to clear. You want to use the minimal power possible. Have you read the manual?"

"Yes sir."

"I'm a warrant, remember. I'm thinking about taking a direct, but haven't done it yet."

"What branch?"

"Infantry."

"I had some direct commissions in my OBC course. One guy only got Second Lieutenant. Two others were firsts."

"They're offering me First Lieutenant! What's OBC like?"

"They don't mess with leadership stuff. Once you've got your commission, they assume you have that. It won't be anything like the WOC program."

"Nothing will ever be like the Warrant Officer Candidate program." He had set the aircraft down again in the grass next to the white tire. He rolled the throttle down to idle, and then showed Randolph how to friction the controls, so they would not move. They both got out of the aircraft, leaving it running. Shanke showed him how to pace off his take-off run.

"Will I need blues while I'm at Benning?" Away from the noise of the aircraft, they had taken off their helmets. There was a steady wind on the small hilltop.

"I brought all my uniforms. Didn't need them, but you never know."

"Warrant Officers have the same type of blues, don't they? I don't need to buy a new set?"

"Get the stripe on the trousers and the blouse sleeves changed. The post tailor shop could probably do it for you."

"Infantry is baby blue?"

"Fort Benning prefers robin's egg blue. You're going to love Fort Benning. It will be like no place you have ever been." Randolph smiled. In his short military career, there had been very few times he felt like a veteran. He was still finding it hard to believe he was talking to his instructor as if he was just another Army officer.

After they climbed back into the aircraft, he let Randolph take the controls and hover to one end of the small clearing, over their paced-off path. After the mandatory pre take-off safety and cockpit list, he initiated the take off. There was plenty of power and room. Seeing the trees recede underneath them gave him a spine-tingling, racy thrill. He did an approach to the same area. Shanke decided they did not have to re-pace the take off, so Randolph hovered back to the same spot and took off again.

They went into a yellow tire area, which had half the open space as the white area they had been in. Again, they frictioned down the controls and got out, this time planning a max performance take-off to best utilize the smaller take-off area. With the exiting and re-entering of the aircraft, the flight period passed quickly.

"My uncle Leslie has taken over as acting CEO." There was tension in Andrea's voice, much different from the fatigued tones of lost sleep. It was later than their usual evening telephone calls. With animated enthusiasm Randolph had been discussing the first flight period of Primary II with Blaisedale, who had the same level of excitement with the tactical tire areas. It was one of the only times in recent weeks they had had any conversation. With a hint of disappointment in his face Blaisedale went into his room when he realized the call was Andrea. Rather than drag the phone into his room, Randolph remained sitting on the couch in the common area.

"Isn't he next in the chain of command? He is the senior vice president. How is your father?"

"He has needles and tubes going everywhere in him. His eyes appear alert. He's talking, asking about unimportant things. They tell us he's doing fine and certainly he does look better than over the weekend." The agitation remained in her tone.

"Your uncle Leslie is only temporary."

"He wants to delay the stock offering. All my uncles have opposed the expansion. None of them support the new alloy products. They think they're trash. They'd rather see Tremblay Bearings stick to its industrial base products and maintain its supposed superior quality. And stay small. If we're not going to compete in the real market, the company will shrink. This is my-our future."

Randolph heard sounds of another voice in the background. Andrea's voice lowered as she held the phone away from her mouth.

"Who is there with you?" Randolph asked annoyed and feeling ignored.

"Sam thinks delaying is not the same as stopping it."

"Isn't it only because your father is in the hospital?"

"You're both wrong." Andrea announced in a loud tone, as much to Samantha as Randolph. "It's stop! Now, they have the chance. Delaying means killing it for good. Scott says obstructing the offering could have a serious impact. Investors will smell the uncertainty. That could affect the price of the stock and the amount of money we expected to raise."

"What does Scott say to do?"

"Do?" Andrea's voice was pensive. "I only asked him his opinion when I found out what my uncles were doing today."

"He would have good advice on what to do tactically in this situation." Randolph heard part of Andrea's additional broken conversation with Samantha.

"Sam agrees Scott would know what to do."

"Do you feel you have to do something? Once your father is better, things will go back to normal."

"If there's no stock offering, there will be no capital equipment or expansion of the plant. Someone has to get this back on track. The stock offering must go forward."

"Who else feels the same way you do?"

"Leland Junior. He's as pissed off at his father and our uncles as I am."

"You have an ally."

"Leland Jr. is no one's friend, except himself. Sam agrees with me on that. She's met him, and thinks he's a two-faced bastard, which he is."

"If you can't go to Scott, you need some more advice. Almost legal, if you're going up against your uncles."

"Sam agrees."

"Am I talking to you or Sam?" Randolph said sarcastically. "What authority allows your uncle Leslie to take over—other than his senior vice president rank?"

"I don't know."

"Find out. Is there someone else who can give you an opinion? A lawyer, an accountant?"

"I'll go see Doran! You're brilliant." The phone again was pulled away from her ear, and there was more background chatter. "Sam wanted to know who Doran is." Andrea said to Randolph. "Oh, he'll know. That's a God-send, Randy."

"Who the hell is Doran?" Randolph demanded.

"Our lawyer, corporate and everything else. I haven't seen him at the hospital. He must know about my father. Someone would have told him, or he's seen it in the paper. I'm actually quite surprised he hasn't called me. My father met him when he was starting the company. He advised on incorporating and helped with all the rules and regulations that came out during World War II allowing Tremblay Bearings to get preferential treatment for raw materials. That probably saved the company from floundering. Each year on my birthday he gives me some surprise gift. His wife died years ago, and they had no children. He's more than our lawyer. I'd trust him with anything I have."

"Why does he remember your birthday?"

"He's my Godfather. That's how much my father trusted him."

Riard got the first dual ride the second day of PII. Randolph got the long bus ride to the stage field. The second period on their single aircraft was Randolph's. Shanke let him find white tire areas, and with minimal comments, silently judged his approaches and landings. Then, they went back to the stage field where Shanke demonstrated touchdown autorotations to the asphalt runways. This was the culmination of the simulated engine failure. During Primary I these were demonstrated to the students by the instructors for the purpose of familiarizing them in case of an actual engine failure while solo. Keeping the aircraft undamaged and the occupants unharmed was the Army's objective. Full stop autos were demonstrated on both the asphalt runway and to the grass next to the runways. On his first attempt to the asphalt, Randolph had a very long run while the aircraft slowed and stopped. Shanke was not overly critical, and merely recounted weak points to improve. On the way back to the Main Heliport, he demonstrated a simulated engine failure with a power recovery at a three foot hover. This precision maneuver to three feet over the ground was designed to strengthen coordination of bringing back full power, while flying to a spot suitable for a possible landing. After they had climbed up several hundred feet, and after some clearing turns to insure no other aircraft were in the area, Randolph was permitted to roll off the throttle to go into autorotation. On his first attempt, his hover was twenty feet about the ground. Again, Shanke did not criticize, but merely emphasized areas to improve.

Covington on his second flight got an unsatisfactory flight, a pink slip, his first. It did not seem to faze him. His facial expressions and everything else remained the same.

Arriving at the trailer, Randolph began to anticipate Andrea's call. Instead when the phone did ring Blaisedale dragged the long cord into his bedroom and talked for over an hour. Occasionally, Randolph heard his deep voice as he laughed or his voice rose with some explanation. His face was bright as he returned the phone to the common living room, but then uncharacteristically he returned to his room rather than sit in front of the colored television set with Randolph.

For over an hour Randolph sat alone alternating his attention to the television screen, the inanimate telephone, and the silence within the trailer. Finally in exasperation he called the apartment. Sam answered the phone then yawned audibly and apologized. Andrea was not at the apartment.

"We've been looking through old files all day at the lawyer's office. Doran seems to be an inspired and knowledgeable lawyer, but his filing system leaves a lot to be desired. He's never employed a secretary for any length of time, and he's changed his own filing rules every year for the past thirty years. We went out for some supper. Andrea told me to come back here and get some sleep. She went back to Doran's to continue looking."

"What is she looking for?"

"A will or something Doran drew up for Mr. Tremblay when the company started to take off after World War II. He believes it allows Andrea's mother to become temporary head of the company in the event of her father's incapacitation."

There was no further news. Frederic was still recovering, chatting contentedly with the hospital people. Andrea had seen him early in the afternoon, and then they had gone to Doran's office.

The next day Covington got a second pink slip. Still, he seemed indifferent, although some dark circles seemed to have permanently shaded his eyes. No one tried to talk to him about the violations putting him two-thirds towards expulsion. That night after Blaisedale nearly tackled the phone after its first ring Andrea was on the line.

"We found it in Doran's screwed up files. It's a way to stop them."

"Stop who?"

"Uncle Leslie is going to issue a statement Friday delaying the stock offering. Doran remembered the old will which has a clause stating that in the event of my father's incapacitation, my mother could take over or designate someone to run the company until the Annual Board Meeting in October. The will is still registered."

"Your mother isn't married to your father anymore. How can that will be still valid?"

"It's enough to get a court hearing just to determine its legitimacy. That may make my uncles back down."

"Your mother knows about this?"

"She wants to name Scott as the temporary CEO. I think it's a good idea except Scott doesn't want to do it. That got my mother pissed off. My uncles don't know any of that. We're gambling that the threat of outside interference by a court hearing might do it, and Uncle Leslie will not delay the stock offering."

"Did you get Leland Jr. to help?"

"I still don't trust that bastard. If he thought it was in his interests, he'd tell his father and my uncles what we're trying to do. He doesn't know about any of what I've got. He's been climbing the walls trying to figure out what the meeting with my uncles tomorrow is about. Doran telephoned my uncle Leslie there could be a legal challenge to his assuming temporary leadership of Tremblay Bearings. That got all my uncles' attention. My mother has a big chunk of stock and will be there. Scott finally said he'd come and try to convince my uncles not to delay the stock offering."

"What made Scott change his mind and get involved?"

"They sleep together, remember." Andrea laughed. "That has certain advantages."

"Really? What about lack of joint bed maneuvers? What do you suppose that causes?"

"I have to watch things here." Her tone suddenly turned to tartness. "With my father in his current condition, it's up to me. My mother's stock could lose a lot of value. Mine would too."

"You have stock?"

"More than my mother. I don't have control of all of it, now. It's part of my inheritance. Doran informed me of that. He thinks I should get on the Board of Directors."

"How is your father?"

"Saw him right after lunch. They've taken some of the tubes and stuff out of him. They were going to have him sit up later this afternoon."

"What did he have to say?"

"Nothing important."

"Hasn't anyone told him what your Uncle Leslie is trying to do?"

"Of course not. He needs to get better, not upset. I must win this. It's for both of us."

"Your uncles ain't going to forget what you're doing."

"My father has always had fights with his brothers about the company. All I'm doing is standing in for him. He wants the company to grow. That's my goal too. As far as my uncles are concerned, we'll still all give each other presents at Christmas."

At the Thursday evening formation, they were reminded of the college ROTC ball that Saturday night. Those wishing to attend were requested to reply to the invitation out of consideration of the sponsor's logistical planning.

"Let's go to this thing," Randolph said to Riard after formation.

"You could have got something going in Fort Worth. Looks like Blaisedale did. It's got to be my turn."

"You've had nothing but missed approaches and go-arounds. You'll never bring the needles together in Fort Worth. Let's move on to touch down autos."

"You go to one of those college things, there won't be any booze. You sit in the corner and watch couples dance. That's junior high school stuff."

"If they're sending out invitations, there's got to be unaccompanied women. It's a diversion to see if there's any tactical advantages. If there isn't, we'll go back to Fort Worth."

"Are you out for full stop touch-down autos or are you just going to do go-arounds?"

"My mind is opening up. I might even be shooting for the grass."

"Did Shanke let you do one to the grass?"

"Did one today."

"Son of a bitch! I'll have one tomorrow. How much of a ground run did you have?"

"A lot less than the asphalt. The grass really slows you up quicker. It's hairy, the grass makes it seem a lot easier to roll over. Asphalt gives you a safer feeling, more like landing a fixed wing."

"How much open runways of asphalt are there in Vietnam?" Riard commented sourly.

Blaisedale was in the shower when Randolph arrived at the trailer after last formation Friday afternoon. This was the first week of duty free Saturdays now that ground school classes were finished. He was looking forward to the colored TV, potato chips, possibly a beer, and some flying talk with his roommate. Blaisedale was in such a rush he forgot to bid farewell as he got his overnight bag stuck in the trailer door as he tried to shut it. A moment later the sound of his car's engine roaring to life quickly faded as he speed over the dirt driveway.

The only sound became the voice on the colored TV. Changing out of his Nomex, he stopped at the refrigerator for a beer, the first Friday night one he had in over two months. When the phone rang, he looked at his watch. It was much earlier than Andrea usually called. His first thought as he picked up the receiver was that something must have happened to Frederic.

"I want some more flying stories." It was Faith. For the next hour Randolph related the high points of his first week of Primary II from landing in the white and yellow tire areas—Shanke had taken him into a red area, and it had been confining—to the thrills of doing touch down autorotations. Faith interjected some giggling, and also with questions when she did not understand something. His beer went flat in neglect.

"Betsy is still wearing Andrew's ring. She was home from school and stopped by."

"You still think that's wrong for her?"

"Definitely, that's something you have to be one hundred percent sure of. She thinks everything will work out. Andrew is using her, that's obvious."

"What's wrong with being used?"

"When it's genuine, you can't fake it. That's how she knew. That's why she's a fool."

"Things have to be tried to make sure it's the real thing."

"Then try me!" Faith did not giggle. They fell silent. Randolph strained to hear her breathing.

"When?" Randolph asked to break the silent standoff.

"Whenever and wherever you want me, I will come to you."

"Why?"

"You're a blockhead at times." Now, she giggled.

"I've thought of it. What would happen to you? What would our families think? That price for you is too high."

"You've thought about us that much?"

"Yes," he was silent for a moment. "I can't let that happen to you."

Faith did not answer him immediately, and another extended silence grew. "Start thinking about what happens if we don't try."

Saturday Randolph found a sports coat, which had traveled with him through Fort Benning, back home and then to Texas, unworn. Blaisedale had an iron, which made the wrinkles disappear. There was a turtle neck sweater Andrea had given him. Riard was wearing a tie, which he quickly shed when Randolph picked him up. It was a longer ride to the college town than to Fort Worth. Although their directions were geographic, once they found the campus, they saw a few couples on sidewalks heading in one general direction.

The men were clad in uniforms. The only thing Randolph recognized on them was the ROTC insignia. They were the familiar round discs for the company grade cadet officers and the diamond shaped discs for the field grades. They wore dress blue officer coats over a white shirt and a black bow tie. As a cadet Randolph had never owned any dress uniforms. Many but not all wore brown, knee-high riding boots indicating they were members of some special group. He wanted to find out, but Riard directed his attention to the women once they were admitted to the hall.

The women wore party or cocktail dresses. Most wore high heels and had their hair piled up on their heads indicating hair saloons in the area must have had a busy Saturday. There was a live band and a long table with refreshments without alcohol. The ROTC instructors from the university were all present in their formal dress blues. Their ranks ranged from Captains to Lieutenant Colonels, and the colored stripes on their dress trousers indicated they were from several different branches. There was an attending audience around a single, full Colonel who must have been the school's Professor of Military Science, the commander.

There were obvious students from Fort Wolters ORWAC classes, who had accepted the open invitation. Most were dressed informally as Randolph and Riard were. The number was surprisingly large. There were a few from their yellow hat class. They exchanged sheepish smiles. The many decorations in the auditorium suggested substantial preparation. There were fifty unaccompanied women; all dressed semi-formally as those with dates, which numbered twice that. They stayed in one geographic area of the vast auditorium. They danced with the accompanied and the fewer unaccompanied cadets. Their main focus was to dance with anyone, including the instructor contingent. Many eyed the Fort Wolters group hungrily, which gave Randolph and Riard some preliminary encouragement. The music ranged from formal waltzes to an interpretation of current rock music, which without the proper instruments was comic. Randolph and Riard danced with several women. No one seemed to be making any formal attachments after an hour of dancing and short, stilted conversation.

"Are these real girls or life-sized windups?" Riard whispered to Randolph as they surveyed the dance floor. The cadets looked splendid in their uniforms. Stiffly, they were as formal as the women.

"We don't have the right uniforms."

"This is a bust. A lot of our guys are leaving."

"There is something plastic about them. Everyone is only interested in being seen." They were sipping a drink that tasted remarkably like Kool-Aid. "In my college we never had anything as fancy as their uniforms."

"Yeah, OCS skipped dress blues. Our only parties were cleaning ones on any day of the week. No one was interested in dancing with the tach officers. Maybe they still have horse Calvary units down here in the South. There's got to be college bars in this town."

"If it ain't a dry county."

"Quaint Texas laws."

They abandoned the dance as did the majority of the Wolters students. From the campus, they drove in circles until they spotted bars. They selected one, which seemed busiest. The motif was the university's sports' mascot, an unlikely animal to have any sports interest. There was loud music, lights, a dance floor, and a bar. There were also several familiar Wolters faces, which had been at the ROTC dance. They bought draft beer at a crowded bar. Getting dance partners was competitive, although there seemed to be many unattached females. The attitude of the college bar patrons all of them obvious students was one hundred eighty degrees from the formal military ball. It was also a different more relaxed atmosphere than the Fort Worth bars, which were snap shots of the current cultural rock music themes. Riard fell asleep in the Camaro's bucket seat on the long drive back to Mineral Wells. Blaisedale's car was still absent when Randolph pulled up to the trailer, which was as silent and dark as a tomb.

The phone rang and rang and would not stop. Gradually, Randolph came to consciousness and realized Blaisedale could not answer it, since he was still absent from the trailer. The alarm clock said it was 5:30 AM, a time Sunday morning the radio programs began their religious programming. Lazily, as he became more awake, he realized whoever it was on the phone was not going to give up. Wearily, he climbed out of the warm bed.

"They're going to issue a press release. The offering for Monday will be postponed. That's tomorrow. We've got to stop that press release. Where the Christ have you been? I've been on this phone since last night."

"This still is last night." His tone was icily sarcastic.

"I've had the operator trying for hours. Where is your Goddamned roommate?"

"He must have found another bed to sleep in. I went out with Riard. He's my stick buddy. You know what a stick buddy is? It's a student flying term. I'm somebody's stick buddy. When guys share the same instructor, that's what we call each other. All the wives and girlfriends know that especially two months into flying You don't know a goddamned thing about what I do!"

"I'm thinking of our future."

"Future? That's something that's in front of you. Like keeping ahead of the aircraft. Do we have a future? Will we ever be together again?"

"Where were you?"

"At an ROTC ball. It was a social event for bachelor, unattached officers. Since I have nothing to attach myself to, I am by definition unattached. About fifty of us went. The women looked like plastic manikins. Some of them could actually move their arms and legs. Some of us danced with them."

"I'm scared."

"Why should you be scared? Your engine hasn't quit! The ground is still way below you and not coming up fast."

"It was too late for Doran to file Friday, but he's going to do it first thing tomorrow morning. That was our best shot, but issuing the press release tomorrow morning will kill that advantage."

"Wasn't Scott able to persuade them?"

"I thought they were impressed. He disqualified himself from running the company because of my mother's stock holdings. Maybe that's why my Uncle Leslie thinks he can get away with it. If he publishes that press release, the stock offering is going to be like a lame horse."

"Turn the nose into the wind then begin looking for the proper place to set it down."

"Make sense, please."

"That's autorotation. Your engine has failed. You have no other choice. Strange, the Army's machines are telling us that."

"Everything right now in this moment in time depends on stopping that press release. The company may never be what my father envisioned."

"Then, stop it."

"How?"

"Your father is talking now?"

"He's coherent. They're talking about releasing him in a few days."

"He knows nothing about what's going on?"

"I've told you, he's not strong enough to handle all this."

"Are you?"

"I'll do whatever is necessary."

"You've got two bullets. Doran and your father. The enemy is about to cross the line of departure. Doran's first shot was a dud. He's still an important part of the picture, though, with the threat of that court action. When we get off the phone, call your Uncle Leslie. Tell him he is to not to issue the press release and let the stock offering continue. You will call off Doran, and the court disposition."

"He's not afraid of the court action."

"That's your dud. You're going to use it again as a live bargaining chip. You need to do a trade with Uncle Leslie. You tell him he's ruining the vision your father wants for the company. You have to let your father know what's happening. If something happens you're putting it right on your Uncle Leslie's head. See if he doesn't back down. Have you got the strength to make that call? You're going to have to be forceful and very threatening this early in the morning."

She was silent for a long time. Randolph knew she was still on the line. "Yes," she said finally. There was a quiet determination in her voice.

The second week of Primary II, Covington got a change of instructors. After two flights, that instructor passed him onto the captain who commanded the detachment of instructors. This commander was rumored to have top ratings as an examiner of instructor pilots. From him Covington got his third pink slip expelling him from flight school.

Covington was not the only one. One other Second Lieutenant of Transportation lasted until the end of the week before he received a third failure grade for flight.

"After more than fifty hours," Randolph said to Riard. "You know how to fly. It's just polishing your technique."

"It's a slap at the P-One civilian instructors. The policy is to cut. They're doing it. You in the same Army as me, Thayer? Competition is how the Army works. That's how they removed candidates from OCS. Chewed them right up and spit 'em out. There probably was a number quota for that too. I stopped by to see Tim. Says he's actually glad it's over. No more pressure."

"This hasn't been like P-One." Randolph said.

"He said they were right. He's not a pilot and doesn't want to be one."

March brought some periods of summer-like weather to Texas. Thermals sometimes pushed the aircraft up, unexpectedly. Those were the only surprises for Randolph while flying. It was a relatively short cross-country distance to the tire areas, past well-recognized landmarks such as stage fields. Randolph and Riard sought the dual periods. They were both beginning to compete on the finesse of touch down autorotations.

Shanke appeared one morning having shed his multi-colored warrant officer bar for a solid silver one. Gone was the warrant officer crest. In its place on his left collar were the familiar crossed rifles of the Infantry. His eyes were a little baggy and drawn attesting to a celebration. His flight detachment had honored his promotion.

"Do you have an OBC reporting date at Fort Benning?" Randolph asked. They were sitting at their table in the Main Helicopter airport classroom.

"Late September."

"That's when I went last year. The West Pointers go first during the summer. They juice things up for the cadre. Do you come back here afterwards?"

"Possibly. I'm eligible for a short tour."

"You just signed up for another Vietnam tour," a student who was a Captain of Military Intelligence smiled. He was sitting at the next desk with his stick buddy, another Captain, waiting their instructor's arrival. "Some wonder in the Pentagon started playing with his slide rule. Why train more guys for the end of the war when you've got a group of veterans sitting around CONUS. How do we entice them to go over again? Two ways. Send them to specialized training courses like Officer Rotary Wing Aviation Course, they've been taunting us with for years, or promote 'em."

"Sir, this is a good career move." Shanke said defensively. His face betrayed his surprise.

"The wings on your chest are the career move. You've got 'em. Look at the number of full Colonels going through. I knew what the cost of flight school was going to be. I ain't doing again as a grunt. Aviators sleep in beds, and the club is close by. It's going to be a lot different with all the major American units withdrawing. We're going to be working with the dinks. What's your educational background, Lieutenant?"

"I've started some courses at the local state college."

"You would have done better to enroll nights in a degree program and kept your warrant. The Army wants education. Combat tours won't mean shit. They're almost a waste of time. I've got thirty percent of a master's done, which I'll continue with in correspondence mode while I'm piddling around on a second tour. That's going to be the main promotion criteria in the future."

With stoicism Shanke looked at the loquacious Captain.

"Now you know the price of your commission." The Captain smiled, cruelly.

"A short tour could mean Korea," the MI Captain's stick buddy said. "Congratulations on your promotion, Lieutenant. You take a promotion any time you can get it. Worry about keeping it, later." His branch was Field Artillery.

It was a half hour past midnight when Blaisedale kicked at Randolph's bedroom door to open it, as he dragged the long-corded phone with him and deposited it next to Randolph, who had been sound asleep. "You didn't hear that?" Blaisedale's face was etched in sleep and annoyance. "It's your woman!" He snarled. "I think she's drunk." He stumbled back to his own bedroom.

"My uncles backed down," she giggled. "The stock offering is going on. Scott got some early information from London. It's selling well. Doran didn't have to file. Your plan worked. My Uncle Leslie caved in. Sam and I are having wine. Say hello to Sam." There was a fumbling with the phone. Randolph heard their jovial voices.

"She just went into the bathroom. Listen, when your boss wants to drink wine, what can I say?" She laughed. From the sound of her voice he knew she was not as inebriated as Andrea. "Some good bennies to this job."

"How is Frederic?"

"We were at the hospital today. He was sitting in a chair eating regular hospital food. Started to ask questions about the plant. Andrea dodged them very well. A day, maybe two, and he'll be released."

"That's why the uncles caved in. Obviously, it's not in their best interest to oppose him. Andrea should have some free time, now?"

"Anyone who opposes Andrea's interest is asking for trouble. She's jumped in on the expansion of the plant. She's horning in on Leland Jr's negotiations for the new equipment. Leland's about ready to assassinate her. She's insisted that she is representing her father. There's a couple of different vendors. They've been giving some pretty fancy diners to get attention."

"Why doesn't' she let Leland Jr. do his job. Why does she have to do everything?"

"Andrea is thorough. She gets into the details and tries to find out if something isn't working the way she wants it. I've never met someone like her at her age. She's a phenomenon. Leland Jr. could be digging his own expulsion. I tried to talk her out of calling you this late, knowing the Army starts early. Sorry, we woke up your roommate. One of the equipment manufacturers gave Andrea a case of wine of all different kinds. We've been tasting since about-I don't know when we started. I've got to get to Atlanta for that upcoming show. Andrea's been insisting I stay here with her. She's out of the bathroom."

Randolph heard her voice before she put the phone to her ear telling Samantha to open another bottle, apparently another type they had not tried. "Your father is doing better?"

"Post hospital care is the next obstacle. There's an argument about having different people stay with him. No on wants to baby sit around the clock. Or, we get twenty-four hour nursing care. Things like that. Nothing's decided."

"Does he know you beat your uncles?"

"I didn't have to use that on my Uncle Leslie. Just calling off Doran did it. That had made him more pissed off, and once I knew that, I had him. I didn't have to fire the second bullet."

"Does this mean the horizon is opening up? You can see ahead clearer."

"My uncle Leland wanted me to go to California. Told my uncle, politely of course—because I am his sincere little niece-I couldn't leave my father at this point. Do they really think they're dealing with a fool? Get me out of the way so they could have stopped the offering." She chuckled, smugly.

"What's going on in California?"

"Jonathan started all the fires out there. Let him solve the issues. That's why I pay him so well. My Uncle Leland must think I was born today—I mean yesterday. Doran and I did it. The stock is being sold. The next step is getting the new capital equipment under contract."

"Why can't you let Leland Jr. do that, or someone else?"

"My uncles would buy tinker toys that would break down, fail, and wouldn't produce the quantities we need. I want that equipment up and running, quickly."

"Is that before you finish the case of wine or after?"

"Actually, the company that gave me the case of wine isn't the front runner. Samantha here is going to test the new market. She's my reconnaissance. That's a military term. You should be proud of me, I'm not forgetting my attachment to the Army."

"This part of the Army would like to see you."

"We'll have time for that. No, there's another white one in the box, Sam, Open that one."

"I have to go to bed." Randolph hung up the phone.

With Shanke's stress free methods of instruction and his increasing self-confidence, solo periods became a desirous means of releasing some of Randolph's excess frustrations. Getting free of the Main Heliport traffic, picking up a heading to the tire areas, he would look out at the horizon gaining a great feeling of exhilaration. Selecting white tire areas, he played with his approaches, going in fast and pulling an armful of pitch to slow himself up, like wrangling in a horse. He did not stop to friction down the controls and pace off a take-off. Most solo students had abandoned that step. Prancing and fooling around the large landing zones in the white tire areas added write-ups by several students about minor blade strikes to trees. Randolph liked the way the aircraft responded with only his weight. Often, he would set the aircraft down in the grass next to a tree. After glancing up and around mostly looking for an aircraft that might have an instructor in it, quickly, he would pull pitch and rise up, almost vertically beside the tree until clearing it's top, then, jauntily tip the nose over and look down through the bubble watching his skids clear the tops of the branches by a few feet. When solo, he had to remind himself of time. It passed quickly.

Faith called him in the middle of the week. There was some relief in talking about his flying with her. She knew how to listen. He worked at hiding his frustrations. The neighborhood gossip centered on the Beckwerths. Meredith was taunted at school for her father and sister Sarah's activity in an anti war demonstration. Apparently, they had been caught by a Boston television station news team. Their appearance and comments were broadcasted. Faith was more upset by that incident than what her father and younger sister were doing. Although there was no mention of her coming to him, she knew by the end of the conversation Andrea still had not been to Texas.

The approach of the weekend brought depressing thoughts. Hearing catches of his fellow students' enthusiasm further discouraged him. Blaisedale disappeared again on Friday night. It was the third weekend of his new life. Still secretive, he gave no hints or indications. During the week, he got calls and as Randolph did, dragged the long-corded phone into his bedroom. Occasionally, his booming laughter would erupt through the thin walls. His calls were a constant reminder of a budding and growing relationship. Also, he lost his permanent drabness, although he remained reserved. Late Sunday night he reappeared at the trailer and quietly completed his preparations for the coming week. Andrea's calls were more erratic and beginning to resemble business conferences. Increasingly, unlike Blaisedale's, there was little gaiety. She launched details, sometimes technical in nature with astonishing speed. Often he was silent and labored trying to comprehend some of the specifications she reiterated. Finally, he became bored and found he was forcing himself to listen. Her calls gradually began to depress him.

Riard badgered him about returning to the Fort Worth bars. He acted as if a woman was waiting on a bar stool for his arrival. Extremely confident of success, this was going to be like initiating a straight-in auto to an open field. Randolph began to contemplate the prospects. Would he find the long-haired girl he had shared two dances with? Was she a regular patron of the clubs they prospected? Would he let something develop, this time? The thought haunted him all week, as Riard continued to harp about the unlimited possibilities that lay before them. On the momentous Saturday night, the methods were of their previous forays. They sortied enthusiastically into each bar and after the usual dismal scouting moved on. Since he couldn't remember which club the long-haired girl had accosted him, his search intensified, and each miss injected further depression. That made him realize he had crossed an invisible barrier. He wanted to find the girl. Did that constitute an indiscretion? Previously, the bar hopping had only been amusement to help pass time. That was the reason he had not pursued the dark-haired girl. Suddenly, he realized he wanted more than just finding the mysterious girl. His despair was complete, adding further dejection to his clouding thoughts. Desperately, as his search increased in intensity, Riard's quest also became frenzied and reckless. As they returned to Mineral Wells Riard was quiet in defeat.

Going into the next week, he learned through Andrea's excited announcements the European stock offering had raised even more money than anticipated. She was now a member of the capital equipment procurement team, if not it's unofficial leader. Leland Jr., she reported gleefully was being compelled by her vice president uncles to accept her opinions and recommendations. Closing a deal was eminent. After two and a half weeks in the hospital, Frederic was released on condition prescribed by his brothers and further enforced by Andrea of having twenty-four hour nursing care at home. After his first full day home, he wanted to go to the plant. It took Andrea to dissuade him. Leslie Tremblay, the finance chief, remained in charge of day to day operations. His tenure was clearly that of a second-in-command assuming temporary control. The implications of the October Board meeting grew as Andrea's influence was making a clear and steady imprint. Doran, the crafty ancient legal mind, upon Andrea's insistence and Frederic's verbal approval, was officially installed as the company lawyer at his requested salary of one dollar a year. Andrea began pushing for his seat on the Board of Directors, a place his substantial stock holdings, some given by Frederic and others clandestinely purchased, entitled him. Samantha's answering of the apartment's phone indicated her continued presence at the plant as the new right hand of the regal daughter. She began to fret over the decreasing time available to prepare for the Atlanta trade show. With minor irritability, she remained at Andrea's side.

Randolph flew every day of the third week of Primary II. It was the first full week without Covington, who now awaited orders to begin his troop duty prior to Vietnam service.

As they filed into the classroom after the short ride from the company area, Randolph sleepily followed Riard to their briefing table to await Lieutenant Shanke's arrival. Riard looked just as sleepy. They had shared a bench seat together during the short bus ride from the company area. Riard had been silent. Snippets of the conversation with Andrea the night before wandered through Randolph's thoughts. While she had been busily attacking the capital equipment procurement and mashing her major opposition Leland Jr., her uncle, who was still her nominal boss, had allowed some of the reps and distributors in California to continue to do business with their old system of commissions. That violated Jonathon's contractual rights. This had been a minor irritability to Jonathon's rising sales numbers. Suddenly, these infringements were being blown into major concerns. Jonathon began complaining directly to her to alleviate the territorial encroachment. Andrea had rambled on and on about the problem, getting into geographic districts which completely escaped Randolph's cognizance. While listening to her continuous narration he realized that she was beginning to lay the foundations for an emergency excursion to California to mend fences with her star salesman. How many weekends would that trip devour?

He felt himself drawn to a comparison of Faith's infrequent calls. Each time the phone now rang in the trailer, he hoped it would be Faith, the forbidden fruit. Why was he longing for her to come to Texas? Was it only for the pleasure of the flesh, which he was sure she would not deny. He tried to sanctify his interest in her. She cared about what he was doing. Listened to his flying stories. Did he want her? Or, did he just want?

Suddenly staring at the scratched top of the old table, he could not remember what day of the week it was. Was it Wednesday or Thursday? Looking at Riard's pensive face, he expected more lobbying for Fort Worth bar hopping since it was getting closer to the weekend. Randolph pondered Riard's silence hoping it might be an admission of bar hopping futility.

"If you tilt rearward with the cyclic just slightly before touchdown, it will slow up your ground run." Riard said. His face had brightened. He looked much more awake than only moments before. Randolph thought about the control movements during autorotation. At the bottom of the glide, the collective was full down to keep the blades flat, and the cyclic was tilted forward to maintain forward air speed. Moving the cyclic only slightly rearward seemed unlikely at this critical juncture of the maneuver. Momentarily, Andrea and Faith evaporated from his thoughts.

"If you're not going forward on touchdown, you could lose your airfoil." Randolph said.

"So what! You're on the ground then. I watched Shanke while he demonstrated one. He did it, so I copied him."

"You still need demonstrations?"

"He likes to do autorotations. He has to maintain his pilot technique."

"He can do a five foot roll which you can't. Maybe he hick-upped just before touch down, and you thought he was pulling back on the cyclic."

"You watch when you get down the bottom, and he will move the cyclic aft. That club with the big white light ball over the dance floor had the most unattached women. We should start there Saturday night."

Randolph did not answer. His moody thoughts seeped back into his silent reflection.

"That place has the best prospects." Riard persisted.

"Your auto roll will be thirty feet in there. At least that's shorter than fifty feet in the other dumps."

Riard's face clouded slightly. "Fort Worth is the only chance of getting anything going. Blaisedale found something. That college town is too far away."

"An hour more. We had to find the hall."

"As soon as we found the campus, we saw those cadets. It was an hour and a half longer than going to Fort Worth."

Purposely, over the past month since the bar hopping had begun, he had avoided mentioning Andrea to Riard. Shanke came into the room with the other instructors with his usual quick gait. His short briefing was to the point. Randolph was flying first period, dual. Riard had to ride the bus. Aircraft were becoming less available at this point in their training.

In the early evening, Blaisedale got a call first and talked for an hour and a half, while Randolph watched the colored television. When he finally brought the phone out to the common area, Randolph dragged it into his bedroom. Samantha was still at the apartment.

"Andrea is out with a company that makes automatic processing equipment. They went to the Top of the Hub Restaurant. That's at the top of the Prudential Building."

"I know where it is." He said testily, as he settled on his bed.

"This company believes it can move mass produced, stamped bearings quickly to a final inspection area just prior to final packaging. Leland Jr. thinks it's unnecessary. Andrea wants it. Leland's father and Leslie the finance uncle don't think we need it. It's becoming a test of wills. Andrea says she'll go to her father to get it."

"I thought you were supposed to be in Atlanta?"

"I know some people going to the show. The Tremblay Bearings showcase did arrive on time today. I was supposed to be ahead of it. I have a good location in the convention hall."

"Is she going to authorize your travel orders?"

"I keep telling her she's winning the battle. We talk for hours about strategy, and how she should handle certain situations. After awhile, we've talking in big continuous circles."

"Half the time I don't know what she's talking about."

"She's getting very involved in the technical stuff for the new equipment. I've already sacrificed seeing my son another weekend. The Atlanta show starts Saturday. I must be on a plane no later than Friday morning."

"Has she mentioned anything about coming to Texas?"

"No!"

"Has she ever mentioned it at all?"

"I wish I could be more positive."

"Your objective is in sight. All you have to do is march on Atlanta. What's going on in California?"

"There's big problems' brewing with Jonathon. She was on the phone with him for over an hour yesterday."

"That means she's going to California?"

"Not before the ground breaking ceremonies. Frederic is supposed to be at that. She won't miss that."

"That's a week and a half away, two weekends."

"Her father's expecting to go and hold the shovel. Andrea's going to be at his right side. He's siding with her in all these little battles and tipping the balance to her. They share the same vision for the company. Sometimes they seem to be out in right field, but they're out there together. They want the contract for the new equipment signed before the ground breaking. It's complicated with timing the installation schedules and everything else. Andrea seems to know exactly what's going on and keeps her father thoroughly informed. She's hardly aware of the day of the week it is. She thought it was Thursday, this morning."

When he hung up, he thought ruefully at least he still had something in common with Andrea with her forgetting what day of the week it was.

241

Chapter Ten

Friday after last formation by the time Randolph arrived at the trailer, Blaisedale was in the shower. Within minutes of Randolph's arrival, he was in civilian clothes, carrying his small overnight bag, and out the trailer door with an almost inaudible farewell. Saturday Randolph slept late, went to coin laundry, and stopped at the PX. He bought a paperback and cigarettes. Returning to the trailer he watched one old movie, then had turned the television off and was engulfed by the silence. The afternoon was half spent.

Thinking of opening a can of beer the phone rang. He did not answer it, although it persisted. Could it be Andrea or hopefully but improvably Faith? Andrea would call at any hour. It was unlikely to be Faith in the middle of a Saturday afternoon. What was Andrea supposed to be doing today? Possibly she had told him. In his downhearted mood, he did not want to listen to the latest activities concerning Tremblay Bearings. The phone stopped ringing. This was the first time he did not want to hear her voice. Was this the beginning of the end of their relationship? What relationship? It was two and a half months since they had been together. When was the last time she had said she was coming to Texas? Touching her skin or running his fingers through her hair were no longer recognizable memories.

The call was probably not from Andrea, but from Riard. Purposely through most of the week he had avoided committing himself to another foray to Fort Worth. Riard must have assumed they would both go again on Saturday night. Since he had driven last week, it was Riard's turn to drive. That meant he could drink too much and fall asleep on the long drive back to Mineral Wells. They would have heard the noise of the bands and the stereo-enhanced music, blinked through the cascades of illumination and colored lights as they gawked at and pursued lithe mini-skirted young women. It would mean another failure. Why go?

Could he find the long-haired girl? Did that girl really exist or was she a figment in his mind? Blaisedale and Riard had seen her and chided him for not getting something started. What if he did find her, and she could not remember him? Memory was tricky, sometimes mixing with wishful thinking. Was she a memory destined only for that night? Even if he found her could he duplicate the magic of those two dances? She existed on that one night which he discarded and lost forever.

Should he try Fort Worth solo? Probably would meet Riard there and have to explain. Riard was his misguided stick buddy. Maybe you owed something to your stick buddy, which meant you could not deceive him. Fort Worth was out.

The college town was the only other place to try to revive his muted sense of touch. What was a woman like to talk to who was not on a telephone? Were there women who wanted to listen and discuss. He knew how to dress to be around students having observed the night of the failed ball. So what if it was much longer than the Fort Worth run. As an Army officer he was a military planner. Leave earlier. It was that simple. In fact, he should leave within an hour; the afternoon was waning, No time to think about reversing the decision. In the shower as the water cascaded over his body, the phone rang again. This time he had a perfect excuse not to answer it.

As he started on the long drive, there was time to continue pondering. If a man had only so much time, and was being ignored, did he have a right or an obligation to seek what he was being denied? Yes, he answered himself. Time could only be lost, never repeated. Would he fail, falling flat on his face? It had been a long time since he had pursued and if he was rusty and doomed, there would be nothing to apologize for. He would waste only a tank of gas. A good military tactician knew to use only an area of operations where the objective was obtainable. The college town, where those small groups of females huddled expectantly, was the place. Riard hadn't seen it when they were there after the ROTC ball. His military mind did.

Clarify the objective. Attractive girls might distract him. Accustomed to attention they had natural defenses, which took too much time and energy to overcome. The target had to be plain and possibly even unattractive. If there was a receptive spark, grab it immediately. Buoyed and jubilant when he arrived, the long drive did not tire him. As he drove through the campus, there were no serious, stern faced cadets, wearing riding boots guiding shop-window mannequins with beehive coiffeurs. There were still many students walking through the spacious campus. He drove around until he found the bar with the school's animal mascot motif. Even at the relatively early hour, it was crowded. From the faces he surveyed he recognized no one, and none extended any recognition to him. His military-cut, short hair did not stigmatize him. This was Texas, not Kenmore Square. There were no long-haired men. Most of the bar's patrons appeared to be students. He found his way to the bar and ordered a beer. His initial observations reinforced what he felt he had seen on the first visit. Larger groups, which included both men and women, came to drink a little too much, do some mild, non-serious flirting, and stay within the confines and protection of their flock. There were other groups, mostly small containing all females. They were there to flirt and mingle. Now that he had defined the objective, all he had to do was find it.

Circulating with dogged persistence through the club, he examined and reexamined the same groups. People left and others arrived. Finishing his beer he elbowed his way to the bar to order another.

The target materialized. Three girls sat at a small table. Having not seen them come in he was sure they had arrived after him. They guarded their tiny piece of real estate as they listened to the local grown band, talked, and giggled. Watching them intently, he concluded no one else was monitoring their presence or even seemed interested in pursuing them. They were a small herd isolated. Two wore dark-colored sweatshirts; the third wore a broad-knit beige sweater. One of the sweatshirt-clad girls had long hair, the others rather short. Half his beer was gone, and he purposely set it down to remind himself not to drink anymore. Of the three, all were potential targets. His preference would have been the one with the longer hair. Andrea's hair was silky. He relished being entangled in it. Quickly, he drove thoughts of Andrea from his mind to bolster his concentration. Intrigued with the target in sight his excitement with the pursuit escalated. Certainly, the longhaired girl was more interesting than the other two. Reminding himself of his pre-mission self briefing that anything making the girl attractive could act as a hindrance, he had to reject her. That was good military logic. Keep the objective unencumbered and in clear view. Having standard equipment was the minimal physical qualification. Each of the three surely was so endowed.

The one he selected was wearing the sweater. She was flat chested and seemed rather cubby. Her face was rounded, and her teeth flashed in frequent smiles in the half-light. The main criteria he had stipulated had been met. She was plain, there, and unattached. With cold military resolve, he studied his intended objective. She did not seem overly made-up. If she was wearing any facial makeup, it was invisible in the cascading light from the small dance floor. Her lips were dark indicating lipstick a deep shade of red or some other dark color. She had to be isolated from the others. If necessary, a confrontation with the three of them would have to be initiated in order to pull her away from her small tribe. That sounded fine in the thinking stage, but how the hell was he going to do it? A stupid opening line had to get her attention, while it served as a measure of potential acceptance. Isolate by getting her onto the dance floor. Then predetermine with rapidity if there was an interest. His tactical plan unfolded as quickly as his racing thoughts. Solicitously, he waited for the appropriate opening, and then wondered what an appropriate opening could be. It became apparent when the two sweatshirt girls got up to dance with each other. His heart kicked into an accelerated beat. The asphalt was clear and open. It was time to level the skids before touchdown. Reaching for the discarded half glass of beer, he hurried directly to the small table.

"Is this chair taken?" He tapped on the back of one of the two empty chairs. His heart was beating so fast, blood pounded at his temples, and he could feel sweat on his palms. Her large dark eyes flashed at him. Her lips curled into a half smile.

"I'm here with friends. If you'd lak to sit there, that's ok."

"I'm really looking for someone to accompany me to a deserted South Pacific island. I think you're the one." Randolph kept his gaze on her startled face. "You've no idea how long I've been searching."

"Ah would say at least ten minutes. We been watching you. Hi. Mah name is Vicki Horwell. Ah love Texas, do you?"

"The lone star state is so lonely when you're alone."

"Ah ain't from Texas, but ah lak it here." She smiled revealing a gap between her front teeth. Her smile was warm and open like her sparkling eyes.

"Can I sit?"

"Ah hope you can. Y'all got something that won't let you?" She blushed such a scarlet color, he could see it plainly in the dim light. He lowered himself into the chair letting his knee touch her thigh. She felt it and did not move away. Finally, the color returned to her face. "I'm sorry. Ah didn't mean to be rude."

"That's all right. I can sit. I can stand. I can do a lot of things."

"Ah know you're from up north. Ah can tell by your accent. Ah been to New York City. We marched in a parade on Thanksgiving Day. Named after the de-partment store. It was our high school band. Ah washed a lot of cars and sold a lot of cookies and cakes to earn the way up there."

"What did you play?"

"The clarinet." Moving his leg to maintain contact with her, she did not move away and pressed her thigh against his knee. "Ah enjoyed playing in mah high school band. Ah love music."

"I've marched some myself."

"Were you in the band?" Her face brightened.

"I wanted to play the flute. I kept looking off to the side to watch which fingers to put over which holes. I'd get out of step and kick the guy in front of me."

"Ah see," her face showed sudden dejection with his mockery.

"I've always admired those that march." He changed the tone of his voice, adding sudden sincerity. "It's an art that takes a lot of coordination most people don't understand, as I'm sure you do. Marching and playing an instrument can't be easy."

"Y'all right, there. Coordination is the key."

"Are you studying music?"

"No, education. Ah wanna teach elementary kids. Ah love children. Ah teach Sunday school here lak ah do back home. That's good practical experience. Ah hope it counts toward mah teaching credits."

Her two companions started back from the dance floor. Briefly, panic shot through him. Her isolation, the first part of his scenario, was about to be lost. Tactically, he had her interest, despite his inadvertent not-in-the-mission-plan rudeness.

"Well, well! The tuba player netted one." The girl with the shoulder length hair said. There was a crooked smile on her lips.

"Ah played the clarinet, Nadine. Y'all know that."

"You don't have the lung power for a tuba, Vicki. Hope you aren't playing beyond your capabilities, again." Nadine eyed Randolph greedily. Neither girl sat since he had taken one of their vacant seats. Other patrons, ignoring them, brushed by. The noise level in the crowded room and that supplied by the local band required them to keep their voices raised. There was an awkward moment before Randolph stood. He felt a tactical loss building, which angrily he wanted to resist, as Nadine stared straight into his face. For a brief moment Randolph was tempted to shift objectives. Nadine seemed far more interesting.

"Do you play?" Randolph asked.

"Not the tuba," Nadine smiled.

"You should. You have the lung power for it, but not the grace." He reached for Vicki's hand, and then pulled her to her feet. Vicki sneered at Nadine as he lead her onto the dance floor.

"Ah want to go to that south sea island, y'all promised. I want to go where-ever." She did not resist being dragged past other thrusting dancers. On the dance floor, closer to the band, the music was numbing loud. The small dance floor was crowded. They found an opening and began gyrating to the sounds, which the band projected through multi positioned speakers. Randolph attempted to let his body flow with the music. Vicki moved clumsily at first, until he realized she was trying to follow his awkward rhythm.

As they danced, his thoughts intensified about keeping the mission on track. His tactical plan was working. The rolling sounds in her southern voice made him giddy. Her face, especially her eyes were intriguing and inquisitive. There was receptiveness. He could feel it and wanted to exploit it. How could he keep her separated from the others? The military pre-mission planning got him this far. With sudden panic, he realized he had reached the end of the improvised plan. The other two were gawking from their small table. The music ended, suddenly. The band had turned off equipment and were about to take a break. Looking around wildly, he saw a single open bar stool. Impulsively, grabbing her hand, along with keeping the initiative of his half-thought out plan, he towed her toward the bar. She did not resist or hesitate. His arms gripped her waist as he helped her perch on the barstool. There was some substance to her waist which her clothing hid. She made no attempt to hinder his touching her. She gazed unblinking at his face, her lips were curled slightly in her resilient smile.

"I'll buy you a beer?"

"Sounds like you're saying bear. Ah love the way you talk." Her voice sounded normal, but he noticed her hand in her lap was trembling, slightly.

The bartender ignored his repeated attempts to get service. He was squeezed in between the stool Vicki sat on and the next one, which someone was sitting on, their back to him. He could not determine if it was a man or woman. The stool had been in use. A girl dressed similar to Vicki, a sweater and jeans, stood in front of them and glared for a moment before moving on.

"Where do we go to get away from all this clutter and noise?" He leaned toward her face and noticed she withheld a flinch.

"Is that the first stop toward that island?" She laughed.

"Maybe! This is your town. You must know someplace we can go."

"Ah need to get mah jacket."

They abandoned the prized bar stool and moved through the dancers, gyrating to canned stereo music, back to her table. Her two tablemates looked at her with envy. Nadine was ready to spar again.

"If you won't share him, Vicki, has he got any friends?"

"I'm solo."

"Can you go get some friends, whatever your name is?"

"This is-what is your name?" Vicki asked.

"Jim." Randolph said evenly.

"Ah see you guys later. We gotta go."

"Don't go too far, Vicki, you'll be lost." Nadine said sarcastically.

They made their way out through the crowded bar into the cool air. Vicki slipped into her jacket, which had the school's sports mascot and slogan.

"Your roommate seemed kind of pissed." Randolph said. "I really don't know anyone else here."

"Those weren't mah roommates, Jim. Just people ah know from class. Nadine's too used being the center of attention all the time. Y'all took the wind out of her sails. She deserved it."

"Why do you hang out with her?"

"She's the magnet. Maybe ah get lucky and catch any over flow. Lik tonight. Cept, ah seemed to have got the whole flow." Randolph smiled as they stopped at his car. "Jim, whatever happens tonight, ah will always believe in that island." She smiled. "Ah like Camaros. Mah daddy has a manual shift. Mumma won't drive his car." Randolph had opened the passenger door. She sat in the low seat, watching his face as he walked around the front of the car.

"Are you hungry?" He asked when he was behind the wheel.

"For many things. Y'all want to get some food, ah know just the right place. Y'all lak roast beef?"

It was a small, well-lit local restaurant. There was a take-out window with several customers waiting for their orders. Inside, it was filled with students. Although they had to wait while placing an order, they managed to get a small table. Vicki removed her school jacket. She was wearing a plaid mini skirt, which showed her thick legs.

"Y'all don't go to our school?" While waiting for his reply, she attacked her sandwich. Randolph also started eating. It was good beef. Strangely, he found he was hungry.

"I'm a salesman."

"Y'all young to be a salesman. What do you sell?"

"Ball bearings."

"Who wants those?"

"Everyone. All machinery has them. They can be made out of metals, plastics and synthetic materials. There are hundreds of different types." Her expression remained skeptical. "My father owns the factory. He said learn sales. So, I'm a salesman."

"What do you wanna be?"

"A vice president. They get a big office and a secretary."

"Where y'all from?"

"Massachusetts."

"Ah thought you were from up north. Our school has people from Boston. Y'all talk like they do."

"It's so nice to meet a receptive person. Most of my day, I'm with older people. You're a big turn-on for me."

"Depends upon what y'all want to turn on." She smiled and sipped her Dr. Pepper. "Ah lak that phrase. It's so relevant to today."

Looking over his sandwich at her plate, he realized she had finished eating. There was nothing remaining on her plate, not even crusts from the bread. With deliberate slowness, he finished eating trying to think of the next move. More students were crowding into the small, brightly lit restaurant. A nearby movie had just finished.

"Ah think they want our seats." Vicki Horwell stood and pulled on her school jacket. She took his hand as they walked out of the restaurant. Hers were very warm. "Ah could show you the campus? It's very lovely. Ah know a lot of people came here 'cause it's so beautiful."

"Where is it?"

"If we walked, about ten minutes. Ah walk this way nearly every day. It's nice and fresh this time of year. The flowers will be coming out soon. The leaves will come back on the trees. Ah have lunch here often. Did y'all lak the food?"

"Very good roast beef. You were right. Let's take my car. It's a nice night to walk, but it is getting late."

Saying nothing, again she smiled and hugged his arm. The campus was large. They drove all around it. It was well laid out. She showed him all the main buildings including the dorm where she had lived during her freshman year. Many of the buildings still had lights on, and there were several walkers hurrying through the spring coolness.

"You don't live in a dorm anymore?

"We all got an apartment. Lucinda Ann will be with her boyfriend. Don't expect to see her 'til Monday. Probably Monday morning, a half hour before classes. That boy is wasted on her. She just don't appreciate him. Keeps running him down all the time. All she ever talks about at the start of a week is, is she pregnant, until about Wednesday. Sue Lee-that's mah other roommate-will be back tonight. She has acne, and they can't do nothing about it. Had a boyfriend once. He was a Chinnaman."

"Was he from China?"

"No, Austin."

"He's an American?"

"Oh, he was born in this country and spoke perfect English. He's still a Chinnaman. Mah daddy would disown me if I ever brought one home. Sue Lee's so nice to everyone. It's a shame she got that acne."

"People should learn to look beyond the physical," Randolph said. "There's beauty in everyone."

"Ah know that. Most people don't see that. Ah can make coffee. Y'all want some? Ah make a real good brew. Mah roomies say they can't get started until they have mah coffee. Y'all bought us a sandwich. Time Ah gave you something."

"With the coffee?" He smiled at her. She turned, and curled in the bucket seat, and reached to touch his arm. "What about Sue whatever, your roommate?"

"Ah expect she'll be home, but she always goes to bed early. Snores, too. Ah hear her through our paper-thin walls. Sounds like a truck going through mah room some nights. We all got our own rooms. Take the next raght."

The apartment was in a three story, red brick building designed to house students. There were dozens of apartments a quarter mile from the campus. A huge lot behind the building had many open spaces. They walked up well-lit stairwells to the third floor.

Vicki called out to Sue Lee as she opened the apartment door. There was no response. The door opened onto a single room. One end was the kitchen area; the other, with a window overlooking the front street, was the living room area. It was cramped. A table in the center of the room took up the bulk of the space. A couch opposite a television on a small stand with a coffee table in-between took up the rest of the room. It was cluttered with stray clothes, stuffed animals, empty soda bottles and stray dishes. On the walls in almost every open space were posters of popular rock bands or singers. One exception was the Dallas professional football team.

Without her expected roommate present in the common living area, Randolph noticed a slight alarm in her face. She hurried around the cluttered room picking up a few mislaid articles. She opened one of the bedroom doors, but did not go in. There was a note on the table. It was written on a piece of lined paper.

"Her brother got sick. They picked her up. Her family's close." She set the note down on the cluttered table.

"I have to use the latrine."

"Y'all in the Army?"

"I was for awhile," he said quickly, angry at betraying himself.

"Y'all been in and out already? Y'all ain't no deserter or protester?"

"I got out on a medical."

"What's wrong with you?"

"I'm allergic to bees. I got stung and nearly passed out. So, they discharged me."

"There's no bees here, so you're safe. Bees?"

"You've never heard of being allergic to bees?"

"Ah never met anyone who was. Ah heard of it, of course."

The bathroom was tiny with barely enough room for the toilet, a tub that doubled as a shower and a wash bowl. Randolph wondered how three women managed in such a confined space. There was no place to set cosmetics or basic toiletries. Draped over the metal bar that held the shower curtain were half a dozen damp brassieres drying. The cups were huge. He had never seen a bra with such a large cup size. Vicki was preparing the coffee as he came out of the bathroom.

"Those are Sue Lee's. Ah wish she wouldn't hang them up in there. Claims the dryers don't get them dry. Ah always said if the fire department runs out of buckets, we just donate Sue Lee's old bras. Ah wish Ah had a quarter of what she's got."

"You ever heard that old saying 'anything over a mouthful is wasted?'"

"Ah have. Ah haven't got even a mouthful."

"Breasts are the most beautiful part of a woman's body. Do you know why?" She shook her head. "They are the key to her essence, to her inner being, to her utmost femininity, to her very soul."

"If y'all got any."

"You have. It's how you use what you have. That is important."

"If ah had any, ah certainly would use 'em."

"You have nipples?"

"That's about all ah have."

"All that extra boob just gets in the way."

"Ah never heard it expressed that way. Ah know boys lak boobs."

"With all that flesh, it takes longer for a woman to understand that inner most joy. You're lucky. Your ecstasy must come immediately."

"You mean Sue Lee with those big honkers has never felt that?"

"She may never feel the true ecstasy. Not like you would."

"Ah lak to feel that. Sure would."

She had set two, tall ornately painted cups with a matching a sugar bowl on a section of the coffee table she had cleared while the coffee was perking. They were obviously a special set, not used regularly. The coffee's aroma filled the room. It was good. Purposely, Randolph sat on the couch. Still, Vicki hovered walking around the room, picking up and casting things out of sight. Her hands were trembling as she picked up, very carefully the fancy empty cups and transferred them to the uncluttered spot on the coffee table. When the coffee was finished brewing, without moving the prized cups, she brought the pot to the coffee table and poured.

Suddenly, as she sat next to him he had an overwhelming desire to leave. He would be betraying Andrea. Even Faith might sneer at him. Unexpectedly betrayal and mockery seemed very serious. Still, he felt abandoned by Andrea and Faith whom he could not have. Tactically, everything had gone well. Could he abandon the mission before achieving the objective? Or, did he already have the objective? No, he did not. Looking at Vicki's pleasant face, she had a very pretty smile and good, straight white teeth. Heat rose from his loins. He was getting an erection, which after months of abstinence felt unnaturally gratifying. He did not want Vicki, merely as he had presumed, he wanted. He began to feel agreeably light-headed as the inside of his mouth dried. Vicki was still moving objects out of the way on the table gradually making the clear spot larger. Some things got pushed off the small table as she protected the cups. The coffee table still held books, notepads and a scarf. He put his arm along the back of the couch becoming more sensitive about his erection but enjoying the sexual feelings shooting through his body. His hand touched her shoulder, and he felt her anxious reaction to his deliberate touch.

"How do you lak your coffee?"

"Just coffee. Plain."

"Not even sugar?"

"I get my sweets in other ways."

"Ah bet you do."

"You're a sweet."

"No, I'm not. You believe what you want. I don't care."

Slowly, he picked up the decorated coffee cup, fighting to keep his hand steady and sipped. "Your coffee tastes just like your roommates say. They are right. It's wonderful." Leaning toward her, he had to reposition his body on the couch. Her lips were warm, and he felt her uncertainty. As he pushed his tongue into her mouth, she resisted, but it melted quickly. While he worked his hand down her back slowly, she moved her body toward him, hesitant but rapidly gaining reassurance with her own moves. There was tenseness, but he felt it disappear as she relaxed in his embrace. With a slow deliberateness, he took the bottom edge of the beige-colored sweater and pulled it up and over her head. Her brassier was like an adolescent's. While she did not stop him from removing the sweater, she put her palms over her flat breasts.

"How can I kiss them if I can not see them?"

"They're my breasts."

"Please, Vicki, I want taste them."

"Y'all crazy."

"How can I give you pleasure, if I can not touch?" He fondled the straps of her brassier that crossed over her shoulders. With the pads of his fingers, he touched her skin, tracing small circles. His fingers moved down over the exposed portion of her chest and sides. He felt her reaction to his touch. "Let me touch your buttons."

"Ah know you'll laugh." Slowly, she relinquished her defensive hold on herself.

"Beauty is what we see. Woman, be the woman you can be. Let me touch the essence of your ecstasy."

"Jim, y'all full of sweet crap. Ah navah heard such stuff." When he did not respond to his name, immediately he knew that she knew of his lie. For a brief instant he saw it in her eyes. Still, her face told him of her willing acceptance. "From a salesman that sells brass balls." She said sarcastically. "Y'all sure got them."

"Steel, brass, and lots of other materials. Ever heard of Teflon?"

"Sure, plastic stuff."

"It's the stuff of the future. You'll see a lot of it."

"Y'all sure ah can't see it now?"

Slowly, he pushed the thin bra straps down over her arms. Impatiently, she reached behind and unfastened the clasp when he started fumbling with it. He pulled it gently off her and put it on the coffee table. Leaning forward he took one of her nipples into his mouth. Sucking gently, he felt it harden. Her whole body shuttered. "Now, I can feel your soul." He mumbled, still sucking on her. "The true you."

"Ah don't know about my soul? Ah goin' to hell for sure. Ah don't care. Ah sure lak that. Stop talkin' and keep doin' that."

"This couch is awfully small."

"Mah bedroom has a bed."

"What a revelation."

She laughed, a laugh that spilled out naturally. "Y'all did this so quick. Now, ah know how easy the devil gets you. Ah know why people fall so fast. Ah really and truly don't care."

Her bedroom was dark and cluttered. He bumped into a bureau. Standing next to her single-sized bed, he undid the clasp of her mini skirt and slide her panties off at the same time in one smooth motion. He caressed her buttocks and thighs, then put his lips to her neck and sucked and licked her skin. Her whole body shook. The sheets were cold but warmed quickly to their bodies. Forcefully, he manipulated her, putting her body in the position he desired. At first, she was hesitant, but once she understood his commands she responded enthusiastically.

When he entered her, she was moist and receptive. Her legs went wide. All his thoughts focused on his rutting, driving himself as deep as he could. At the moment of release, he felt a flood, as he had never felt it before with Andrea or any other woman. He paused a moment before withdrawing. She had just started to moan, when his cessation of movement caused her to pause. He was disappointed but satiated. Rolling off her, he let himself sink into the bedding, savoring the long, desired release.

For possibly ten seconds, she was deathly silent, then her breathing exploded. "Mah Gawd. Ah feel like I'm full. Ah nevah dreamed it could be so. Y'all right? You didn't die on me?"

"I like to be quiet afterwards. That way the enjoyment lingers." His senses were still enjoying the physical discharge. Was it a sexual awakening with the hint of indescribable future pleasure? Had he discovered that plain, unadorned girls could give more and so were truly a better arrangement. There would be no competition with other things which naturally distracted a relationship. No job, only school, as when Andrea had been a student, and all her attention directed at him. That distraction and other desirable physical attributes were an important part of a bond. Or, were they? What did this chubby girl do, other than lay there while he concentrated on nothing but himself. Careful, he cautioned himself, you've taken the objective. Think about escape. Clearly, the mission and all the tactical stuff in between had been accomplished. There was no need to post flight. It was time for the stage field bus back to the Main Heliport.

"Ah want to scream this out to the world! Y'all beautiful. Oh, ah loved that. Ah be quiet. Ah promise. Oh Gawd, ah be quiet for you." She cuddled next to him and tried to lay still. Her body was shaking with her excitement.

As his eyes adjusted to the darkness, there were posters on every open space of her walls. They were more rock bands. The most notable exception was the familiar face and beckoning hand of Uncle Sam enticing enlistment in the Army. Maybe she always wanted one of those ROTC cadets with the riding boots. Andrea worked at making the Army non existent. Possibly he should get a poster for Andrea's bedroom, which brought a silent smile.

"How did y'all come to find me in that club?" Her voice was still etched in breathless excitement.

"A customer recommended I come to this town. In my job it gets lonely."

"Ah understand lonely. Y'all don't have to tell me about that. Ah'd lak to thank that customer whoever he is."

"Where did you get the recruiting poster?"

"In a de-partment store. Y'all miss the Army? Y'all tried your best. Ain't your fault if you're allergic to bees. Ah don't fault you for being thrown out."

"I wasn't' thrown out. Medical discharge." Inching toward the edge of the bed, it was difficult disengaging himself from her. When he sat up and put his feet on the floor, he had to push her slightly away. While leaning forward searching for his underwear, she kissed his back.

"I'm thirsty." He had managed to slide his underpants on and was groping through the dimness for his pants.

Quickly, she rolled off her side of the narrow bed and pulled on a worn bathrobe.

"Ah get you something. Whatever you want." When she opened the bedroom door, light flooded into the small room. He was able to locate more of his clothing. As he pulled on his pants, he eyed her looking through their refrigerator and moving things. He found his shoes and one sock. As he searched frantically for the second one, she was back holding a can of soda as he finished buttoning up his shirt.

"That just makes me thirstier. I just want a sip of water and to use the bathroom."

She followed him, trying to stay close, which annoyed him. Carrying his shoes and one sock, the uncarpeted floor was cold. Her bathrobe was dull pink and grayed from numerous washings. She followed him to the bathroom door and stood in front of it as he closed it on her.

He urinated, and then sat on the toilet to put on the one sock and his shoes. There was a window in the small bathroom, which opened by a crank. The crank made a slight noise as he turned it. Fresh air rushed into the silted staleness displacing the bathroom odors. The fresh air gave him a feeling that made him giddy. Quickly, he shrugged it away to concentrate on organizing his escape. After patting his rear pocket where he kept his wallet and the one where he kept his car keys, he opened the bathroom door. She stood, awkwardly in her worn bathrobe staring at him. There was a pleading in her face, which suddenly made her pitiful.

"Mah roommates won't be back 'til late tomorrow. We got the whole place to ourselves."

"I gave you something. You know that."

"Ah want more. Why can't ah have more?"

"We all want more. If we went back in that bedroom, it wouldn't be the same. It was unique. We'll always have that."

"I'll take half as good. Ah be happy, I promise Jim....or whatever...." Tears gathered in her eyes.

"I forgot my cigarettes. They're in my car."

"Y'all must have your cigarettes." Tears overflowed her watery eyes and rolled down her cheeks.

Her face was flushed. It was the last vision he retained of her. With a full, lead-like feeling in his stomach he rushed quickly past her, out the apartment's entry door and down the well-lit stairwell. The image of her distressed face stayed with him for a long time. He felt spent, but without the relaxation after being with Andrea. Damn her. There was hollowness in his chest, which stayed with him until he reached the safety of his Camaro. Betrayal? No, it was Andrea's fault. None of this would have happened, if she had only come to Texas. And, it was Faith's fault for not being able to come to Texas. He had betrayed Faith's sincerity and honesty in her feelings for him. Damn her too.

Irritable driving through the well laid out campus, he relaxed when he reached the comfort of the Interstate. Finally, he pulled the Camaro off the asphalt onto the dirt, stopped and got out. Standing next to his car, a few headlights of passing cars illuminated him. He peed into long dried grass that stopped at the pavement's edge. The relieving of the pressure in his bladder reminded him of his debauched thirsts with Andrea. Back in the security of the bucket seat he felt at ease with himself the first time since leaving Vicki. Putting the car in gear, he slowly accelerated to the posted speed limit. The vibrations of the engine increased his relaxation as he settled in the comfortable bucket seat for the long drive back to Mineral Wells.

Sunday morning Randolph slept late waking to the trailer's silence. With Blaisedale's weekend absences the trailer seemed unnaturally quiet. Images of Vicki's apartment, her small bedroom, the posters of rock bands on the walls, her fancy set of coffee cups, and parts of her plump, naked, and smooth body repeatedly floated though his mind. Getting up out of bed, showering, dressing and eating gave him minimal purpose. Staring at the phone, he was apprehensive about it ringing. Conversation with anyone especially Andrea might expose his betrayal. If Faith called, he knew she would guess something was amiss. Slipping on a winter parker, he left the trailer.

He walked. The old dirt road in back of the trailer finally met an asphalt one, which he followed until there was an intersection and a new, undetermined direction to follow. There were billowy clouds which caused crispness to the March Texas air. Occasionally the wind nipped at his clothes. The feeling of having done something abhorrent began to recede. Still, he rationalized a man did what he needed to do. What he had done with Vicki Horwell was a normal activity. The only depravity was it was not who he wanted to be with. There was nothing to be ashamed of. So, why was he? He needed, and she gave. It was an even transaction. In every thought about what had happened, as he kept reviewing it, the sought-after release, one hell of a good one, accomplished its purpose.

Realistically, had he betrayed Andrea? Or even Faith to stretch their non existent relationship. He owed nothing to Faith. What if his one night stand had been with her? Possibly that would be a true Andrea betrayal. How would he feel afterwards? Would he still feel as if he had done nothing wrong?

What would the true soldier feel? Get over it, Thayer. You're a soldier, aren't you? It was an extra bit of authorized fornication. When it's over, you move on to when you get the next one. The professional has only one bond, to his unit and organization. That is the heart of the real soldier. Betrayal had nothing to do with women. Being improper at soldiering would be betrayal. Ideals could not be betrayed. Ideals had nothing to do with feeling. That's why a one-nighter for the real soldier is only one night of passing pleasure, then forgotten. The true soldier didn't have the answer he wanted.

Why was he so concerned? Andrea was not a Faith and would never know about it, unless he talked in his sleep. It was her fault for being away so long. That made her equally, at least half equally, at fault. This kind of ridiculousness in his thoughts had to end.

Hunger drove him back to the trailer in early afternoon. After eating he resumed walking. When it started to get dark, he knew he was lost, although it did not discourage him. He kept walking, his pace neither hurried or slow. Eventually in the darkness he recognized a section of road, turned onto it knowing he was several miles from the trailer. Arriving, it was very late. Blaisedale's car was parked in its usual spot, but he had gone to bed, leaving a note near the phone indicating Andrea had called. More hunger forced him to open the refrigerator and forage.

Lying on his bed still dressed his mind was sharp and clear although his body was fatigued from the uncounted miles he had walked. What had happened at the college town was a failed mission. Of that, he now felt positive. The walking, not the uncompromising true soldier had resolved that. He wanted Andrea, to see and touch her. The solution was to bring her to Texas.

When he heard Blaisedale's alarm, he woke. On the post in the parking lot, milling around waiting, Randolph wanted to avoid Riard who arrived in the parking lot a few minutes before the formation was called. When the student flight leader signaled, they hurried to their normal formation spots. However, Riard eyed him suspiciously as they climbed on the bus taking them to the Main Heliport.

"Where were you Saturday? I even drove by your trailer, and it was all dark."

"I did a solo to the college town."

"Did you score?" Riard's eyes lit up.

"College kids. Drank beer and listened to a lot of bad imitation rock. It was a long ride."

"I knew that would happen. You should have gone to Fort Worth. I went with Collins and Edwards. There was this one blonde, beautiful. She wouldn't dance with me though. Said her boyfriend would object. Why the hell was she in that club?"

When they reached the Main Heliport and filed off the bus, Randolph felt the stiffness from the walking. Moving helped clear away the feeling. He was ready to go back to flying. He got a solo aircraft for first period, and then he was to turn the aircraft over to another student. Riard drew a dual ride with Shanke.

That night Blaisedale was on the phone for nearly two hours barricaded in his room. There were no other calls. Tuesday he had a dual period with Shanke in which he excelled while doing autorotations. Even Shanke gave him some rare compliments, rather than his quiet hints for improvement. The flight period made him feel confident. For the first time since Saturday night, he felt normal in body and mind. That evening Blaisedale used the phone first, but was on it for only about thirty minutes. When it rang, he knew who it was.

"You need to get an answering service. Get it installed and send me the bill. Sometimes I have specific things that I want your opinions on."

"I won't get an answering service. If I wanted one, I'd pay for it myself." His voice rose more than he intended it to.

"I know you're working during the day, but evenings I must be able to reach you."

"Then come to Texas!" He snarled.

"The ground breaking is Monday. I have to be there for my father. I've got to go to California. Afterwards, I'll stop on my way back here. I'll try to make it a weekend."

"You're to come here Saturday." His tone was cold.

"Are you giving me an order?"

"Call it that, if you want. I want to see you Saturday."

"Don't be ridiculous. Everyone has been waiting for the ground breaking. We've got local news coverage. The whole industry will be watching us. Sam's done with the trade show in Atlanta. She's going to be here, even giving up a visit to her son. Her show proves there is definitely a new, potentially large market for the new alloy products. If you weren't in the Army, you'd be here, too. This is the start of something that is going to continue moving. It's our beginning."

"I don't want to hear about Tremblay Bearings, ground breaking, increased sales of any of that other crap. You and I are nearly at the end of all that. I'm going to rent a room in the Holiday Inn by the entrance gates of Fort Wolters. I'll be there all day Saturday. If you don't come, there is no more us. Either come or forget about me for the rest of your life."

"You're not being rational." For the first time there was shock in her voice. "There are other things I'm working on. I can't drop everything and leave."

"I'm not going to be alone anymore"

"All I've been doing has been for us. How can you be so selfish?"

"Be here on Saturday or forget about us." He hung up the phone.

A glass slider door allowed him to stand outside on a cement slab of the Holiday Inn room he rented. The door faced the pool where the solo ceremony had been held. The water in the still uncovered pool looked cold. On the colored television there were still Saturday morning children's cartoons. He walked around to the front of the building where the parking lot bordered the road that went through the main gate of Fort Wolters. The huge green and white sign, the Holiday Inn trademark, was a glaring reminder of his safety violation. Staring briefly at the sign brought back the panic sensation of having drifted out of the daisy chain in the pattern and making a blind turn back to capture a spot. He remembered his fear and the reward for successfully reentering had been a pink slip and no Andrea.

His thoughts during the long wait drifted to Faith. She had become a substitute for the missing Andrea. Although she listened to him and was genuinely interested in what he was doing, it was only the absence of Andrea that had perked his interest in her. Had Andrea made frequent visits, he would not have allowed her to seep into his thoughts. He wished her no ill will. His sister was right. She had to resume her life. His was full.

Had he created the leverage to force Andrea to come? His apprehension began to rise as noon turned into early afternoon. Each night during the remainder of the week she had called and Randolph refused to take her calls. Blaisedale was annoyed by his behavior, but seemed to understand it. Each night he pulled the phone toward Randolph only to get his negative response. Blaisedale would intone into the receiver, "he's here, but not tonight."

This day was the one week anniversary of his brief night with Vicki Horwell. No longer did he feel like an unmarried adulterer having broken an implicit and unwritten oath. The only wrong committed against him had been enforced loneliness. There was no Army regulation for governing the handling of solitude. With a month left of Primary II, if she did not show, several weekends remained with nothing enticing except bar hopping with Riard. The long ride to the college town could be an alternative. If there had been one, there could be more. Feeling unrepentant as he now did, he was ready to consider it.

His mind drifted into neutral as he lay on the double bed watching an old movie in black and white on the colored television. Stiff from lying on the bed for long intervals, several times he got up and stretched, looked at his watch and began to ponder her supposed itinerary. Since she was the only one who knew he was at this Holiday Inn, the phone ringing would have to be her. Several times he stared at it wondering if it was to be their final connection. The gentle knock on the door nearly went unheard. Blood rushed to his head as he quickly jumped off the bed.

"I came to you, again." Her face was neutral and blank. She held her suitcase, then her face exploded into warmth. "I want points for this." Dropping the suitcase, she extended her arms to hold him. He smelled her hair, her skin and perfume so quickly he was slightly dizzy. Holding her he turned her head toward his. The taste of her mouth made his knees shake. Her eyes watered, and then tears rolled over her cheeks.

"I can feel your heart beating." He said huskily.

"I can feel something, and I don't think it's your heart." The lascivious smile that spread over her face was the old Andrea. Randolph picked up her suitcase. They managed to get through the doorway, and awkwardly, he shut it. They groped each other as they helped remove each other's clothes. The sheets were warm where he had been laying watching the television. Touching her skin brought back all the old feeling and memories. He concentrated on withholding. She felt him struggling but became lost in her own exploding sensations. His release was very quick. It surprised him. "I'm sorry," he whispered to her.

"It's okay." She sighed and chewed on his ear lightly as they settled into the bedding remaining entwined. "You made me think this past week. Would you really have cast me away?"

"How else was I supposed to get you here?"

"Sam scolded me when she caught me balling my eyes out. Told me to get my ass down here. I couldn't get a direct flight. Everything was sold out. I had to go to Chicago to get here. Why can't you understand what I have been doing in the company?"

"This is March, I haven't seen you since last year. What you have been doing, you enjoy. It hasn't been all for us."

"Sam has told me other things about the Army. She learned a lot from her ex husband, the lifer."

"Have you ever thought about why men like him follow this profession? Give up family and love ones?"

"This killed it for us in college. I thought you had changed?"

"I would like to know why Faith's brother, Arthur Beckwerth did what he did!"

"He killed himself. Doesn't that tell you what war can do to men?"

"But why? His manhood wasn't affected. It was his leg. He could still have brought satisfaction to a woman and received it. His failure as a Marine overwhelmed his desire to continue living. I told Faith he needed to be with his dead comrades. She didn't buy it."

The mention of Faith's name caused her to flinch. He felt it and rolled away from her. Looking at her face a mask seemed to have developed. She was staring up at the ceiling and had not moved.

"War messed up his brains." She said in a low tone, as if talking to a young child. "That drove him to it, not any failure."

"Soldiers have been around since the first organized governments. Usually, they were centered around a king, whom they claimed loyalty. Were they soldiers dedicated to their king or to the fact of being soldiers? I'm not an Infantry soldier. I found that out at Benning. The type of soldier I am going to be is at the forefront of this war. If I don't do this, and allow myself to fall into your splendid life, will there ever be a me? I'm not saying I don't want to work for Tremblay Bearings some day. I want you, and you are Tremblay Bearings. That will be my life some day. If I don't do this, for the rest of my life, I will have to say I gave something up which was very important to me."

"There have always been soldiers." Her voice was again toned down. "To most of them it was probably the best paying job around. Vietnam is not worth it." Randolph lay on his side staring at her. She remained on her back having not moved, looking up.

"It's not Vietnam. A soldier fights in a war. What makes him face all that possible destruction? It's important to me. You've got to see that."

"See you get killed or become mentally deranged like that Arthur kid?"

"Do you want me, or a substitute who sold out and became a shell?"

She did not move. She closed her eyes. "A minute ago, you just survived another minute in the Army. In the next minute, that will be a second minute. Eventually, all those minutes ad up and your time in the Army will be finished. Would you take an alternative assignment away from Vietnam, if the Army ordered it?" This time he did not answer. She opened her eyes and moved her head to look at him. His look was reflective. "It's a simple, honest question." She prodded. "The specs have been changed, so the assembly has to go back to engineering for updated blueprints. It could happen. How would that make you feel?"

"If the Army legitimately doesn't need me over there, I won't go. Time is running out. I want some with you. You've no idea how many weekends I had to get through when we could have been together. It made me very frustrated."

"On this crazy journey to everywhere to get here, I had plenty of time to think. I have been sacrificing time. It hurt you most. You've said you'll come to me and Tremblay Bearings. That's made this whole trip worthwhile." Purposely again, she was silent, but a smile spread slowly onto her lips as she extended her arms to embrace him.

They spent the rest of the Saturday in the Holiday Inn room, leaving only to find a restaurant and buy convenience store snacks. Piling up cushions and pillows on the single bed, they watched the colored television, satisfied with old black and white movies, one of their few common enjoyments. Their long separation created an excitement of being physically close again. During the long night, each slept for short periods and waking reached out to touch the other for reassurance. Since she had taken a bus and then a taxi to the Holiday Inn, they left at checkout time Sunday to make the drive to the Dallas Fort Worth airport for an early afternoon flight. Monday, she was on time for the ground breaking ceremonies.

During the following week, the telephone duel between Blaisedale and Randolph resumed. One night Blaisedale commandeered the phone using it for three hours forcing Randolph to leave the trailer to seek a public one. A growing sense of depressed anxiety developed in Blaisedale. His normally reserved manner remained the same. He was under some unnamed pressure. Once, he threw a coffee cup across the common room. It smashed into pieces against the wall. Calmly, he then swept up the mess. Often days passed without even cursory verbal exchanges. His face darkened with lines of deep almost permanent torment. As the remaining weeks of Primary II passed during the month of April, their common living experience deflated under the tension. Still, Blaisedale departed the trailer on Friday nights returning at later times each Sunday evening. Once, he returned Monday morning allowing himself only enough time to shower and change into his Nomex.

The weekend following her visit, Andrea went to Los Angeles to hammer out an agreement with the old distributors to minimize the infringement on Jonathon's contractual rights. Her dictate was no sales were to be lost due to commission disagreements. She pulled Jonathon into the disputed terrain forcing him to take a greater and broader responsibility for what was his territory, all the West Coast. His mild protest fell on her unfeeling and cold senses. Bluntly, she reminded him his compensation during his first year of employment with Tremblay Bearings would be nearly triple his previous year's salary.

In mid April, two weeks after her first visit, Andrea returned to Texas. Renting a car at the airport, she booked a return flight Monday morning, giving them two nights together at the Holiday Inn.

At the plant she invaded an unused office next to Frederic, which had been reserved for a secretary who, when employed, never lasted for extended periods. Her move out of the sales area was symbolic of her growing power base. She began to task Samantha with more responsibility beyond trade show coordination. Purposely, she kept Sam in Massachusetts when either on the road or visiting Randolph. With little reluctance, Sam was induced to become her source of intelligence. As the summer began, increasingly, she sent her to the mid west to check and evaluate the existing distributors and reps who sold Tremblay Bearings, all under the guise of scouting potential trade show participation. Her findings went directly to Andrea bypassing Leland senior, who was still the nominal head of sales. While executing Andrea's field orders, Sam established a special relationship with a particular salesman from Ohio, which quickly developed beyond professional association. Closing her apartment in Pennsylvania she rented one within a hundred yards of Andrea's. While searching for a suitable New England prep school for her son, she complained about their high cost. Andrea told her she would pay the difference of the tuition the boy's father did not provide.

Securing Doran's legal input, she reviewed with her father the final capital equipment contracts and the detailed installation schedules. Doran's impact with the threat of stiff monetary penalties to the multi-faceted contract virtually assured Tremblay Bearings of strict adherence to schedules. These were now fully under her control. Frederic's work week was still limited. Increasingly, he relied on Andrea for information about the company's expansion operations. Leland Jr. was relegated back to his position in the purchasing department.

In late April, Scott Lynder shocked his family announcing he would take the Nixon Administration position. Leaving his business interests in the capable hands of his law partners, the shift required renting an expensive apartment in an exclusive area of D.C. Fresh from her decorating of the new South Shore home they had built, Sylvia plunged again into the world of contractors and furniture salesman. Scott's title was bureaucratically impressive. His rank was that of an under secretary.

Andrea at first speculated the move was to please her mother. Scott's two younger children opposed his move vehemently. His second son, Samuel had recently passed the bar exam and was threatening not to join Scott's law firm. A series of quiet but intense meetings resolved their differences. One of Scott's first official trips was to the Far East to meet with financial and diplomatic interests, the position and influence for which he had been courted. Whether on his agenda or trip itinerary, he used his enhanced diplomatic powers to make a side trip to Vietnam, where a short visit with his son, CPT Lynder was arranged.

Andrea reported that the Captain was pleased with his father's new employment, supporting it wholly and enthusiastically unlike his siblings.

"Scott doesn't do anything that will not benefit Scott." Andrea reported to Randolph. "By meeting all those important financial people, he's laying the foundation for his law firm's interests once China is opened up."

"Doesn't that sort of make a big conflict of interest he's putting himself into?" Randolph asked.

"At Scott's level influence is what you sell. He has already set his sights on what he wants. This is his chance to meet all the players who will be important in the future."

As the weather turned warmer in the late spring, Primary II ended. The unrestricted freedom of the solo flights to the tire areas was gone There were check rides. Flight Eval provided military pilots. Randolph drew another CW2. He was a veteran, polite, efficient, and militarily correct. At the stage field, they did two straight-in autorotations, one terminating in a power-recovery at a three-foot hover, the other to an asphalt lane where his sliding roll was scrutinized but apparently acceptable. In the tire areas they went into a white one Randolph had been in before. The IP had him talk-out the mental planning of the approach. On the ground they rolled the throttle down, frictioned the controls and got out to pace the take off run. It had been so long since Randolph had actually done that part of the maneuver, he did some colorful adlibbing. It satisfied the check pilot. En route from the tire areas, there was the simulated engine failure, which this IP also had him terminate at a three-foot hover. Fortunately, Randolph had picked a wide-open field without obstructions.

"You would be surprised how many guys do that maneuver perfectly and end up landing on top of a tree. That was well done, Lieutenant." After this compliment the remainder of the ride was anticlimactic. The entire yellow hat class passed without incident.

Faith continued to phone periodically. Usually, her main topic was neighborhood gossip. Her father still supported the antiwar movement, but no longer was directly involved in demonstrations. This caused friction with his daughter Sarah as her activities expanded. Faith listened when he spoke about his flying, asking questions, or giggling at the appropriate times. Without comment but with subtle innuendoes she knew Andrea had finally visited him in Texas. Still, she maintained her boisterous and candid humor. Randolph found her calls still relaxed him and he looked forward to them.

At the end of Primary II, the mounting visible tension in Blaisedale broke. His face in radiant tones of joy exploded when he announced to Randolph they would not he sharing a trailer together in Alabama. He had convinced his girl, who he now revealed was six years older than him, to temporarily give up her job and go to Alabama with him while he finished flight school.

When Riard heard of this event, he announced that he would share a trailer with Randolph, becoming his new roommate. Randolph had quietly decided he had had enough of Blaisedale and did not object to Riard's proposal.

At the end of April Andrea arrived in Texas for the move to Alabama. They were together for a week, their longest time together since their college days. They stopped in New Orleans as did most of the yellow hat class and walked through the French quarter. Each night of the driving trip to Alabama was similar but different. They slept for longer periods and felt more relaxed while together.

One muggy night in a motel room that had an air conditioner that produced a steady low pinging noise, which at first was extremely annoying but then became tolerable, he woke to find her standing outside their room in the humid air. Light from the parking lot spotlights silhouetted her. Her arms were folded over her chest. Pulling on his pants he joined her, standing quietly beside her. He was thinking of lighting a cigarette when he noticed her face. Two streams of tears rolled down her cheeks. Encircling her crossed arms, he held her close. They stood quietly for a moment and he felt her tension lessen.

"I feel like I've been in control. Then, I get like this."

"Congratulations, you really are a woman."

"Did you want something else?"

"If you changed anything, it wouldn't be you. Everything is going to be all right." He whispered into her ear.

"Is it?" She shuttered and he felt it go all through her body. "I don't want things to end. I don't want you to go."

Disengaging his arms from her, he stepped a few inches away. She did not move or respond, but remained holding herself standing still.

"What's the good of survival if everything inside is terrorized into mush?"

"Many people have faced this and survived." He speculated on her thoughts. Was she frustrated over not being able to change anything? His original set of orders was still in force. With everything going her way in the Company, it must have been galling not to be able to control his future. She would always be a strong willed woman. It was enlightening to discover that deep inside her there were actual, feminine emotions.

In the second half of the Aviation Officer Rotary Wing Course at Fort Rucker, they did not wear colored hats. They wore regulation olive drab baseball caps with their insignia of rank on the front of the hat. For two months, May and June the students saw very little from the air of Alabama. Cardboard hoods attached to their helmets limited their view to the aircraft's instrument panel. Basic instruments were followed by advanced instruments, which gave the students fifty hours of flight time. Randolph referred to this training period as the 'I follow needles' time. Upon graduation, they were to be considered temporarily qualified having gained a 'tactical' instrument rating. Some instructors cautioned them that their limited knowledge was just enough to get them killed. "Don't fly in the clouds," they warned. "Some who did, they are still looking for."

Chapter Eleven

On the living room floor of his trailer, Randolph worked over maps for the final student flying period the long cross-country flight. The topographic maps with grids marked off in kilometers represented the land from Fort Rucker, Alabama to Eglin Air Force Base in the Florida panhandle. The mission was to pick up Ranger candidates and ferry them several miles to another set of coordinates. Randolph wondered if the fledging Rangers knew their pilots were also students nearing completion of their training. Graduation was the first Friday in September. This Monday, the last day of the long humid August was the final week of flight school.

Final formation for the day had been at mid afternoon, allowing commander's time to be devoted to navigation and map preparation for the cross country flights scheduled for the next day. This long flight was the culmination of the last section of training labeled simply 'contact.' During the twenty-five hour period of transitioning into the Huey's, the Army's main troop carrying helicopter, they learned the aircraft's fundamentals and characteristics. At this point in their training, the students had enough flying experience to be tasked professionally to learn a new aircraft's limitations and capabilities. The main consideration was gaining the feel of the much heavier multi passenger Hueys. The UH-1 was much more aircraft than the three-place OH-23 trainers in far-off Texas. Basic flying technique remained the same although gone forever was that exhilarating feeling of being solo in a machine with controls that connected directly to the senses. In the Hueys there were tubes filled with fluids necessary to manipulate the tremendous torque to maintain control over the standard helicopter flight apparatus, petals, collective, and cyclic. Randolph compared the sensation to holding a stick in a bowl of soup.

After cutting and taping maps together, he plotted a rough course. He had planned to work with Riard who along with several other students had been called to the orderly room after formation. Oddly, he had not returned immediately to the trailer as Randolph had anticipated. Having changed from his Nomex to shorts and a shirt, he worked on the floor. Their small kitchen table was not large enough to lay out the maps. This central area of the trailer was much cooler than his bedroom. In three and a half months, neither he nor Riard remembered ever shutting off the air conditioner. It was hot and muggy, August Alabama weather. Sometimes it rained which really added no relief, and only brightened the red soil of the surrounding farmland. Randolph got up off the floor where he had been working and went to stand in front of the air conditioner. There was perspiration on his forehead and the exposed skin of his arms. Each day on the flight line when he finished preflight his T-shirt and crotch were moist. At night the bedrooms were too far away from the single air conditioning unit. Riard kept claiming he was going to buy one for his bedroom, yet still had not done it. The veterans said the Alabama weather was similar but not the same as Vietnam. Lately, the subject of Vietnam entered his thoughts often. Within two months he expected to be there.

The trailer had the same layout as the one at Wolters. Each had a bedroom. Randolph had drawn the smaller one. Riard was not much of a housekeeper. His bed had been made only twice in anticipation of an overnight guest. In both events she did not materialize. Dishes and cups remained in the sink until food and liquid would have solidified if Randolph did not wash them. Dirt or clutter did not offend Riard.

The afternoon passed into dinner time. Randolph went back to his maps, reviewing the plotting and course lines. When they got the weather briefing before the flight, actual headings could be figured. He began to wonder what was detaining Riard. They had discussed the map preparation and each knew how much time and work was needed. The maps, because of the scale they were issued, when tapped together were the size of small blankets. Randolph expected Riard to stop on Post to get fast food. He seldom prepared his own meals, as Randolph did. Cooking, along with his lack of house-keeping skills, was not one of his assets. With all of the plotting finished on his maps, he now anticipated Riard merely copying what he had done onto his maps. That was Riard's way. Hunger caused Randolph's stomach to rumble, so he went to the kitchen part of the common area to look for something for supper.

Andrea's last visit had been two weekends ago. His lust for her had started to surface as usual after the second abstinence weekend. She had been punctual through the summer, regardless of her business activities or of the sticky, humid Southern weather. She had allowed nothing to deter her, unlike the first half of flight school. She would be at the graduation having booked a Thursday flight. He had been lobbying unsuccessfully for her coming a few days ahead. Wednesday would be preparation for the ceremonies and turning in uniforms and equipment. Thursday was open for families. His parents with Teddy were scheduled to arrive that day also. He had reserved a room for them at the Holiday Inn, where he stayed with Andrea during her trips, their usual custom. Already, he envisioned the possible complications of openly staying with Andrea. If nothing else, he knew his mother would cast a certain look at him, designed to cut to his bones. He anticipated it, but had decided it did not matter. If he was scheduled to go fight in a war, however his mother looked at him he could withstand. Andrea still had never seen either of the trailers he had lived in during flight school.

With some travel time to his home of record added to his thirty days of pre Vietnam leave, he would have four and a half weeks before reporting to McGuire AFB in New Jersey for transportation to the Republic of Vietnam. The Army would forget about him during this period, and he was free to go where he wanted, so long as it was within the continental United States. Andrea had scheduled to drive from Alabama to Massachusetts with him, so they would have many nights together. She had thoughts of stopping in Virginia for a few days. Her only vacation time taken from Tremblay Bearings had been the week she had spent driving with him from Texas. He also knew she was planning on taking more time in September during his leave.

Part of her travel plans to Alabama and her inability to get there earlier for his graduation revolved around Samantha Brown. Their relationship had grown during the summer, beyond employment. Her son was about to start school in Massachusetts, and her activities going to Ohio had also increased since meeting her salesman. She often flew there on weekends, when Andrea did not have 'tasks' for her to accomplish. Thomas Bernard, the salesman had traveled to Massachusetts for Samantha. Thomas was divorced, in his mid thirties, the father of two children and had been involved with sales all his adult life. During one of his New England trips, Andrea had gone out to dinner with them. Thomas was an accomplished salesman, and knowing her importance to Samantha, had managed to charm Andrea.

When the phone rang, it surprised him, although he immediately thought of Andrea. It was early in the day for her to call. It was Faith. Her calls still came regularly perhaps once a week. Randolph never cut her short letting the conversation last as long as she desired. Her voice brought the feeling of home and despite himself, he was interested in neighborhood gossip. He never called her and allowed the conversation to enter any topic, although to her credit, she never mentioned Andrea the cement block between them.

Tina Michaud gave birth to a boy during the summer. Connie Anacio had gone to New Jersey to see her and the newborn. The baby looked more like Tina. Connie speculated that even Tina might not know the actual father of the child. Connie earned the dean's list the second half of her sophomore year and worked in a drug store during the summer, her anti war activity at an end.

Another call had been spent on Betsy and her fiancé Andrew Tanlewood. He had earned a slot in John Hopkins Medical School in Baltimore. Betsy was searching for a college near there to transfer to. She was about to enter her third undergraduate year and had spent the summer on the Cape at the Croteau summer home. Her skin was the color of bronze and hair bleached out to almost white, the normal summer colors for Betsy. Faith no longer editorialized on Betsy's engagement status.

One call had Faith nearly in tears. This time it took Randolph's consoling tones and patient listening to soothe her. Sarah got herself arrested at an anti-war demonstration. Although sympatric, Mr. Beckwerth came down hard on her, grounding her for a month during the summer. Finally her mother was emerging from the mourning for her older son and backed the stern punishment. Sarah's actions created a lot of tension in the Beckwerth household.

"How do you feel now that you're almost finished with the course?" As usual her voice was buoyant and cheerful. He knew she wanted to make these calls and struggled to limit their frequency. It struck him deep in the gut, when he first heard her voice. That never changed, and he found himself, afterwards, wondering why.

"I'm already qualified." He had to swallow to contain the tightness in his voice. "I have logged over two hundred hours. That's the minimum to get the rating as a military pilot."

"Are you still flying? Friday isn't that far off."

"There's one more major flight, tomorrow. We're going to Florida."

"Is Florida that close to where you are?"

"It's within an hour and a half of flying in a Huey. That's our max."

"Everyone here is very proud of you. You've really accomplished something. Helicopter pilot."

"Army Aviator."

"That sounds even better. Will you mind if I come to your graduation? I want to be there when you get your wings."

"It's a lot of money only for two days."

"Your grandmother is coming, Al and Judy, too."

"When did they decide to come?" No one had told him about their attendance at the ceremony.

"I've been officially authorized to tell you." She giggled. The sound of her voice even over the long distance wires sent a tingling feeling down to his toes. "Your whole family is going to be there. Please let me come."

"I can't stop you."

"If you don't tell me its ok, I won't come."

"Faith, you're like my sister."

"I never want to be your sister, but I want to be there to see this important event in your life. Your wings! I'll stay out of sight as much as possible."

"If my whole family is going to be here, it wouldn't be right if you weren't."

"Thank you! Betsy and Connie are going to be bride's maids in Judy's wedding. They still haven't been able to rent a reception hall."

"Are they going to do the tent thing?"

"It's leaning toward that."

"When are you coming?"

"We were all able to get tickets on the same flights. Everyone's coming together." Randolph wondered if Andrea would be on their flight. When their conversation ended, he held the phone for a long time before setting it on its cradle. In addition to the neighborhood news, he realized he had been waiting for her call.

During her tri-weekly visits which allowed her mental relaxation from stress, usually Andrea arrived Friday night and departed Monday mornings giving them three nights together. They seldom ventured away from the Holiday Inn. The food was adequate, and she preferred not to spend time seeking restaurants. Randolph also found relief, especially during the two month tedious instrument period. Their quiet entertainment remained watching old movies on color television. Andrea even purchased a paperback encyclopedia on movie actors to settle their trivia contests which sometimes they argued passionately. Once he asked her if she wanted a tour of the Fort Rucker's flight facilities.

"It's just like any other Army post, isn't it? We didn't have much luck at the officer's club at Benning." Her continued complete lack of interest disappointed him.

During their July Fourth weekend, which Andrea referred to as their black anniversary, while lying on top of the bed in bathing suits after a pool trip, and letting the air conditioning dry their wet skin, Randolph raised the subject of where they first made love.

"Was it at the Fens?" Andrea asked. The Fens was a small park a few blocks from Northeastern. "We used to walk over there and sit on the grass when we first met. We started necking there, and then moved to your car."

"I can't believe you can't remember the first time."

She laughed. "It was too crowded. Too many people walking around."

"That's why I had the blanket in the back seat."

"I remember the blanket. We used it in the main parking lot."

"We used the main parking lot and got close. We were still in the heavy necking stage. You were slowly allowing me access to certain parts of your body."

"I had to keep you interested," she sighed playing along with his memory game.

"Remember the frost on the inside of the windows? That and the blanket gave us privacy."

"In the woods near my house?"

"Eventually, you nixed the main parking lot. You can't remember, can you?" Randolph laughed again. "You can remember complex business details, but you've forgotten that."

"It was under the blanket in the back seat of your Volkswagen Beatle."

"That's right, but where were we? We had been at it for what seemed like hours. I was getting very frustrated, you felt it, and I think you were too. It was time, but we didn't have any place to go. I drove a couple of blocks away from the school into a residential area. It was quiet and dark. I found an open parking space, and we got into the back seat with that blanket."

"What day of the week was it?"

"It couldn't have been a Tuesday or a Thursday! I worked those nights."

"It was a Wednesday."

"How do you know that?"

"My period was due in two days. I didn't get it." Randolph lay very still for an extended minute, until she looked over at his anguished face. "You screwed up my cycle, not me. I got my period a week later, and then I went on the pill to normalize my cycle. I knew where we were and even the day of the week, which you forgot. It was time for us."

After another desultory look at his maps spread out on the floor, he went back to the air conditioner. Standing in front of it, he let the cool air strike his face. What was combat going to be like in a helicopter? Aviators had faced battle in other wars. Had they ever confronted it at low altitude right over the trees when their main opponents would be ground troops? The senses would be apprehensive. That part would be the same, regardless of where the soldier was. How would he react? What thoughts would be racing through the mind? The day would be like any other day. Sunny. Raining. Hot. Cold. The possibility of utter personal destruction would loom ahead. That made it different. It would be a feeling someone stuck in Boston commuter traffic would never feel.

"Hey, damn, you ain't going to believe this," Riard shouted as he opened the trailer door. He tossed his helmet bag onto the cardboard-hard couch that was part of the furnishings. "My orders have been changed." He waved a sheaf of mimeographed papers. Orders indicating a change of duty station were always issued with multiple copies. "Those other names that got called out with mine, we'll all Field Artillery. We were all on orders for 'Nam. Everyone got changed." Randolph had not paid any attention to the additional names read off after his roommate's at final formation. A dozen, including a few Captains were in the group. No alarms were raised since routine administrative communication was handled through formations. Randolph, still holding his arms out in front of the air conditioner was stunned. "I'm going to Fort Leonard Wood, Missouri. The allocations for Field Artillery officers in Vietnam have been cut."

"Your assignment as an aviator is branch immaterial."

"Field Artillery apparently doesn't recognize that." Riard smiled. "I wanted Vietnam. That's where the flying is. I've been psyched to go for months. I am really disappointed."

"You almost-rated, piece of shit. Wanted to go, my ass!"

"Orders, old boy." Riard beamed. "We in Field Artillery follow orders to the letter."

"How did they others take it?"

"I thought one of the Captains was going to kiss the company clerk."

"No one knew this was coming?"

"If things are starting to slow up with withdrawals and everything, the other branches will start doing the same thing."

"Infantry will be the last. Good old we'll take the hill, Infantry."

Riard threw a large package of Hershey chocolate bars on the small kitchen table. "Put some of these in your helmet bag. They're for the Ranger candidates. We're not supposed to give them anything, but they'll be expecting it. It's a tradition. They've been eating off the land for the past couple of days. They'll be very hungry."

"Who told you that?"

"My instructor."

Since their arrival at Rucker, they had not been stick buddies. During basic and advanced instrument training, the aircraft were two-place, ancient OH-13T, crammed with instruments. The instructor not the student started and shut down the aircraft. Since there was only room for two bodies in the aircraft, stick buddies saw each other at common briefings. The final phases of flight school were transition into the Hueys, then the tactical flying or 'contact'. Riard's instructor was a CW2 and Randolph's a Captain.

"What are you going to do at Leonard Wood?"

"I'm assigned to a training command. I gotta call home and tell 'em. My parents will be glad. Hell, I'm glad!"

"Don't you want to fly?"

"Sure. Leonard Wood will have an airport. I want my flight pay. This Florida mission will be the first time we've had paxs on board. Hope we don't get an A-model. My instructor says they sometimes bleed rpm with a full load."

Randolph went back to the floor area to fold his map, and then brought it into his room. In his excitement Riard had forgotten his map preparation. He would probably use his stick buddy's. Stretching out on his bed, he listened to his excited voice as he related the news over the phone. Should he tell Andrea, or wait until she found out about it? Not telling her would make her angry. In a few minutes he heard Riard leave the trailer probably going to the fast food restaurant on post. He wondered how long Riard would survive if fast food hamburgers were no longer available. There were no restaurants like that in Vietnam, but then again his roommate no longer had to think about that.

Edwin Martin, Second Lieutenant of Transportation was Randolph's stick buddy for transition and contact. Except when doing autorotations at a stage field, the stick buddy in the UH-1 no longer stayed on the ground waiting. He rode in a jump seat mounted behind the two pilot seats. As a Transportation ROTC flight graduate, Martin was headed for a Chinook transition after graduation. They were walking toward the flight line. Their instructor, Captain Greenlee bounced his helmet bag against his leg. He was a recent returnee and had flown with the 101st, which had been operating in the mountains of I Corps. Randolph and Martin were his first students. Rows of aircraft, models A, B, C and D Hueys were parked on cement slabs. They were painted standard olive drab except for the cargo doors, which were bright orange. They arrived at their aircraft, a "D" model, which had the larger cargo doors with two small windows rather than a single large one on the A, B, and C models. It had been configured with seats and seat belts, along the bulkhead in front of the transmission and in the crew chief and gunner's wells on the sides. They could take five passengers in the seats. The familiar jump seat for the non flying student was missing.

"Guess I sit back with the Ranger candidates," Martin said. Randolph had been designated to fly first period. Greenlee read the logbook while the Second Lieutenant students started the pre flight.

"Typical boneheads." Greenlee commented as he opened the left pilot's door and turned on the battery and then the radios. After hooking up his helmet he put it on. They heard the slight static hum as he transmitted. The crew chief was a Staff Sergeant, wearing a First Aviation Brigade patch on his right shoulder. He was driving a three-quarter ton. The brakes squealed as he arrived.

"It was written up to take five passengers," the Sergeant whined. "Wish someone could make up their goddamned mind." There was a jump seat in the back of the three-quarter ton. He manhandled it from the truck and took it to the aircraft. Captain Greenlee glared silently at the sergeant while he installed the seat. There was sweat discoloring his armpits when he had finished.

"In the 101st our crew chiefs understood what they were supposed to do. They also showed their respect for superiors." Greenlee said to him.

"People should know how to write things up."

"Write things up, *what?*"

"I wasn't talking to you, sir." He stopped and looked directly at Captain Greenlee. "Making a comment to myself so I won't misunderstand another write up."

Captain Greenlee's lips twitched as he stared at the Sergeant. "Where was my second student supposed to sit?"

"On his ass, sir." The Sergeant walked quickly to the three-quarter ton and slammed the door shut with excessive force. Some dirt spun from the wheels as he left.

"Who put a hair up his ass?" Randolph broke the silent tension.

"I could write him up for insubordination." Greenlee was still angry by the sergeant's outburst. "If I did it might cost him a stripe. Maybe even a bar to reenlistment. Most E-6s you see want to stay in. One Hundred and First was mostly volunteers and were jump qualified. I'm still getting used to this stateside Army. You guys are going to have to deal with what's left over there. Lot of American units leaving. My unit had good NCOs. You didn't have to spell things out to them. That Sergeant will never make it to reenlistment."

When they had finished the preflight, they stepped away from the aircraft to the shade of the tree line as they waited for the signal to crank. They noticed other students and instructors getting out of the sun, also. "Sir yesterday, you were telling us about Charlie's radio capabilities. We got side tracked." Randolph said.

Captain Greenlee smiled. "Their radio procedures were thorough. They listened to everything. Each time we changed our tack frequencies within a day or two, they found the new ones. Guys told them everything we were doing. If we gave a place a nickname, they could figure it out without much problem. We got compromised so many times: it had to be our sloppy radio procedures. That's the stuff I would advise you guys to think about. Remember, you ain't going to have much left on the ground. Let's go." They all saw one of the flight lead crewmembers raise his arm and twirl it like a rotor. It was the signal to crank.

From the right seat, Randolph went through the start-up checklist. Greenlee monitored him closely when he pulled the trigger to start the turbine. The starter had to be disengaged at the appropriate moment to avoid a hot start, which could damage the engine. Greenlee's first comment upon their first encounter with the Huey was that a hot start would "cause a lot of additional paperwork, we don't need." Sitting six feet in front of the mast from Randolph's perspective made the blades appear smaller. Once during the twenty-five hours of transition into the Huey, Greenlee had put the nose of an aircraft in front of a tree, and they had watched the track of the turning blades as it went between branches. He was demonstrating how close they could maneuver to an obstacle.

"Wish I could do my lawn like this." Carefully, using the rotor wash, he isolated a few leaves and then disintegrated them with the turning blades. "My wife won't cut the lawn. Captain or no Captain, says it's my job. She paid someone to do it while I was in I Corps."

The Huey's controls seemed more fluid to Randolph. Gone was that sense of directness in the OH-23. Being a larger aircraft, the control response was slower, since the movements of the controls had to go through tubes filled with fluids. Gone was the mere thinking of movements. It had to be followed with positive actions. The noise of their turning rotors joined the others cranking. Following directions from the tower, Randolph hovered to a position on the grass where the flight was forming. Under Greenlee's gaze, he carefully turned the aircraft in the direction of take off, and then lowered it. Part of the rear skid touched the ground first. Small flights of four or five aircraft were lining up in the huge open space in the center of the stage field. Randolph had begun to develop a definite feel for the controls. Their aircraft was to be chalk three of their flight.

"Roll it down to idle. No sense in wasting the fuel."

Randolph rolled off the throttle to flight idle. "Sir, good you're conscientious about the government's money."

"Uncle has plenty of money. He prints the stuff. I'm concerned with how fast we're consuming fuel. These hogs all burn at different rates. I don't want to get in the middle of the lift and have the twenty-minute fuel light go on."

Martin, sitting in the jump seat was folding his blanket-sized map preparing to navigate the first leg of the flight. Plugged in, he could hear all conversation and transmissions on his headset.

"Always know where the refueling points are wherever you end up over there. You've got to be able to guess when you'd be getting into your reserve. Warning lights can malfunction. Fuel consumption is no joke. We had one guy who was always running low on fuel. Every time he refueled, the 20-minute warning light was on. Some front seats didn't want to fly with him. Said he stretched that too much."

"How many refueling places were there in I Corps?" Randolph asked.

"We might have to go as far as thirty minutes from fuel. All the other Corps areas-everyone I've ever talked to-that was about the same. You don't let the twenty-minute light come on. If I teach you guys anything, I hope it's that. This guy in our unit finally ran out of fuel. Fortunately, he had just made an approach to a refueling area. He did a hovering autorotation, unexpectedly. Thereafter, his front seat, whoever he was, had the main responsibility to monitor fuel consumption. They should have pulled his aircraft commander orders. You can't do that kind of shit and get away with it all the time. Got to think ahead, or these monsters will eat you. Charlie can shoot at you and miss. Your own stupidity gets you a direct hit."

Once they were positioned with the flight, the lead aircraft took over the radio procedures. They heard flight lead ask for clearance. Greenlee used the UHF radio to communicate with the other instructors. The VHF was used for the tower. As they lifted off, the rotor wash from the other two aircraft in front of them beat against their aircraft's controls.

"Good thing we didn't get an "A" model. If we did, you'd feel this a lot more. In the H-model being used in the land of the two-way gun range, there's plenty of power. That was the major improvement over the "D." Bigger engine, I think. Remember not to run out of power because you're overloaded. Slick drivers are always saying, 'yeah,' I'll take one more. Then when they try to pick it up, they run out of left pedal. Huey drivers are mostly in lifts, anyway. It's the Command and Control's responsibility to specify how many pax in each lift. That should be based on the weakest aircraft in the flight. You can throw in the known abilities or lack thereof of the pilots. When the slick drivers do a single ship mission, that's when they run into trouble." Randolph still on the controls listened intently. Martin seemed preoccupied with the huge map.

"That coming from a gunship pilot?" Randolph asked.

"Naturally," Greenlee laughed. He was proud of his past, Cobra gun ship tour with the 101st Airborne. "Somebody had to protect the slick drivers."

After leveling off with the smooth cool air slipping by the open windows, Randolph concentrated on maintaining his position in the flight, a forty-five degree angle off chalk two. After ten intense minutes sweat was dripping down his flanks. He tried to make minimal corrections to maintain his position. If he allowed his attention to wonder, even momentarily to the instrument panel, he had to make corrections to stay where he was supposed to be in the formation.

"I see a big graveyard," Martin dodged to each side of his seat as he strained to look out through the windscreen or the side windows of the cargo doors. Randolph could feel his movements through the controls. "I think we're a little south of course."

"Look for water towers. They usually have the name of the town painted on them. Then you know where the hell you are. Thayer, I'll take it. You look like you're going to bust. You got to learn to relax and let the aircraft do the work. I have the controls."

Randolph stretched his arms and legs and looked around. He wondered if there were many water towers in Vietnam.

Greenlee's head was turned to the left as he flew on chalk two. His movements on the controls seemed effortless. They stayed in formation. "After a while, you'll get to know certain streams or buildings or even single trees. You'll know where you are. If you're any good, you have to know that all the time. Even if you do become a slick driver. That will take some time, though. You won't get that the first flight."

"You make it look easy." Randolph wanted the controls back.

"I didn't do much formation flying in I Corps. All Slick drivers brag. They claimed the gunship pilots only learned how to make donuts in the sky. Slick drivers could look at a hole in the canopy and tell you whether they could get in there or not. Course, they always said they could get in anywhere. If they went into a tight hole, generally it was without a load. Then they picked up their paxs and have a heavy ship. That's when the trouble started. Think ahead, guys. I can't stress that enough. You can have it back, Thayer."

Back on the controls, he tried to relax. Again he was fighting over-controlling.

"Gunship pilots had to learn how to navigate. Most slick drivers, as long as you had a good flight lead, didn't know where they were half the time since they were in formation."

"What about Chinook drivers?" Martin looked up from his map.

"Anything with too many transmissions and two main rotors should mean twenty rotor disks is just fine for formation." Greenlee laughed.

At the controls, Randolph got tired again, but fought it. For more than half an hour, the only thing he saw were the skids and Jesus Nut at the top of the rotors of chalk two. His concentration fixed on the surfaces and connecting mechanism of chalk two's main rotor. He began making control movements when he saw them move.

"I think we're almost there," Martin announced breaking a long silence in the cockpit. He had been folding and refolding his blanket-sized map as he followed the progress of the flight.

"We'll see how good flight lead's navigation is." Greenlee said.

"I see red smoke," Martin said quickly. Again, he was pulling at his seat belt on the jump seat straining to see outside the aircraft.

Randolph glanced down once through his chin bubble, and did not see any of the signal smoke, but did see the outline of an old airstrip, which was to be their landing zone. As the smoke was spotted, flight lead's instructor began talking to the people on the ground over the FM radio. The cadre on the ground began telling them where they were and how many Ranger candidates there were to transport.

"They screwed that up." Greenlee announced. The flight began a slow turn and descent. Randolph was still concentrating on holding his position in the flight. "Whenever you're talking to people on the ground, you make the radio contact first. If they have a call sign and use the correct tactical call sign that verifies who they are suppose to be. If I hadn't worked with them before or didn't know the voice I was talking to on the Fox Mike, I'd ask them some dumb question only an American would know. Ask about one of the jokes in the latest issue of Playboy. Or a sports question. Anything the gooks might not know. Then, you request they pop smoke. They throw a smoke without mentioning what color. You identify the color of the smoke. The NVA had smokes, and they'd pop 'em to get you to come down. A helicopter and the crew for the cost of a smoke."

When they were on short final, the rotor wash from lead and chalk two beat against their aircraft. Randolph easily over-rode the interference. More smoke grenades had been popped by the Ranger instructors, and the rotors tore into the dark smoke and dissipated it.

"Make the approach all the way to the ground. Always do that if you can. Get the blades flat. Get the collective down. I don't want us rolling around on the ground."

The Ranger candidates waited without moving for the order to board the aircraft. They wore camouflage paint on their faces and on the backs of their hands. They did not have steel helmets but wore cloth caps. Each wore a harness with ammo pouches. Their cadre approached the aircraft when the blades were at flat pitch, then signaled the candidates. Each got onto an installed seat and were ordered to fasten the seat belts. Their groups were divided into four to five man sticks. As they were strapping in, Randolph looked back into the cargo area at their faces. There were red lines in their alert eyes. Under the camouflage paint there was obvious tension and fatigue. They kept looking furtively at their instructors. There were no smiles. They were all very serious-looking. Relief began to show on their stern faces as they leaned back in the small canvas seats. Martin gave them candy bars. Without hesitation, they grabbed them. Some stuffed them into their equipment hiding them from their cadre instructors.

"One guy ate the wrapping too. He didn't even open it." Martin said into the intercom.

"All that for a little piece of cloth," Greenlee said. "It's been cooler. These guys don't smell too bad. When I was going through methods of instruction, we picked up a group that really smelled."

"Look at all we've done for a little piece of metal." Randolph said.

"You got a point, there, Thayer." Greenlee said.

Two of the Ranger candidates, after gobbling down the candy, let their heads rest against the bulkhead oblivious to the noise of the whirling machinery inches away. Some actually started to doze. Others had vacant stares as fatigue overtook them, and they realized they had reached a place where no one was watching them.

Flight lead ordered them to prepare to pull pitch at the count of ten.

"Light on the skids. Watch the torque. You will feel the additional weight. Watch lead. You got to stay with him." Randolph felt the skids as they became light and then left the ground. The aircraft settled slightly, and he felt Greenlee's hand on the collective. The aircraft bobbed as it caught some of the rotor wash from lead before going into translational lift and surging upward. They managed to climb only a thousand feet before the flight began a slow descent. Air born, Randolph could notice no difference in how the aircraft performed. However, when they started to descend, he could feel the weight of their passengers in the controls.

"You can feel it." Randolph said to Greenlee. "Lot different than an empty ship."

"Get used to it. If you're going to be a slick driver, this is all they do." Greenlee said.

The flight made shallow turns and a gradual descent. Only after the aircraft were on the ground and the blades at flat pitch did the candidates unbuckle their seat belts and rush to the cover of tall grass. Lifting off, the aircraft was light and felt normal to Randolph. They flew to a tactical refueling site where they did hot refueling. Metal gratings had been set up as refueling pads. The engines were rolled down to flight idle with the blades at flat pitch. Greenlee saw his students' apprehension. On the flight line at Rucker contract civilians did the refueling when the aircraft was completely shut down.

"This is the only way you refuel in Vietnam. Usually, you top off before you leave on the flight. You make up the fuel used for cranking. Every pound can be important."

The site was manned by Army enlisted men, although this was an Air Force base. While they refueled the aircraft wearing helmets, gloves and dressed in the same two-piece Nomex flight suits, Randolph and Martin switched places.

They returned to the deserted airstrip where they picked up more Ranger candidates and slipped more candy bars to them. The field was open without obstructions other than a few bushes that were only a few feet tall. Again they made gradual and shallow approaches with wide slow turns. Martin performed the same take-off and landing as Randolph had. He flew the aircraft back to Rucker while Randolph made a half-hearted attempt to navigate. Finally, he folded the huge map and stuffed it in his helmet bag.

Captain Greenlee did not seem to care if he navigated or not. Randolph settled back in the jump seat, watched the countryside beneath them and felt like a tourist.

"I'll take Teddy to the pool," Faith said. Teddy had been badgering his mother and everyone else since check-in to take him for a swim in the Holiday Inn's pool. He had seen it as they drove into the parking lot. The outside pool, surrounded by lounge chairs was crowded. Many of the hotel's guests were there for the graduation ceremonies the following day. Randolph had gone to the airport in his Camaro to help transport the Thayers, Grandmother Willis, Faith and Al Garber. His father and Teddy went with him in his car. Everyone else rode in the oversized van Al Garber had rented. It had plenty of room for everyone including baggage. The flight had arrived at three in the afternoon from Atlanta. Everyone except Teddy was still flush from the flight, which had departed Logan at 8 a.m. His grandmother had gone to her room, which she would share with Faith. Teddy had already explored their room insisting that he be allowed to sleep there. Grandmother Willis ordered him a roll out cot. Judy was expected to sleep on a cot in her parents' room. Al Garber had his own room. He had parked his luggage, and then returned to be with the Thayers.

The flights were the first plane trips Judy had taken. She was animated. Faith had flown commercially before. Grandmother Willis was an accomplished traveler. It was the first flight his parents had taken in over twenty years. Maggie Thayer made comments about the changes that had occurred during the past two decades. Judy was sitting on one of the two double beds next to Al Garber, their bodies touching. Randolph sat alone on the second bed; listening to Judy ramble and watching his mother unpack. His father in one of the few easy chairs in the room was enthroned before the color television. When Faith made her announcement, she paused next to Judy, Al Garber and Randolph. "You could come swimming with me and your brother." She said to Randolph, gently.

"I didn't bring a suit." Randolph said.

"Where is Andrea?" Judy asked, after Faith left the room to go to hers to change into a bathing suit.

"Delayed, "Randolph answered her without hiding his obvious frustration. "Last night she was ready to go to the airport. I thought she might be on the same flight as you."

"Let's go outside for a cigarette," Al Garber said to Randolph. The dejection in Randolph's face had grown. Judy did not object or offer to go with them. Randolph noticed the knowing look she gave Al Garber as he stood. The air was heavy. They walked through the large parking lot past the pool, finding some chairs beneath shady trees. Al Garber was silent as he watched Randolph light a cigarette. When Randolph looked at Al Garber's face, he noticed the expectation.

"Andrea's been very punctual visiting me here over the summer. We stay at this Holiday Inn, not my trailer. She was here two weekends ago. I really expected her about the same time you guys arrived."

"Maybe she'll take a cab from the airport." Al Garber said. "Guess you'll have a job when you get out of the Army."

"I'd be pretty dumb not to work for her father's company. With her father's heart condition, Andrea has fallen right into it. She's nothing like when we were both students."

"It might be nice to start near the top," Al Garber smiled broadly. "That's something I'll never know."

"Nice of you to rent that van. I should have thought of it."

"My contribution." Al dragged deeply on his cigarette, and then exhaled. He stared silently until he had Randolph's complete attention. "I want you to be my best man."

"That's what I saw in Judy's face back in the room," Randolph smiled.

"With your leave and travel time, were you planning to go anyplace? That's what everyone doesn't know."

"Andrea's mentioned the Cape for a week. I won't let that interfere with your Saturday. Isn't there anyone else who's close to you?"

"You mean a lot to Judy. More than you know. I'd like us to be more than just brothers-in-law."

"If that's what you guys want, of course I'll do it." Randolph smiled as Al reached to shake his hand. They both saw Judy trotting toward them. They stood when she got nearer.

"You have a call, Randy. It's Andrea. She's pretty upset." Her gloomy face exploded into a smile when she saw Al Garber's face and knew instantly what her brother had said.

Randolph did not remember any of the distance he covered through the parking lot and into his parents' room. The phone was suddenly in his hand. The image of his mother's face swam before his racing thoughts.

"Scott Junior is missing. He was on a helicopter that went down yesterday. They've flown over the wreck, but there's nothing of any survivors. I'm in D.C. Sam and I drove down last night. My mother and Scott have been trying to get more information. Samuel is here. Sandra's in Europe. They're still trying to contact her."

"With who he is, being Scott's son and everything, you'll get all the information that's available. That's an advantage, Andrea." Randolph's perspiration beaded on his forehead.

"That doesn't change his status. He's still missing." Her voice was harsh. He could feel her tension and escalating anger. "Why can't they get anyone on the ground near the downed ship?"

"There's no American troops on the ground there."

"We control everything over there. We'll get people to him."

"That's how much you know about it!" She snarled. "American troops are stretched thin over there. That's U.S. policy now. That makes a big impact on troops who are there. I know what I'm talking about."

"The Marine Corps doesn't leave people behind. They will get to the wreck. It might take a little time, but they will."

"Scott is taking this very hard. This stupid war! It destroys the people it shouldn't." She was silent a moment. Randolph was staring at his mother, who stared back at him, noticing his anguish.

"Obviously, you won't be here tomorrow."

"I can't leave my mother and Scott." Her tone had become openly hostile. "It had to be a helicopter. The things are not safe. Goddamned helicopters!" The line went dead in his ear.

The graduation exercises for the Officer Rotary Wing Aviation Course were shared with three other aviation classes. There were two Warrant Officers' classes, one fixed wing with less than a dozen graduating and the rotary wing with over seventy. The third class was the Officer Fixed Wing class of an even dozen of which eight were Captains, attesting to the difficulty and perseverance of gaining a slot in that course. The Fort Rucker commander, a two-star general introduced the guest speaker, a one-star general from the Pentagon. His talk was short, direct and somewhat technical about the future of Army Aviation, which the two hundred graduates through award of their aviator badges, their wings, were entering. A post chaplain's speech was moral, upright and short urging the new aviators to uphold their spiritual powers and strengths when entering their first assignments, most of which would be Vietnam.

At the conclusion of the formal ceremonies, everyone filed out doors into the sunlight where wives, mothers or girl friends pinned the wings on the new aviators' chests. Maggie Thayer about to pin Randolph turned to Faith and beckoned her to help. Only when Randolph signaled affirmatively did Faith step forward to complete the little ceremony.

Since it was still mid afternoon when all the formal procedures were completed, Randolph took his family for a tour of the newly established aviation museum. There were several obsolete aircraft, including a Russian one captured during the Israeli-Arab seven-day war three years before. The Thayers and Grandmother Willis took many photographs while everyone posed with the new Army Aviator. Randolph displayed adequate smiles for picture taking. They went back to the Holiday Inn. Teddy easily bored with the static aircraft display was eager to get back into the pool. The long afternoon with the glaring absence of Andrea played a toll on Randolph. His face was drawn, nearly haggard.

Since Randolph and Riard had parted, turned in the keys to their trailer, Randolph stayed in Al Garber's room. Judy spent her second night on a fold-up in her parents' room. Teddy again slept in Grandmother Willis and Faith's room. They had breakfast together before returning to the rooms to pack for the return trip. Randolph's face was still gaunt and, mostly, he was silent. Faith quickly finished her packing and rushed to the Thayers' room.

"Randy is obviously upset. He may try to do something rash, like try to drive straight through home. That could lead to an accident. If I go with him, he won't push himself like that because of me. I can do some of the driving." Faith stood, her feet almost in a boxer's stance facing Maggie Thayer's lengthening frown.

"You traveled with us. Your mother will be expecting you back with us."

"When she knows I'm doing something to help Randy, she won't object. This may be the only thing left, I can do for him."

"What about your tickets? You might not be able to get a refund." Maggie Thayer's scowl dissipated only slightly.

"That's only money. I don't care about it."

"Will he take you?"

"He says I'm like his sister, so he better."

Randolph protested about her going, but meekly as Faith had predicted. Actually, he was glad for the company. Plainly he saw his mother's moral dilemma smashed by Faith's tactical victory. It was the only thing that morning that brought a smile to his lips. With Faith firmly lodged in the bucket seat of the Camaro they left the Dothan airport after seeing everyone off. Having signed out of Fort Rucker that morning, and with his car fully packed, his travel time began tacked onto his long period of leave.

At first for long intervals of driving they did not talk. Faith was interested in the country they were passing through. Her steady trickle of comments eventually opened him up. He talked about his college days at Northeastern. She told him interesting stories about her job as a legal secretary. Grudgingly, he shared the driving allowing Faith to put in a couple of hours behind the wheel. Late in the evening they both saw the sign welcoming them to Virginia.

"We need to stop. I'm tired, sticky, and hungry for some real food. After I eat something, I want a shower and to stretch out in a comfortable bed. We've been on the road a long day and you can't see anything in the dark. The country is interesting, I'd like to see more of it."

"We've stopped for meals and breaks. It'll be light soon."

"Bull! Look at your watch, daylight is hours away. We'll miss all this scenery. Driving through the night is not worth risking an accident and damaging your car. You don't want to be without a car on your leave. We'll get up early and start. You're not even sure where she will be. She may still be in D.C."

Her mention of Andrea startled him. Through the long afternoon of driving as with all her telephone calls over the summer, she had not mentioned her. Reluctantly he realized Faith was right about not knowing where Andrea was. Although the call had come from D.C. he had no address for the Lynders' Washington apartment. She might have stayed at a hotel.

"If we stop at one of the bigger name motels, their rooms usually have two beds. We don't have to sleep in the same one, although I wouldn't mind. Or, we can get two rooms, if you prefer. That's dumb because it's much more expensive. You're the pilot, make the decision."

The driving and being cramped from sitting in the same position so long was giving him a big-headed sensation, a clear signal of fatigue. With minimal hesitancy he agreed. They began looking for motel signs before the highway exits. The first exit they passed had motel names they didn't recognize. The second had a Holiday Inn. Randolph turned onto the exit way. Within a few minutes, they had stopped in the motel's spacious parking lot. They got out of the car and stretched. It was a nice warm evening. The air was thick and moist. There was a fast food restaurant across the street from the motel. They ate sitting on bench seats. Faith attacked her food. Randolph picked randomly.

"One or two rooms?" Faith asked. She was studying his face intently as they left the restaurant and walked back to the car.

Consciously, he avoided her gaze. "Who is it you don't trust? Me or yourself?"

"Both."

"I'm flattered. Also disappointed."

"This is a difficult time for me. You should understand that."

"My sentiments, also! So near yet still so far." Her broad grin was both mysterious and lusty.

Randolph opened the small trunk to get their suitcases. He carried both of them, as they went in the main well lit entrance. At the registration desk, while Faith did not even blink once, he asked for one room. As they went through a dimly lit corridor, he did notice the triumphant smile that parted her lips slightly. There were two beds in their room, both doubles. With a chivalrous shrug he offered her the shower first. Settling in an easy chair, he felt his tired muscles and actually yawned a few times as he turned on the colored television. She was quick in the shower, perhaps ten minutes. Opening the door to the bathroom, she emerged, stark naked with the exception of a huge bath towel wrapped partially around her wet hair. The big towel hung down touching her shoulders.

"Forgot my hair dryer. I was using your grandmother's."

"Faith!"

"Everything is the same, like it was that one afternoon so long ago. It's all still here." She turned completely around a few times, displaying herself. Stopping, she faced him, still rubbing her hair. "You got the one room. Don't blame me." She snickered. Slowly taking the towel off her head, her wet hair fell to her shoulders. She watched his eyes as he studied her body. Standing perfectly still he stared but did not move. Finally, she turned away from him and darted back into the bathroom, wrapping another huge towel around herself. She sat on the edge of one of the beds facing his chair. He still had not moved. There were the beginnings of tears in her eyes, which she dabbed at, briefly. "Do you know what it took to do what I just did, and then have you not want me?"

"It's not that you're not desirable. You're beautiful. I'd be crazy if I didn't want you. Right now feeling like I do, it would be kind of perverted. You made me feel good all the time we've been in the car this afternoon, talking and laughing. Honestly Faith, I haven't felt that way in a long time."

"Then complete it for me, tonight."

Randolph swallowed a few times, but did not look away from her. "I'd like to, but I can't. Please understand."

"I do, but I don't want to understand." Her eyes watered again quickly.

"I understand want and desire."

"Do you?" She could not stop the tears from rolling down her cheeks.

"It would be a lie for me. Does that make sense?"

She sucked in a deep breath and let it out audibly. "Yes, I don't want a lie. We've never had that between us. This isn't the time to start."

After an extended silence, Randolph stood up from the easy chair. "I need to take my shower."

"A cold one?" Looking at her face in the dim light of the room the tears were gone, replaced with her usual broad smile.

"I like you, Faith. That will always be so."

"You have to start someplace. I'll take that for now."

He went into the bathroom.

Chapter Twelve

When they stopped in front of the Beckwerth house, it was 2:00 AM Monday. The neighborhood was deathly still. Street lamps made shadows of the dark leaves under their arching light. Faith leaned across the console and kissed him lightly on the cheek. The move startled him, but made him realize also how tired he was. She had relinquished the wheel for the last time in Northern New Jersey.

"Thanks for the ride. Just like commuters at the train station. Except, they usually get home before this hour." Her smile was genuine and warm despite having spent nearly one complete rotation of the hour hand in a bucket seat.

"You made the trip okay. I didn't have a chance to brood. The difficult part is still in front of me."

"At least I did something right, finally."

"You always do things right. Some guy is going to get real lucky. You deserve the best."

"Can I have one thing before we say good night? This was a long drive. I earned it."

"What?" His tone was suspicious.

"One real kiss. The kind you suck the air out of me type."

He looked at her face in the half light. There was sincerity as well as an open pleading. A flash of the last look in Vicki Horwell's face crossed his mind. He reached slowly for her, putting his arms around her. They were cramped and their positions were awkward over the small console between the seats. Her lips were warm and the inside of her mouth tasted different. He worked the kiss for a long time, and felt her body responding. Afterwards on the short drive home, the sensations of her lips and mouth remained with him.

The Thayer house was deathly still and quiet as he pulled into his usual parking spot on the street. He did not unload his car, other than taking an overnight bag and crept through the darkened house. Going upstairs toward his room, he knew where each step creaked from his weight. He recognized gashes and scratches in the woodwork. In his room, the bed, the bureau, and his desk were as he remembered them. Nostalgia made his knees tremble and reminded him of how tired his cramped muscles were. His narrow bed was neatly made up, his closet door open, with his clothes hanging as he had left them at Christmas nine months before. Everything was the same, but different. He was different. Undressing to his underwear he slid beneath the cool sheets. The bed was familiar and felt small after the numerous larger beds he had used in the past year. He was home.

His solid sleep was interrupted by the incessant, distant ringing of the phone. His bedroom door was open, so he knew his mother had come in to see him before she left for work. The ringing would not stop. Sleepily, he pulled his pants on and a shirt, and padded wearily down the worn stairs to the living room. It was Andrea. She was still in D.C.

"Scott Junior walked out of the hostile area on Friday. It was actually only two days he was listed as missing in action. They hit trees, but they all got out. Some on board were hurt. On the ground, he took command as the senior officer. He helped carry one of the injured, and they avoided NVA soldiers who were looking for them. They're talking about a big medal for him. It will really help his career."

"When did you learn all this?"

"Saturday, we were at Scott's office. That's when we got the news of his return to friendly forces. He wants to return to his unit. Scott wants him to come home. I called your unit. You had already signed out. Your trailer phone was disconnected."

"Graduation was Friday. There was no reason for me to hang around."

"I called yesterday but your mother said you hadn't arrived home yet."

"What brought the ship down? Was it a mechanical problem or enemy fire?"

"I don't know."

"What altitude were they at?"

"Nothing was that detailed. He was in a helicopter that went down. A helicopter!" She answered testily.

"I've got four weeks of leave before I report. Are we going to spend any of it together? Mike, my roommate had his orders changed. He's Field Artillery. There were twelve FAs in my class, and they changed all of their orders. None of them are going to Vietnam. The way things are going, I might not do a whole tour. Anything is possible."

"Why didn't that happen to Infantry branch?"

"It's got to be a mistake. Mike will end up in Vietnam. We're considered branch immaterial for aviation assignments."

"I've heard that term before. Why was it just Field Artillery that was changed?"

"It's the Army. Stupid things like that happen."

"Remember what you told me, if they didn't need you, you wouldn't go. You can stay in CONUS."

"My orders haven't changed. I was told I'll get supplemental travel orders by mail in a few weeks. Right now, the time I have with you is dwindling rapidly. It's kind of hard to get started when you're there, and I'm here."

"We should be back by Wednesday. We have to stop in Pennsylvania to pick up Sam's son. He's already missed some school. Sam insisted on driving down here with me. I didn't want to wait for Logan to open up. It was good of her to do that. She didn't have to."

"You've got your car?"

"We drove down here in my Mustang."

"Let her drive your car back. If the kid has any stuff to bring, with three of you it's going to be very crowded in that type of car. Get on a flight today and I'll pick you up at Logan."

"I can't leave today."

"Why the hell not? You found out about Scott Junior. What else is there for you to do down there?"

"I have to meet with Scott. He's got a list of contacts in the Far East that could be potential customers for us."

"Why can't he send you the list?"

"One of the contacts, Scott thinks is actually here in D.C. on a low level unofficial trade visit He's here to feel out Americans on business prospects. Scott says it's very important to meet with these people face to face. If he can arrange just a quick meeting with this man, he will remember me, and that will be an 'in' later, when we do business with them. The Orient's a huge potential market. If Scott can pull it off, I've got to be here." Her tone seemed to increase in pitch as she ran on with this explanation. To Randolph, it sounded almost as if she were convincing herself. He listened patiently without interrupting.

"This is my time. If I had known you were going to stay in D.C., I would have stopped there on my way home."

"I'll do what you say and not drive back with Sam. I'll be on the shuttle early Wednesday morning. I've got some things to finish up this week when I get back, but I'm taking the whole week off next week. We'll go down the Cape. It's September and still nice down there. There'll be less people, so it will be better. I need this day. You've got to understand how important this could be for Tremblay Bearings. Big important!"

Randolph was silent.

"Go to my apartment. You remember where I hide the spare key?"

"Why? Without you there, it's just empty rooms."

He watched her, sleepily, as she dressed. She wore a frilly white blouse under a black pin stripe jacket, mannish but unable to mask her blatant femininity. As she finished applying makeup, she stood then bent over to pick something up from the floor and the matching pin striped pants went snug. He could almost feel her

302

skin as he stared. She smiled at him when she caught his leering gaze, and came back to the bed. Sitting on the edge next to him, he could smell the fresh application of makeup mixed with her perfume.

"What are you planning on doing today while I'm gone?"

"I'm going to let my sperm count increase."

"That sounds ambitious." She smiled.

"You could call in sick, stay here and work on continuing to decrease my count."

"I have things I have to follow up on, especially if I'm going to be away for a week."

"You'll stay off the phone during that time?"

"I can't promise that." She smiled again. "There may be some things that need my attention"

"You're looking at the main one."

"I'm doing the vacation. I'll try to limit the telephone, monster that it is."

"You've gotten very important for those tight breeches you're wearing."

"They aren't tight."

"They're tight, you know it, and torture lesser animals than I am. Course, I have an in with that wonderful ass. It happens to belong to me."

"You work on that sperm count. That sounds about your speed these days."

"I'm a soldier on leave. We live close to a liquor store. The world is wonderful!" He put his palm on the back of her neck and pulled her down toward him. Her hair fell onto his face and neck. Its silkiness tickled his skin. She allowed him some increasing liberties as his hands wondered over the fabric of her suit. When he started to displace some of it, she stood up quickly to break his embrace.

"The diplomatic thing would have been perfect. You could have got posted to Europe. I'm going to have to face the sales situation over there eventually."

"That job is for a Captain." Looking at her pensive expression, he wondered why that subject suddenly arose. Her gaze was riveted to him as if she were looking for a reaction. Then conscious of his returning stare, quickly she turned her face away. "I'm not even officially a First Lieutenant. I haven't got any order giving me that rank."

"It happens after a year, automatically."

"You know that?"

"I have my sources," she smiled smugly, which annoyed him further. "Bye," she blew a kiss to him as she walked out of the bedroom door. He heard her open the apartment door and close it. Then the silence entwined him. He remembered her once mentioning a diplomatic job but had thought the subject was long past. He had worked diligently during the leave to avoid any controversial issues. They seemed to have had a fine time together, enjoying non-stressed filled days.

He had picked her up after plowing his way through the commuter traffic into Boston early on a Wednesday morning, leaving his parents' house with a suitcase full of his civilian clothes. They had spent the rest of that day together mostly in the apartment and in bed. She had risen early Thursday and gone to work. During that day he had gotten his fitting for his tux completed, the only pre-wedding task he had been given. Judy's ceremonies were approaching rapidly in just over two weeks. It was Friday. He had been a rated Army Aviator for one week. They did not celebrate the anniversary. It felt strange for him not to be flying or having any other duties. He anticipated with some excitement going to the Cape, a place that was always slightly exotic to him. Andrea hadn't committed to leaving work early so they could get a head start on the traffic. Randolph expected it to be heavy, one week after Labor Day and with good weather forecasted.

Judy's wedding was on schedule. Reserving the church was the least of the frenzied planning activities. The reception was slowly winding down to a last possible alternative, a tent in the Thayer back yard. Since reception halls and large restaurants within twenty miles were fully booked, and possible cancellations weren't forthcoming, the tent was becoming the primary plan. They had located one to rent. It was in Worchester, which added substantially to the cost. Their honeymoon was to be only a week.

Judy wanted to be back in time to see him off. His reporting date was the second Thursday in October.

Andrea stayed at Tremblay Bearings until six. She had to change and wanted something to eat before they started for the Cape. They got stuck in the Friday night traffic in the bottle neck roads before the bridges. She had reserved a week at a rather large and expensive hotel with a section of its own ocean beach as well as indoor and outdoor pools. They played miniature golf, drove miniature drag racing machines around an oval track, and went to movies, although they preferred watching television at night in their room. The weather cooperated remaining generally good, although a distinct autumn coolness enveloped some of the mornings. They read paperbacks sitting on the beach and made sand castles. Andrea bought an overpriced sand bucket with shovels with her plastic money at the hotel's gift shop. They enjoyed each other's company content to shut out the world around them. She limited her business calls which were mostly to Sam, who gave her briefings on activities at the plant. Production for the new alloy bearings had started. Jonathon's California customers were creating a steady flow of orders. Others were beginning to come in from other industrial areas of the country.

Late in their week while on the beach, suddenly, she excused herself to go to their room saying she needed to use the bathroom. She was gone a long time. Finally without any feelings of concern other than missing her, he walked to the hotel. As he was passing through the main lobby he surprised her getting out of a public phone booth. She was startled by being discovered. Her face seemed to go blank, an unusual condition for her.

"Why didn't you use the phone in our room?"

"I had just finished talking to Samantha," she said quickly. "She was on her way out of the plant. I thought of something, and I wanted to make sure she knew it. I was afraid I'd miss her." The color started to return to her face. Still, she did not smile at him. Randolph accepted the strange explanation, thinking it must have been something at the factory causing her concern. Thinking to redirect her thoughts, he rattled forcefully about restaurant prospects for the night, as they walked slowly back to the beach.

They extended their stay through the second weekend, returning to Andrea's apartment late Sunday. More than half his leave had been used. She was up early the next morning and went to work. This was the start of the week of his sister's wedding. Judy planned to work until Wednesday. Al Garber planned to stay at his job until Thursday when his parents were expected to arrive from their retirement home in Florida. The tent was scheduled to be delivered and erected in the Thayer back yard on that day also. Randolph had been away from the frenzied preparations, but numerous notes on the huge kitchen table made him aware of the frantic pace to get everything done in the limited remaining time. He had come home to check his mail, expecting the supplemental travel orders. These would have flight and bus vouchers for his trip to McGuire Air Force Base. He checked the counter space his mother reserved for his mail. There were two envelopes from different military commands.

Opening the first letter, which he selected randomly, it appeared to be a copy, which had been reproduced numerous times. There were several different types of print, some slightly blurry, and the copying had made the ink quality different from tones of nearly gray to dark black. The form told the Army's policy statement about annual leave changes from short tour assignments to reassignment to Continental U.S. Army Commands. It reminded him it was the individual's responsibility to contact the gaining command concerning leave. As usual in any Army document there were references to Regulations, circulars, and directives. His understanding of his leave was it was granted prior to starting a short twelve month tour in Vietnam, where normal leave would not be granted. Why would they pick this time to remind him of leave policy for CONUS when he wasn't assigned to it? He had a reporting date with a bracketed hour frame during which he must sign in. Why had he been sent the form? Possibly it was a usual Army mix-up.

The second envelope was official correspondence addressed to Second Lieutenant Randolph Willis Thayer requesting he make a selection from the following list of available language courses. There were a few dozen courses listed, and the Army posts, ranging from Virginia to California, where they would be taught. There was a return envelope for his reply requiring no postage as long as if was mailed within the United States.

His first thought was that he had been reassigned, like his roommate Riard. That would explain the odd leave policy letter. Riard had still been at flight school, so the school did the administrative duty of reproducing orders. While on leave, how would that be handled, other than by correspondence? His knees felt wobbly, and he had to sit at the kitchen table. He studied the letter. The phrase "officer's request" struck him. That seemed odd. He had not requested a change, and certainly he did not want more schooling, especially language training. It had to be a mistake.

Taking one of the clear pads of writing paper placed on the huge kitchen table obviously for wedding related notes, he went into the living room to the Thayer phone. There were no telephone numbers on either the letter or the correspondence. His first thought was of Fort Devens, the major active Army post in New England. He called. Over an hour and a half later after being disconnected twice, being left on indeterminable 'hold' a few times, he was finally routed to an Adjutant General's detachment, where a female civilian finally listened patiently to his concerns about the official correspondence.

"If you requested language courses, they would reassign you."

"I didn't request that." He was angry, but tried not to antagonize the only friendly voice he had heard.

"Read me the letters in the upper left top of the form. I can tell you where it originated." He did as she directed. "That's officer management. Infantry Branch is corresponding with you. There're in Washington. I've got a toll free number as well as an area code one."

"Please give me both." The free call number put him into what he thought sounded like a recruiting command. The person he talked to never hung up on him but put him on hold several times trying to determine what department to transfer him to. Finally, with his patience quickly ebbing away he shrieked into the phone, "I'm an Infantry Officer who is also an Aviator!"

"That's special assignments, Infantry. I can connect you." With that, he lost that gentle soul as he was transferred.

"Special assignments, Infantry. Captain Yanty. May I help you, sir?"

"Sir, I've got a request to select a language course. My name is Randolph Thayer. I'm a Second Lieutenant and just graduated from ORWAC this month. I didn't request this. How did I get it?"

"Thayer, Randolph? Your name sounds recent. I think I saw your folder."

"Graduated on the fourth of this month, sir. I'm on my pre-Vietnam leave. I don't want language school. I had all the flight training, I want to use it." Randolph quickly reiterated the facts of the official letter.

"It came from this office, Lieutenant. Infantry is honoring your request for a change in assignment. That's a dream assignment. You could end up with some major command or even in an embassy somewhere in the world, depending on which language you choose. Hold for a moment while I locate your folder."

The phone went into 'hold' sound. He stared at the wallpaper of the Thayer living room, which had not been changed in ten years, and began seeing things in the pattern he had never noticed before. CPT Yanty returned to the phone within what could only have been a few minutes. "This is a request initiated by the individual. There is no letter signed or anything. Looks like it was done via a verbal request. That's not too rare. I've seen it on occasion, Lieutenant. I'm a rotary wing aviator, too. Looks like you'll be flying the same model desk as me."

"Can I get back to my original orders?"

Captain Yanty was silent for an extended moment. Although he knew the Captain was still on the line, he was tempted to ask if their connection was still functioning.

"Who the hell are you, really, Lieutenant?"

"I'm a nobody, a Second Lieutenant who wants to use what the Army spent so much money training me to do."

"This request doesn't indicate that."

"I never asked for the change."

"Somebody is looking out for you, Lieutenant. My boss's cubical door's been closed a lot the past week. Usually when that happens he's planning his golf matches. Usually brings a couple of clubs into the office. I haven't seen any this past week. Curious. I often wondered how grown men can get any enjoyment out of walking around with a bunch of sticks hitting a tiny ball trying to miss man-made miniature lakes and deserts. Then again, I'm not a Colonel. I've heard things are getting tougher. My tour was 1967-8."

"You were there for Tet?"

"They caught us with hour pants down, Lieutenant. We got waxed."

"All the Field Artillery officers in my ORWAC class got their orders changed from going to Vietnam. Is Infantry starting to do that?"

"Not yet. I heard something strange like that going on down the hall. Wasn't sure it was true."

"It happened two and a half weeks ago at Fort Rucker. If I don't go, what happens to my slot?"

"Some unsuspecting soul will get orders for a short, unaccompanied tour."

"An infantry officer?"

"Flying assignments are branch immaterial. It could be another Infantry type."

"I don't want some unsuspecting soul doing my tour."

"I can tell you what you can do. Officially, you need to vacate this request. A letter signed by you should accomplish that."

"Where do I send it?"

"You sure you want to do this, Lieutenant?"

"Absolutely! I want to fly."

"Got a pencil handy? I'll give you the mailing address."

He typed the letter out on his school portable typewriter, which was still in the closet of his room. When it was finished, he went directly to the post office and sent it overnight mail to the address CPT Yanty had given him. Then, he began to wait.

The specter of the problems at Fort Benning began to haunt his thoughts. Once again, somehow Andrea was involved. The linkage was much more subtle and potentially had a greater impact. Asking her directly was something he still wanted to avoid. His original set of orders had not officially been revoked. Was CPT Yanty right, and had he done everything possible with a single letter to avoid a new set of orders? Impotence plagued his existence broken only by the mail deliveries.

Monday night at the restaurant they selected, Andrea detailed the growing problems in the Midwest, which she felt were hindering sales. Sam's obvious influence was noticeable. There had been open lobbying for the hire of a new territorial salesman, Sam's Ohio boyfriend. Andrea using her stepfather's law firm resources, discretely checked out Samantha's friend. He was a moderately successful career salesman of industrial products, who could fit into her growing sales organization, which she felt needed new blood. There were many details about Midwest distributors and reps, which she narrated down to a boorish level. Randolph wondered where she got such information, but decided against asking fearing an additional torrent of wearisome facts. He feigned interest. When she was finally finished, they had little else to discuss, and their conversation lapsed into extended periods of silence. That night they made love with a desperate urgency. For a long period they were both awake, each sensing the other's restlessness but neither was willing to address it openly.

Tuesday, he hoped his overnight letter had arrived. He was tempted to call CPT Yanty, but realized it could still be in some bureaucratic in-basket and might take days to be directed to an eventual destination. Randolph squandered the day fretfully, until Andrea returned from work. Immediately, he perceived in her a silent sense of expectancy. She also was waiting for something extraordinary to happen. Would it have to do with new orders for him? It added to his growing sense of foreboding and suspicion. Again their love making was desperate and frenzied. Afterwards each retreated from the other, not touching yet aware of each other awake and waiting. He dozed and when he woke with a start, it was past 3:00 AM. Andrea was not in the bed. He found her in her second home office bedroom. There were signs of its infrequent use, now that she had a complete operating office at the plant. She was staring out the window which overlooked the apartment's parking lot. Her arms were folded over her chest. She was standing perfectly still. Wrapping his arms around her, she did not resist his touch but did nothing to encourage it.

"Are we coming to the end?" Andrea's tone was nearly a whisper.

"I still have more leave."

"I don't mean that!" Her voice exploded like the crack of a bullet.

"In flight school we had days of separation, and we survived. I will bring you with me in my heart wherever I am."

"I won't be here, alone." Her tone was bitter. "There's still time for change? It must!"

Slowly, he removed his arms from her and stepped away. She remained motionless looking out the window as he had found her. Silently, he turned and went back to their bed.

Wednesday, he was at his parents' house when the mailman arrived. It was the last day the house was silent and empty, before the wedding preparations would keep members of his family away from their jobs in order to complete nuptial tasks before Saturday. Randolph had picked up his tux, his only assignment. There was no correspondence or other mail for him. He wondered if it was too early for any response unless CPT Yanty was waiting for his letter. Would the Captain risk antagonizing his boss, a Colonel? He might. He was an Aviator. Risk was part of the avocation.

That night at dinner in another restaurant, Andrea lobbied for him to go with her the following week on the Midwest trip. She had not planned to go until after he left in October. Voiceless developments for the approaching Board meeting, which would have a huge impact on her standing in the company, were beginning to mount. She wanted the mid west trip completed.

"Bureaucracies work in strange ways." Andrea stated bluntly, capturing his wavering attention immediately.

"They also have their own language." He retorted.

"I should be getting a new title, once the Board meets next month, and I'm on it."

"That's a forgone conclusion?"

"Yes," she said softly.

"What title do you get?"

"Bureaucracy isn't limited to government. Business has it own little quirks. They can force people to make decisions whether they want to or not."

Knowing the trip could not start until after his sister's wedding Saturday, he was non committal. His main concern was that he would be away from the mailman, who could be carrying his future. Again their bed session was intense, followed by long silent hours of wakefulness.

Thursday, while Andrea was at the plant, again Randolph went to his parents' house. Judy was home waiting the arrival of the tent, which was scheduled to be erected only two days before its expected use. The tent company arrived in a task force of two trucks and half a dozen workers. The supervisor of the group was rather young, but aggressively persuasive. Judy knew where she wanted the tent which differed with the supervisor's assessment of the labor and time involved. Judy soon grew flustered. Randolph, sensing the mounting confrontation, inserted himself, giving specific and definite instructions where the tent was to be put up, and where the main openings were to face. Verbally, threatening the supervisor in front of his gaping and snickering work force, that he might have to inform his boss for the reason in returning all the way to Worchester with the un-rented tent and no payment check, caused all argument to cease. The tent was erected per Second Lieutenant Thayer's instructions. Judy expressed her gratitude for her brother's intervention.

Randolph waited impatiently for the delivery of the mail. There was an official envelope containing travel vouchers for a plane ticket to Philadelphia and a limo bus transporter company which would take him to McGuire. There were no amendments to his orders. The account numbers on the vouchers matched those on his original set of orders. He was going. His flight would depart from

Logan at 10:00 AM. Thoughtfully, the Army would allow him time for a final breakfast with his family.

He went back to the apartment to wait for her. Turning on the television, he could not concentrate on the programs. Getting up, he wandered aimlessly from room to room. In the second bedroom where he had found her standing staring out the window, he stood for a long time looking out the same window. Suddenly, it was as simple, yet as complex as ever. I'm ready. The inner uneasiness was settled. Certainly, it was still there, insulated by the remainder of his leave. What had caused him to seek this path? Was he like the Roman Legionnaires? The doughboys? The GIs of World War II? Did anything ever change historically? Millions had endured what he was about to face. Were there true soldiers in those armies? Still he did not have an answer. He was going to the one place to look.

He was standing in the kitchen area when she opened the apartment door. As usual she was wearing a business suit, a skirt with a matching jacket over a white blouse. He had seen the outfit before which made her look much older than her twenty-three years. Expectation covered her face. Silently, she stayed where she stood after closing the door.

"It didn't work." He said smugly "Why didn't you have them send me to an aviation unit here in the United States? Maybe, I wouldn't have questioned that. When you told me you accepted me being an Army officer that was a lie."

"At first I did. We were back together, and that was the important thing. You wanted me back so bad it didn't matter what I thought. And, I didn't care what I thought. We had plenty of time. Things were going to change. This long stupid war would get over."

"You changed. I didn't."

"Yes, I have changed. Our lives together are at stake."

"All that I am isn't important to you. You never learned anything about me. I swore an oath and put on a uniform. Obviously, you don't know what that means."

"You are caught up in this thing like millions of other draftees."

"I'm a volunteer, going by my choice. I have a contract with the Army. You understand contracts."

"You've got three years from your graduation date. Then you can be a civilian again. Our lives can really start. I'm insuring it will be a good start."

He was silent for perhaps a minute. They stared at each other as neither moved. "Why language school?"

"To eat up time before you're a Captain. That's the minimum qualification for a diplomatic post. Language school is a good requirement toward that."

"I'm an Aviator."

"With Scott's influence I can get you the diplomatic slot. That is better for me and how I feel. Getting to know the thing that's got under your skin was just like finding out what made our distributors tick. What made them produce sales or push your product? What made them sit and do nothing? I had to find out in detail. It was easy to find their motivation. Money. Yours, I can't understand."

"I want to find out why men choose this path."

"Is that worth your life? Is it worth mine? You don't want to think you sold yourself out, if you don't go. That sounds so noble. It's selfish!"

"Some other poor bastard has to take my place, if I don't go. How is that suppose to make me feel?"

"Good, let them! Just the fact that they would listen to a "request by the officer" means they don't need you over there. You promised me if that happened you wouldn't go. Your roommate Riard had his orders changed just because he's Field Artillery. All the other Field Artillery Officers in your class had their orders changed. Why? Because they're not needed over there. You are not needed either."

"The Army made a mistake. They will correct it."

"Look what happened to Scott Jr. when he went missing. There's too few Americans over there now. I've been told its more dangerous now than when there were half a million troops over there."

"Who told you that?"

"Samantha."

"How the hell does she know anything about it?"

"She lived with it for years, while her ex-husband gloried in it, and forgot about her and his own son."

"Somehow you used Scott's influence in the Administration to mess with my orders."

"Any officer can do that. It's one of your Army's sacred Regulations. They can either deny it or approve it. You told me you would do it."

"So you did it for me hoping I'd think it was the Army."

"The Army will only lead you to trouble and anguish. Or worse, like that Arthur kid. The way out of Vietnam is there. You just refuse to believe it. That is the truth!"

"Truth? You don't understand truth! Truth is being true to what you are. You still refuse to accept what I am. I'm a soldier! The day I was born, I was one. Don't ask me how I know, I just know. You refuse to see it in me. I could have been in Caesar's legions, and it would have been the same."

"You're blabbering nonsense! I came back to you. What we had, we both discovered was real. We almost lost it. Most people don't have that kind of second chance. Ours is unique. Don't throw it all away, when all it takes is a simple, 'request by the officer.'"

"I got my supplemental travel vouchers in the mail, today. I'm going!"

"I can't do that year with you over there."

"Then I'll be doing it by myself." Taking his jacket from a kitchen chair, he brushed her arm as he walked around her to open the apartment door. She did not move as he closed it behind him.

Judy's wedding had been planned to manageable details. Al Garber did much more than any typical groom. Judy was sure of Al. Of much more importance, Maggie Thayer had been won over. Judy was twenty. Maggie Thayer had not been much older when she married.

Randolph was a minor element of the ceremony and was used as major leverage. When their church informed them two weddings were scheduled for the requested Saturday, Al Garber did not hesitate to go directly to the minister, who happened to be a former Army Chaplain. When informed of Randolph's key role and his next destination, Judy's ceremony became the third scheduled wedding for that day. A group from the plant where Al and Judy worked, volunteered to prepare the church for her four o'clock ceremony, after the second wedding at two.

Gloom was the only description that fit Randolph through Friday, the day after the breakup and also the time of rehearsal and the wedding party dinner. Faith hovered near him guiding and helping prepare for the rituals of a wedding. That night she remained with him as he drank half a fifth of scotch in the vacant reception tent in the Thayer back yard. When he spoke, she listened without criticism or scorn. She was there. She guided him up to his room and put him to bed. On the wedding morning, she poured coffee and aspirin into him and cooked his breakfast in the Thayer kitchen.

When formal pictures were taken Randolph smiled appropriately although there was a darkness in his face. Faith remained near him prompting him when he forgot his functions during the ceremonies. Judy was an adorable bride, young, robust, and pretty. Many of the neighborhood, who had known her all her life, in addition to distant, rarely seen relatives, watched as she was united in love. It was natural for everyone to gravitate to the huge tent in the Thayer yard for the remainder of the celebration. Judy and Al finally left the tent at about 8:30 PM. With shoes and cans tied to Al's Firebird rear bumper, they drove into the darkness to begin their week of honeymooning. Randolph was tipsy by that time, but was able to throw rice and confetti at his sister and new brother-in-law. The tent remained full of people. When the band was scheduled to leave at nine, a collection was initiated to keep them playing for another hour. Faith began watering Randolph's scotch. Again she remained close, jealously warding off potential flirtations. When the band finally packed up their instruments and left, Randolph needed to remain sitting, although he continued to imbibe. Even when the dancing stopped due to the band's departure, people remained huddled in groups at rearranged tables. By eleven, a few revelers were stretched out on folding chairs passed out, while the table groups became fewer but not less boisterous. No one would interrupt this party since there were several town policemen present with the celebrants.

Finally Faith prevailed and guided Randolph through the still partially crowded house up to his bedroom. The murmur from the tent was muted even with his window open. He sat on his bed, holding his last drink, which he had insisted upon bringing. Faith settled in his easy chair. She still wore the apricot colored maid of honor dress. It was slightly rumpled but still clung to her slender figure.

"Want to find out why men become soldiers."

"It's better than being a house painter." Faith yawned. She had nursed several drinks throughout the evening, but was stone sober.

"I suppose you could fall off the ladders and get killed. That would make it a more dangerous job. Most people probably don't know that. There's risks in occupations like that. That's a dangerous job too, like being a soldier."

"Then take the right precautions. Make sure you do."

"I have to find out."

"If that's what you need to do, then you will."

"What do women want to find out?"

"Whatever they need to know to get what they want."

"She conquered the factory. Was going to seduce me with it. It would have been a sweet life."

"Tonight, it wouldn't matter. You're too blown away."

"She didn't understand me. I never saw that in her. Wanted to think she understood me."

"You saw what you wanted, like most people. Just like tonight, what you want is right in front of you, and you still can't see it."

"I loved her. Now, she's gone." He started to cry. Faith stood, rather unsteadily from the fatigue of a very long day, then sat next to him on the bed. She cradled his shoulder with her arm.

"Let it go. Get it out of you." She whispered into his ear.

"Men–soldiers aren't supposed to cry." He snuffled and attempted to stop his tears.

"Bullshit! Make yourself clean and free."

"I have this question I must have answered."

"That again," Faith sighed. "So they can break things and do other things people normally don't do."

"You think soldiers like to destroy? They keep telling us, we're saving people."

"As you blow them up with bombs?"

"I am really going to seek the truth."

"You need to seek until you're satisfied. Then, that will be out of you, too. Then you'll be at peace with yourself."

"Like Arthur?"

"Don't you even think of doing something that stupid! I'd rather see you back with her. Life is important. God gave it to us. Don't spend it stupidly, like my brother."

"You are a smart cookie."

"Then aim at me. Whatever you hit will be a bull's eye."

"You're too good, I can't do it."

"You won't remember any of this, you're too drunk."

"Not too drunk. Some drunk, but not completely drunk." He smiled at her. "You believe what you want to believe. Like people who want to do things most people don't normally do."

"One for you, Randy! You'll forget, because you'll say you were drunk. I know men."

"You don't know soldiers."

"There is only one I want to know, and right now he has to go to bed."

"Why? What is there in the morning? It's all gone."

"In the morning, you can start the first day of your life. I'll be here when you wake up."

"You're too good. I can't do it."

"Try."

She put him to bed, helping him undress after a last, unsteady trip to the small upstairs bathroom. When he was finally laying flat under his bedding and beginning to snore, Faith sat in his easy chair opposite him and cried.

Flipping another cigarette butt into the dark water caused a muted singe as the flame was instantly extinguished. It was past 1:00 AM, cool but not cold on this long October night. With only a light jacket and sitting on the unsheltered rock by the lake, he thought should have made him cold. It didn't. The rock was the place beckoning him. Since breaking up with Andrea thirteen days before, he had avoided coming, but knew eventually he would. Leaving had shrunk to a mere eight hours. He might never see the rock again, a prospect he let creep into his thinking. It had been a big part of his life, a place for decisions. Things got sorted out here, and made sense, finally. It was time for that before he went.

Going to war unencumbered emotionally was what he had wanted. He had used that as a rationalization right after they broke up at Northeastern when he needed something to get himself through the final intense months of school. Soldiers, like anyone else, he had decided, brought their emotional baggage. Some hide it better than others. Right now, his felt like a raw, open wound. Would marriage have made a difference? At Christmas when she had eagerly opened her present, the desire for a ring was definitely there. Al Garber, now his brother-in-law craved marriage to his sister. Neither of them wanted to wait an additional year. Betsy Croteau's med student, Andrew, wanted it for security and help getting into medical school. The spectrum of reasons was out there. Why shouldn't it fit him? This hurt from the loss was real. He had felt the impact every day. Nothing dulled the pain. It had rubbed itself raw in his conscience. It had worked its way though his thoughts as a test of wills. His or hers? Neither would accommodate. So, his only baggage would be what he carried in his duffle bag.

The sound of footsteps approaching through the dried leaves caused him to look away from the black water. From the shadows a figure emerged, climbed onto the rock and sat next to him. It was Faith. She did not say anything but stared into the dark water as he had been. He did not look back at the water, but stared at the outline of her face.

"They're getting concerned. You left after supper without saying anything. They don't want you to miss your plane."

"I'm not going to miss being where I'm supposed to be. Officers don't miss troop movements. How did you know to come here?"

"Once I saw your car in the lot, I knew you were here. I followed you once when you came here. I hid over there," she pointed in a direction behind them. "I wanted to see what you were going to do."

"What did I do?"

"You just sat here like you are now. For a long time, too. I got cold and went home."

"Was that for the cellar playroom escapade?"

"No, it was before that."

"I spent a lot of time here because of that crazy afternoon."

"Really," she smiled and he saw her teeth flash in the darkness. "If I had known that, I probably would have come here to be with you. I thought you hated me after that. You barely talked to me for weeks."

"I was afraid we'd made a baby."

Faith sighed. "We'd have a four year old now. Teddy's only nine. My brother is seven. They could have grown up together. What would you have wanted? A boy or a girl?"

"If that had happened neither one of us would be sitting here tonight. I'd probably be working in Judy's factory. You'd probably be there too. Your mother or mine would have raised what's his face."

"You would have wanted a boy. The male response. Must have that boy to continue the name. Can I write to you?"

"It will be something to look forward to."

"I'll make my letters as interesting as I can. Are you scared?"

He did not answer immediately, but finally said, "Yes."

"Then that makes you very sane. I'm glad to hear that. I know you're on a quest, you must follow. Those that love you can't follow. I may never know why. One day you'll be at peace with yourself, and your life can continue. I only hope I'm with you."

"You will be."

"What's the main thing for you to get out of this war?" He did not see the smile that had exploded from her lips. "Is it about cowardice? Do men think about things like that a lot?"

"I'll be strapped into a seat in a helicopter. I won't be able to run away. I've lain in bed and broken into cold sweats thinking about where the piece of metal will hit. What will it feel like? That's what I can't prepare myself for."

"That's only fear. That's normal, especially for war. Everything I've read and heard puts that right on the bull's eye."

"I don't know how I'll handle that."

"You'll do it. When we were young, I remember that summer you ran around with your Davy Crockett coonskin cap and carrying that long plastic rifle. You were the boy-soldier then. You were preparing for what you're about to do now."

"My father was never a soldier and could never have been one. One of my grandfathers was. What makes those two men so different? Why has it been passed down to me? Is it hereditary? Maybe it skips a generation now and then."

"It's something my father has forgotten. Once, he was a good Marine. It was the inspiration for his whole life. He raised us with those ideals. Losing Arthur changed him."

"Your father and Arthur paid their dues in combat. Maybe that gives your father the right to criticize war."

"God won't forgive Arthur."

"God sent him to war and killed him. He was a warrior, of warrior stock. He made a mistake—stepping on the mine. It was probably hot. He was sweating and miserable. They had been going through miles of swamps and jungles through a long day. He knew he got careless. For a moment he relaxed and would go down this path like the dozen other slippery paths earlier in the day. Maybe he was thinking about how many more hours it would be before they dug in for the night. Going down that path was a mistake, which his fatigued mind permitted-allowed him to make the mistake—that's what he could not forgive himself for. That caused him to seek the philosophy which would allow him to do something—namely take his own life—which was completely alien to his Christian beliefs. A warrior can not make mistakes-but God allows it—and forgives them. He rests with his comrades."

"That's the biggest crock of shit I've ever heard!" Faith's silence was broken by her belly laugh as if echoed off the water. "You tell a good story when you don't know the facts." She turned her head to Randolph's stony face. "Warrior stock? Where the hell did you get that term? Some Marines who were there when Arthur was wounded talked to my father on the phone. That was last spring, maybe April. I can't remember exactly. Guess you didn't hear the story. Arthur had just eaten breakfast chow. He was supposed to relieve someone within the perimeter on guard. No one expected Charlie to have gotten inside their camp to set booby traps. They did that morning. Arthur was in the wrong place at the wrong time. He wasn't hot, miserable or exhausted. He had just eaten breakfast after sleeping all night. Why did he kill himself? My father will never admit it. He couldn't accept life that he had to face, as a cripple. He was a coward. That's what my father can't accept."

"Charlie got inside their perimeter to set booby traps?"

"An act of war, which is unexplainable and cruel."

"Why was it Arthur and not one of the other Marines?"

"You tell me. I've wondered that question so many times. It was fate, bad luck, or maybe it was God. Mainly, it was war."

"God wouldn't deny him the chance to be with his comrades, and those he loved. It wasn't your brother's fault. He was a casualty, the same as many others. He didn't come back in a body bag, but his mind died when he was wounded."

"That, I'll agree with. Something in him died when he lost his leg. That has happened to many others, and they manage to live with it."

"Since the beginning of recorded history, there have been soldiers. What made them be soldiers? I want to know! It's one of the world's oldest professions."

"Not the world's oldest profession." Faith giggled. "That's reserved for women. We wait, and we give." She was quiet for awhile, and they listened to the gentle lapping of the water against the rock. "She really didn't help you, did she?"

"Andrea took no interest in what I do. I refused to see it, or face it. I had my own selfish reasons."

"She couldn't see a snot if it was hanging out of her nose!" Faith was silent again before she asked, "It's not over, is it?"

"It can't be anything else. She left me no room to maneuver. Interfered with my orders. I was a sap. She set me up. Told her if the Army genuinely didn't need me over there, I wouldn't go. A hint dropped in the right place by the right people. Still, it was my decision."

"I wish she had succeeded, and you weren't going."

"Why? You've always supported what I wanted to do. I have to take my chances like anyone else. That's part of being in the military."

"You're not like my brother. You're entirely different. I don't want to go to another funeral with a flag draped coffin." Again Faith lapsed into silence, and they both listened to the water tapping the rock. "You were my first, and maybe you're the only one for me. I slept with two others. Mostly, it was to see if it was different than when I was with you. They were both terrible. They only made me realize it was you."

"It wouldn't be fair to you." Randolph looked at her in the dim light. She had turned to face him again. Her expression was stoic and majestic. "I don't want to hurt you. Maybe I wasn't meant to love anyone, at least a normal person like you. When you've had a relationship like I had, it will always be part of you."

"I accept you had a relationship that will be with you throughout your life. You're human, and what you did and felt was real. I'd never pretend it didn't happen. That wouldn't be real. Don't you let this ruin your chances of survival. If you won't come back for me, you do it for your mother, or Judy and Al, and your brother Teddy. If you don't come back, and I hear it was because you didn't care, I will personally go and rip her eyes out of her face."

"I promise to be careful." He smiled. Now, tears rolled freely down her cheeks.

At five a.m. Faith complained of stiffness and the cold. She was hungry and suggested they find someplace they could eat, which would also be warm. When they left the lake Randolph was not particularly hungry, but when they arrived at an all night diner, his stomach was rumbling. After they had ordered, Faith insisted on calling his mother to assure her that he had been found, and they would be home with enough time to prepare. In the small diner there was an assortment of typical morning people. Mostly, they were blue-collar workers who got up early. With Andrea out of his life, even with a college diploma, he realized he could become one of them. Or, he could remain in the Army. Not being involved with Tremblay Bearings created new horizons, not all of them desirable. His thoughts further depressed him. After eating, they drove to Faith's car parked at the lake, and she followed him. His mother who had been dozing on the couch woke immediately when they came into the kitchen. Fatigue showed in her worry-lined face, but it disappeared quickly. This day, although different, was still another day, with normal activities to get done. As Faith started a pot of coffee, he went upstairs to shower. Judy's room was obscenely empty. Al Garber had leased a bigger apartment for them. Judy had taken all her furniture and possessions to her new home.

In the small bathroom used by his siblings, he looked around. Every chip in the tile floor and every stain on the walls had a history. The familiarity crowded in on him. The shower revived him relieving the tightness in some of his muscles from being awake nearly twenty-four hours. As he had done innumerable times, he stood at the small sink and shaved. The only difference upon finishing was not putting his shaving gear in the cabinet. Instead, it went into a small travel bag. In his room, his duffel bag was on the floor next to his bed. His uniform lay on the bed, where he had set it the night before. He began dressing, starting with civilian underwear never having adapted to the baggy military shorts, and a clean white T-shirt, a requirement for the uniform. From his bed, he took the blouse of the TWs, the lightweight replacement for khakis, officers and ranking NCOs, were authorized to wear. Folds were tailored into the material, one crease down through the breast sections and three down the back. Its light weight caused it to feel unlike a uniform. The pants were of the same material and did not bind or pull in.

Transferring the insignia from his greens, which he had left hanging in his closet, he placed a Second Lieutenant's gold bar on the right collar of the shirt. On the left collar he put the gold crossed rifles of Infantry branch. After passing his first active duty anniversary, which had occurred during his leave the gold bar would turn into silver. The new First Lieutenant insignia was packed in the duffel bag. It was one of his final purchases in the PX at Rucker. Although tempted to wear the new rank insignia, he decided he would wait for orders. Checking the greens again, he pondered taking any other insignia, deciding on the black and white nametag, which he pushed into his toiletries bag. If he got killed, the Army would give him a new set of greens to wear in the box. Thoughtful of them, he reflected, as he sat on his bed to dress his feet. The low cuts, the shoes that went with the TW uniform were dull. He spent several minutes brushing them, bringing back a partial shine. These were the same shoes he had received when he joined Advanced ROTC and was issued his first non returnable uniform. Since he had usually worn boots in a volunteer group at Northeastern, the shoes were in good shape and could still hold a decent shine. His only decoration was the National Service Ribbon, a being-in decoration, which hung over the left pocket of the blouse of the TWs. Above the single ribbon were his wings, which would tell everything about him. In the mirror hanging on the wall over his small bureau, he inspected himself. He was sure all the insignia was in the right places. He was ready. He would start off to war, unarmed but at least in comfortable clothes.

What about the true soldier? Maybe he had met him. Although only a student in the Army, some wearing uniforms he had met might be close. His last instructor, CPT Greenlee cared about his students and purposely passed on much of his combat experience. Was that the mark of a real professional? Did it matter what profession was followed? Betsy's father Dr. Croteau stayed in the blue collar neighborhood where most of his patients lived. He could have moved to a richer part of town, but he stayed. Were there true doctors? Andrea's father, Frederic, was a good businessman. He had started with only ideas and built a solid, professional industrial company. Saddled with his brothers' animosity and lately his ill health, he still possessed the insight to forge ahead. The new alloy products he was introducing had a ready market. Being good at what you do is the mark of true man. Faith would be happy if he had found his answer.

Hurried steps bounding up the steep stairs distracted him. The distinct sound meant his mother, moving a lot quicker than she usually did. From habit, he looked around his room looking for anything that should be hidden from her sight. He smiled at his self-concern. It didn't matter what she saw.

"Andrea just drove up." His mother's breath came unevenly from her unusual quick ascension of the stairs.

As he passed through the kitchen, Faith's face was etched in open pain. Her eyes followed him, as he quickly looked away from her. She rose from her seat at the huge kitchen table. As Randolph opened the back door, momentarily he grabbed at the doorframe to steady himself to avoid falling. His throat was completely dry. He swallowed to ease the discomfort, but it did not go away. Judy stood and tried to hold onto Faith, but she broke from her grasp. Following Randolph through the open kitchen door, once outside, Faith ran around the house into the back yard. Judy had followed her outside, and watched as she sprinted through the Thayer back yard and disappeared into the neighbor's. She was running full force.

Andrea stood next to her Mustang, arms wrapped around her chest. As he approached, her face looked pained. Closer, he could see tears were streaming down her cheeks. The only other time he remembered her crying was when they broke up at Northeastern. Momentarily it stunned him, so he stopped a few paces from her.

"I had to come. I had to see you one more time. I got to thinking maybe you wouldn't think I love you. And, that was no good. I had to come here and tell you. Face to face. Even if you wouldn't see me. I couldn't let you go to that place alone, without me. You understand?"

"Perfectly."

"Let me learn and understand it. Please! I want to see what's inside you. If you're a soldier, I may still hate it, but I've got to understand it, or I'll go nuts. That's where I was wrong. I'm sorry. Please forgive me."

"You're here." He put his arms around her. "That says it all."

"I took a wrong turn."

"Give it some pedal, and you'll get the tail back in trim. Then your flight will be smoother."

"You make it sound so easy. Please hold me. Tighter! I know that's flying stuff. I'll get to know it, I promise. I'm going to get to Vietnam. It's a country and I've got a passport and connections. I'll get there somehow."

"Maybe someone over there needs ball bearings." He smiled looking down at her face. Her eyes were red and watery.

"If they don't, we'll make them think they need them." She attempted a smile, but could not. Her body was trembling. "I don't like you going. Don't misunderstand that point."

"I'm not telling you to change the way you think. You wouldn't be my Andrea."

"I can be mad at you now. Last night I didn't have you, so I couldn't be mad at you. Now, I can." She smiled. "I'm still pissed off at you! You're going to make me do this year. You get your way. You'll have the easy part. I have to be here, alone, waiting and wondering."

"My poor Andrea."

"You've got to hold your piss as Samantha says, regardless. That's a woman's place. I don't know if I can learn that. Nothing has been simple these past few weeks."

"I've got to understand where you're coming from, too. I'm putting a lot on you."

"When are you eligible for an R & R?"

"I have to get there first."

"You'll tell me when you are?"

"You'll use other means of communication besides the telephone?" He laughed.

"I can write. I already bought some fancy stationary. You've been promoted. Why are you still wearing a gold bar? You're a First Lieutenant, Army of the United States. I know Army stuff."

"Are you coming in for coffee?"

"Do they hate me?" Her face became apprehensive.

"Doesn't matter. I love you, so they have to."

"How much more time have you got?"

"An hour, maybe. I'm all packed. Had nothing else to do for two weeks."

"I'm sorry."

"Me too, for the two weeks we could have had together. That's over. Let's not think backwards. Let's get that coffee."

END